Making It Home

Also by Teddy Jones

Slanted Light

Jackson's Pond, Texas

Well Tended

Nowhere Near: Stories

Making It Home

a novel

By

Teddy Jones

NEW YORK, NEW YORK

Published by MidTown Publishing Inc.
1001 Avenue of Americas
12th Floor
New York, NY 10018

Publisher's Cataloging-in-Publication data
Names: Jones, Teddy, author.
Title: Making It Home: a novel / by Teddy Jones.
Description: New York, NY: Midtown Publishing, 2021.
Identifiers: LCCN: 2021935079| ISBN: 978-1-62677-026-3 (hardcover)
| 978-1-62677-028-7(paperback) | 978-1-62677-027-0 (e-book).
Subjects: LCSH Family--Fiction. | Ku-Klux Klan--Fiction. | Racism--Fiction.
| Race relations--Fiction. | Marriage--Fiction.| Man-woman relationships--
Fiction. | Texas--Fiction. | Women--Fiction. | BISAC FICTION / Small
Town & Rural-Fiction | FICTION / Women | FICTION / Family Life /
General
Classification: LCC PS3610 .O632 M35 2021 | DDC 813.6--dc23

Praise for Making It Home

Making It Home could not be a more timely book. A large extended family living in western Texas collides with a growing ring of white supremacists. As the gang become increasingly menacing, the threat underscores the need for courage, and for the kind of love that doesn't flinch or wilt in the face of persistent danger. There's a fierce, sometimes wild river running strong through these pages. As it flows, it reveals that there are no easy answers for combatting human ignorance and hate, there are no endings that will remain happy forever. We live in an imperfect world, but it is still possible to think, imagine and make things better. The cast of characters in this strong family affirms this through their hope, decency, and tenacity. And as an added bonus, what wonderful, lively dogs live among them! Eleanor Morse, *Margreete's Harbor*

In *Making It Home*, Teddy Jones continues the rich, century-spanning saga of the Jackson family that she began two books ago with *Jackson's Pond, Texas*. Jones' talent for creating indelible characters endures, as does her way with a compelling plot. Indeed, Jones' new novel boldly explores and exposes the existential threat posed to 'home' (dwelling/town/state/country/world) by white supremacy, homophobia and xenophobia. This is a timely page-turner. Robin Lippincott *Blue Territory: A Meditation on the Life and Art of Joan Mitchell*

In *Making It Home*, the latest gripping installment of Teddy Jones' highly engaging Jackson Pond, Texas, series, the contemporary rural town is at the crossroads of survival versus succumbing to a slow demise. As Mayor Ray Banks choses rejuvenation and forms community action groups to carry out his vision of a flourishing Jackson Pond, a dark threat makes its presence known with white supremacist graffiti and vandalism. This emerging gang of domestic terrorists targets the extended Jackson/Banks/Havlicek family. Even as the family battles against these attacks, a long-buried secret reveals their own patriarch's unwitting involvement and cover-up of a Ku Klux Klan murder perpetrated on the Jackson family ranch a century ago. The family must unite to save themselves and others from the escalating violence and confront their own need to atone for the sin from their family's past. Their vision of a peaceful, inclusive, and thriving future for Jackson Pond's citizenry hangs in the balance. Sue Boggio, co-author of *Sunlight and Shadow, A Growing Season, and Long Night Moon.*

Acknowledgments

It's likely that every person I have met, whose work I read, or on whom I have eavesdropped has influenced my work in one way or another. I thank them all even though I couldn't possibly name each one.

There are others whose positive influence on this particular novel as well as on this writer can be specifically identified. This is to thank each of them. First, there are the members of the John Dufresne Taos Workshop 2017 who read and critiqued the early manuscript of *Making It Home*: Jill Coupe, Karen Kravit, David Norman, Cully Perlman, and Peter Stravlo, plus John Dufresne, our workshop instructor.

Next, John Dufresne deserves a repeat serving of gratitude because he has become my continuing mentor, having worked with me in eight separate master classes over the past ten years and advised me on numerous other writing-related matters. Three others merit my lasting gratitude for shaping my approach to writing fiction—Robin Lippincott, Eleanor Morse, and Philip S. Deaver (now deceased), members of the faculty of the Spalding University MFA in Creative Writing Program. And my friend and colleague Martha Burns, my steadfast first reader and critic, must be listed. Her value to my writing cannot be overstated.

In addition, thanks go to Elizabeth Trupin-Pulli of Jet Literary and to Michael Zealy, who gave me permission to apply the word "fabulous" when speaking of him as publisher. Finally, I am grateful to each reader who chooses my fiction.

Teddy Jones, 2021

Making It Home

a novel

By

Teddy Jones

CHAPTER 1
Legacy

Albert Jackson had always thought of home as peaceful. After the war it seemed dull. But the article circled in this week's *Floyd County Tribune* told him things were changing out there. He read aloud to Delia, his bride-to-be, as she sat on her parents' living room sofa, straight as a poker, perched like a wren near the edge of the cushion. He'd tried to prepare her for the article by saying he didn't want her to be afraid, just to know the kind of thing that had happened near his hometown.

"This is from last week, dated December 1, 1920." He pointed to the article on the front page, making sure Delia saw it. "'Sunday, C. C. Jackson contacted the county sheriff in Calverton saying that he'd found a body on his property that morning. The deceased was a Negro man, tentatively identified as Lincoln Berryhill, age thirty-four, from Bosley, Oklahoma. That identity was based on items found nearby. Deputy Asa Moore described the condition of the corpse as follows: 'completely naked, except for a tattered sock on the right foot. Appears to have been killed by a blow or blows to the back of the head, which has a bashed in appearance. Both legs are broken below the knees, with bone visible sticking out from both.'"

Albert paused, then said, "I worry about Dad finding him. It could have worsened his heart condition."

If Delia reacted at all to the gory details, he couldn't tell from looking. The expression on her face, pleasant and somewhat distant, a carbon copy of her mother's, had not changed since he began reading the article to her. Come to think of it, her women friends he'd met while visiting Longview all wore similar faint, far away smiles.

Wondering why he hadn't thought before about that intentionally vacant expression, Albert hesitated. Today, exactly as he had each week since he and Delia Carson became officially engaged, Albert Jackson sat with her in the front parlor of her parents' Longview, Texas, home. Doing his best to fit in, for the time being at least, with the way things were done in her family and in East Texas, he visited from Fort Worth. His Model T made the five-hour trip easily. But as far as he was concerned, the two towns were worlds apart. In Fort Worth, he could stretch his legs, hear talk of men dealing in cattle and land, feel the same as he'd always felt back home in the Texas Panhandle where he knew he was a man involved in the important work of helping feed the country. Everything about Longview felt cramped, a place more like the old South, full of manners and formal courtesies and open secrets.

He'd received an edition of the newspaper he held in the mail each week from his father, C.C. Jackson, since they reached their understanding. First, his father had sent that telegram letting Albert know in no uncertain terms that the fact he fought in the Great War didn't mean it was the last work he'd ever need to do. Even though there had been a few more words on that yellow paper, Albert got the message from one short line—*Get a job or get home.* Right away, he'd gone home to Jackson's Pond and explained to his father he was courting a woman he'd met in Fort Worth and had to be there to win her hand. After a long talk they reached an understanding that got him a bit of a reprieve. They both knew his mother's dying last year had left the house in need of a woman.

Now that he and Delia Carson were engaged, plenty of things required his presence in her hometown. Since that Western Union delivery from his father, he'd managed to bargain for several more months in Fort Worth. Composing a proper marriage proposal, getting to know her friends and family, engagement parties, fittings for a wedding suit, and a few other things he made sound urgent or compulsory did the trick. But his father let him know, with this regular news delivery, that he was watching, and the clock was ticking. After the wedding three weeks from today, Albert and his bride would make their way westward across the more than four hundred miles from Longview to the Jackson Ranch, home.

Delia spoke, returning his focus to his purpose today. With only the slightest change in her placid exterior, she said, "Surely he would have let you know."

He wasn't so sure about that. Dad would be upset if he knew Albert even mentioned his heart condition to another person. As far as C.C. Jackson was concerned, one way or another, he was and always would be a permanent fixture on the ranch he'd bought back in 1895.

Albert straightened out a fold in the paper and read on, "Found nearby were overalls and a red union suit, an empty billfold, and a letter introducing Lincoln Berryhill. The letter stated Berryhill was working his way down to Fort Stockton, Texas, to stay with an elderly uncle who once had been stationed there as a Buffalo Soldier. The letter, torn into four pieces found scattered near the clothing, also said Berryhill was a good worker and trustworthy. It was signed Marshall Lee, President of the Bosley, Oklahoma, First National Bank. By press time, no relatives have been located to verify identification, and Mr. Lee has not replied to our inquiries."

She asked, "What does that have to do with us?"

"Nothing, I hope. But it could mean the KKK is trying to stir up problems out there. They kill people for no other reason than being Negro. I've also heard they aim to get elected to office and run the big cities in the state. Dallas, Austin, even Wichita Falls."

Delia leaned forward a tiny bit, deposited her teacup, still full, on the end table. She turned to face Albert and said, "That's not necessarily a bad idea. Women right here in our town know we're safe primarily because of the protection of the Klan. My mother told me that when she was a girl, one of those free niggers who thought he was as good as anybody leered at her sister when she went downtown to Harper's store. Her sister told their daddy and it wasn't long before that buck wasn't hanging around the town square anymore."

Albert asked, "What happened to him?"

She shrugged. "Mother never knew all the true facts. Her daddy only told her the Klan took care of the situation, and she didn't have to worry anymore. Said he and all like him had been taught a lesson. You can see why something had to be done—all them menacing decent women, and their nasty kids doing their best to take over what didn't rightly belong to them after the war between the states."

"Sounds to me like vigilantes took the law in their own hands."

"I'm glad I didn't live through that. But the men, the white Christian men, did what they had to to keep them in line. And the Klan's still watching." After a brief pause to retrieve and sip her tea, she said, "How can women feel safe out in West Texas if there's no one keeping the order of things?"

"That's what the sheriff's department's for. And courts."

"Justice sometimes must be swiftly administered. People who can't or don't want to live like the rest of us have to be taught a lesson."

Such ignorant talk from the girl he'd thought would be his wife! And worse than that, his dad would probably agree with her. Albert ought to leave before he said what he thought. Arguing with Delia in her family's living room probably qualified as bad manners.

He said, "Can't or don't want to live like the rest of us could take in a lot of people. And who's to decide?"

"Albert, you are being intentionally dense. You know exactly who I mean. Field hands, people who don't speak our language, all that other riffraff." She focused on him, as if he'd just come into view. "If I didn't know better, I would think you were trying to start an argument with me. And here, so near to our wedding."

"I'm trying to have a discussion, to understand what you believe. If that sounds like arguing, well so be it." He stopped talking, made a show of checking his watch.

She said, "I think I am due an apology."

"I have to go. I need to get out to the ranch. I'll be back next week."

That note in his father's handwriting that he'd wadded into his pocket, the few lines that came with the newspaper, said, "There's more to this story. It may die down, but we need to talk, face to face. Now." This morning, as soon as he read it, Albert telegraphed his dad that he'd be home in no more than two days.

Delia shot up from the sofa. "You'll do no such thing. Critical preparations for the wedding and our honeymoon must be attended to."

"This is more critical."

She stamped her foot, noiselessly because of the thick rug, but he saw the movement. She said, her voice louder than he'd ever heard, "That's debatable."

"No, it's not. And in case you don't know it, married or not, I'll always decide my own plans." He turned toward the front door, then turned back and said, "And another thing. I fought overseas to make sure we live in a democracy. That takes in all kinds of people, not just white, Christian people."

She followed behind him as he went to the door. He'd expected tears, but when he turned, he saw a face she'd not shown him before—skin splotched red, mouth pursed, eyes narrowed. Her voice ragged, she said, "If you leave now, don't bother coming back."

Albert took his time walking toward his car. Halfway down the path, he heard the front door slam.

By the time he'd made it back to Fort Worth late that evening, he'd figured out a way to apologize without saying he'd been wrong. It was expected that he bring home a wife and get situated to take over the ranch. After his mother died, Albert's dad had surprised him with the news he was ready to retire. So, Albert didn't have time to go through courting someone else. Plus, it wasn't just Delia he'd had to court. Winning her mother's approval had been just as important. All the other available girls were probably the same—could only love a man if Mama approved. He'd gotten this far with Delia, her mother, all the plans. Starting over and finding another girl—all that could take forever. No, it was settle this or end up a bachelor living on a ranch out in West Texas miles from anything, alone.

So, he had to smooth this over pronto, plus handle whatever had his dad in an uproar. Once he adjusted to the idea he couldn't rest on his status as returning hero who'd survived the fighting in France, he'd felt himself growing eager to move into running the ranch. As for finding a wife, he understood the need. A man of substance, operating one of the largest ranches, not counting the Matador, had to have a wife and one or more sons.

Married women he knew seldom acted, at least publicly, counter to their husbands' wishes. Once they were married and set up on the ranch, Delia would learn to occupy herself with suitable causes. She'd involve herself in ladylike things that didn't include arguing about law enforcement and secret societies bent on keeping the ways of the defeated South. The Great War changed the world. People had to change to live peaceably together in it.

Not that he'd say any of that to her right now. His excuse for having spoken harshly would be his worry about his father. He'd remind her about his obligation as the only son of a man whose wife had recently died, and how he'd only been able to talk his dad into letting him stay in Fort Worth because he'd told him about the wonderful girl he was seriously courting and hoped to bring home as his wife, right away. Then to top it off, he'd leave her in charge of their honeymoon plans. That should please her and her mother. He stopped at the first telegraph office he saw.

A reply waited for him when he reached Jackson's Pond late the following evening. "Moving ahead with honeymoon plans. Mama very pleased all wedding plans remain on schedule, even though family obligations took you away. Eager for your return, my love."

Driving from town out to the ranch, Albert thought about her message. That woman would go far among other women. She had a knack for saying things in the nicest possible way while getting exactly what she wanted. He folded the telegram and stowed it in his pocket.

It felt good getting back home. The masses of trees and greenery over on the east side of the state had begun to press in on him, made him realize how animals accustomed to grazing free must feel when penned. And it smelled odd over there, moldy, reminded him of sump holes in the trenches. Some days the scent of flowers grabbed at his throat the way he'd seen men choking from mustard gas.

C.C. Jackson paced on the front porch of the ranch house as Albert drove up. Ten at night was way past his bedtime. Albert left his suitcase in the Model T Ford and took the front steps in two big strides. "What are you doing out here this time of night, Dad?"

A double-barreled twelve-gauge shotgun leaned against the front porch rail. His father wilted into the rocker nearby. "It's time you got here. I've held out by myself since the paper come out. They'll be back for sure."

He'd never seen C.C. Jackson's hands tremble before. Now that he stood closer, he could see beads of sweat on his dad's forehead. "Who?"

"Klan."

He sat in the other rocker, scooted it around to face his father, stalling, hoping the old man's breathing would settle down. "Out here? Why?"

"To keep me from talking, put a scare in me, or worse." He leaned forward and moved the shotgun to his lap. "I'll have a surprise for 'em. Both barrels loaded with double-aught shot."

"Have you slept any at all?" He'd seen men in trenches who looked better. "I'll get my bag. We'll go inside so you can tell me everything."

He moved slowly on purpose, getting his dad settled in the oversized wingback chair in the living room, the shotgun within reach. "Put your feet up on that footstool and rest a minute while I wash up and get something to eat. Then we'll talk." He didn't give him time to object. As he headed to the kitchen, he said, "Been on the road non-stop since morning."

Snoring from the vicinity of the big chair said he'd been correct. His father hadn't slept, probably in days. Albert made a sandwich from bologna and cheese he found in the ice box and took that and a glass of milk with him to the living room. Around midnight, his father yelled, "What the hell are you doing in my house?"

Albert grabbed the shotgun just as his dad reached for it. "It's me, Albert! Settle down!"

"I been trying to tell you but you won't sit still."

"I'm sitting. Tell me now."

C.C. straightened in his chair, rubbed his face with both hands, then leaned forward. He said, "Last Saturday evening, right at dark, I was out in the barn, cleaning up tack. A truck, one of them International Harvester kind we seen in Fort Worth, no one round here has one. It came up the drive. Never seen it before. Four fellows, two in front, two in back, all covered with white sheets and wearing masks. No way for me to pretend I wasn't here. So, I come out, casual like, carrying my coal oil lantern and a pitchfork—only thing in the barn that might be a weapon. I stopped just outside the barn door."

Albert laid his sandwich aside. The bite he'd taken threatened to choke him, his throat was so dry.

"Damned if they didn't drive right up to within a foot of where I stood. When they did I heard a pitiful sound coming from the back of the truck. A cross between crying and moaning, sort of quiet like. One of those in the back yelled, 'Shut your mouth or you'll have something to moan about.' After that, the sound stopped. I said, 'There's nothing here for you, so turn that thing around and go on.'"

Albert said, "You didn't recognize the voice?"

"Can't be sure. Then the one riding shotgun says, 'You need to get in back. You're going to help us.' I'm pretty sure that was old man Forney from over near Lockney."

"Soon as I began to get a notion of what was happening, I said, 'I don't want no part of whatever you're doing. Now get off my property.'"

Thinking it would be a good idea to keep C.C. calm, Albert said, "Hold on. I need some water. Be right back."

He took his time dipping a glassful for each of them. In the living room again, his dad took a long drink, then leaned back against the chair cushion. "You can guess they didn't leave, or I wouldn't still be all lathered up. So, I did what they said, got in the back. There lay a black man, about your size. He'd been hogtied, so he was on his face." He shook his head. "I can picture it yet. Pitiful sight a human treated that way."

His hand trembled as he drank more water. "I said, 'Why in hell are y'all doing this?' One of them said, 'Have to stop this one or there'll be more. Teach him a lesson. We don't and there'll be more. Like rats. Let one live, they multiply.'"

Albert gave up on eating the sandwich, and pushed it away. He thought he'd seen all the killing he'd have to see in this life. Now, this kind of trouble. Here at home.

"When I started asking more questions, the same one said, 'If you know what's good for you, you'll shut up or get worse than he does.' I'm pretty sure that was Reese. His boots showed from under his sheet, all run over at the heels, a hole cut for a bunion on the left, like a sharecropper. Seen 'em lots of times in town. All this time they're driving off to the east side of our place, where it drops off the Cap into those mesquites. Then all of a sudden, we stop and they cut that back rope holding his feet, jerk him out on the ground and make him stand up. The driver says to me, 'Get out, you're going to strike the first blow and then forget everything you've seen.' I didn't move so they pushed me out onto the ground."

His dad pulled up a shirt sleeve and showed a long scratch and bruise. "One of them pushed a baseball bat into my hands, intending for me to use it on that man. I dropped it and decided right then I'd find out if they meant to do me in. Better then than waiting, I thought. So I said, 'Tell me what he's being punished for.'

"'For bein' in the wrong place, for asking for food in town, for vagrancy.' They all chimed in. I argued, told them if he was a vagrant to call the law. 'We are the law. You're with us or we'll punish you, too.' I still refused. Then one of them said, 'You take the first blow and keep your mouth shut, we let you go. We'll do the rest.'

"None of it made sense, and I said so. Asked 'em, why bring him all the way out here from town? Why on my place?"

"'Out here we can take our time. Besides, your place has the only trees for miles, even if they are scrubby mesquites.' Reese, if that's who it was, pulled out a pistol from under that sheet, and said, 'You'll get worse than him, and we'll make sure everyone knows about that woman you had out here.'"

Albert didn't ask what that meant. His dad was right—none of it made sense.

His father stopped talking, stared off into space and shook his head. "I heard about them over in Wichita Falls, but I never had any idea they were out here, too. Klan."

The rest was more than his dad could get out, Albert could tell. He waited, trying to control his temper and breathe normally until his dad would say more.

His dad leaned back again and closed his eyes. Without opening them, he said, "Nobody in the world deserves what was done to that man. And I did what they said, struck the first blow. My only consolation is I used my fists, not that baseball bat, and I only hit him in the chest. He was sturdy, thick-chested. After I did, one of them drove me up to the barn and pushed me out, then took off again. The other three stayed there."

After a minute or more, he sat straight again. "You saw in the paper what I told the law. Far as they know, I just found the fellow when I checked fence the next day. That's true, far as it goes."

Albert noticed his dad's voice had gone flat, like he used up everything he had just telling what he was ashamed of, but was determined to finish. "I went back out there to see if they were gone. They were. He wasn't. Now that I've told the sheriff, I expect they'll be coming for me again."

Another silence stretched between them. Then Albert said, "I'll sleep with the gun tonight. You go on to bed. I'll lock up. We'll decide in the morning what to do."

Like a child shamed for lying, his father hung his head and went straight to bed.

The next morning, Albert was still awake. When his dad got up, Albert made him eat eggs and drink coffee before he'd talk with him. Then, as they sat together on the front porch, C. C. said, "I didn't explain what they meant about the woman. I hired her to come out from Calverton to clean. She was real nice and did a good job. When she offered to cook supper, I told her if she would, and would stay the night, I'd pay her more. She did. I did, but only the one time." After a hesitation he said, "A man gets lonely."

Albert kept a straight face. War had shown him lots worse behavior than that. He said, "Dad, that's of no consequence. Don't worry about it getting out. The other's lots more important. Let's talk about what to do to make things right."

"I want to tell the law the whole thing, confess. That's the only way I'll feel right ever again. What do you think I should do?"

"Tell the truth, I don't know. We have no way of knowing about the two you think were local. We don't know if the sheriff's in on it or if not, whether he'd investigate. You tell, and you might end up being the only one ever blamed for any of it."

They both studied things out on the horizon, too far away to see clearly. Albert's mother had been forever asking one or both of them what it was they saw out there where there was nothing to see. She never understood that was the point.

Then Albert said, "Let's pack up and go to Fort Worth. I'm getting married in less than three weeks. You can rest up in a hotel until then. When we get back out here we can decide together what, if anything, needs to be done. Let's let the lawmen have a chance to do their jobs."

"That's probably the sensible thing. Son, it's sure good to have you here."

"Let's get you packed."

Floyd County Tribune
Wednesday, January 26, 1921
Grand Jury Returns Verdict

The Floyd County Grand Jury returned verdicts of NO BILL in the case of Silas Reese, C.C. Jackson, and three as yet unknown others in the death of a Negro man found on the Jackson property November 28, 1920.

Jackson testified to finding the body and having no other involvement with the dead man. Testimony offered no explanation for the charges against Reese and the unknown others beyond Jackson's assertion that "four men came up on my property the night before I found that body. They were wearing hoods and I didn't recognize the truck. The only one I thought I knew was Reese, based on the shoes I saw. I ran them off and that's the last I saw of them."

The Sheriff's department stated that after numerous attempts to contact, no family has come forward to claim the body. The unrelated individual in Bosley, Oklahoma, who provided a letter of reference found on the dead man declined further involvement with the matter. Given the circumstance, the body of the deceased will be given a Christian burial at county expense at an undisclosed site.

CHAPTER 2
Buried

What began as a quiet conversation between Melanie Jackson Banks and her husband turned louder. The first to raise the volume, she surprised herself. She hadn't realized how strongly she felt about the City Council's new planning committees. No one in town was better equipped to lead the education and child care committee than she was. She and Ray started breakfast slightly later than usual since her preschool was closed for Labor Day. After only a few bites, she told him she wanted him to appoint her chair of that committee.

He topped a half slice of toast with scrambled egg, bit into it and chewed. She watched without a word as he worked through most of the eggs and all the toast. Finally, he said, "You are the best qualified. But you have to see that appointing you chair could be seen as nepotism, or if Garland Thames doesn't know that word, cronyism, or stacking the deck, or whatever else our previous Mayor Thames might want to call it."

"Since when did you start worrying about politics again? I thought you left that all behind when you quit the Governor's staff. You said being mayor of Jackson's Pond was going to be your contribution, not a career step."

She jerked her plate off the table and carried it to the sink, threw her toast in the trash. He followed her, his empty plate in hand. He said, "We quit arguing like this years ago. Is something else besides committees on your mind?"

He moved closer, put an arm around her waist. She flipped on the garbage disposal, then pulled away and faced him, wiping her hands on a dish towel. "Politics. The same reason the Calverton School District chose an ex-coach with little administrative experience and a quickie doctorate for Superintendent over me. Just one more example to prove qualifications don't count when politics comes into play."

"This is a different situation. I know you're the best qualified. I doubt anyone would dispute that. It's not a hiring decision like that was. Years ago."

"If all that's true, appoint me chair, and I'll recruit a committee."

"Are you prepared to deal with a backlash, if it comes? The effect on you, your preschool? You know I don't care if I'm ever reelected mayor. Truth is, if there was someone else who'd get this town back on its feet, I'd resign right now. Problem solved."

Melanie took a deep breath. "Sure you would. You'll be lying if you say you don't love every minute." She'd told herself she finished years ago with attacking him, blaming him for every disappointment or wound. Lashing out at him instead of admitting . . . She said, "No. You shouldn't resign. Jackson's Pond needs leadership."

She tossed the dish towel on the counter, and turned her back. Head down, she said, "You're right. There is something else. It happened last Friday, the fifth day of school."

He took his usual seat at the table. "Tell me."

She dragged out the chair opposite. Its scraping against the floor tightened her jaw as she sat and faced him. "Okay, Mr. Mayor, if you actually care, I'll tell you. I had just gone to lock the front door. All the parents had left. You know I encourage them to bring the children in rather than letting them out at the sidewalk for the first week. It makes the schoolroom a familiar place for the children and shows the parents toys and books that can stimulate three and four-year-olds' interests."

She stopped, remembering how her hands shook minutes later. "I saw Justin Reese coming toward the door, his wife scurrying along behind him. They left their little boy alone in the pickup. I opened the door and greeted them. Neither one said a thing. He walked right past me into my office."

Ray said, "The child was enrolled?"

Melanie nodded. "The mother brought him the first day. He was in my class and joined in all the activities. Seemed to have a good day. Then he was there Tuesday and missed the next two."

"That's the Reese who brags around town about building a bunker out on his family's place?"

She nodded again. "He demanded a refund for the month's tuition his wife had paid. He said she shouldn't have enrolled their son. But now she'd gotten her priorities straight, and would homeschool the boy. Right then I wished Dolores had been with me, not in the second classroom. I had offered them chairs, but he ignored that and kept standing, her cowering behind him. He moved toward me and spoke so loudly I wanted to back away. I didn't, but I wanted to." She exhaled a sigh. "Something made me ask if there was a problem with the school, or simply a family decision."

"Let me guess. He doesn't want his child in school with Hispanics."

"Clearly, only he used the most derogatory term possible. And then what upset me so was he said, 'I might have overlooked that. Wetbacks have their place. But I'll not have a—and he used the N word—teaching my boy anything.' That's when I was glad Dolores hadn't been in the room. Him talking about her that way. My hands shook so I could hardly get the check written for his refund."

"Did he make any threats or do anything illegal?" Ray sat still, but his face had reddened. "I'd like to have a reason to call the sheriff on him."

"Nothing direct. But I watched after I locked the door behind them. That poor wife never said a word, and trailed him out like a servant. When he got in the pickup, I could see him shouting at her. The little boy climbed up in her lap and put his hands over his ears."

"You did the right thing, making him admit his reason."

"No, if I'd done the right thing, I'd have had the courage to tell him bigotry has no place in education and that I wouldn't tolerate his speaking about the other pupils and teacher in those hateful terms."

She couldn't help it, retelling the episode started the crying she'd held back since Friday. Ray reached for both her hands, held them tight, and waited until she moved to dry her eyes. He said, "I'm glad you told me. I'll be watching him."

Melanie said, "There's something else. I'm going out to talk to Mother this afternoon, but I want you to see it first." She went to the room they shared as an office and returned with a single piece of yellowed newspaper. "You remember when I told you I was reading Grandmother's diary. At the beginning, I found exactly the sort of thing I expected, the things a twenty-year-old would write while preparing for her wedding. Pages of details —who her bridesmaids would be, arguments with her mother, the bridal gown, guest list, that sort of thing. Oh, I also figured out she lied about her age. She called herself twenty, not twenty-one. People would have thought she was an old maid." She paused a second and thought about her grandmother, always so proper.

She said, "Grandmother also wondered whether Albert Jackson was a 'good match.' Called him handsome, but often moody, still thinking about his experiences in the war. One line was, "He'll need to put all that behind him. A married man has to take up the family business and make it succeed.""

Ray pointed to the paper she held and said, "Looks like you found something else."

"Stuck in between the pages." She handed it to him. "Read it. I couldn't believe that Grandmother never told me."

She watched as he read the article. He mumbled, "Grand Jury. Your great-granddad, right? Silas Reese. The Klan. I'm not surprised Delia never told you. Your grandmother didn't strike me as the sort who'd mention any hint of scandal in any part of her family."

"I'm going to ask Mother if she remembers the Klan ever operating out here. Or maybe Daddy knew something and told her." She held the article, staring at it intently. "What if that poor man was buried out on the ranch? No funeral, no family, probably no marker."

"You've had lots on your mind. Are you sure you want to dig into this now?"

"I can't get if off my mind."

Ray sighed, then said, "Nothing I can do will change the past. But I can watch for trouble from the current Reese family member. Let me know if there's anything else you want me to do."

As she drove to the ranch, Melanie passed the shrunken pond that had once been so important that the town was named for it. She shook her head and tried to focus on positive things, images of her grandmother as a twenty-year-old, aflutter with fussy preparations for her wedding, seeing the grandfather she'd never known through Delia's young eyes.

But by the time she knocked on her mother's front door, thoughts of Delia Jackson's wedding dress and of handsome Albert Jackson had been replaced by hooded men in white robes.

She gave her mother a brief hug, then said, "Are we alone?"

Willa frowned slightly. "Robert? He's over at Chris and Andrew's. Are you upset about something?"

"Puzzled, I'd say." She sat on the couch and faced Willa, sitting in her chair nearby. "I found this in Grandmother's diary yesterday." As her mother read the article, Melanie said, "Do you remember, as a child or later, hearing anything about that incident, or about the Klan being out here?"

Willa said, "Give me a second. I'm trying to recall. Nothing comes to mind immediately. I doubt my mother-in-law would have told me or her only son. Something as potentially scandalous as this, she'd have wanted to remain buried."

"I think it's what's buried that bothers me most. That poor man. First, he's treated inhumanly, then there's no justice, and finally, he's put in some grave without family present, probably not even a service or a marker. To me that's a scandal, too."

"Since Mamie has the library open again, maybe she knows where burial records might be. Even though the cemetery's been closed to new burials for years, I think there's a legal requirement that records be maintained. Of course, who knows if he was even buried in the cemetery here, or at Calverton, or maybe not in a cemetery?"

"Exactly. Maybe even out here on the ranch." As soon as Melanie said that, she regretted even thinking it.

"C.C. Jackson's guilt offering?"

"Maybe I read too many mysteries. But doing what I can to make this right is important to me."

Willa said, "The Calverton newspaper publisher should be able to tell you where their archives are kept, possibly at the Southwest Collection at Tech, or maybe available online."

Melanie leaned back against the couch cushion, and closed her eyes. Without opening them, she said, "I might not be so upset, except for what happened Friday." Then she told Willa about the Reese encounter. "Maybe that just set me thinking that there may still be Klan or something like it out here, that might do harm to someone." She opened her eyes. "Do you think I'm overreacting? I know I sometimes do."

Willa smiled and said, "I'm smiling because no one's immune, me included. Push the right button, and off I go. But no, I understand there are hate groups cropping up everywhere. And they don't harm just one person. Entire communities are affected."

Melanie sat quietly. Then she said, "Yes, even though we like to think of ourselves as more enlightened than back in the twenties, intolerance seems to be growing."

She pushed away a recollection of her own treatment of her son, Chris, years ago. Her rejection of his lifestyle had been an emotional reaction to some buried prejudice, one that made her unreasonable and unloving. Realizing that had taken her years. His forgiveness had come swiftly, but she still had moments when she hated the person she had been.

After a few silent minutes, Willa said, "On a happier note, Robert and I are thinking of getting a dog."

Just then Melanie heard the back door open and close quickly. Robert stood in the doorway from the kitchen. Her reaction to seeing Robert was, as always, a smile. Perhaps that was because he always managed to find a way to make her laugh, even though she would have preferred to be able to keep her distance. He greeted her, then said, "I heard the word *dog* as I eavesdropped my way in. She said yes this morning and made me a happy man."

Melanie saw him wink at her mother, then move to stand behind her chair and place his hand on her shoulder.

He said, "Since I was a boy, I'd always wanted a dog. But there was my sudden immigration to New York City, close quarters with relatives, then off to university, later living in apartments, then my townhouse in Austin and my travel made it always impractical."

Melanie said, "A puppy?"

Willa said, "No, a young, grown dog. Not a tripping hazard." She chuckled. "Beat you to the punch on that one, didn't I?"

Melanie had to laugh. After a couple of serious talks about her constant comments on safety hazards, they had agreed—her mother appreciated her continuing concern, and Melanie would do her best to reduce the more obvious evidence of her vigilance.

"You might want to mention your mystery to Robert. He loves searching for clues. And you can trust he keeps confidences well."

Melanie patted the space on the couch next to her, and Robert sat there. Willa went to make coffee. He said, "You've unearthed a mystery?"

Melanie hesitated, then repeated the evidence she'd found and described her reaction, her reasons for wanting to learn more. She finished by saying, "I know it may take a while to find the answers."

"Not to worry, my dear. When the university attaches Emeritus to your title, it means get out of the way. I work only on projects of my own choosing now. And I may never leave here again. Don't tell Willa, but for the first time since I left Ireland, when I'm here, I feel as if I'm home. Now give me an assignment."

They agreed he'd check Internet archive sites for newspaper mention of the murder and the grand jury trial. If he found nothing, he'd contact the newspaper office directly, but only then, since she preferred to keep her inquiries subtle, at this point. He also suggested that he would search for the murdered man's obituary or death notice. "I'm quite familiar with the genealogy sites. You know how we Irish are about those that came before us. I have a subscription to one of the best sites. I will report my findings by week's end, Madame Sherlock."

He'd done it again, gotten a smile from her. After the three of them drank coffee and discussed the construction plans for Chris and Andrew's house, she said, "I feel better for having told you this. Thanks, both of you, for listening." She checked her phone. "I need to get home before long, but if you have time, there's one more thing."

Robert said, "Time in abundance, and happy to be able to say so."

Willa said, "What is it?"

"You know about the planning committees Ray intends to set up?"

They both nodded.

"What are your thoughts about who should chair those? I know you've both been on lots of committees in many organizations."

In their own ways, both Willa and Robert suggested important attributes for a committee chair—one who understands the process of getting ideas from the group, not pushing a personal agenda; a respected person, known to be fair; someone with little to lose, who cares about issues; and from Robert a plug for women as chairs, his reason being that they tended to move the process in an orderly way.

Melanie said, "What about me as chair of the education and child care committee?

Willa shook her head. "Even though you're the most knowledgeable in those areas, you shouldn't be the one. Not any of the committees. Not Claire or me either."

As she felt her face edge toward a frown, Melanie said, "So you agree with Ray."

"I don't know Ray's thoughts, but I think he shouldn't appoint anyone in the family. Consultants, even maybe as a member, but not as chair."

Melanie sighed. "Anything else?"

Robert said, "If I were appointing a committee, I would want to try to appoint at least one person, maybe the most vocal, who's likely to oppose change. Better to have them in the tent than out. It's a good way to identify obstacles to change early."

Melanie set her coffee cup on the end table. "You've given me a lot to think about. Thanks, even if you agree with Ray, not me."

As she backed out of the drive, she waved to Willa and Robert as they stood at the front door. For some reason, tears clouded her view. The looked as if they belonged there together.

Floyd County Tribune
Thursday, August 28, 2014

Jackson's Pond Strategic Planning

Following the Jackson's Pond City Council meeting August 25, Mayor Ray Banks announced the Council's decision to develop a strategic plan for Jackson's Pond's future.

"This is an effort to make our town an outstanding example of a community's commitment to working together to make a town survive and succeed. Central to this effort is participation by all citizens in one or more activities of the planning process. Please contact the City Office if you are willing to serve on one of the following committees: public health and safety, education and child care, housing, city infrastructure; and business enhancement.

"This will be a lot of work, but it's important if we want our town to prosper. The new business created by RBJ Data Solution's choosing us as their home site can be the beginning of lasting improvement that will assure our town thrives in the 21st century." (See related article on the strategic planning process, page 3.)

RBJ Data Solutions Office Opens

The first three employees of RBJ Data Solutions opened the doors of the company office at 223 Main Street in Jackson's Pond Monday, August 25, 2014. The renovated site of the former drugstore brings a new look to the corner of Main and Bond.

Administrative Director, Clay Gomez; Office Coordinator, Lucinda Perry; and Administrative Assistant, Tonya Johnson will be joined in the near future by at least five other RBJ personnel. Gomez explained, "Even after the data and research facility is completed, this office in town will function as the gateway for employee recruitment and public information. So, we're a new fixture on Main Street. We encourage local people to drop by and learn about RBJ."

CHAPTER 3
Civil Twilight

Willa closed the back door soundlessly. Robert always slept lightly and late. She stepped out onto the patio behind her house. The darkness had begun to ebb but stars still shone brightly. Light pollution didn't yet reach out here beyond Jackson's Pond, Texas. Not willing to spoil her morning, she left the outside light off and used her walking stick to guide her as she carried her coffee mug to the glider.

Her early time alone each day was one more of the benefits of the differences between her and Robert Stanley. Her long-time friend, now constant companion, kept a routine of reading and listening to music until after midnight, then sleeping until eight, which qualified him as a night owl. She rose at least thirty minutes before sunrise, no matter what the season. Though some would have called her a lark, she preferred to think of herself as a raven, coming off the nest early, soaring, watching the rest of her world come alive as the sun climbed. A short nap at midday, a luxury in her earlier years, was now a requirement. It maintained her energy until around ten at night. Studio time occupied part of each day. That, plus her ballet work with Elisa and Amy, and the always present family and ranch activities kept her productive and feeling necessary. As yet, she'd never questioned whether she still had a purpose.

"Do you have the cook fire started and the coffee on to boil, my dear?" Robert's deep voice startled her. His thick Irish accent made her smile. It remained faint, just a lilt, when the situation was formal. The first time she'd heard one of his art history lectures, she'd barely noticed it. But when he relaxed, it returned, and with it came the charm that made each day they were together memorable, if for no other reason than laughter they shared.

She said, "I'm sorry if I woke you."

"Although my first thought was of you, that didn't wake me." He carried a cup of coffee and sat next to her on the east-facing glider. "Are you entertaining long thoughts this morning, Willa darlin'?"

"I was on your mind?"

He nodded, then sipped his coffee. "Indeed."

"Anything I need to know about?"

He winked at her above his cup's rim. "It will all be revealed in time."

She made certain he could see her expression, an eye roll and a bit of a smirk accompanied by a "how important could it be" shrug. "To your question, yes, long thoughts about twilight."

"And what did you think?"

"I always loved the early and late light, an emotional response I never really understood. Then I learned the specifics about twilight in my first studio art class, years ago at UT. I can still recall parts of that lecture. I doubt I need to tell you. You probably included that in one of your lectures as well."

"Not necessarily," he said. "Mine were duller stuff, I fear. Art history isn't nearly as dynamic as studio art. But I've often wondered why twilight as a metaphor seems reserved for the near end of things—the day, one's life. Not accurate, as twilight happens at the beginning, too."

She scooted to the side, leaving room for him on the glider. "That's exactly the reason I was thinking of it. Twilight is a visible signal of impending change," she said. "At my age, I prefer to focus on the beginnings. Change energizes me. And as sure as this is September first, we are about to face changes."

"And you know that how?"

She looked toward the eastern horizon. "It's a feeling I have." After drinking more coffee, she pointed toward the single star still visible. "See there, astronomical twilight becomes nautical twilight as the edges of objects and the horizon become visible." They sat without speaking, observing the changing light. Then, turning toward Robert, she said, "Because of that, for example, I can now see you haven't combed your hair or shaved."

"Ouch! You know how to hurt a man. This early, I require coffee before all else."

She patted his arm. "Watch. The part I love best comes next."

"Civil twilight." Chris's voice came from the north side of the house. Her grandson walked over and joined them. He said, "Okay. I was eavesdropping, but only the part about nautical twilight. Did I miss anything good?"

Wearing boots, Wranglers, and a khaki shirt, he looked fit for the range. Willa asked, "Ready for work so early?"

"Thought I could beg a third cup of coffee before we get started this morning."

Robert said, "Is Labor Day not observed in this part of Texas?"

"J.D.'s starting to plant the wheat today, and I'm assigned to check fences on the grass. So, no holiday for me and Britches."

He went inside and came out carrying a mug and the coffee pot.

Robert said, "What about your contractor? Does he work on Labor Day?"

"You're a step ahead of me again." Chris raised his cup, toast style. "This coffee isn't the only reason I came over here. Ranch work's going to keep me busy all day. Would you meet with him? You know what we want changed on the plans. I'd hate to have to cancel the appointment. Andrew had planned to be here, but he called last night, said he'd be late getting back from Taos. Couldn't find a rental moving truck until yesterday and packed until late last night."

Robert said, "I'll do it. What time?"

"Nine-thirty. Thanks!" Chris drained his coffee in one gulp. "Okay, got to go. The boss doesn't know I'm carrying my camera. Just after civil twilight's my favorite."

One day, he'd shown Willa a series of pictures featuring the wind turbines for a photo essay he planned. Among the images so far, he'd captured different views of birds; cows with calves; a horse; and a lone bull, each in combination with one or more of the modern windmills. That day he'd said, "Peaceful coexistence, I'm thinking for a title. Or maybe acculturation."

After Chris left and Robert disappeared indoors, Willa went to the studio she'd added to the house she'd grown up in. The remodeling project had transformed it from the simple two-bedroom frame house into a metal-roofed, stuccoed, hacienda-type dwelling. Since her return from Taos last October, she'd watched the transformation as each phase seemed to create need for the next. The final part, adding a suite of bedroom, bath, and study for Robert, had been completed last spring. It had been delayed after the highway accident that nearly killed J.D.

Since then, it had been as if the whole family, Robert included, had drawn closer together, and that the Jackson ranch had become their common concern, second only to J.D.'s healing from the fractures and other injuries.

A whole new energy, larger than the group from which it emerged, had grown in these past three months. Now Chris had ranch work each day and a new art project. Andrew seemed happier than she'd ever seen him—changing careers from nursing to working as an assistant with the vet, and taking online courses for vet assistant certification. Any idle time he filled with long talks with Claire about nursing, with helping on the ranch, and haunting horse sales to buy one of his own. And now the house that he and Chris would build to replace the "palace on wheels" they'd lived in since arriving would soon be under construction.

Even if the new vitality hadn't touched Willa, seeing her grandson and his partner so happy would have been enough. But she also felt inspiration. The result sent her this morning to her studio and the easel holding a small sketch and a larger, twelve-by-eighteen-inch piece of watercolor paper. She'd chosen hot press paper, unlike the cold press, her usual favorite. And last night she'd placed tubes of opaque watercolors and white gouache on her work table. All the paintings she'd shown and sold before had been transparent watercolors.

Robert, now freshly shaven, poked his head in the doorway. "I'm making a bit more coffee. Will you have any?" He walked nearer her work table, leaned to peer at the sketch on her easel. "What's this? A Willa with a human in it?"

"Not to worry, my dear. No portraits from me. It's an experiment. Looking at ways our landscapes affect the people who populate or visit them. We'll see."

"I love watching you at your work." He touched her shoulder. "I'll make brunch for us when I finish with the builder."

Focusing her attention on the sketch, she said, "That's a deal. And I'll take that coffee you offered. No need to deliver. Just go on about your rat killing, Muldoon."

Over the years she'd known Robert, more than ten now, her initial admiration for him as an expert art historian and art businessman had grown. As time passed, she'd come to rely on his professional advice and support.

Today, as she mixed gouache with the first color to apply to the bare white paper, she referred again to her sketch. In a High Plains landscape, a man, seen from the back, walks up a slight incline toward a traditional windmill. He carries a knobby wood walking stick and a medium-sized dog runs near him. She planned to add a hint of a jackrabbit in the tall bluestem grass for that dog to chase.

If this painting worked out as she hoped, it would be Robert's eightieth-birthday present. That gave her plenty of time. In all the years she'd known him, he'd never mentioned his actual birthday. There'd never been a party or gifts. He probably thought she believed he was a leprechaun. This year the family would celebrate him on November first, if her plan worked. Beyond her trust, Robert now held a spot in the place in her heart reserved for family.

Colors mixed, Willa selected a moderately stiff flat brush to begin laying in background color. She stepped back and eyed the color she'd begun with. Observing from different distances was a habit. What she saw pleased her, thus far.

Next, she added a dab of water to the green she'd begun the foreground with. Moving to the blue she'd mixed on her palette, she tested it on the upper portion of the paper, then continued. She stepped back again to check the color and the texture she'd used to create the matte effect she hoped to achieve with the opaque paint.

A tiny squeak reminded her to spray the back door hinge with WD40. But Robert beat her to it. He had the can in his hand when she walked into the kitchen. He said, "Just a tiny noise, but annoying nonetheless."

"Through with the builder?"

He wiped a bit of oily excess from the door. "Yes, and he's to return tomorrow, ready to begin. Now we're alone, my dear."

In three steps he stood beside her, took her right hand and gathered her in a waltz embrace and led her in a few steps accompanied by his hummed version of *The Blue Danube Waltz*. Melanie would choke if she saw them.

Since Willa had told the family of her cerebellar degeneration diagnosis, her daughter wore vigilance like an overcoat, always prepared for the worst—a fall, creeping invalidism. Not Robert. He'd promised they would dance as long as either of them could stand. He'd never let her fall from his arms. After Frank died, so many years ago, she'd never expected to find such warmth and comfort with anyone again. She'd chosen not to search for it. But Robert brought it. Another of life's gifts, she thought.

After a slight bow, he said, "You're especially light on your feet today."

She kissed his cheek. "You do know how to charm a girl. Is that your way of recruiting cooking help?"

"Ever so slick, wouldn't you say?"

"I'll set the table and any other menial task you require."

Working together, they prepared migas, flour tortillas, and refried beans. Sliced oranges and apples covered a small purple plate. The aroma of green chiles and comino followed them to the kitchen table.

She asked, "Any problems with the builder?"

"Not at this point. It's as they actually do the work that one must watch. Some subcontractors occasionally slide in shortcuts to raise their profit." Robert ate the large serving of the egg dish quickly, then leaned back. "That came just in time. I was near famished."

Willa took her time eating. She could feel him watching, a clue that he had something on his mind. He drew a deep breath and leaned forward, elbows on the table. "There's something that I need to ask you. Do you need to get back to your work or do you have time now?"

"I have time. Now that I've begun, I can see where I'm going with this piece." She leaned across to take his plate, stacked it atop hers. "Making space. I'll clear away later." She took a final sip and added her coffee cup and saucer to the stack. "Ask me."

He folded and then unfolded the purple napkin she'd chosen to brighten their brunch table. "I might as well just out with it. Your family will certainly want to celebrate your eighty-fourth birthday. September twenty falls on a Saturday this year, so that day will be taken. And Chris and Andrew may need my help. So sooner is better..." He paused, then continued. "Since I've been out here . . . seldom have trouble saying . . ."

Willa said, "Maybe if you began again."

"Right." Robert sat back from the table, shaking his head. "It's that I want to ask this in just the right way. You've told me this is my home as often and as much as I want to be here." He paused again. "And you haven't said anything has changed even though I've been here constantly since May . . ."

Willa said, "If you're wondering, I'm not tired of your being here." She paused when a knock sounded at the front door, then said, "If you need more room, we can rearrange things."

He raised a hand and shook his head. "No, it's nothing like that."

Before she reached the door, Jay Frank yelled, "Gran, Mr. Stanley, come look." Then another knock on the door. As Willa opened it, he said, "Come watch. O'Keeffe's walking on a lead."

She stepped out onto the front porch. Robert followed. He said, "That's really good. Two months and he's already trained to a lead. You know, it's probably the Irish name."

Jay Frank had waited a week to name the goats after choosing them at the sale. Sitting on their front porch, he'd said to Willa and Robert, "About names for the goats. I need your help. See, since you two bought my show goats for this year, and art is what you do, then I'll name my goats for painters. Will you give me a list of really good painters to choose from? Maybe six or eight."

Willa had frowned a bit, to show him she was considering his request carefully. She said, "Robert's the expert on artists' names. He can give you eight, probably right this minute, no strain."

No surprise to her, the boy had come prepared with pen and pad. Robert said, "Male or female?"

Her great-grandson looked up at Robert, as if in serious thought, then said, "I don't think they'll know the difference."

"Okay. Ready?" Jay Frank nodded. Robert reeled off names. "Rivera, Monet, Van Gogh, Gorman, Hockney, Hopper, O'Keeffe—a good Irish name—and of course, Jackson, that's Willa Jackson."

That last name got a smile from the eleven-year-old. He said, "I'll look these up and decide which goats they fit."

Two days later he had Willa and Robert go to the pen with him to tell the four goats their names. O'Keeffe was the largest, then, in order of size, Jackson, Hopper—he chose that one because that goat was feisty—and finally Rivera, because he liked the sound of the muralist's name. Watching Robert's face as the boy explained his decisions, Willa had thought Robert would have been a wonderful grandparent, or in this case, great-grandparent.

Now, after they both praised O'Keeffe's accomplishment, plus that of his handler, Jay Frank left, saying he had work to do at the pen. As they walked back inside, Robert said, "He's such a mature child. And very formal. You notice he always calls me Mr. Stanley."

Back in the house, Robert pointed to the large leather couch in the living room. "Let's sit here."

He waited until Willa was seated, then sat near, turned toward her.

She said, "Before you say more, tell me, do you feel at home in this house?"

"More than anyplace I've lived."

"Fine, then you mustn't treat me as if I'm the landlady. You should do what you want."

"But still…" After a few seconds, he said, "Even so, what I want to ask involves both of us."

Willa nodded, made a beckoning motion. "Let's hear it."

"First, now that you've agreed to having a dog, let's discuss the particulars."

Without hesitating, she said, "Any *particular* type—size, breed?"

He leaned back against the cushion, smiling. "Housebroken. Companionable, but not a lap dog. No particular breed."

"There hasn't been a dog on the place in many years. I love dogs."

"We should adopt from one of the shelters. You know I have a soft spot for orphans."

His brogue now made him sound young, excited, and eager to bring home their dog. They agreed to go Friday to the Humane Society shelter in Lubbock. He said, "After we find our dog, we'll shop for a suitable house, food, all that. If you agree. We'll make a day of it."

She said, "You really didn't have to ask."

"Yes," he said, "I did." She moved to rise, planning to clear the table. He said, "Wait, there's one more thing."

Another knock at the door halted him. Willa went to answer, and Robert headed to the kitchen. For the next hour and a half, they heard Melanie's news of the possibility of a family secret she'd discovered and her obvious distress at the injustice surrounding it. After Robert's offer of help, they moved to another topic, the committees that Ray planned to appointment to head plans for Jackson's Pond's revitalization.

All the while, Willa watched her daughter's face. She could tell that Melanie would not rest until she'd done all she could possibly do. Who could fault her intention to see that social justice prevailed? Willa would have been proud of her even if she weren't her daughter.

After they waved goodbye to Melanie, Robert took Willa's hand and led her to the living room. He said, "Let's return to our earlier conversation."

They settled back on the couch, and she waited, watching his face, seeing uncharacteristic hesitance.

He said, "I planned to wait, but . . . Well, it's time." After a deep breath, he said, "Darlin' girl, will you marry me?"

For most of his lighthearted banter, Willa usually played the part of second banana, laying out lines he could turn into jokes. They'd been together so often, for so many years, she could usually keep up her end of the conversational bargain. And though he often amazed her with his wit, he seldom took her completely by surprise. They had never once spoken of marriage.

"You've finally done it, truly surprised me. I believe you're serious."

He raised his right hand. "On my oath. Never more serious in my life."

She didn't speak for seconds that stretched to a minute, then probably two. He said, "You don't have to answer now."

"I couldn't . . . couldn't answer now."

She barely managed to speak, much less sort the many thoughts that had to be examined logically—would her family be disrupted—Chris and Andrew in favor; Claire, J.D. and the children neutral; Melanie heartbroken and threatening legal action? Could Robert and she bear being the reason for a rift in the family? Did her happiness and his matter that much? Was she an old fool? As quickly as the thoughts assembled, they evaporated. It wasn't only her thoughts that swirled; her chest filled with emotions easier to name, but no less confusing to experience. Sadness, for her first love, Frank long absent, but seldom far from her; love and tenderness for Robert, steady and constant, and always ready to create memorable moments; excitement at the possibility of finding more light in her waning years, making new memories even now.

Watching his face, she saw the twinkle, a smile around the eyes that betrayed a coming punch line. But he only nodded, then said, "I understand. I can wait."

She shrugged to loosen the muscles that had suddenly clamped her shoulders. She said, "Please tell me you're not pregnant."

Robert's laugh sounded a release for both of them. "Okay, now you got me!" He gathered her to him in a tight hug. "That's just one of the reasons. I'm serious, though, and I hope you'll answer me soon. I love you more than you can know."

"And I love you. But we must both think about this."

He nodded. "I have. A great deal."

"We'll talk soon."

He said, "At twilight?"

Who wouldn't love such a romantic and love being in love with him? But marriage? She kissed his cheek and said, "Yes, someday soon, at twilight."

She meant it. Bringing order to her thoughts, making a careful decision would take some time and effort. Entertaining the mixture of emotions would, however, be a pleasure. How fortunate she was at her age to have more reasons than most people to feel love and excitement and very little of what many dwelled on through their later years, regret.

Floyd County Tribune

Wednesday, February 2, 1921

Town Talk—Heard Around Here

Social Niceties

Methodist Ladies of Jackson's Pond, Texas, honored Mrs. Albert Jackson with a Welcome Tea last week. The new bride is at home on the Jackson Ranch outside Jackson's Pond. A member told this Editor that Mrs. Jackson would definitely be a fine addition to the group. "She's a graduate of Miss Troufant's in New Orleans where she learned many important skills that will benefit our group and our town. Plus we have already recruited her to sing alto in the choir. We were lacking in that area."

Following Recent Events

In his continuing effort to follow stories to their conclusion, this Editor spoke to a member of the Commissioners Court this week. When asked what disposition was made of the remains of Lincoln Berryhill, who was found murdered in our county, the elected official replied, "Taken care of. It's best for you and your paper if you let it lie." Since that encounter, no further information has been gained.

Time to Pray?

The windstorm that moved dust from the west side of our county toward the east all day last Saturday brought only grit and grimness. A farmer I encountered the following Monday muttered, "It's going to be a long year, spring weather starting in January. We sure needed some moisture out of those clouds. I'd have been happy with sleet and ice, anything but dirt. I think it's time to start praying."

CHAPTER 4
Gang of Three

After she returned home from the ranch, Melanie changed into her workout clothes and threw herself into exercise on her elliptical trainer. Since she and Ray remarried twelve years ago, she'd changed many of her attitudes and lots of her habits. Actually, the changes occurred before, gradually during those long years alone after she and Ray divorced, and helped her realize the value of the man she remarried, recommitted to. But daily exercise remained a constant. Today she hoped it would help her focus. Too many thoughts competed for her attention—how to convince Ray she should be committee chair, the possibility that a not-so-distant ancestor had participated in murdering an African American man on their ranch, that the man might never have received a proper burial, her mother and Robert's getting a dog at their age, and the possibility there were more like Justin Reese right here in Jackson's Pond.

Minutes later, as she began to perspire, she felt clarity about only one thing. She was often guilty of being too quick to judge. Tempted by her considerable intelligence—she had grades and certificates to prove that—and a well-honed logical thought process, she reached conclusions swiftly. Maybe it was age, Ray's influence, and perhaps her bitterness at having been passed over for the school district superintendency years ago, or all of those, that made her a bit more open now to others' ideas. But quick conclusions about people and about the solutions to problems still often winked at her, a seductive force difficult to ignore. At least now she was aware that same force could create prejudices and too-simple answers to complex questions. As she headed for the shower, she repeated what she hoped was true, "Fifty-nine years old and I'm still a work in progress."

With no mission in mind, she went to her office and stood staring at the four boxes of Delia Jackson's papers. Her grandmother could have done well as an office administrator, given the records she kept—household expenses, receipts for remodeling work on the big house, minutes from the clubs she belonged to and often presided over. Then it struck Melanie. She'd only looked at the full contents of three boxes. When she found that clipping in the diary in the third one, she'd stopped. And that diary didn't fit with the rest of the materials in those boxes. It was personal. The other things were less so.

She pulled a stool from under her desk and sat near the fourth box. A faintly familiar scent met her when she lifted the lid—Delia Jackson's hand lotion, glycerin and rosewater. She'd loved snuggling next to grandmother in the big bed they often shared for naps, where waking smelled like roses and the end of a nap started an almost new day. She lifted out a diary which looked exactly the same as the other she'd found. The first entry in this one was January, 1923. She set it aside, along with six more like it. More interested in finding clippings, she got her wish as she lifted out a large framed photo of Albert Jackson in his WWI uniform. That picture had hung in the bedroom, Melanie recalled. Under the photo, the rest of the box was filled with clippings. She heard Ray come in the door from the garage. The clippings would have to wait.

Then one near the top caught her eye. Her grandmother's name. It only took seconds to read the old-fashioned prose describing Delia Jackson's introduction to Jackson's Pond society. So soon after her arrival, much had been expected of her, apparently.

From Melanie's perspective, much had been given in return. In a time in the early twentieth century when women's clubs offered social opportunity as well as a platform for effecting social change, even small towns benefited from those organizations. Without them there would have likely been no libraries, no charitable funds, no town beautification, no Red Cross volunteers, or many of the other functions that civilize a community. Although by current standards the clubs with their fussy rituals seem quaint, they served their purpose. The Federated Women's Clubs House still stood unused in town. If she were still alive, Grandmother would never have let that happen. That building should be celebrated and vital.

Following the article, just below the fold in the clipping, the next piece of local gossip caused her to stop. The editor was warned away from asking further about disposal of the body of Berryhill. She placed the clipping on her desk and closed the box. When she looked up, Ray stood watching her from the doorway. He said, "Find something interesting? Something positive maybe?"

"Troubling. Nothing I can do anything about right now, though." She crossed the room and put her arms around him. "Any chance of getting a kiss from the mayor?"

"Not a chance. No ma'am. It's a guarantee. Anytime, anyplace." He kissed her behind her right ear, then on the mouth. "How's that?"

"Not bad for an elected official. Let's have a glass of wine before I make supper."

The next afternoon, Melanie, Willa, and Claire sat at the small table in the break room at Banks Preschool. Willa said, "After you left yesterday, it occurred to me that Ray shouldn't have to decide about committee chairs without the benefit of some input from outside the City Council. So here's some breaking news—I have some ideas about the committees. We'll be the first to provide input."

Willa sounded the way Melanie remembered her in the past, as if hopes of setting Jackson's Pond on a progressive path has sparked her energy. Years ago, that feistiness had irritated Melanie, the earlier version of herself she so often regretted. Back then she'd wanted a mother who sang in the Methodist choir, attended Garden Club. Instead, after she was widowed, Willa managed the Jackson ranch, became a force in the statewide Cattle Raisers Association, worked tirelessly for Democratic Party candidates, and won prizes for her watercolor paintings.

She asked Melanie, "Do you know if the other council members are committed to this planning process?"

"Ray said it took a lot of discussion, but they finally all agreed it's either that or watch Jackson's Pond, Texas, dry up completely." Melanie remembered he'd first mentioned strategic planning several months ago. "I recall he said the RBJ business would be the perfect stimulus to make planning for progress critical."

They sat silently for what seemed like a long time. Then Claire said, "How do you think Daddy will react to our offering to help?"

Melanie said, "It'll depend on how we present it. And who. I imagine he'd take advice from Mother more easily than from either of us."

Willa frowned. "You two know more people here in town now than I do."

Melanie said, "He might not admit it, but he's very serious about his responsibility as mayor. About being fair and unbiased. And he won't like feeling ganged up on. I can tell you for certain."

Claire asked, "How did he react to the idea of your being the education chair?"

"I barely had it out of my mouth before he said a flat no."

Willa said, "Maybe he'll be more open when you're not the topic."

"I know you agree with him, but I'm not convinced either of you is right."

"We might as well come up with our suggestions now, including education, before we worry about how to offer them to Ray." Willa looked toward the cabinet and sink. "Does that coffee pot work?"

Melanie hustled to make coffee. Thinking about convincing Willa and Claire, she emptied enough drip grounds for eight cups into the basket, then realized she'd only poured water for six. She added two more cups of water.

Claire said, "Let's start with infrastructure."

Willa shrugged and nodded.

Melanie said, "Why infrastructure? You have someone in mind?"

"Garland Thames," Claire said. "A former mayor should have some ideas and would know more than a lot of people about city services, water supply, tax income, things like that."

Melanie remembered Thames' whispering campaign against Ray, insinuating he'd be a tool of people downstate, as if anyone downstate cared about Jackson's Pond. "He wasn't exactly a gracious loser in the election."

Willa said, "That could be a good reason for Ray to appoint him. Only a generous man would appoint his defeated opponent."

After they discussed a few more factors, ending up more pro-Thames than con, Claire said, "Are you both okay with tentatively including his name?"

Melanie shrugged, and Willa nodded.

They quickly agreed on Mr. Patel, the motel owner, as their favorite for the business enhancement committee. And even more quickly they agreed that the town Realtor, Sam Landrum, was a good fit for the housing committee.

"I'll be surprised if those two aren't already on Ray's list," Melanie said. "I guess that's a good thing. Not so much to have to sell him on."

Just to show they were also open to input, the unappointed advisors chose the retired owner of the local convenience store as an alternate for Mr. Patel. Now they were down to the two Melanie considered most important and most difficult, health and education. As surely as Ray had nixed her for education, he would veto Claire for health just as quickly. Melanie said, "Either of you want more coffee?"

They both shook their heads. Claire said, "I don't live in town, so I'm not eligible to head the health committee. But I do have an idea. Heath Goodman, minister at the Cowboy Church. He's very interested in the community. He and his wife have three small children and live here in town, but he works at an implement dealership in Lockney. A couple of years older than me."

Willa said, "I don't know. He sounds like a busy young man. Maybe too busy."

"We need some young people involved in this. His church is where lots of them attend."

Melanie said, "But is he old enough to be wise?"

Claire said, "Mother, really!"

As soon as Melanie had said it, she leaned back, both hands raised and said, "Erase that. You'd think as many times as I've complained about racism and sexism, I'd be more sensitive to other prejudices." She stood, shaking her head, "You're right, Claire. I was wrong even thinking that. I'm getting more coffee."

Willa said, "If he's too busy, surely he'd say so. I'm okay with Heath Goodman, if you two are." They both nodded. Then she said, "If there's only one thing that each chair must be able and willing to do, it's to get people talking, committee members and others in town. Get ideas circulating. If Ray hesitates about any of these, we need to have evidence that they can and will do that."

Nodding, Claire said, "I agree about wide input. In graduate school, I thought I was destined to lead, and others should follow. But eventually our community health practicum made a believer of me. I knew I had all the right ideas for how our project should be implemented, and I nearly made my first failing grade ever before my classmates convinced me the instructor was correct. From the very beginning, she had repeated a phrase like it was a mantra: 'All of us are smarter than any one of us.' So much for the leader being the source of all ideas."

Her daughter's capabilities as a nurse practitioner had, from the beginning, awed Melanie. Claire had gone from late adolescent to competent professional almost overnight, it seemed. Now here she was offering wisdom that had long eluded Melanie. She couldn't help smiling as she thought, "Too soon old and too late smart."

Willa said, "Aside from yourself, do you have ideas about a chair for the education committee?"

After a long silence and a deep breath, Melanie said, "Yes, I do. Marisol Quintero."

"There's another name I don't know. Tell us about her."

Before Melanie could answer, Claire said, "Yes, why didn't I think of her? She was my junior high counselor before she went to work for the migrant program."

"Would she do as good a job as you?" Willa leaned toward Melanie.

"I wouldn't have admitted it before now, but she'll probably do better. She's very good at encouraging others to find solutions and more patient than I can ever be."

Melanie summarized the list they would offer Ray. Then she said, "Now, back to who'll pass this priceless information on to the mayor."

Claire said, "I think we should also tell Daddy we're coming back next week with suggestions for consultants. I'm putting your name at the top of the list. Do you mind?"

"Yours should be at the top. If there's any area where the committees will need consultation, it's health and safety. By the way, I heard the Texas Health Solutions clinic may close."

"I heard that, too. But I doubt it. Not yet, at least."

Not the reaction Melanie had expected. Claire seemed genuinely uninterested. She turned her gaze on Willa, who looked healthier than she had in a long time. And definitely enjoying herself. Melanie said, "Back to the messenger. I think you're the one, Mother. Ray respects you and knows you have no personal agenda. If it's me, he might resist a bit, based on having to make clear he's not going to appoint me, that he's in charge."

"What about Claire?"

"She could convince him. He respects her. But you are the smoothest. Men always listen to you. It's some kind of magic you work, I think."

"I agree, Gran. It's you."

Willa said, "Magic? Gray hair, I think. Okay, I'll do it. But don't think for a minute I won't invoke both your names as needed. As Claire's teacher said, 'All of us, et cetera.'"

Wednesday, just as she and Dolores ushered the last pupil and parent out the door after school was over, Melanie saw Willa and Claire park behind the last pickup in line. She waited for them at the door. As they came up the sidewalk, Melanie noticed Justin Reese drive past, slowly, come nearly to a halt directly in front of her. He raced his motor, then drove to the end of the block and turned right onto Main Street. The sticker on his back bumper said, "America for Americans."

Willa said, "I just stopped to drop Claire off and let you know I'll be back after my appointment with the mayor."

As Willa turned back toward the curb, she lifted her right hand, showed them her crossed fingers.

When she returned more than an hour later, Willa was the only one at the table without a bowl of ice cream. "We gave you an hour, and when you weren't back, we started without you." Claire pointed with the tip of her spoon toward the refrigerator. "I'll get you some while you tell us all about it."

"No, thanks." Willa turned toward Melanie. "You were right, he had never even thought of the former mayor."

"What took so long?"

"I'll tell it in sequence. First, I explained that these suggestions were offered in a gesture of civic participation. We want to smooth his work in this important process." She cut her eyes toward Claire. "I saw you smirk, Missy. It was a sincere comment. Before we started, I told myself to behave as if he were a stranger and this was strictly business. So, yes, he probably wondered why I was so formal. But he never said anything about it. I led with the Garland Thames suggestion. Debating that took a while." She leaned back, then said, "I believe I will have some ice cream."

Claire returned with a dish of strawberry. "I wasn't smirking. Rolling my eyes, maybe." With a flourish, she produced a large serving spoon from behind her back. "This will help you catch up with me."

Melanie smiled watching the byplay between the two. Her daughter and her mother had always enjoyed one another so. They were a lot alike. Although seeing them happy together pleased

Melanie, she couldn't help wishing everyone found her as easy to be with as those two.

Willa summarized by saying Ray agreed with all the rest, and complimented them for their work. Until she began talking about consultants and members, it had been easy, she said. He'd argued that neither Melanie nor Claire should be consultants. After some fast talking on her part—Melanie could just imagine—he'd agreed that if someone on a committee suggested either of them, he'd agree. Then when she brought up Justin Reese, using Robert's notion of bringing the likely resistor directly into the process, he never did agree.

"That young man's treating you badly left a strong negative impression. I couldn't convince Ray." She raised her hands as if helpless. "I failed. But actually, I was proud, too. I like knowing he's protective of you."

Melanie nodded. She'd always been able to rely on Ray. She said, "Is that how you left it?"

"Except for one thing. He asked that we put some time into urging some people to volunteer as committee members. The response has been disappointing so far. Only five names on the sheets at City Hall."

Claire said, "Before we leave, let's make another list. People to contact."

"You start. I have ice cream to finish." She took a bite. "Oh, he did say one other thing. Something about how he'd been ganged up on before, but never so gently."

Melanie knew Ray wasn't the only one who'd been ganged up on. She pushed aside her wish to be the education committee chair. Marisol would do a good job. She also pushed the clipping she'd found away from her thoughts. It was a subject for another time, when something could actually be done. Whatever that might be. She said, "Here's a start on contacts. I'll talk to Mamie. She'd give anything to get the library open full time again."

Floyd County Tribune
Thursday, September 18, 2014
Planning Committee Members Sought

Jackson's Pond Mayor Ray Banks announced today that spaces are still available on the five strategic planning committees. "The work of the strategic planning process will be vital to the future of our town. It's important to have broad participation.

"Each of the five committees will have four members plus the chairperson. Committee chairs have all agreed to serve, plus eleven of the members. We continue to seek nine additional members to fill these important jobs. Please contact the City office in Jackson's Pond if you are willing to be a member."

Banks also said he hopes that the full membership of the planning committees can be announced in time for next week's edition of the Tribune.

CHAPTER 5
Gradually, In the Heart

Robert drove Saturday night to Claire and J.D.'s—the big house on the Jackson Ranch. Willa had said they should walk; the exercise would do them good. But he cajoled her into riding in his relic of a Volvo station wagon. He said, "Just once more before I trade it for that Land Rover I've had my eye on."

"Don't try to kid me. Now that you have access to a barn, you'll stash it away under its own special cover forever. You men love your cars, name them, and attach all your best memories to them. It's the same out here with pickups. You might get something else to drive, but there's no way that Patrick—you thought I didn't know its name—will ever be traded away."

He drove at a crawl. Claire had told him to arrive after 6:30. He said, "The sunset is going to be lovely tonight. Perhaps we can watch from the porch before supper is served. Want to take a detour by the pond?"

"I know what you're doing."

"What's that, my dear?"

"Distraction won't work. There's going to be a surprise party, the thing I begged Claire and Melanie not to do. I told them that overlooking it entirely would be the best birthday present they could give me."

"If, and I say *if* because I don't know any more than you do, there is something celebratory afoot, I know you'll accept it graciously." He turned left, toward the pond. She fiddled with her blouse, adjusting the collar to show her necklace. He said, "I love it when you agree with me."

"Ha! Silence from me is not ever to be taken as consent."

"Well. . ." He parked at the gate near the pond. "Maybe you could give them a surprise, turn the tables on them."

"How's that?"

"Tell them we're engaged to be married."

"But we're not."

"We could be. This is the perfect spot, right here, for you to give me your answer."

She looked at him, smiling. "The fact that you proposed is a wonderful birthday present. That's quite enough for now. I need time." She turned away, her face placid, seeming to focus on the single bull grazing near the almost dry pond. A few seconds later she said, "Speaking of time. We should go. Don't want to be late for whatever's happening at the big house tonight."

Although he knew Willa's preference, he hadn't tried to dissuade Melanie and Claire. They wanted to plan a surprise. He promised to bring the honoree and not to tell her a thing.

When they arrived, Jay Frank opened the door. As if he hadn't expected them, the boy said, "Oh, hi. Did you come for supper? I think it's going to be tacos tonight." He pointed out the door to the porch chairs. "I was coming out to watch the sun go down. Want to sit with me a minute? Dad's not in yet, and I don't know where Mom is."

He told his great-grandmother she looked pretty, asked if her blouse was new. What an actor—chatting on at top speed. Then, after some comments about the weather, all sounding like a full-grown rancher hoping for more rain, he said, "Okay, I guess we should go in."

They followed the boy and were met in the living room by Claire and J.D.; Melanie and Ray; Chris and Andrew; the Montoyas and their two boys, Tag Burley and his wife and two sons; Maria Chavez, Mamie, the librarian; Laverne, who had worked with Claire at her clinic; Laverne's husband, R. W., and her daughter, Wendy. Elisa Montoya and Willa's granddaughter, Amy, were nowhere among the crowd.

Minutes later, as guests greeted Willa and talked among themselves, J.D. got attention by ringing a cowbell. As soon as the noise settled, he said, "We are all supposed to go upstairs now to the ballroom. Excuse me, to the ballet studio. At this party, entertainment comes before food. Follow me."

In the large mirror-walled room that filled the upstairs, sounds of soft music met the group as they filed in and seated themselves in folding chairs arranged at the end opposite the stairs. Jay Frank disappeared into a small side room, the one Willa had told Robert had been a seating area for attendees at parties in the ballroom. The lights lowered; the group waited in silence.

Then Jay Frank reentered and announced in a voice surprisingly strong for an eleven-year-old, "Please welcome Elisa Montoya and Amy Havlicek performing dance selections to music from Grieg's *Peer Gynt Suite*." Then he led applause. He disappeared again and the music began.

Robert recognized "Morning Mood" immediately. The two ballerinas, each in pink leotard and tights with rainbow-layered tutu and pink slippers, danced intricate mirror images of one another. When the music stopped and the dancers paused, applause came, perhaps punctuating the small audience's surprise and delight.

The tempo changed with the next piece, "Anitra's Dance," in which each performed a solo to a portion of the piece. Elisa appeared first, displaying deft, rapid footwork and a stunning smile for the audience. Amy reemerged, now wearing toe shoes. Her short solo, danced en pointe, showed strength and smooth, relaxed gestures interpreting the joy in the music. A run of pirouettes displayed developing technical expertise. As they joined in a bow to the audience, Robert saw Willa nodding, hands clasped above her heart. The two dancers must have seen it, too.

For their final number, they performed an intricate dance to the strains of "In the Hall of the Mountain King." At the finale, their deep curtsies told the audience the show was at its end. Everyone stood, except Willa, who sat smothered by the two ballerinas and a large bouquet of mums and other fall flowers, all filling her lap.

Jay Frank, the perfect emcee, notified the crowd that after supper, served downstairs, the ballroom would be open for dancing to recorded music. "Golden Oldies," he said.

After supper, by eight-thirty, Willa had graciously accepted the rest of the birthday festivities—birthday cards, the cake with its single candle, and the singing. And then she danced with Robert to a song he had requested as soon as Claire told him there would be dance music, "I Could Have Danced All Night."

"I recall when we first danced to this," he said. "Do you?

Willa leaned back to look up at him, then shook her head and laughed. "How could I forget? I was the envy of every gray-haired woman on that cruise ship."

Robert held her closer and said, "I remember what you wore—a black taffeta blouse with a portrait collar, a matching skirt, waltz length. And you wore the same emerald necklace and earrings you're wearing now. You told me Frank gave them to you. I also remember because that's when I knew I had fallen in love."

She leaned her head against his shoulder and said, "And here we are, nearly ten years later."

"How fortunate I am. Thank you and happy birthday, dear Willa."

"You're making me cry. People are watching."

"If it's Melanie, she'll think you were overcome by too much birthday cake. Chris and Andrew understand, and Claire is one who also cries when she's happy. So cry if you feel it, as long as the tears are happy ones." Then he led her into a series of three swooping turns that ended just as the music stopped. He heard applause. The only reward he needed was the smile she gave him and the way she held tightly to his hand as they walked downstairs.

When Robert opened the door the following Monday afternoon, Amy and her friend Elisa stood smiling up at him. From where he stood, it seemed they had both grown taller by at least two inches in the past three months. Ah, puberty! Even though he had no children of his own, his memory of his youth, and of the girls in his village, made him certain these two were poised on the cusp of the great adventure known as the teenage years. Always, it was the girls who led, as he recalled.

"Do come in. How nice to have you visit. I loved your dancing at the birthday party. Very impressive." They both shrugged, then glanced around the living room. He ushered them into the kitchen-dining area. "It's a decent hour for an afternoon snack. Can I offer you some cookies and fruit?"

As he moved the fruit bowl to the table, Amy opened the pantry and peered inside, then backed out with a bag of pretzels in her hand. "We just came to visit. Do you have time?" Before he could answer, she said, "Is Gran here?"

"She is. In her studio painting. Shall I call her?"

Both girls chose chairs at the table. Amy said, "We don't want to bother her. We'll see her tomorrow for our ballet lesson."

Elisa took two of the shortbread cookies offered. Amy held her hand out toward Elisa and said, "No. Pretzels are better for dancers. Fewer calories."

Elisa lost the smile she'd been wearing. "You promised. No more trying to lose weight, neither one of us. And you promised your parents." She placed her two cookies side by side on a napkin.

Amy said, "Who put you in charge?"

"I did. I won't dance with an anorexic, and I won't be one, either. Not even for you."

Robert moved to the sink, turned on the water and washed his already clean hands. He saw Amy pretend something in her backpack fascinated her. Elisa said, "You promised."

This time the words carried a hint some consequence would befall a promise breaker.

Amy stared at her friend, who returned the gaze without looking away. Then Amy placed two pretzels on her napkin and inch by inch rolled the bag top down to the level of remaining pretzels. Next, in what looked like a complex ceremony, she took one of Elisa's cookies and traded it for one of the pretzels, then each of them took one bite of a cookie.

Robert dried his hands and exhaled. The girls each chose an orange, and stacked bits of peel on a single napkin, together building a graceful orange tower, glancing occasionally to where he sat on a stool at the countertop bar.

Watching them, he saw two gazelles, slender muscles ready to spring from grazing to full speed fluid motion at the first hint of danger. In Elisa, the combination of her Hispanic father and African-American mother produced exotic beauty—mocha-hued skin and velvet brown eyes—alert eyes, occasionally wary. Amy's olive complexion, dark curls, and emerald eyes spoke of a genetic line from her great-grandmother Willa, through her mother, Claire, skipping her blond grandmother, Melanie altogether. Amy would be the dauntless one leading the herd, he had no doubt.

In his limited adult experience with teenagers, Robert had concluded that more often than not, girls had an agenda, a mission, while boys frequently did little more than breathe and eat. So these two stopped in for a reason. After all, they'd walked at least three miles from the big house "just to visit."

After most of their oranges had disappeared, the pretzels and two additional cookies had been consumed, Elisa said, "Mr. Stanley, do you mind if I ask you some questions? We have reports to write."

"I'll surely do what I can to help. Ask away."

All business, Amy put her telephone in the middle of the table. "If you sit here with us, we can record so we don't forget things."

They produced notepads and pens from the backpacks they'd carried in. He asked, "What's the subject? Art's the only thing I really know much about. So, I may not be very helpful."

Amy said, "It's not for a class. We're starting a blog. It will have all kinds of subjects. This is about immigration. Now I'm recording. Today is September twenty-second, 2014 and this is Amy Havlicek. With me is Elisa Montoya. We are interviewing Mr. Robert Stanley."

"A blog? Do you have a website?"

"Not yet. That's next. We need to have content ready for the first post." Elisa wore a tiny frown as she glanced from him to the phone. "There's a free program, but we're having a little trouble with all the instructions. We may have to ask Jay Frank. He's smarter than he acts."

Amy said, "So you say." She pushed the phone nearer to Robert. "You're Irish. So that makes you an immigrant in this country. How long ago did you come to the United States?"

Willa walked in and said, "Are you three conspiring?" She stood behind Robert. "What time will we leave? I can be ready in ten minutes."

Elisa said, "We can come back."

Robert nodded. "That may be best, if you have many questions."

Amy slid her phone into her pocket, and followed it with two pretzels. "We'll be back after school Wednesday if that's okay. Ballet tomorrow." She waited as Elisa zipped her paper and pen in her backpack. As they walked toward the front door, she said, "Thanks for helping us."

He said, "Between now and Wednesday, please look up the term *editorial review*."

As they left, Willa said, "Actually, I'm ready now. I heard them come in, but didn't hear what they wanted."

"I'll tell you on the way. Who's driving?"

"Let's take the pickup," she said. "I'll drive. You still haven't mastered Lubbock streets."

After they left the ranch, Robert told her about the girls' idea for a blog. He hadn't had time to learn the reason for their interest in immigration.

Willa, eyes on the road, said, "You'd be surprised at some of the things those two are aware of. They talk about the usual teenage things, but also about deeper subjects. Eavesdropping on bits of their conversation before and after ballet has opened my eyes."

He said, "Are you certain about Laddie?" The first time they went to the shelter was last Monday. He'd envisioned walking in at the animal shelter, both immediately falling in love with the same dog, and whisking the grateful animal away to a plush life on the ranch. But from the first step inside, they had been drawn to different dogs.

The same thing happened on their second trip, Friday morning. Robert had spotted Laddie, a newcomer, from across the room. The russet-colored dog had the regal bearing and wise eyes of a herding animal. The shelter volunteer said their vet had identified him as "mostly Australian shepherd, but smaller." Then she paused, and they both watched Laddie raise his nose as if scenting something. "I think he's got a hunting breed in him. When he's in the outdoor play area, he's always scouting around, digging."

At the same moment Robert was chatting up the volunteer, Willa was charming Peggy, a female dog with mixed colored curly hair. The volunteer, who likely as not made her breed guesses on the spot, said Peggy might be part Airedale or other large terrier. If she'd said either of those dogs was an Irish wolfhound, he'd have been certain her volunteer function was sales, not animal care.

He and Willa had each considered all the other dogs present, just to be fair. After at least an hour of enduring sad eyes and wagging tails, they returned to Peggy and then to Laddie. No decision. The animal care woman looked a bit deflated when they told her. She'd mentioned twice that Peggy and Laddie might both be gone before the week was over. "Real charmers, both of them," she'd said.

The first thirty miles of the trip back, they'd debated, each mentioning the merits of the other's favorite. Her insistence he should have the dog he wanted had surprised him. She'd said, "You're the one who brought up the idea of having a dog. You've never had one. It's settled. We'll go back tomorrow and bring Laddie home." She'd even made him stop at the feed store in Calverton, and buy dog food and a bed. They'd never actually argued before.

Now, as she parked at the animal shelter, he said, "I have an idea. If both dogs are here, we can compromise."

"Half a dog each?"

He arched an eyebrow at her. "No, both dogs. They'd be happy to have a companion when we're busy or traveling. Both have been neutered. So, puppies won't be a problem."

"Why aren't you happy getting what you want?"

"Because, Willa dear, I love you and want you to have what makes you happy, too."

She gave him a steady look, like estimating the truth of what he'd said. Then she leaned over and kissed him, there in public, right on the mouth.

On the way back, they laughed about the two dogs standing on the small back seat, leaning over into the front, panting and wagging their tails. He said, "Back seat drivers. I'm glad you're driving. Happy dogs always distract me so."

They stopped again at the feed store for a second bed. This time Willa chose—one covered with bright red flowers.

As promised, Elisa and Amy turned up at the front door soon after they got off the school bus Wednesday. Robert had prepared a snack. Pimento cheese sandwiches, cookies, pretzels, and apple slices awaited them on the table. After they ate and played with the dogs, they got down to business. Amy put her phone on the table again. Both had pens and paper ready. After several questions about where he came from and why he left and when he arrived in the U.S., he managed to interrupt. He said, "Flattered as I am by your interest, I wonder what set you onto immigration as a topic."

Amy said, "We heard some people at school talking about immigrants taking jobs away from U.S. citizens. Real Americans, they called them."

"Yes," Elisa said. "And when they saw us listening, one of them said, 'Just wait till they finish building that wall in Arizona. They'll send *them* back.' He was talking straight at me." Her smile disappeared and tears welled in her eyes. She sniffed and said, "Just because I look different."

Robert said, "Ignorant people often say unfortunate things."

"I wanted to punch him. If Elisa hadn't made me leave, I would have."

"You've chosen an intelligent response, this blog. Using a personal example to explain the facts can be very effective." He pushed the plate of pimento cheese sandwiches toward them.

Elisa tore a tiny sandwich in half and handed part to Amy. He asked, "Did you look up editorial review as I asked?"

Elisa nodded. Amy said, "That means you get to check our work before it's public."

He said, "What are your feelings about that?"

Amy shrugged. "It's probably a good idea. I might want to say something that would make things worse. I'm still mad."

Elisa nodded. "She has more of a temper than I do."

He recalled being their age and new in the U.S., still tender from his parents' deaths. More than a few times he'd fought bullies who spat the word Irish like a curse. Nineteen forty-eight had been a hard year for him. Living with relatives he'd never met, moving from a village in the south of Ireland to New York City. The worst part had been enduring the hatred targeting him, not because he looked different, but because he came from another country, spoke with an accent, and probably because he and the bullies were all young teenagers. They were ripe with raging hormones.

He heard Willa speaking to someone in the living room. She and Melanie came to the kitchen. Interview suspended, he occupied himself watching the four females and sneaking bits of sandwich to each of the dogs.

Melanie said, "I guess I interrupted something here, other than snacks."

The girls explained their mission, without explaining why, only that they were going to start a blog and "Mr. Stanley is our first interview." Amy said, "No need to leave, Grandmother. We only have one more question today."

Robert said, "Fire away."

Elisa read from her notes. "Is an immigrant always an immigrant or does that ever change?"

"Interesting question. If one becomes a naturalized citizen, I suppose that should make a person no longer an immigrant— becoming a U.S. citizen, therefore an American. But that's a matter of legal status. In a person's mind, being an immigrant may not change by legal decree. I think it's what one feels in the heart that makes the change. That may follow long after becoming a citizen. I think that having close family in the new country could make it easier. But until that person feels at home, no longer displaced, he or she remains an immigrant."

He felt Willa and Melanie watching him. Meanwhile, both the girls concentrated on their notes. Then Amy picked up the phone, put it her pocket. She drilled him with a gaze he recognized from Willa—intelligent, curious, searching. She said, "How do *you* feel? Are you still an immigrant?"

He took a deep breath. This deserved a serious answer, not his usual tossed-off response to personal subjects. "For a very long time—most of my life—I was an immigrant. That change in the heart I spoke of has been gradual. Finally, now I feel at home. So I am no longer an immigrant. I just happen to have an accent I can't entirely rid myself of."

The girls studied his face for a second or two longer, then thanked him and collected their reporters' gear. Backpacks on, they headed to the front door. "We'll bring what we write for your editorial review."

He called after them. "It was an honor to have been your first interview. I look forward to reading it."

The front screen clacked closed. Melanie said, "I wonder what got them started."

Robert shrugged. "I'll leave the dining area to you two." He whistled a three-note warble. The dogs rushed and sat at his feet.

Melanie said, "Please don't leave. There's something I want to show you." She took a small newspaper clipping from her purse. "More from grandmother's boxes." After he read the two entries, he passed it to Willa. Melanie said, "I found it a few days ago, but didn't mention it, thinking I'd see if I could find more. But no luck in any of the other boxes. I haven't read the diaries yet, but I'll be surprised if Grandmother included that." She waited until Willa looked up. "Do you agree that the column leads you to think there's not going to be an official burial record found?"

Willa said, "Sounds as if the people in charge wanted the whole episode buried, not just the body."

"I wouldn't give up on finding more information just yet," Robert said. "There may be no county record, but there could be something. I've been doing some research, as I promised. Your librarian friend Mamie, quite an interesting person, seemed delighted to show me the existing records for the Jackson's Pond Town Cemetery. After it was closed to burials some years back when all the plots were filled, the library became the official home of the records. The Cemetery Association kept excellent books over the years. Entry number one was an infant, buried in the first grave plot sold. Family name Goetze, died January 5, 1900."

He'd spent several hours reviewing not only the burials-by-date record book, but also the minutes of the association and the financial records which included purchase records for plots. "The final reckoning of available plots a few years back shows all accounted for, used by owners and family members up until the time the cemetery's final plot was used. I had thought the burial might have been in some plot owned by the town, a potter's field of sorts, but according to those records, that's not the case."

Willa said, "That leaves Calverton and some of those little cemeteries out where townships started and then shut down. This could take a long time."

"I know you have other things to do, Robert," Melanie said. "I'll just have to either find the answer myself or forget that man who was killed."

"No, you don't. I'm on the case now. Let me continue at least until you three have finished with your subversion of city politics. If I've had no luck by then, we'll hatch a new plan."

"You don't mind, really?"

"Not meaning to sound ghoulish, but I love it. Never put any kind of an historian onto a search for facts from the past unless you want every possible stone turned. If you don't mind, I'll copy that clipping for my file."

When he came from his study to return the original to Melanie, she and her mother were standing near the front door.

He heard Melanie say, "I can't imagine how you'll deal with two dogs underfoot. Please be careful."

Willa's reply made him smile, "No need to worry about me. If they trip anyone, it's likely to be Robert. I caught him doling out treats from his pocket."

As he crossed the room, he whistled the three-note signal, softly. Both dogs trotted behind him to the door, toenails clicking against the tile floor. Melanie hugged Willa and said goodbye. Then she surprised him. For the first time since he'd known her, she hugged him.

Floyd County Tribune
Thursday, September 25, 2014
Jackson's Pond Planning Groups Named

Jackson's Pond City Council announced five committee chairs and the members of the strategic planning committees for the city. Mayor Ray Banks emphasized as he made the announcement that membership reflecting varied points of view has been sought. He said, "The planning process will only be successful to the extent that the committees' recommendations reflect a broad consensus of the citizens of our town. Care has been taken in these appointments to assure diverse input." Chairpersons and the committees listed are as follows: Physical Infrastructure—former mayor Garland Thames; Education and Child Care—Marisol Quintero, School Counselor; Business Enhancement—V.I. Patel, Motel Owner; Public Safety and Health—Heath Goodman, Minister; and Housing—Sam Landrum, Realtor. (See related article, page 4, for full committee lists.)

RBJ Groundbreaking Set

A press release from the City Office in Jackson's Pond included the following:

"All Jackson's Pond citizens and friends from all over the county and beyond are encouraged to attend the RBJ Data Systems groundbreaking ceremony at 11:00 a.m. September 26, just outside the current city limit of Jackson's Pond. Signs at both ends of Main Street will direct visitors to the site. Refreshments will be served."

Mayor Ray Banks elaborated with details. Those include that the event will not only celebrate the beginning of construction for the RBJ Data Systems facility, but also will introduce principals in another new business that will be coming to Jackson's Pond, to begin construction in the near future on a site adjacent to the facility. He said, "We hope everyone will be on hand to celebrate this important event."

CHAPTER 6
Breaking Ground

Claire heard her grandmother say, "If you're the Avon lady, come on in." She walked toward the sound of Gran's voice and found her in her studio, painting. Willa said, "Caught me." She reached to cover the painting, then stopped and nodded toward the easel. "That's a secret. Can you keep one?"

Claire moved closer. "It'll cost you."

"Will ice cream seal your lips?" Willa took the walking stick leaning on the edge of her painting table and started toward the kitchen.

Claire could tell she intended to herd her out of the room. "Definitely. But tell me first."

"That's for Robert's birthday, November first. One part of the secret is that he doesn't want anyone to know when it's his birthday, but I think he's already busted on that one."

When they reached the kitchen, Claire went directly to the refrigerator, opened the freezer compartment, and peered in. "You never said there was a selection. Two half gallons and two pints. Treasure!" She pulled out chocolate and strawberry. "You've been making banana splits, the way you used to when Chris and I were kids. I need to come by more often. Maybe every afternoon."

The aroma of the chocolate ice cream triggered a reflex; she closed her eyes and saw herself at age six, just home from first grade, eating from a tiny bowl. Being six for a few seconds made her smile.

As Claire dipped out a scoop of each flavor, Willa said, "Move over. I'll get the toppings. There's a banana in that bowl." She pointed toward the fruit bowl in the middle of the table. From the refrigerator, she handed out pineapple and strawberry toppings, chocolate syrup, maraschino cherries, and a closed container. "You'll need to get the vanilla, too." Lifting the container, she said, "And this is real whipped cream."

Claire assembled two miniature banana splits, quickly, as if she'd worked behind a soda fountain for years. Seconds later, she lifted her first bite, then stopped. "So what's the rest of the secret?"

She began eating and was into her second bite, when she heard Gran say, "No, dogs don't eat ice cream." She looked up to see both of the new dogs sitting at attention near her grandmother's feet.

"Some dogs do, and Jay Frank's goats. Are you worried about spoiling the dogs?"

Willa said, "No sense worrying. If I don't, Robert will."

"I remember when I was little, you and Granddad Frank had a heeler." Claire took another bite of ice cream, one she'd topped with an equal amount of whipped cream. "What happened to that dog?"

"Died, poisoned. I never saw your Granddad more upset. He was sure Junior Reese did it."

"Justin's father?"

Willa nodded, and then focused on her bowl.

Claire leaned back from the table. "I've been worried about Mother, her safety. She told Daddy Justin drives by the school every afternoon. Revving his engine, driving slowly. Staring at her and Dolores while they're outside sending the kids home."

"Have you told her?"

"Well, no. But I do worry. In high school he was always mean, sneaky."

"You should tell her. It would be important to her to know you care."

Claire attacked the ice cream remnants, a spoonful followed by another. "She knows I care."

"When there's a grandmother around, and the grandkids love her, a mother can wonder."

"You wondered? I can't imagine that."

Willa nodded. "I've never told you, but Delia Jackson was a formidable woman, and she absolutely doted on your mother. Her only granddaughter. Who wouldn't have? Your mother was such a pretty child, all dimples and smiles. And when she was three I gave her to Delia."

Her grandmother smiled that sort of smile that says regret lurks behind. Claire said, "Don't tell me if you don't want to, Gran."

"You need to know this."

She listened, watching Willa, who sat perfectly still as she described her depression after baby George's death. How she disappeared, as she put it. For a whole year, she barely ate and did only what was necessary for Melanie. Gradually, she let her daughter go, knowing she couldn't be the mother Melanie needed.

Claire touched her great-grandmother's shoulder. "Oh, Gran, how hard that must have been. I'm so sorry."

"If it hadn't been for Delia, I don't know what would have happened to me or to Melanie. I was ready to die. When I finally realized that I'd lost her, that her grandmother had replaced me, I worked very hard to undo that. I would never want Melanie to feel she'd lost you. So it's important for her to hear from you that you love her. Part of loving someone is being concerned about them, their safety, happiness, health."

Willa took in a deep breath and exhaled long and slowly. She smiled at Claire, then poked her spoon at the mound of strawberry ice cream in the middle of her bowl. "I think you came here today for something other than ice cream. What else is on your mind?"

"Dad, too. He works harder than he should. Getting ready for this groundbreaking, he's been at the city office late every night. Can't be good for his blood pressure."

"You're the health care professional, maybe he'd listen to you." Willa reached with her spoon and picked a cherry off of Claire's chocolate ice cream. "You didn't want that, did you?"

Claire shook her head. "I've had enough." She twirled her spoon through the melting ice cream, a tri-color puddle in her bowl. "Daddy did tell me they filled all the committees. I looked at the list. I think the three of us helped make that happen, from the names I saw."

Willa said, "Let's go back to the studio. I'll show you the secret."

On the way, Claire trailed the dogs, which both walked a few steps behind Gran as if warned she might be unsteady. As she passed Gran's bedroom, Claire noticed the unmade bed, covers flung back. Dented pillows on both sides told her two had slept there. She smiled and followed Willa and the dogs on down the hall. It felt like Gran had revealed three important secrets already today.

They stood at her easel. The painting lacked a finished appearance, which Claire knew was usually the last thing to emerge in Gran's paintings. But she immediately noticed there was a human figure in the painting, a man. Ravens often appeared in Gran's paintings, and occasionally a deer or other wildlife. She'd never seen a "Willa" with a person in it. The man was flanked by two dogs resembling the two that now had retreated to their beds in opposite corners of the studio.

"This is Robert, isn't it?" She saw the shock of gray hair, the broad-shouldered wide stance. The figure leaned a bit forward as if walking up a slight incline toward the fence line and mesquites beyond. Far in the distance on the left side of the painting, delicate brush-stroked lines hinted that wind turbines dotted the horizon. The man carried a walking stick, not for support, but horizontally, as an accessory. In a pasture on the right, a massive black bull wearing an ear tag with the ranch's brand stood near a barbed wire fence, placid, observant.

"It is," Willa said. "What's your opinion?"

Claire stood looking at the painting for at least another minute or two before she spoke. She moved back, then nearer again. "Amy told me that when they interviewed him about being an immigrant, he said he now felt at home."

Willa nodded.

"I hate to make a suggestion. You're the painter. But since you asked, I think he should be coming forward, not leaving, not seen from the back. He's home now, and in this painting, he's coming home."

Willa cocked her head to the left, gazing first at the painting and then at Claire. She hugged her granddaughter. "You're exactly right! Why didn't I see that? Now don't forget—it's a secret. I doubt he'll let me give a party, but if you happen to drop by after supper on November first, you'll be able to see the finished product."

As Gran placed a drape over the painting, Claire asked, "Did you ever paint Granddad Frank?"

Willa nodded. "The only other time I did a human. I had a feeling I needed to do it. It seemed urgent. I never told anyone. The year he died, I started it before he was diagnosed with multiple myeloma. I painted all through the wheat harvest that year, anytime I wasn't driving the grain truck. It shows him as an adult at the same place he proposed to me when he was a young man, at the pond. Back then it was larger. In the painting, he and his horse are watching the sunset. That's where he often went to think. Someday I'll get it out so you can see it." She reached toward Claire. "Are you crying, sweet girl?"

Claire nodded. "I'm sorry. It's not about what you were telling me. I think I'm crying for me. I'm scared, Gran. Ever since I nearly lost J.D. and he was in the hospital for so long, I've had a feeling I need to be vigilant, make sure nothing happens to him. As if I could even do that. I wish I could stop feeling this way. I know it's irrational.

"And then when Justin Reese started in on Mother, I remembered J.D. said when Justin approached him about buying our north pasture he got nasty when J.D. told him we weren't interested in selling. Then he got even nastier when J.D. offered instead to buy the piece of their land abutting ours."

"It's only been a few months since the accident, Claire. It takes time to get over."

"And I wasn't even the one near dying. I wasn't even injured. But now, I'm all neurotic, worrying about the people I love."

"You *were* injured. In a way."

Claire wiped her eyes. "I feel better now. I need to go see Mother while she's on my mind." As she neared the front door, she said, "When you see Chris, would you tell him I want to talk to him about a photo. . ."

Before she could finish, Chris stood in the dining area and said, "Tell Chris what?"

Claire turned away from him and spoke to Gran, "Tell Chris he's a snoop. He's as bad as Jay Frank, always hearing everything, always just around the corner."

"What photo?"

"See what I mean?" She turned to her brother. "Oh, look who's here. I wanted to ask if you'd make a print of that picture of J.D. the first day he got back on his horse."

"What's it worth?"

"What's it worth for me not to talk to the boss and get you fired, Cowboy?"

"It'll never happen. I'm essential personnel."

"Essential personnel don't have time to snoop around in the middle of the afternoon. What are you doing here?"

"Looking for J.D. He told me to keep an eye out for poachers. I think I might have found something."

Chris told them he'd found some bullet casings, not empty shotgun shells. "Don't let Jay Frank go up north by himself until we get this checked out. Do you have a number for the game warden?"

Claire shook her head. Chris said he'd look for J.D. at the ranch office. As he headed toward the back door, he said, "I'll print that picture for you this evening."

"Thanks. Snoop." She hugged Gran. "I'm going to Mother's right now."

On the twelve-mile drive to town, Claire replayed in her mind Gran's words about letting her mother know her concerns, and how care and concern showed love as much as the words *I love you* do. She didn't doubt it. But she did wonder why she, as a professional nurse, had to be told that, had to hear Gran's example of feeling she'd given away her daughter to Delia, to make it real for her. The parallels were obvious. The truth was, since she was a child, she'd always preferred Gran, and had pretended as she grew older that she lived with Gran and not with her own, always-busy, always-serious mother. Only as she had grown older had she recognized so much of her mother in herself—the love of learning, the goal of being recognized as a competent professional, the drive to achieve.

At Banks Preschool, she pulled into a space behind a parent picking up two children. She sat without moving, waiting to see if Justin Reese made an appearance. As if on cue, he roared around the corner, then slowed to a crawl as he passed her and went on by the building. Near the end of the block, he revved his engine and squealed around the corner.

Neither her mother nor Dolores Montoya was outside to witness his display. She found them inside cleaning chalk drawings off tabletops in the front classroom. They both stood and greeted her with hugs. Dolores told her she'd see her tomorrow when she picked up Elisa after ballet. She couldn't stay to visit, she said, having lots to do at home.

Her mother offered her a cup of tea. As they sat in the break room, Melanie spoke about a child she'd had to send home with a fever. She said, "I hope his parents have money to take him to the clinic. I've heard of people being turned away. You wouldn't have done that to anyone."

"No, I wouldn't. But Texas Health Solutions provides healthcare as a business, not a service."

"I know it must hurt, though, seeing what you worked so hard for disappear."

Claire hadn't put it into those words, but her mother was right. She shrugged, nodded agreement. "I came by to see if you've had any more trouble with Justin Reese."

"Nothing overt. Only his daily drive-bys. Don't worry. I choose not to reward his behavior by paying attention to it."

"That's why I came. Please don't ignore what he does. If he makes any threats or does anything menacing, call the sheriff. I want you to know I am concerned. I love you, and I don't want any harm to come to you or your school."

The look on her mother's face told Claire she'd done the right thing—that expression and the fact that she said, in a very soft voice, "Thank you. Hearing you say that means more than you can know."

Claire heard a noise in the front room; she pushed away from the table and was in the doorway in seconds. She whispered, "Stay there." Then she shouted, "School's closed. Who are you?"

Her dad shouted back, "It's okay. It's just me."

By the time he turned around from locking the front door, she was standing beside him, laughing. She said, "Did I frighten you?"

"Got my attention."

They walked together to the break room. He hugged Melanie and asked, "Everything okay?" He sat next to her at the table. "The door wasn't locked."

From across the table, Claire saw his face was flushed, noticed shallow breathing. She said, "That's my fault. I came in just as Dolores left, distracted Mother." She hesitated, then said, "After you've been sitting for a few minutes, I want to take your blood pressure."

He shook his head. "Don't bother. It's fine. I had it checked last month. And I take the medicine."

"Humor me." Before he could protest further, she was on her way to the Suburban. Her equipment bag always traveled with her. When she returned, he'd taken off his sports jacket, leaned back in his chair and extended his left arm. She placed the sphygmomanometer cuff, put her stethoscope in her ears, and pumped the bulb on the cuff, all in the space of a few seconds.

As the dial's needle declined from 200 downward, bounced at 180, she heard the corresponding muffled beat. It disappeared at 95. She said, "We'll wait while you rest a few minutes and repeat it to be certain."

He said, "It's probably up a little."

"Shhh."

She checked her watch, intending to wait seven minutes, doubting he'd be still any longer than that. Smiling at him, then nodding at her mother, the fact that she'd continued wearing her work watch every day told her she hadn't quit when the clinic closed, not really. She nursed J. D. from the time he left the hospital; now here she was tending to her dad.

The second blood pressure echoed the first—180 over ninety-five. Her mother's eyes widened.

Her dad said, "Okay. What do you want me to do?"

"You're not going to argue?"

"I don't want to have a stroke. But I don't have time to get in to see my doc. Just tell me what, and I'll do it."

She reviewed the medicine list he carried in his billfold and explained which two doses to increase and by how much. "But just upping your doses isn't enough. I want you to rest one hour after lunch every day and get seven to eight hours of sleep each night. Go to bed earlier or get up later, but get that much rest. You know about deep breathing and relaxation. So do it."

Her voice sounded harsher than she intended, but it reflected her concern. "I don't want you to have a stroke, or a heart attack either. But if you keep this up you certainly could." Then she asked questions about chest tightness, shoulder pain, headache—all the usual suspects. Satisfied he'd been lucky so far, she told him to carry aspirin in his pocket and chew one if any chest pain occurred and call EMS immediately. "I'll hunt you down tomorrow and recheck. And every day until your next appointment with your doc."

Her mother said, "Our daughter has spoken." She and Claire watched as Ray put on his jacket. "I'll help him do what he needs to do. Ignore him if he grumbles."

Claire said, "I've got to get home now. Please remember what I said, both of you."

Her mother said, "I won't forget."

Driving toward the Jackson Ranch, on the same road she'd driven countless times, something felt different to her.

Different from the weary trips after long days of school while pregnant, pushing to finish her master's degree before Jay Frank was born; nothing like the hurried, child-scented mornings taking toddler Amy and infant Jay Frank to day care, then a year or two later, to pre-school or returning home with them nodding in their safety seats.

The same twelve miles of road she'd been on between home and town had not changed substantially in any way. The miles rolled before her, familiar like pages in a well-thumbed dictionary, orderly, reliable. But today, something said to her, *you've been here precisely in this way before, experienced this same lightness, this same fullness.*

When she reached the gate near the pond, she pulled off the road and stopped. She looked from the road to the gate and past to where the bull grazed and saw nothing she hadn't seen many times before. She stared out to the pond, shrunken during her thirty-four years from a substantial body of fresh water down to a shallow vessel surrounded by marshy grasses. That had changed, but so gradually it was barely noticeable from one day to the next.

She leaned back against the headrest, closed her eyes, and her memory came clear. This was the calm she felt going to or coming home from a day with people whose homes she entered, was welcomed, and where she left knowing she had helped improve their lives, their health, if only for a short while. She'd forgotten because so much time had passed since that had been her work, forgotten because her mind had been filled with worry. First it was worry she might lose J.D. to that other woman, then it was that Amy might descend into a full-fledged eating disorder, then that Jay Frank could die from the bite of that rattlesnake. Later she knew she might lose herself in that depression that lurked and laid her low. Dread took over when she lost her clinics. And then real fear that J.D. could die from his injuries in that awful accident loomed just as she'd thought she might find this feeling again. She'd let concern for her husband and her parents turn into a rolling, growing mass of worry.

She'd allowed events, real and imagined, to rob her and make her lose purpose and lightness. But just then, there, near home, she reclaimed her purpose, her will to achieve that calm, light sense. What was left now was finding how to make it real again.

She started the Suburban and drove home, taking her time. She could wait for the answer. When it came, she'd be cautious.

Floyd County Tribune
Thursday, October 30, 2014
Green Power Partners Plan Announced

In a press release Green Power Partners, Inc. of Dallas announced today that its feasibility study of Jackson's Pond as a site for their first facility has been completed. Based on the study's favorable findings, the company will begin site preparation for the plant which will fabricate generators of wind energy for homes and small businesses.

The three sizes of generators the plant will produce are the result of extensive testing and improvements to earlier models produced by the Swedish company, Scanpower, which is a corporate partner of the Dallas-based company.

Company representatives attended the groundbreaking for RBJ Data Solutions last month and announced at that time the plans for the feasibility study. The press release stated, "Now that the decision has been made to locate in Jackson's Pond, we expect to move quickly in order to begin production within twelve months."

Annexation Finalized in Jackson's Pond

Following City Council approval, documents were signed this week annexing the 640 acres owned by RBJ Data Solutions which adjoins the current city boundary on the north.

Mayor Ray Banks announced the agreement. He said, "RBJ has agreed to annexation, and becoming a part of Jackson's Pond's tax base. Further, the only consideration required on the part of the town is extension of city water and other services, to be purchased at the commercial rate, and a one-year, fifty-percent abatement of city taxes.

"This is far more generous to the city than is typical in attracting new business. RBJ tells us they want to be good corporate citizens."

CHAPTER 7
Varmint

Chris's morning started off fine—actually, better than fine. He'd gotten up before the sun, early enough to have his camera ready to set on its tripod to catch the first rays glinting off the blades of the wind turbine about a mile from the house. THE HOUSE was what he'd begun calling the place that was moving rapidly toward looking like a place to live. After more than three months that seemed like three years living in the trailer, he and Andrew were more than ready. The first week construction actually began, back in September, he and Andrew had made it their mission to check each day's progress, but only after the workmen left. No sense annoying them. Then once a week ever since, either he or Andrew called the contractor to mention any shortcuts or errors noticed. They also made certain during those calls that they passed a compliment on one or more of the jobs' subcontractors.

Since they were several miles out of town, the workers couldn't take a break at the convenience store. The second week, Andrew began making enough coffee each morning to fill a two-gallon insulated container. Apparently that was a big hit because they drank almost all of it, every day.

Now, in forty-five to sixty more days, if everything held together—materials arrived on time, the new electric line was strung, and the flooring tile arrived from Mexico, the paint Chris had chosen looked as good on the wall as on the chip— they'd be out of the trailer and in their new home. That was fast construction, but the house was simple. It would be the first one they'd be able to call their own, not leased like they'd had in Austin or Taos. They'd agreed that if everything went well, this is where they'd stay.

This morning, when he went out to bring in the coffee pot, he lifted it and found a note underneath, obviously written with one of those flat-sided carpenter's pencils—wide black letters said, *Best job I ever worked on. The coffee's great. Thanks.*

Andrew, up early too, said, "Wonder what we'd get if I made a batch of chocolate chip cookies?"

Chris shook his head. "Nope. They'd slow down to make the job last longer to get more cookies." He leaned against the counter in the kitchen space. The two of them had to turn sideways if they were both there at the same time. "You have to be out with the vet early today?"

Since they'd moved to the ranch back in May after J.D. was sidelined with injuries, Andrew had become the local vet's right-hand man. Two weeks of unpaid audition, then he'd been hired at a surprisingly good salary. His nursing background translated well to the care of four-legged patients.

Andrew shook his head. "Sounds, odd noise, woke me about an hour ago. Gunshots, rapid fire."

"Did it last long?"

"Just a couple of bursts. Like sound effects in a war movie."

Chris frowned. "Could you tell which direction?"

"No. Might have been a bad dream."

"I haven't seen any shells since those I found last month. But it could have been the same place up north. I'll check."

He waved as he left, carrying his coffee. "Don't want to miss the best light."

Before he made the six wide steps to the trailer's door, Chris stopped and returned to where Andrew stood. Chris kissed him on the cheek and said, "You don't have to say what you're thinking. I *will* be careful."

He pulled the pickup onto the short access road to the turbine, got out, and set up the shot he hoped to get. Any bird that might drop by would be a welcome extra. So far he'd had to be satisfied with cattle, a big buck whitetail deer, and a couple of jackrabbits.

The cattle had just started grazing, rising with the sun, but they were too far away to make an appearance in the shot. He stood appreciating the expanse that seemed vast, unencumbered by the mountains he'd become accustomed to in Taos. Being able to see to the horizon all the way around stirred his urge to paint.

The trailer was too small for even a tiny painting studio, so he'd been using his camera. Skill with photography had earned him good money at the newspaper in Austin. His easels and paints would have to wait until their house was finished. The time away from the paints had helped him put the disturbing dark period he'd painted through before they left Taos in perspective. It was all a part of things unconscious, things he still couldn't put into words or full thoughts. But coming back here, to the ranch, had settled whatever had worked its way into his painting. Some of it, he knew, had to do with acknowledging that the hurt his mother's disapproval of him as a teenager caused could be put to rest, finally. There'd been more, but this place and the feeling his family was whole and that he and Andrew would be a lasting part of it had restored him. He'd loved what he did in Taos, but this felt right, like where he was supposed to be.

After several shots that looked promising, catching the turbines' long shadows cast against the bluestem by the early twilight, he folded the tripod and put the camera in its case. He'd head north to the fence line and look for spent shells. He doubted Andrew had dreamed that burst of gunfire.

As he neared the northwest corner of the ranch, he slowed, then stopped. He walked east along the fence line, taking his time, watching the ground for casings. After about a quarter mile, he returned to the pickup. Being exposed and on foot might be a bad idea.

He drove parallel to the fence, heading east. About a half mile on, he heard motor sounds, rolled down his window, stopped the pickup but left it running. He reached for his binoculars in the console. Scanning right to left, he fixed on two four-wheelers kicking up puffs of dust as they tracked west. Painted in desert camouflage, the vehicles stood out against the October-faded green of the grass. Bad paint choice, boys.

As he watched, one of the riders pointed in the direction of the pickup, and both of them swerved and turned south, coming toward him. He opened his door, and as they roared toward him, he punched "record" on his phone, stuck it in his shirt pocket. At his feet, as he stepped out, he saw bullet casings, about a dozen, just below the door, about three feet on the Jackson side of the fence.

The first rider skidded to a swerving stop, like a snowboarder. The other one pulled the same stunt. They left their motors idling. Turned sideways as they were, each one displayed an assault rifle mounted on the right side of his ATV. Chris said, "Morning."

The first one said, "Yeah. What's up, Banks?"

Just as he thought, it was Justin Reese. The helmet and goggles didn't disguise that hateful tone and flat, nasal, West Texas twang. Sounded the same as he had in high school.

Chris pointed to the cluster of shells on the ground. "Just out checking fence, finding some things that don't belong over here. What about you, Reese?"

"Hunting."

Chris let the one-word answer hang there while he toed the pile of shells with his boot. Reese revved his engine, then said, "Yeah, hunting birds."

Chris eyed Reese's gun, nodded toward it. "Anything left of 'em when you use those weapons?"

"Seldom."

"What about deer?"

"What about 'em?"

"Just wondered. Season's not open yet, but I thought I'd remind you this property is posted. No hunting of any kind. Signs on fences all over this place, in case you hadn't noticed."

Reese revved the engine again, angled the front wheels toward Chris. Then he let the machine lurch forward until it nosed into the fence. "I've noticed more than you know. Take this as *my* warning. On my property, I'll shoot whatever and whenever I want. Anything that strays over here."

Chris said, "Even you know the difference between Angus and whitetail deer, right? Our cattle don't stray."

"I know what belongs where. And for your information, you don't even belong in this county."

Chris knew what was coming next. He stepped closer, hoping the recorder was getting every word. "How do you figure that?"

The other rider shifted on his seat, then revved his engine, backed his machine a few feet. He said, "Let's go."

Reese kept staring, ignoring his companion. He said, "Decent people don't want queers and jungle people in this county, not anywhere in West Texas."

"Care to name some of those decent people?"

Reese smirked. He said, "You'd probably be surprised."

"I doubt it. There's a characteristic odor. It's pretty strong out here right now, especially on your side of the fence." He made an obvious check of his watch. "I have work to do. I'll be seeing you."

Chris took his time climbing back in the pickup. Reese's clone saw him watching and shot him the finger, which Chris ignored. Then they both herded their ATVs north. Chris checked his phone. The recorder had worked. He opened the door again, got out, and scooped up the spent shells. Then he punched in J.D.'s number. When he answered, Chris said, "You dressed? We need to talk. I'll meet you at the ranch office."

He got there before his brother-in-law, who turned up about five minutes later carrying a thermal cup full of coffee. J.D. lifted the cup and said, "I couldn't leave without this. Let's go inside. We got trouble starting early today?"

In the office, Chris gave a quick version of his encounter with Reese. Then he played the recording. J.D. listened without comment. Then he said, "Find anything dead out there?"

Chris shook his head. "I'm going back to look around. Standing at the fence where I found those shells, they could have hit something a hundred, two hundred or more yards away. Tell the truth, I doubt they shot anything. I think it's an intimidation tactic. Queers beware, all that."

J. D. said, "According to Claire, he's an equal opportunity hater. Get her to tell you about your mom and Dolores's face off with him." He frowned and drummed his fingers against the coffee cup. "Tell you what, while you go back to look around, I'm going to call the game warden and ask him to come out. I doubt there's anything he can do, but the more people who know, the more likely we can cause the local Klanboy some trouble."

J.D. drank some coffee, then sat staring at a pen on his desk. Chris looked around the large room, remembering it as J.D.'s parents' house when his dad worked on the Jackson Ranch. He knew he and J.D. were doing the same thing, waiting to cool off, push away the memories of the times J.D. had taken up for Chris at school until he got big enough to take up for himself. They'd been pretty good fist fighters back then.

If they didn't calm down, they might do something as stupid in its own way as the things Justin Reese did. J.D. sighed first, just before Chris let himself exhale loudly. He said, "Just like old times, huh?"

They both laughed and stepped out onto the porch. J.D. put a hand on Chris's shoulder and said, "Keep in touch by phone. I mean it. Stay safe."

"If you come back and notice the pickup here and my horse gone, don't worry. I'm riding when I go back up there. Easier than bumping over that clump grass in the pickup. Right now I'm going to Gran's. I think she has what I'll need."

He drove the five or so miles to Gran's house. Waiting at the door after he knocked, he waved at the contractor making a site inspection at their house next door. Gran pulled him in with a hug. She said, "What's going on?"

"Do you still have Granddad's saddle gun?"

"I'd never get rid of that. Why?"

"I need to use it. And the scabbard?"

She raised a hand and said, "Wait right here. I'll bring it."

About five minutes later, she returned, gun in the scabbard in one hand, her walking stick in the other. He said, "Are you having balance trouble?"

"No, it's preventive. I promised your mother. And I'm living up to my promise. Find a coyote den in the calf pasture?"

"Some kind of varmints." What he said next sounded like an afterthought. "I heard from J.D. about Justin Reese causing Mother some trouble. Do you know anything about it?"

Willa's look told him he'd never be any good at spy work. She gave a brief summary of the Reese episode and his continued drive-bys at the preschool. Then she said, "He's making more trouble?"

"He might. I guess you wonder why the gun."

She nodded.

"He needs to know he's not the only one with those Second Amendment rights that he's so proud of." He paused a few seconds. "Don't worry, I'm not going to shoot him."

She said, "I recall when he was born—the baby of that family, late child. If he's anything like his father, he's not to be trusted. Watch yourself."

"Let's don't say anything about this to Mother. At least not yet."

Willa shook her head. "I think you should. If you don't by tomorrow, I will. Sorry, it's the best way."

He sat on the couch, the gun across his knees. She was right, he knew. He leaned back against the cushions.

Then she surprised him by saying, "Speaking of things that should be told. Here's something I'm planning to tell your mother, so I'll tell you now, and Claire later. Robert has asked me to marry him."

He sat forward. "Really? Amazing. What did you say?"

"I've been thinking about it. I'm sure he knows I'll eventually talk with all of you before giving him an answer."

"What are you thinking?"

"If it's important to him, and I believe it is, then I will probably say yes."

"Mother will be the one to resist, if anyone. I'd be willing to bet on that."

"It wouldn't surprise me. But she does like Robert."

"Yes, she seems to." After a long pause, he said, "If my

opinion's worth anything, I think it's a great idea. For a long time, I've worried about him. Being his age, alone, no family. Lots of people admire him. But he'd only let a few people love him, I'm pretty sure." He watched his grandmother's face. "You've been good for him."

"We've been good for one another. And I do love him, full of bull as he is." She pointed to the gun. "Don't worry about that being in working order. I haven't fired it, but I've cleaned it several times, just the way your granddad taught me. Bullets are in that bag below the scabbard."

As he walked toward the door, she said, "Be careful."

At the corral near the ranch office, he leaned against the fence and whistled. Dobie, J.D.'s horse, looked up from where he stood across the corral, but didn't move. Britches trotted over and followed Chris into the barn. He'd swear that horse enjoyed their rides together, the way he made getting saddled up so easy. It took longer than usual today because he'd never attached the holster to the saddle before. Never used the saddle gun, in fact. When he and his granddad hunted deer or wild pigs, he'd shot his 30.06 that had the standard-length barrel and a scope. Granddad was such a good shot, the shorter-barreled saddle gun was fine for him. They usually only went out once a season, for deer. Frank Jackson believed in hunting for food but not simply to kill. But they'd hunt the destructive feral pigs as often as they got into the fields.

The other thing that made getting ready to ride slower was the fact that he stopped to practice drawing the gun from the holster with his right hand. A left-hander, he'd learned to shoot right-handed rifles, but he'd never had to draw with his right hand from a scabbard on horseback. When he finally satisfied himself he was ready, after considering switching back to the pickup, he mounted up.

J.D. honked once as he stopped at the corral gate. "Hold up. Give me time to get saddled. I'm going with you."

As soon as they closed the gate behind them on the north pasture where he'd had the run in with Reese earlier, they split up. J.D. rode toward the northeast corner and Chris toward the northwest. He'd gone about a half mile when he noticed two of the young bulls together off to his right. Even those young ones tended not to be too sociable. He rode toward them at a lope, then slowed as he got nearer. No sense getting them stirred up. Closer, he saw a swarm of flies rising near the bulls. He hit J.D.'s number on the phone. He didn't wait when his brother-in-law answered. "Something down over here. You see me?" He stood in the stirrups and waved his hat.

The fly swarm marked the spot. The two of them joined up and walked the horses toward it. The two young bulls backed away, then turned and ambled off, each in a different direction. Chris and Tag had put the little bachelor herd of eight two-year-olds on this half-section about a month ago. J.D. had said he hadn't decided which or how many to keep, and it wouldn't affect the rest of the herd to let those boys have the pasture for a while. Grass flourished all over the ranch thanks to the rains that had fallen at intervals since the end of May.

"Looks like you were right," J.D. said. "What do you want to bet he didn't die of natural causes?"

Chris dismounted and J.D. followed. Squatting, Chris said, "Not dead long, still warm. Looks like someone just bought themselves an expensive bull." He pointed to the bloody wounds on the bull's neck and chest. "Any luck and the vet'll find a slug or two that made those holes. Want me to call or you?"

J. D. said, "You get the vet to come do a post on site. I'll call the Special Ranger from the Cattle Association and the sheriff."

Busy with their phones, they both turned toward the north fence line. Chris finished his call while remounting. He urged Britches into a trot toward the sound that alerted him—the same types of motors he'd heard earlier this morning. As he closed the distance, about 200 yards, to the fence line, three ATVs, all alike, roared toward him. He felt for the butt of the saddle gun.

Within shouting distance of the lead vehicle, which stopped near the fence, he yelled, "Still hunting?"

"None of your damn business." Reese again.

"It is my business since someone in your crew killed one of our bulls."

Reese said, "The law can decide that."

Chris heard J.D. ride up, saw him stop off to his right about fifteen feet.

J. D. said, "You boys might as well stay close. The sheriff and the Association Ranger are on their way. Save them the trouble of hunting you down."

Reese revved his motor and the other two followed suit. "Let 'em try."

Reese raised a gloved hand, motioned like a squad leader. Then, in an imitation of a military maneuver, they all three turned right, then right again and roared back the way they'd come. If it hadn't been for the weapons on both sides of the fence, it would have been laughable. As it was, Chris had seen the weapons mounted in cases on the sides of all three vehicles and hoped they had better sense than to do any further damage with them.

J.D. said, "Might have been more interesting if I'd let you start a shooting war."

"I'd have been outmanned and outgunned. The vet said he'd be here right away."

"The others, too. You have those shells you found this morning?"

Chris patted his saddlebag. "I do."

They rode slowly back toward the downed animal to wait. Chris felt a surge in his body, something he recognized from a long time ago. Anytime he'd had a fistfight in high school, his hands would shake and his pulse ran rapid, but only *after* the fact. In the face of trouble, he was steady and fierce. Right then, remembering that, feeling his heart accelerate, he held tight to his reins to stop his hands shaking.

Side by side on horseback, they traded observations about Reese and his "men." J.D. filling Chris in on the gossip about Reese and his survivalist-type bunker; Chris telling a rumor from a friend that a Klan-type group had emerged from a non-denominational fundamentalist church in Amarillo. Their targets, so far, were anyone who might be lesbian, gay, bisexual, or transgender, and any facility performing abortions. But to this point, none of what they'd heard involved armed conflicts. They were two guys trading wisecracks about the unfounded stuff they were hashing over.

Chris said, "Gotta wonder where they went to get radicalized."

J.D. said, "I wonder what line of work those guys on the four-wheelers are in. Out here shooting up my beef, and this a work day for most people."

They both laughed. Chris reckoned it seemed a lot like old times, the two of them here, working together. He knew he was lucky to have a brother-in-law who was like a brother.

The vet made the scene before the lawmen. He got right to work after saying to Chris, "Andrew was worried when I told him where I was headed. Maybe you ought to give him a call."

As Chris got on the phone with Andrew, Marty Broadus, the Cattle Association Ranger, arrived. He was the one who recovered J.D.'s stolen bull some months back, so they huddled, talking while the vet took a scalpel to the bull. Chris finished his call and heard Broadus say, "I'm on it. Whichever one of them did this will face charges. That's an expensive bull. We might be able to charge the shooter with a felony. Criminal Mischief Misdemeanor at the least. Big fine, prison penalties."

Chris said, "Couldn't happen to a nicer bunch of guys."

About that time the sheriff rolled up, driving slowly in his big Suburban. Chris watched as Broadus made it clear he'd already taken the lead, so he opened his saddlebag and handed the ranger the shells, which the man put into an evidence bag and labeled. All business. The sheriff stood up close, hands stuffed in his pockets. Useless as teats on a boar, one of Granddad's sayings, came to Chris, made him smile. Then a thought of running for sheriff in the next election occurred to him, which made him want to laugh.

The vet stood, groaning as he did, to let them know it was a chore. He held up a slug. "I pulled out two of these. Definitely the cause of death. I'll be happy to swear to it."

After all the evidence was collected, the lawmen had listened to the recording on his phone, and they'd told their story more than once, he and J.D. stood alone with their horses and the dead animal. J.D. said, "I can't see just sending him to the rendering plant. I'm calling Tag to bring the front-end loader. We'll take that bull out in the pasture near the pond and give him a decent burial." He took a Leatherman tool off his belt and snipped off the bull's ear tag. He said, "Number 5422."

Back at the house-on-wheels, Chris had trouble being still. He checked the photos he'd made that morning and downloaded the best ones to the computer he printed from. He avoided going outside because he didn't want to bother Gran and Robert, who'd see him and expect him to come next door. So he drove into town and parked in front of Banks Preschool. He waited until all the other cars on the block left after picking up their kids. He found the front door locked and he knocked.

When his mother opened the door, he surprised both of them—he hugged her before saying a word. The look on her face told him the surprise was welcome. Inside, he said, "I don't want to interrupt your work. But I need to tell you." Then he laid out an abbreviated version of the morning's excitement. She listened and didn't interrupt.

Then he said, "I heard Reese has been menacing you. Has he stopped?"

"This was the first day he hasn't done one of those creepy drive-bys. So maybe he has stopped."

"I doubt it. More likely he's still dealing with the Ranger. Have you reported him to the sheriff?"

She shook her head. "Your dad wanted to, but I think ignoring him is the best thing."

Now he shook his head. "I disagree. I think part of this started because of me, and I'm sorry my being here might have caused trouble. I did enough of that when I was young. But I've learned some things about bullies in my life. The main one is that if they think you're weak, they'll never quit."

He paced a few steps, then back to face his mother. "I worry about you, Mom. Please report him to the sheriff, and maybe file for a restraining order."

She put an arm around him. "If it matters that much to you, I'll talk with your dad about getting the sheriff involved. Okay?"

"Today?"

She nodded. Then she said, "I'm glad you're here. I hope you don't ever leave again."

He wasn't sure there was an answer for that. "I'd better get back to the ranch." He started toward the door. "It's good you're locking the door here. Do the same thing when you're at home, please." After he was outside, he went back to where she was standing in the doorway. "If J.D. didn't think of it, I'm telling Claire to pick the kids up at the bus every day and warn them to watch for Reese or anyone they don't recognize out at our place. I want all my family safe."

As he opened the pickup door, he heard his mother say, "I want you safe, too. I love you, Chris."

He couldn't remember their ever saying that to one another, at least not in a very long time.

Early the next morning, Chris waited at the ranch headquarters. J.D. had called and said they had plans to make. Chris didn't have to wait long. J.D. walked in, followed by Marty Broadus. J.D. started talking right away.

"Marty has a friend with ATF. He and the sheriff took the statements we made and got a warrant. Besides killing the bull, there's the possibility those guns weren't legal."

Broadus nodded, said, "My ATF buddy said they'd had an eye on Reese for a while, wanted a chance to search his place. They suspect he's building up a supply of illegal guns to equip a militia group. Maybe selling them to other like-minded types. Said Reese was heavily into Klan activity over in East Texas before he came back here."

J.D. said, "With any luck, they'll measure those gun barrels and find some that need registering and aren't.'"

The three of them traded some facts about legal and illegal guns and lapsed into speculation about why the Bureau of Alcohol, Tobacco, and Firearms was interested in Justin Reese. Broadus mentioned a concern about cooperation and jurisdiction. "This could get complicated if we get in a pissin' match about which guns fired the shots and who confiscates. I need to be able to get ballistics tests, no matter what length the barrels are. Legal or not."

Watching as Broadus fidgeted and checked his phone twice in about thirty seconds, Chris wondered if the Association's lawman had held back something. He said, "So the warrant's based on suspicion of killing the bull and the use of possible illegal guns?"

The ranger nodded and said, "That's what I'm waiting on. Supposed to hear from the lab we use in Fort Worth. If they promise they'll expedite analysis, then we'll be ready to execute the warrant, seize guns, and I'll carry them and the slugs over there for ballistics analysis." After a pause, he said, "Yeah, I don't trust anyone else to get it there. Call me paranoid. And all that assumes we don't have to argue with ATF."

J.D. said to Chris, "I already asked, and the answer is no, we can't be there when they execute the warrant."

Then the three of them talked about the possibility the gang on the ATVs might have gotten rid of the gun. Broadus said, "Maybe not. We figure they think they skated on this one, since no law enforcement turned up on Reese's place yesterday."

The ranger's phone rang and Chris and J.D. waited and listened to one side of a short conversation. "Broadus. Confirmed. I'll contact you as soon as I have the weapons, and we'll go the RBJ facility from there." As he headed for the door, he said, "I'll let you know what I can, when I can."

Chris and J.D. sat silent for a few minutes. Then J.D. said, "I'm going to go see where Tag buried that bull in the pond pasture."

Chris said, "I'll check all the cattle while you're doing that. Anything else you want done this morning?"

"Save that north pasture till last. From now on, I want two of us going anytime we work up there. Better safe than sorry. I'll find you when I get through at the pond."

"Did you tell Claire? She knows to meet the school bus and keep an eye out?"

J.D. nodded. Chris said, "I'll be sure Gran and Robert know. Having the workmen at the house worries me a little. All strangers."

They sat a while longer without speaking. Then Chris said, "I hate having to be suspicious of people."

J.D. said, "Yeah. In a way it's behaving just like those Klan types." He stood and slapped his gloves against his leg. "It's a damn shame."

Chris found a fence down on the east side and spent quite a bit of time splicing it, then counting the cattle in the pasture, and after lunch, returning to confirm his count to satisfy himself all the cow-calf pairs were where they belonged. By two he'd finished all the fence and cattle except for the north pasture. He hadn't heard from J.D., so he drove to the pond. Tire tracks in the grass and an area about four feet by six with grass replaced and tamped down told him the bull had been laid to rest. Still no word from J.D.

He went to the corral near the headquarters and fed and watered the horses. Around 2:30, J.D. pulled up, followed by Broadus in his big diesel pickup.

He could tell from Broadus' widened eyes and rapid breathing that he had lots to tell. Sure enough he started talking before the three of them even got inside the office. "Looked like a big raid by the time all of us got organized, wearing those windbreakers with big letters on the back. First off, the gate to Reese's place was chained and locked. So, we had to talk about whether to use the bolt cutters or call him and give him a chance to open it."

"I guess you voted bolt-cutters," J.D. said. He opened the refrigerator and raised a beer and a Dr Pepper. Chris and the ranger both pointed to the Dr Pepper. Then all three settled at the table.

Broadus said, "Ended up calling and Reese came wheeling out in a big, old, camo-painted Ford truck. Sounded like it was burning well-head drip or needed a valve job bad. Here's a surprise—when we followed him out to that thing he calls a bunker, turns out it's a cargo container like they transport merchandise across the ocean, but it's been buried and has a ramp down to the doors on the end. The warrant said we could search for guns, so he leads us out to a metal pole barn behind that bunker and points to three four-wheelers, each one with a gun mount on the right side."

J.D. said, "Did he deny shooting the bull?"

"Didn't say a word when the sheriff handed him the search warrant, never asked a question." Broadus shook his head. "I'd swear Reese had rehearsed it. Him and that other guy."

Chris said, "There were three."

The ranger laughed. "Yeah, those two and the one they threw under the bus. Gave us a name and said he was from Mineola. Said he left last night to get back to work."

Chris could tell that Marty Broadus was intent on telling every detail. So, he leaned back in his chair and tried to keep quiet. It would take as long as it took. Pretty soon, J.D. stopped asking questions, too, and just nodded as the ranger continued.

"We took all three guns from the four-wheelers and searched the barn and that bunker. Reese had bills of sale from a gun show on all three. They'd been fired. Some rounds were missing from each of the fifteen-round clips. Only other things we found were a crossbow and two thirty-eight pistols and lots of ammunition. Unless we missed something somewhere." He paused a second. "I keep thinking we missed something. My ATF buddy said the same thing. His sources thought there were lots of guns, based on what they'd heard."

Then he took off telling about the way the bunker was set up. Chris thought he'd probably draw a diagram next. Broadus said, "That place has solar panels, a couple of laptop computers, bunk beds to sleep eight, a chemical toilet, a camp stove, and more military ration packages than an Army-Navy store." He took a long draught on the Dr Pepper. "And there was some printed stuff in a trunk—old Klan pamphlets, some the sheriff called white supremacy trash, anti-everything."

A ringtone sounded and all three of them looked at their phones. It was for Broadus. After he answered, he listened for a long time, then said, "Okay. Will do." He hung up, and sped through a summary of the rest. "There's a warrant out for the guy from East Texas. The other two admitted shooting, but said no one shot your bull. The sheriff had to release them pending ballistics, told them not to leave the county. If the ballistics fit, they'll be arrested and charged for killing the bull. We'll see if one of them rolls over on the other two." He slapped his phone back in its case and said, "I'm off to Fort Worth. I'll let you know what's next, soon as I get the ballistics report."

Chris and J.D. walked outside with the ranger. As he got in his pickup Broadus said, "The ATF will be keeping an eye on them and on Reese's place. Till this is settled, be extra cautious."

Watching Broadus wheel out, Chris said, "Is Tag up to speed on working in pairs for a while?"

J. D. said, "Yeah, I called him before Marty turned up. Then I had to listen to a long song and dance about how pissed it made him to have to bury a perfectly good bull. I'll give you the honor of telling him the rest. I'm tired of listening, talking. Hell, I'm tired of thinking I can't trust my neighbors."

Chris thought about saying, "Welcome to my life." But he decided it wouldn't help. So he said, "Let's drink a beer."

Floyd County Tribune
Thursday, November 6, 2014

Jackson's Ranch Incident Nets Raid

Floyd County Sheriff's office received a report October 31, 2014 of a registered Angus bull's having been shot at the Jackson Ranch outside Jackson's Pond.

Following investigation, Floyd County Sheriff's deputies, a Special Ranger from the Cattle Raisers Association, and an agent of the Bureau of Alcohol, Tobacco, Firearms, and Explosives raided a dwelling and outbuilding owned by Justin Reese, age 34, of Floyd County. Reese and Erich Bryant, 31, of Clarendon, were held for questioning. Following ballistics tests, they were released and a warrant issued for Boyd Barker, age unknown, of Mineola.

At press time, Barker had not been apprehended, according to law enforcement officers in that jurisdiction.

CHAPTER 8

Relatives

Sunday afternoon, after church, while Ray napped in his recliner, Melanie made cookies. The aroma of baking cookies often calmed her, made her feel like a well cared for child. That same day she began reading her grandmother's diaries in earnest.

Between batches of cookies, she saw Delia Jackson's life unfold in the early days of her marriage. Her entries varied little, alternating between details of household activities and her triumphs as a new member of several women's groups in Jackson's Pond. Melanie recalled her grandmother's commenting once about Willa's working the ranch with Frank and spending time alone, painting. She remembered Delia's saying she couldn't understand her daughter-in-law's apparent pleasure in tending to life's quotidian details. As if Melanie could understand, her grandmother continued, contrasting her own life, filled, as she put it, with concerns of the "higher things of life." As a nine-or ten-year-old, Melanie had fixed on the word quotidian and had checked the dictionary for its definition. Now, reading Delia's diaries, she realized that comment had been evidence of one of the major differences between those two women. Her mother, whose art was definitely a higher thing in life, had been a mystery and a threat to Delia, a woman consumed with club meetings and frequent redecorating projects. And certainly in the early days of her marriage, her detailed records of schedules for housecleaning and menu plans, all executed by hired help, were evidence of dwelling on the quotidian. Melanie paused her reading of her grandmother's diary and thought—these are stories we tell ourselves, hoping to rise in our own estimation taller and better than those around us.

She scanned the diaries through 1926 and found little difference among them other than a change from daily entries to weekly ones. The 1927 diary began much the same, but beginning in February, she noticed a change—a return to daily recording and a difference in the tone. Club meeting minutia disappeared. Delia focused details almost exclusively on her thoughts and feelings about pregnancy. It was her first. She hated "losing her figure" and had problems with constipation; she wondered how she could have gotten pregnant, saying she had taken the precaution of "forced abstinence during fertile periods;" and arguments with Albert about that very thing filled several days' comments.

Then in April, a single terse entry that could have been a report from someone else's life occupied only a few lines. *"A female stillborn was delivered of Mrs. Delia Jackson on April 18, 1927. The unnamed child, small for four months' gestation, was buried in the Jackson family plot at the feet of her grandmother, Corrine Jackson."*

Melanie closed the diary and closed her eyes. How devastated Grandmother must have been by that failed pregnancy. The image of her grandmother, hovering and guiding her, had dominated all the memories of her early childhood. For many years, her grandmother's voice, patiently dictating proper deportment, issuing gentle reprimands, and praising her appearance and accomplishments, echoed in her mind. She knew that her parents had moved into the big house with Delia after Albert's death in 1958, when she was three. But for all the years of her childhood, even with her parents present, she'd somehow felt her grandmother was the source of all that was important. As if her own parents were tiresome visitors who never left.

Eyes open again, Melanie turned page after page of entries about caring for Albert's father as he declined. Then came the entry that stopped her reading and stirred agitation that the scent of cookies couldn't cure. But she couldn't stop reading. After removing the cookies from the oven, she turned page after page.

Father Jackson passed today, peaceful at last, I hope. He was so different from my own people, coarser in many ways, less voluble, and definitely more familiar with physical labor. Until his heart began to fail, no operation on the ranch could be undertaken without his direct supervision and participation. Albert is like him in many ways.

As his heart weakened and moving about became a chore, he yearned for my attention, wanted me at hand, in his room, regardless of whether I was reading silently or writing, or performing some simple household tasks. It wasn't that he needed me for physical care—we had a nurse for that. He wanted the comfort of family near, someone to hear him, as if he'd spared so many words all his life, stored them, he needed now to express them all. And at the end, one of the things he wanted me to hear was a confession of sorts.

It was good that at least he told me. He had no use for the clergy, so he would never have confessed properly. I knew this was his way of cleansing his soul, knew it when he swore me to secrecy, even from Albert.

He began by telling of the killing of the man from Oklahoma here on the ranch, back in 1920. I had read the clipping Albert had shown me at that time, and had known of the official verdict about the death. He retold those things, and I didn't interrupt. Perhaps his mind was wandering as it does with some during illness. I sat with folded hands and listened. Then he said, "That was all lies. I was as big a part as the other three in that killing. No part of me hated that man, but when they said I had to help kill him, I helped. You know why? I was, am, a coward. Three of them, one of me, I thought. I didn't want to end up dead. Better him than me. And when they decided to bury him, they threatened to expose me. So, coward again, I let them bury him here on the place. The County Judge was involved in that, part of the cover up. Only thing is I didn't watch them throw that poor man in that grave. I'd paid my debt by keeping my mouth shut."

He stopped talking, stayed quiet for a long time. I said nothing. Maybe he had more to tell and was working up his courage.

A bit later, I heard him draw a deep breath, which in his condition could also have been his last. I went to his bedside. He grabbed my hand and held it tight. He said, "I've tried to live right since then, to make it up in God's eyes. Do you think I'm forgiven?"

I thought, "Who am I to grant any kind of absolution?" What I said, after a minute's careful consideration, was, "My church teaches that if a person confesses a sin and strives not to sin again, God forgives."

He was silent again, still holding my hand. His eyes remained open and seemed fixed on my face. Was he waiting for something more? I said, "If you want peace before you go, you must also forgive yourself."

He closed his eyes, and nodded. Soon he was asleep, snoring. He died during the dark hours of this morning.

For the past three days, and again this morning, those diary entries had occupied Melanie's thoughts. Although she managed to wade through the school days, each evening she spent more time than usual on her elliptical. Exercise demanded her focus and settled her until bedtime. But again today, Melanie couldn't make herself sit still. She'd gotten home from school around one. To compensate for arriving at seven each day, she left early on Thursdays. Ray worked most days at the Mayor's office, and she enjoyed having the house to herself. But today, since she'd walked in the door, she'd alternately paced and sat, neither choice suiting what stirred in her mind. She was saved by the doorbell from wearing a path in the carpet.

When she opened the door, seeing Robert there brought her usual reaction. Something about his robust good humor caused her to feel an eager warmth much like what she felt upon seeing Jay Frank or Amy. It was as if she'd been waiting for him and hadn't known it.

She led him to the family room off the kitchen. Robert accepted her offer of coffee. She pointed him to Ray's recliner, and went to the kitchen to set a new pot to brew.

Though she'd known him less than a year, she'd already deduced that Robert never turned down a cookie, so she filled a small plate with shortbreads she'd baked Sunday.

They chatted about her cookie recipe and she agreed to give him a copy. Then he said, "That's not the reason, well not the *only* reason I stopped by. First, I wanted to thank you again for visiting on my birthday. What a pleasure it was to see first one, then another of the family members on my eightieth. So much nicer than a party because each person or small group was the focus of attention while they were there. Not the usual crowd scene a party creates where conversations are only synopses, seldom complete and lacking in essential detail."

"I wouldn't have missed coming by. Seeing your present from Mother unveiled was a real treat."

"I may be biased, but it's my all-time favorite piece of art. Your mother is an amazing artist. Amazing woman." He hesitated a second, then said, "She's the light of my life, you know."

It wasn't that Melanie didn't agree, just that she didn't quite know the words to use. So, she did what her grandmother had taught her women should do; she nodded and smiled. Who could disagree with those lovely Irish-accented words?

Robert took the last cookie from the plate, raised it like a toast, and popped it into his mouth. "Never tasted better." After chasing that with a sip of coffee, he said, "The second thing I came to tell you about is this." From his jacket pocket, he produced a notepad. "The kind woman who works in the county records office found financial records books from the early nineteen-twenties, at my request. She believed my story about doing research on the expenditures made by rural counties in West Texas during their early years. I introduced myself as an historian interested in that period. While that is true, I was cautious not to go further and enmesh myself in lies."

He smiled in a way that told he enjoyed the intrigue. "I copied this from the February, 1921 ledger." He handed the pad to her. She marveled at his ornate Spencerian handwriting as she read: "Pauper burial in eastern part of county on donated private land—cost of supplies and labor = $5.00."

She said, "Nothing more about where or who?"

He shook his head. "Sadly, no. But if we had any other corroborating source, historians would qualify it as accurate."

"We do. Wait here." Melanie went to her office and returned with Delia's diary entry from 1927. "I copied this from my grandmother's diary. She'd have had no reason to fabricate such a detailed account, particularly since she was sworn to secrecy."

Robert sat back in the chair, reading the copy, nodding as he did. "Yes. Leads me to believe the body rests somewhere on the ranch." He handed her the sheet and said, "Imagine that poor man, suffering guilt for all those years. Dying, hoping he had atoned."

Again, Melanie had no quick response. But she couldn't shake the feeling there was more to do. Finally, she said, "Do you have any ideas about how to find an unmarked grave on thousands of acres of land?"

"I have no experience in that area, or any resources on such subjects that spring to mind."

"I wonder what makes me feel guilty and responsible to do something about this injustice now. It'll soon be a hundred years."

Robert smiled at her, reminding her of a movie priest, someone loved and trusted by his parishioners. He said, "I can only imagine it's because you are a kind person who believes there's no limit on when to do the right thing." He leaned forward. "Think about this, and I'll help with whatever you decide."

He stood. "I'll go now. The dogs have learned to tell time, and I don't want to be late for their walk."

She went with him to the door, then waved as he drove away.

The next day at four-fifteen, Melanie was in the front yard, gathering fallen, ripe pecans when Willa parked in the driveway. When she got out of her pickup, she handed Melanie a small plate covered with foil. She said, "Robert sends his regards and requests that you see if his shortbreads measure up. He worked hard shaping them the way he recalled from his childhood. No cookie cutters at the house."

As soon as they were inside, Melanie put on coffee to go with the cookies. "He must have gone directly to the kitchen when he got home Sunday."

Willa nodded. "He enjoys cooking, loves trying out new recipes."

Melanie bit into one of the star-shaped cookies. "Have you tasted these? They're excellent."

When she pushed the plate toward her mother, Willa shook her head. She said, "Already had my share."

Melanie had one more, and then covered the plate. "Thanks for the delivery. Everything all right at the ranch? I saw the paper today."

"All quiet for now. We'll see if that lasts."

She watched as her mother gathered herself, sitting up straight in the kitchen chair, then leaning slightly forward. She recognized it as Willa's "all business" posture, a signal Melanie had learned the meaning of as an adolescent. Its effect on her produced acute attention to her mother's every following word and gesture.

Willa said, "There's something we need to discuss." Her mother's faint smile let Melanie know the something could either be amusing or explosive; Willa enjoyed seeing fireworks nearly as much as laughter.

"Robert has asked me to marry him and I'm considering it. Your opinion would be helpful, as will Chris and Claire's."

Of all the possible topics Willa might want to discuss, a marriage proposal was not even on Melanie's list. She told herself to think, not react on impulse. She said, "Robert? That's a real surprise."

"I suppose you assumed he was gay." Willa drank some coffee. Then she said, "He's not."

Melanie shook her head. "No, no. It's just such a surprise. I don't know what to say."

"Whatever comes to mind—your immediate reaction, questions, whatever. I have time."

"Is your mind already made up?"

"No. If it were, I wouldn't be asking your opinion."

Melanie felt herself shaking her head again without really intending to.

Willa said, "So your immediate reaction is no?"

"Not exactly." She clasped her hands together under the table. "It's more a question of . . . why." After a moment's hesitation, she added, "Why now?"

"I have no idea. He's always been one for the romantic gesture, I think mostly because he knows that women secretly want that sort of thing. But he asked me in all seriousness."

Melanie stared at her lap. "Why at your ages? Why not just go on as you are?"

Willa pushed her chair back from the table a few inches. "Did you ask yourself these questions when you decided to remarry Ray?"

"That was different." Her mother was waiting, not speaking. Melanie's voice sounded childlike to her own ears when she said, "How could you love someone else?"

Willa stood, walked to the patio doors. Speaking without turning to face Melanie, she said, "Other men have asked me to marry, or come close, and I refused, cut them off, because I knew I didn't love them." She turned to face her. "You may not believe this of me, but I feel that love is a necessary basis for marriage. I love Robert. Not instead of your father, but in addition, and in a different way. I'll never forget Frank, nor will anyone replace him in my heart. But there's room for more." She turned around, and faced Melanie.

"Yes, even at our ages."

Melanie wiped away the two tears sliding beside her nose. She sniffed and breathed deeply. "No one can replace Daddy for me, and it hurts me to think you don't feel the same." With each word, her voice grew stronger.

"I've talked to your father, to my memory of him, many times. The same answer comes each time, the thing he said to me once. He said, 'If anything ever happens to me, I want you to live your life and enjoy it.' That's the kind of man he was. Never selfish."

When Willa returned to the table, she said, "I asked for your opinion. There are some other things you should know that might affect how you feel, although it's apparent you aren't likely to change your mind."

"Such as?"

"If we marry, there would be an agreement. Nothing would change financially. Robert's a wealthy man. There would be no loss to any family members due to our having married. I suspect it would be exactly the opposite. Although he hasn't said it, I believe Robert wants to have a place as a part of a family."

"He's like part of the family now."

"Not really. As long as he's Mr. Stanley to Jay Frank and Amy, he's separate."

All Melanie could think of was her father lying in that hospital bed, shrinking. She'd never gotten to say a proper goodbye. She avoided looking at her mother when she said, "You feel sorry for him. It's not really love."

Willa said, "I know the difference between pity and love."

Melanie stood, and moved away from the table. "More coffee?"

A silence hung between them, a coffee-scented curtain. After several long seconds, Willa said, "Thank you for being honest. I'll let you know what I decide." She toyed with a cookie, then bit into one. "There's one other thing. It may be impossible for you to understand my feelings, my thoughts, because you've never been my age. Being eighty or older doesn't mean a person no longer wants love, romance, or, most important, to have someone to share intimacy with. One day you'll know that. Unfortunately, I won't be here to see it."

"Mother, you'll do what you want. You always have. I think we should change the subject."

Willa shrugged and to Melanie she looked elegant as she did it. Her mother said, "I wish we could agree." She rose and said, "I'll leave that little plate. It was your grandmother's." Then she surprised Melanie by hugging her tightly and saying, "I love you."

As she opened the door, a gust swirled fallen leaves in the front yard, kicking up some dust. Willa stepped back inside and zipped her light jacket. She said, "November's first cold front is on its way, I think."

After her mother left, Melanie cleared away the cups and poured the cold coffee down the drain, returning the room to its usual tidy condition. Then she changed clothes, went to her elliptical trainer, and began striding.

Floyd County Tribune

Thursday, November 20, 2014

RBJ Begins Interviews December 1

Beginning December 1, the Jackson's Pond RBJ office will hold interviews to fill five mid-level management positions to work at their new Jackson's Pond facility.

Applications and resumes will be accepted beginning November 21, 2014. Contact the Human Resources manager at the RBJ office in Jackson's Pond for position requirements. Those selected will begin orientation Monday, January 19, 2015.

Management positions are the first of several types to be filled for the new data storage and computer assembly facility.

Vandals Strike in Jackson's Pond

Sometime between 10 p.m. Sunday night, November 16 and 7 a.m. the next morning, vandals broke two windows and painted the slogans "America for Americans," "White is Right," and "Speak English, This is America" on the windows of several businesses on Main Street in Jackson's Pond.

The County Sheriff's office investigated. No suspects have been identified at press time.

Texas Health Solutions Clinic Closing

Jackson's Pond's only health care facility, the clinic operated since last year by Texas Health Solutions, will close its doors for the final time on December 23, 2014.

Daniel Jennings, of the company's Dallas headquarters, said, "As a for-profit company, we cannot continue operation in Jackson's Pond, given the current regulatory climate." He further stated that the fate of the Calverton clinic is also under consideration.

CHAPTER 9

Herding Cats

Usually, when Ray arrived at the office, he met with the City Manager briefly, to let her know he, as mayor, was available, and to hear any issues she cared to mention. That latter seldom happened because she'd been in the job more than ten years and knew what was necessary to keep the minimum processes of the town operating—trash collection provided on time; water and sewer systems operating; finances, meager as they were, managed; and Mayor and City Council informed or warned as the situation merited.

Today, he waved to her as he came in and went directly to his office. Before the day was over, he had to figure out a way to get the five strategic planning committees functioning smoothly. That's what he intended to accomplish. But before he got his laptop open, the City Manager, Stephanie Jacobson, stood in the doorway. She said, "Four people have called this morning asking if anyone has been charged with the vandalism. They'd seen it in the paper. I referred them to the sheriff. One of the new people from the RBJ office who called seemed surprised to hear that we don't have a city police department. I had to explain that lots of small towns in larger counties depend on sheriff's deputy patrols. People don't get how expensive a police force would be."

He said, "Maybe that will change eventually." The cost estimate he'd gotten from Regional Planning for setting up a minimum level of police force had told him it would be a topic for later, perhaps much later.

He waved a hand toward the small sofa and side chair across from his desk. She chose the sofa. If appearances were any indication, she'd had a hard weekend. He didn't ask. There wasn't a thing he could do about her family problems—ill, elderly parents and a husband disabled in a cotton gin accident last year. She leaned against one of the two plump cushions at the sofa back and closed her eyes. After a few seconds, she opened them and sat up straight. She said, "Here's a positive note. Mrs. Goodman has offered to volunteer in this office, helping with typing and general assistance."

"It's up to you. Having someone who could type and occasionally answer the phone, just a few hours a week? Would that be more trouble than it's worth to you?" He knew better than to make the decision. He could easily ruin the positive working relationship they had by failing to attend to the line between policy and implementation.

She appeared to be thinking about her answer. Maybe she was just resting a little more before getting back to her office and the mountain of paper it held. He heard her inhale. She said, "She's a nice young woman, wife of that minister who chairs one of the planning groups. Seems smart. Offered three hours a day to us after she brings her kids to school. I'd say it's worth a try."

He nodded and then said, "I know . . ."

"Yeah, I'll be sure to give her the speech about confidentiality and do it in the nicest possible way."

With that, she pushed herself up from the sofa, then turned and looked at it. She said, "That's too dangerous to have in here. A person could easily get stuck. Next time I go to Lubbock, I'll see if some secondhand store has something less comfortable."

Ray looked around what he laughingly referred to as his office, the room at City Hall that had previously held an ancient, useless computer tower and its huge green-screened monitor; boxes of Christmas decorations for the park; the old-fashioned printer, military surplus judging by its color; and four partially empty boxes of lined computer paper that printer had required, if it had ever worked. Before he was elected, apparently no one threw anything away at City Hall.

Except for the Christmas decorations, those items, plus unfiled documents too numerous to inventory, had littered the room long before he became mayor. He'd declared on his first day that he needed an office. Now it looked like a room where work could be accomplished and where visitors could be received, even though much of the furniture came from a secondhand store in Lubbock. Maybe she was right about that sofa.

His desk held a telephone, a blotter, his laptop computer that he brought from home each day, and a lined notepad. The bookshelves, donated by the library, held binders full of State of Texas rules on municipal government, current financial documents, City Council agendas and minutes, and materials related to the current strategic planning project. If he allowed himself to, he'd spend even more hours here than the forty each week he'd promised Melanie he'd limit it to.

Jackson's Pond, a small town (3,023 in the 2010 census) could, like many others, continue sliding toward oblivion with far less effort from its mayor than Ray was willing to dedicate. Most of the small Texas towns functioned with a City Manager/Financial Officer along with a City Council and a mayor whose main function was to break tie votes. Some places the City Manager had an administrative assistant. He'd learned about this structure when he met the officials from several other small West Texas towns at the Regional Council and later read the state rules on municipal structure. But not a one of those towns on the skids had attracted new light industry and none of them had citizens hoping for their city to thrive rather than to only survive.

Nothing in the state's municipal government rules prohibited a mayor from attempting to lead, even though his main prescribed function was to assure that Council votes didn't end up deadlocked in a tie. At his age and stage, with adequate income and no personal axes to grind or scores to settle, Ray saw his mission as mayor—one term at the most, he hoped—to set in motion plans to help Jackson's Pond do more than survive. It was a small town no different from many others. Even though he became a citizen of Jackson's Pond only after he and Melanie married the first time, it was his home. He saw too much of value in the town to let it die.

From his perspective, the strategic planning process was far more than an exercise in community engagement. It was vital to gaining eventual approval of what he knew would be a next step—a bond issue and corresponding tax increase to support the goals and projects that those planning groups would develop. So today, he began a list that he stopped at twenty names—people in city government he'd met through Regional Planning Council, a few from his days as the Governor's Executive Assistant, and some others at Texas Tech.

By noon, he'd talked with ten on the list. In the low-threat, good-old-boy way of gathering information so familiar among Texas politicians, he sought suggestions specifically about formal planning processes in which they'd been involved. What succeeded and what didn't. In each case, as he listened, he imagined himself not so much sifting through the elements of those conversations for the useful kernels as wading through bullshit to find the prize. There was always a prize. He'd learned to expect that missions such as he'd set himself today would net one good idea per four hours. More than that would be a banner day.

He left the office to go home for lunch smiling. He'd already written two prize ideas on his notepad. A friend, a fraternity brother, now a city council member in San Antonio, offered the first. He'd said, "Let them thrash around a bit, then when some of them decide the whole planning process is a crock, offer to find them a facilitator."

His friend's explanation made Ray glad he hadn't offered the committees help at the outset. As he listened, the guy he recalled as a lean, handsome, girl-magnet who came from South Texas ranching money dropped his gem into a story. The tale was about a city-sponsored planning retreat he'd been to, the only one that ever produced any worthwhile outcomes.

Getting around to the point, he'd described himself at the time as divorced, depressed, and fat. Ray had a hard time changing his mental image of "the fastest man in the frat" as he listened. But soon, the prize surfaced. "Our group was in chaos, sniping at each other, resisting, all that. We couldn't agree on anything. Some thought a staffer in the mayor's office probably had our recommendations written before we left town, and that we'd just been sent to that dude ranch in Bandera for the weekend for show. Others thought it was our duty to come up with a plan, but didn't have a clue where to start. Just as I was about to suggest we give it up and all go to the bar, the City Manager came by and asked how our 'process' was going. Everybody turned mute.

"Finally, I laid it out, and described the mess we were in. The city manager offered us a facilitator. Someone he'd brought along in case there was a need, he said."

His friend had paused, stretching out his story the way Ray remembered he always did, like ranchers will when they spend a lot of time alone between conversations. Then he went on, "I'll make this long story shorter. The facilitator knew her business. By Sunday evening, our group was proud. We produced work that ended up as part of the San Antonio Renewal Plan for the Nineties. If she'd come in too soon, before we were frustrated, we'd have ignored her, I have no doubt. That's the reason for my advice about thrashing." Then he went silent.

Ray heard him chuckle softly. "Smartest woman I ever met. Decided I'd marry her if she'd agree. Took some convincing. Cured my depression, too." A few minutes later, the prize written on his notepad, Ray promised they wouldn't go so long between visits again. Nearing home, he wondered if that smart woman still worked as a facilitator. He made a note at the top of the pad as he paused at the stop sign on his block.

From the intersection, the Banks' house was fifth on the north side of the street, straight ahead, the one with a seasonal arrangement of pumpkins, cornstalks, and a scarecrow on the porch. A black pickup backed out of the driveway there as Ray pulled away from the stop sign. Any doubt about who'd been at their house disappeared when he saw the bumper sticker and heard the engine roar as the vehicle sped north. Justin Reese.

Not sure what he expected to find, Ray used his remote to open the garage door and pulled inside. When he got out, instead of entering through the kitchen door from the garage, he walked to the front of the house. None of the screens on the windows were damaged; no signs or symbols marred the exterior; the front door was locked and the glass storm door was intact. But both pumpkins lay smashed and smeared on the porch, the cornstalks broken, and the ears strewn onto the lawn.

His doctor had agreed with Claire's changes in his blood pressure meds and emphasized resting midday, just as she had. So far, he hadn't missed a day of resting an hour after lunch. Well, an hour including lunch, which he ate alone. Melanie ate at her school, but always left something in the refrigerator for him, even though he'd told her a grown man should be ashamed if his wife had to make his every meal. That didn't stop her. Today would be a test. If he could settle down after finding and cleaning up the evidence of Justin Reese's "visit," he'd deserve a medal.

After clearing the mess out front, he closed the garage door and entered the kitchen, telling himself to breathe calmly even though he'd have preferred storming through the house, shouting. Instead, he ate the half sandwich, soup, and grapes Melanie left for him. Then he extended the footrest on his recliner and closed his eyes. No one said he had to sleep. So, he mentally replayed the other prize-offering conversation from the morning. The mayor of another Panhandle town, respected by most in the regional planning group, had congratulated him on being brave enough to get people involved. Then, because he had a meeting to attend, he'd said, "I can sum up all my advice before I have to hang up. Got your pencil?"

Ray assured him he was ready to take notes, and the veteran city official started again.

He said, "Involving citizens in planning is like herding cats. You have to close any doors you don't want them to go in, aim them in the right direction, and then stand back. How to get them to go that way? Feed them. Literally and figuratively. Feed them snacks at the meetings. Create occasions that include food to reward any and all progress toward accomplishing the planning. And feed them useful information."

Ray had wondered if that was the full summary. Before he could ask, his friend said, "What not to do? Don't try to tell them how to get where you want them to go. They only go if they can go in their own way, at their own pace. Feed them information, all you have, but don't force it. And don't take it personally if some of them stray off. That's cats."

Ray woke, startled by the sound of the refrigerator's ice maker spilling cubes into the bin. He'd actually napped for fifteen minutes. Finding those two prizes had let him relax in spite of the issue of vandalism that waited on the fringe of his awareness. That should please his wife and daughter. He lowered the footrest. Sitting upright, he allowed himself one more mental image of a herd of cats. Then he stood, rounded up his keys and his notepad. In the garage, before he turned the ignition, he wrote on the notepad, SNACKS. He'd call Melanie before she left school for the day. No sense ruining her day by telling about the "visitation."

Back at City Hall, Stephanie stopped him just inside the front door. She said, "You have a visitor. Mr. Patel. He apologized for coming without an appointment. As if anyone else ever worries about such niceties. Says he needs to talk about his committee, and right away."

"How long has he been waiting?"

"Only about ten minutes. I gave him some tea. He sounds English, so I doubt he likes coffee."

When Ray entered the office, Mr. Patel stood at military-drill full attention. Ray said, "I'm so sorry to have kept you waiting. Let's sit and you tell me how I can help."

The motel owner sat, seeming to balance just on the edge of the chair he chose. Watching him, Ray thought of Melanie's grandmother, Delia Jackson, and her stiff-spined way of occupying a chair.

Patel said, "Mr. Mayor, I regret to inform you that I must tender my resignation."

After he made that statement, the man inched forward, positioned to stand again. Ray saw an envelope in the motel owner's hand. Ray said, "Do you have time to talk about this? It would be a shame for you to resign, especially if there's something I can do to help."

Mr. Patel's starched posture lost a bit of its crispness. He exhaled, then said, "I had such high hopes. An all-volunteer committee, a common desire to enhance and enlarge the business base in town—surely we should be able to arrive at a plan to propose. I fear it is I who am the problem."

Ray was tempted to agree. Even though Patel had lived in Texas for more than ten years, and was succeeding at his business, his manner had remained formal, respectful and courteous, but reserved. Some folks had a hard time warming up to that. "Have you talked with any of the other committee chairs to see if they're having problems, too?"

Mr. Patel seemed to be searching the bookshelves, perhaps hoping he'd see an answer there. Eventually, he locked eyes with Ray. "Pastor Goodman came to see me. He is experiencing many of the same difficulties. In meetings, people either don't talk at all or some monopolize, and disagree with others' opinions without any facts to support their own."

"Is it fair to say they are thrashing around?"

"Quite fair. And rather colorful." Mr. Patel finally smiled, appeared to relax a tiny bit more. "I've seen children at play do better with cooperation."

Ray said, "I might be able to get you some help. Would you be willing to have a person work with you, with the group, someone from outside whose only interest is in helping the group create a plan the members can agree on? A facilitator."

"You know such a person?" Patel frowned and returned to his study of the bookshelves. After a silence, he said, "Yes, I believe the members, each in his own way, want to do the work. If that is true, a person of that sort could be helpful."

"Would you be willing to poll the other chairs to see if any of them want someone to aid their groups?"

As if newly energized, Patel said, "I shall do it promptly. May I contact you again today with their answers?"

"I hope you will."

Then Patel stood again, and surprised Ray by offering his hand. The firmness of the handshake told him something he hadn't known about the man, his resolve.

Later that afternoon, when he called to tell her about the ruined decorations, Melanie surprised him. Rather than being upset about the Reese encounter, she'd only said, "It's predictable. Apparently, he and his friends were busy today. I'll lock the doors when I get home and I'll see you at supper."

At home that evening, telling Melanie about his day, Ray reported, in order, his prize ideas, the meeting with the motel owner/committee chairperson, and the stroke of luck at not only having all the chairs agree they needed help, but also at being able to secure the services of a team of two people from Wichita Falls who came highly recommended by none other than the former Speaker of the Texas House of Representatives. The committee chairs, as a group, would meet with them Thursday evening. Then each committee would have one or the other of the facilitators starting right after that.

When he paused, Melanie said, "So, should I make cookies?"

"Cookies. For what?"

She patted his arm and said, "One of your prize ideas included feeding the cats. Making cookies is the least I can do."

He laughed. "I guess I got a little wound up by the prospect of something that might resemble progress. Skipped right over that one. Yes, if you have time, that would be a nice touch." He reached across the end table between their chairs and caught her hand. "If I haven't mentioned it today, I love you."

Her smile and return squeeze of his hand didn't match the sadness in her eyes. She'd held something back. He said, "What's wrong?"

"I hate to tell you. You have enough on your mind, and you're just getting your blood pressure back in control."

"I can handle whatever it is."

"Claire came by the school. She showed me pictures from her phone. Just awful."

"More dead cattle?"

"That would be easier to take." Melanie shook her head. "It's so hard to believe this is happening here." As she stood and moved toward the kitchen, she said, "I'll show you."

She returned with her phone. "Claire sent these after she came to town and showed me." Her hand shook as she passed the phone to him.

"This is the Family Heritage marker at the ranch gate, right?" He saw the words, This Isn't Over, painted in red across the face of the sign. Below, there was a red circle outlined in black, with a white cross in the middle, and in the center of the cross, a black-outlined diamond, white in the center, with a red symbol resembling a comma in its center. Ray said, "That's Klan, right?"

"I intend to look it up. But that's what I'd guess. Look at the next one."

The picture was a Posted, No Hunting sign, common in rural areas where farmers and ranchers don't want hunters on their land. Across the sign, red paint spelled OPEN SEASON ON QUEERS.

She said, "That sign is about a hundred feet down the fence, east from the gate."

"What have Claire and J.D. done about this?"

"She called J.D. and he called the sheriff. At first, J.D. didn't want to report it. Just clean it up and keep a watch. He thinks the attention is what they want."

"What changed his mind?"

"Claire said it was Chris. He told J.D. he knew he was trying to protect him and Andrew from gossip. Told him it would be wasted effort. So, they called. The deputy came soon after and pronounced it the work of the same vandals who marked up the town."

"I doubt that. Unless the vandals from town are that crew of Reese's." Ray was out of his chair now, looking at the pictures again, as he paced the room. "Intimidation, creating fear and suspicion among neighbors. That's what they want."

He handed her the phone and sat again. "Did the kids see those?"

"Claire drove them right past the gate, on down to the pavement to catch the school bus, as soon as she noticed there was something odd. Said she told them she'd make it easy for the bus driver. But you know Jay Frank. He seldom misses a detail. Claire and J.D. intended to talk to them this afternoon."

Ray leaned back and closed his eyes. "I'm trying to remain calm, but it's damn hard when our family's a target, and there's not a thing I can do. I feel more like punching the wall." Relaxing intentionally seldom came easy for him, but he'd listened when Claire had explained that he could choose his reactions under stress rather than allow stress to control him. So he sat still and listened to his breathing. Claire's prescription. After a couple of minutes, he said, "Did the deputy try for fingerprints?"

Melanie nodded, then shrugged. "For all the good it will do. If those painters have any sense at all, they wore gloves."

He closed his eyes again. Then he said, "Can you see what I'm doing?"

"Taking a nap in the face of crisis?"

"Funny girl. No, really."

He opened one eye when she sat in his lap and leaned against his chest. She said, "Doing exactly what you're supposed to. Relaxing, consciously." He closed that one eye and nodded.

She planted a kiss on his cheek. "I'm proud of you."

When he wrapped her in a hug, she snuggled closer. "I'm calmer now, too. You're a good influence on me, Ray Banks."

His eyes still closed, he smiled. "We'll do what we can, whenever we can."

Wednesday evening, at the Patel's home, Ray arrived with Melanie's cookies and the two facilitators, Lucy and Mark, fifteen minutes before the meeting was scheduled. Mrs. Patel had supplied coffee, and when the other four committee chairpersons arrived, all assembled used a few minutes with introductions and compliments for the refreshments. None of that was accidental.

Lucy had prompted Ray to arrange things, right down to the timing, just that way.

Three hours later, when Melanie met him at their front door, he hugged her and said, "I'm a genius!"

"I never doubted that. What makes you so sure tonight?"

"I used the resources I had. I gathered information from lots of different people, put it all together and boy, did those two from Wichita Falls do a good job. If it wasn't so late, I'd take you out dancing."

She pulled him inside. "The neighbors will talk—mayor drunk, shouting at his own front door. Come on in, have a seat at that bar, and I'll pour you a glass of wine."

For the next several minutes, he told her about the two facilitators and how they had gently instructed the chairpersons in the process of group decision-making. Never once could they have been accused of talking down to the group, or of implying that the committees were in disarray. Then they walked them through the process they would use when they met with the five groups, and provided a handout. He finished by saying, "I think they will be a huge help. What you see before you, Mrs. Banks, is a hopeful man."

He sat, smiling, and sipping his wine. Then he said, "Oh, and there's another thing. Heath Goodman asked if we could talk separately, afterward. He followed me to the office."

"Sounds clandestine."

"He said his wife told him today that Reese's wife had called her and talked a long time about being worried her husband and, as she put it, some of his cronies, were planning to cause big trouble. He said his wife told him exactly what Mrs. Reese said was, 'There are more of them coming out every weekend. They meet over at his bunker. Last weekend there were eighteen. He gets phone calls and whispers so I won't hear. He got up after midnight Sunday, night before last, and left. I heard voices and more than one vehicle. He came back alone before daylight. I was afraid to ask him where he'd been, so I acted like I was asleep the whole time.' His wife is concerned the woman's in danger."

"What did he want you to do?"

"I'm not sure. What I did was tell him he should go in and report it to the sheriff. Goodman didn't want to put Mrs. Reese in danger, but said he probably would talk to the sheriff. I don't know if that's what he wanted from me, but it was all I could think of. That and remembering that the vandalism happened on that Sunday night."

He watched Melanie cradle her wine goblet in both hands, and stare at the deep red liquid she swirled. Then she said, "I wish there was a way to help her. Poor thing must be frightened to death. Is it okay for me to tell Claire? You know she can keep confidences."

He nodded. "It's probably good she knows. I'm still concerned something more is going to happen out at the ranch. I think those guys are just getting warmed up."

Later, in bed, Ray stared into the dark and silently prayed, "Please, God, keep my family safe and don't allow evil to overcome the good in this community."

It had been a long time since he prayed. Too long, he thought.

Floyd County Tribune
Early Edition
Wednesday, November 26, 2014

Texas Health Solutions to Close Calverton Clinic

Texas Health Solutions announced Monday that their Calverton clinic will close December 31, 2014. The closure of their Jackson's Pond clinic was announced earlier. No mention was made in the announcement of sale of the clinics or of any arrangement for a replacement for their services.

Vandalism Reported at Jackson Ranch

Personnel at the Jackson Ranch in the east county notified sheriff's officers of vandalism which apparently occurred the same night as that earlier reported in Jackson's Pond. The Family Heritage marker at the ranch and a Posted sign were both defaced. Deputies gathered fingerprint evidence and photographed the damage. No comment was available regarding suspects in either vandalism case. Investigation continues, according to sheriff's officers.

Arrest in Bull Shooting Case

Boyd Barker, of Mineola, was arrested as a suspect in the shooting of a breeding bull on the Jackson Ranch earlier this month. He is reported to have been returned to Floyd County jail to await trial on the charge of felony criminal mischief. If convicted, he can face both a fine and a jail sentence.

CHAPTER 10
Give Thanks

Melanie and Ray had taken separate cars out to the ranch for Thanksgiving. She stayed to help Claire clean up and he had gone on into town to take care of some things at the city office. Now she was on her way back home, driving slowly. As she passed the pond, she stopped, backed up, and parked at the dirt road leading from the pavement to the pasture. There the remnant of that odd natural feature stood out as a miniature green swale surrounded by the knee-high native grass of the rest of the pasture. It had been out of the ordinary because it was a steady-source pond in a semi-arid land where, after rains, water pooled in playa lakes, then disappeared soon after.

She walked toward the gate, wondering if her son-in-law had moved the bulls to another pasture nearer the house. J.D. thought ahead. He and Chris would probably have moved them right after the shooting in the north pasture.

Right, no bulls. That foresight of J. D.'s was an admirable trait, and one of the reasons she was glad her mother had chosen him as ranch manager, then later made him partner many years back. He'd been Chris's friend when they were teenagers and there was no doubt they were as close as any brothers could be. Their working together now that Chris and Andrew were making the ranch their home seemed natural, good for both of them.

Melanie pushed open the unlocked gate and walked toward the pond. Her memories included nothing of significance about the pond named for her family. As a child, she'd been aware of it, but not interested, primarily because her grandmother had warned her away. A lady doesn't muddy her clothes, nor wade, certainly not in water of unknown depth. Still beautiful, if only for its difference, the pond she'd ignored as a young woman drew her today, for no reason she was conscious of. Her thoughts roamed.

She walked to the far side where three large rocks offered a place to sit. Facing southwest, she bathed in the long rays of late afternoon, soon-to-be-winter sun. She watched as it spread her shadow against the already-brown pasture grass.

Today she felt liberated, no longer warned by her grandmother, no longer urgently needed by her two children for the daily vigilance she'd marshaled years ago. They were adults. She was no longer responsible for enforcing rules, for watching what they ingested or inhaled with whom or where. No longer waiting until they were in bed to guiltily smoke one cigarette a day in the bathroom with the window open just a crack, or drink a glass of wine. Never again needing to be the immovable object in the path of irresistible forces.

Gone, the days of being the responsible model of deportment, conducting all adult conversation out of their earshot and never swearing. She was now free to be foolish, irresponsible if the mood struck her, and to be a whole person, not simply a parent. Now free also to regret the mistakes she'd made living that half-life she'd thought a parent must. Today she considered herself truly fortunate that her children had begun to know her as an adult. She wished she'd realized long before now that her own mother was not simply her parent, her duty, but also an adult she could know and admire. Although some of her mother's choices would always mystify her, like her considering marrying Robert.

As the sun fell lower, she started back toward the car. Claire had asked her to come again tomorrow. As far as Melanie was concerned, as delicious as dinner had been, the best part of her day had been that request. The words, "Give thanks," came to mind as she started the car. She drove forty-five miles per hour all the way home.

The next morning around eleven, she parked in front at the big house. She heard Jay Frank's voice, faintly, but couldn't locate it until he yelled, "Wait there, Grandmother. I'm walking O'Keeffe. I want you to see him." He was coming up the drive, a large goat walking on a leash behind him. When he and the goat were about six feet away, her grandson said, "Now watch." He put the goat through a series of stances, all designed to show off his musculature. Then he dropped the leash and walked toward her after telling the goat to stay. "He's going to win the blue ribbon this year. The others are good goats, but he's the best."

He hugged her around the waist. Then he said, "O'Keeffe, come."

The goat trotted to him and nuzzled at his pocket. Jay Frank said, "He knows where the treats come from. I've got to work the others, then I'll be in. Don't start without me."

She went onto the porch where Claire waited, standing inside the screen door. Claire said, "I heard what he said. I told them that when you came, we were all going to talk about some important things we want them to think about."

Claire walked ahead of her mother down the hall to the den. She said, "I thought I knew what I wanted to say, but yesterday I realized I'm not sure. Two different ages, two different developmental levels. And the subject . . . I'm not sure where to start. As a teacher, you know better than I do how to go about getting them to understand." She sat on the couch, patted the place beside her. "And besides, I needed moral support. They don't need to see how angry it made me finding those signs."

Melanie said, "I don't know that it's wrong for them to know it made you angry. You're human. Those words were hateful and the act of putting them here was intended to frighten anyone who saw them."

She sat, thinking for a few seconds. Then she said, "I think it's best to start where they are, find out what they think they know, then go from there. Children need to know they and the people they love are together, protecting one another."

Claire nodded. "That makes sense, at any age."

The front screen slammed and seconds later Jay Frank appeared at the door. "I'll get Amy."

The two of them returned together. Amy, a now taller version of the toddler she'd been, with wild black curls and full of sparkling energy, glided into the room as only ballerinas can. Jay Frank, also grown taller, still seemed the intense little boy she'd held on her lap every chance she got. They both wore serious expressions, and stood in front of their mother and grandmother. Claire said, "You're not in trouble. Please sit down so we can talk."

All it took to start them was her saying, "We think you know about the signs that were on the gate and fence this week. You probably have questions; maybe you're worried. We want to try to help you understand."

Jay Frank gave Amy a look suggesting they'd talked already. He said, "I could tell it made you really mad, Mom. I was afraid to ask questions."

Amy jumped in, "I told him you might have been really worried and just looked mad."

"It was silly of me to try to keep it from you. You're both old enough to know."

Jay Frank, the family fact gatherer, said, "What exactly did you see? I know it was painted on the sign. First words were 'This isn't.' But we passed too fast for me to get it. Then it was gone when we came home."

Amy said, "I told him someone had painted lots of things, vandalized, in town. Hateful things. And it was probably the same stuff. I was texting and didn't see it."

Melanie watched Claire's face. A moment passed as she closed, then reopened her eyes. That was her "wheels turning" expression, the one Melanie first noticed when her daughter was about four. Spinning out the fabulous tales only four-year-olds can, she'd pause for breath, close her eyes, then open them, and off she'd go again.

Claire pulled her telephone from her shirt pocket. "I'll show you. I took these before the sheriff came, before I scrubbed them off." The two peered at the photos. "Can you see why that made me angry?"

"You had to clean it off?" That was Amy.

Jay Frank said, "It was meant to scare us."

"Yes, to both. But mostly it was because someone was trying to scare us. Remember those girls who bullied you and tried to scare you last year, Amy? And those boys saying things about Elisa. I felt a lot like you did those times, I think."

Amy frowned. "Grownups did this?"

Melanie said, "People of all ages try to make other people feel afraid—people different from them or who have different beliefs."

Jay Frank said, "What's that mark?" He enlarged the picture, focusing on the red, black, and white circle.

Melanie waited. When Claire hesitated, Melanie said, "There are people, adults, a sort of gang, who call themselves the Ku Klux Klan, who use that symbol. And they often hide behind masks and robes, to make themselves even more frightening."

Claire said, "That's what made me the angriest. If there are people here who are part of that, I want the law to deal with them. And if they're people who just used that sign to make us afraid, they got it wrong. It just makes me mad."

Melanie said, "Have either one of you ever read about the Klan, heard about it in school?"

Amy was quick to respond, recalling something from her Texas history class. But she didn't stop with that. She and Jay Frank both spilled out questions, listening quietly to answers from both their mother and Melanie as they explained about Klan symbols and people who are targets of hate groups such as the Klan. And they both wondered aloud why any adults would behave that way.

Melanie had watched the two of them, saw the initial interest in their eager questions, and now heard fear tinge their voices. She said, "I think we need to also talk about how to make sure everyone stays safe."

Claire nodded and sat straighter. Just as she began, Jay Frank waved a hand. "Wait, I have one more question." Amy gave him a nod. He said, "What does this mean?" He'd located the picture of the other sign, the one saying "Open Season on Queers."

Amy rolled her eyes. "It's a hateful name for people who love people of their same gender. Like Uncle Chris and Uncle Andrew."

Melanie took note of Amy's choice of the word, gender. She said, "Did you learn about that in school?"

"No. You know how people around here are. Narrow-minded. I read a lot."

Melanie tried to remember herself as a teenager and could only envision a completely naïve child, concerned with her appearance and making good grades. Amy knew the words but that wasn't the same as truly understanding. She would need more opportunities to explore many ideas. Claire and J.D. had their work cut out for them.

Jay Frank's eyes widened. "So, someone wants to scare them? Mom, are they going to hurt Uncle Chris or Andrew?"

"To scare all of us, I think. Let's go back to what we can do. Your dad and I have talked and he and Uncle Chris talked to the sheriff when he came out."

Melanie could see Claire watching the children as they talked and had noticed Jay Frank fidgeting on the ottoman where he sat. Claire said, "Now, I want to tell you the important things about staying safe. Ask questions when you think of them."

Before she could go further, Amy said, "Do you think whoever did this is going to come back? Will they try to hurt some of us?"

"We don't know. There's no way to know."

"Does the sheriff have any idea who it is?"

"He said it's probably more than one person. They're investigating. And there are lawmen watching the people involved with shooting our bull. Under continuous surveillance."

Claire wrote a list as she explained what she called the new family safety rules. They listened without questions and when she finished, she handed the list to Amy to duplicate on the copy machine. Seconds later, Amy was back with four copies.

Then Claire asked them to give her their phones. "I'm going to set the GPS locator function. That way if you ever should be missing, we can locate you if you have the phone."

Jay Frank's eyes lit up. "Then we keep them with us, turned on, all the time."

His mother said, "Exactly. And remember, you must check in with either me or Dad anytime you leave the house, or leave somewhere else. That's so we know where you are, and that you're safe." She handed back the phones. "I know you understand what we talked about. But it's a lot to remember. It would be a good idea to keep the list in your pocket until you get in the habit of doing all we agreed on." They both nodded. "Okay then. You probably have other things to do."

Amy left the room, then poked her head back around the door frame. "I'll be upstairs doing my barre work."

Jay Frank said, "Thanks, Mom. I'm going to my room to memorize this list."

As soon as they left, Melanie told Claire she was impressed with how she'd dealt with the situation. They were standing at the cabinet looking out toward the back yard, each holding a soft drink can. Without looking at her mother, Claire said, "It helped a lot that you were here. Thank you."

Melanie didn't move. She didn't want to change what she'd recall of this moment. "Thank you for asking me to be here." Then, as Claire reached over and hugged her, she had to continue looking toward the cattle grazing in the distance. Otherwise, she'd have cried.

Later, while Claire cleared the table and reset it for lunch, Melanie sat at the bar and read the list Claire had titled New Family Safety Rules.

1. Stay alert. Be aware of your location at all times.
2. Keep phone with you, with all family numbers and emergency (ICE) numbers up to date.
3. Check in with a parent or designated adult each time you go to another location. Adults do the same.
4. If any stranger comes on the ranch, call parent or designated adult immediately.
5. Do not accept rides with anyone other than family or the Montoya family or Tag.
6. If anyone asks about the bull that was shot, or about the vandalized signs, tell them to speak to parents. Official answer from children is I Don't Know.

7. If anything scares you, or you're worried, talk to a family member. We share.

8. Don't post your location on any social media, ever. And don't accept any new friends. Remember there's no privacy on the Internet. It's not possible to know who reads what you post. Use actual phone calls rather than social media or texts.

Claire said, "I'll be through here as soon as I get some burger meat from the freezer." She handed the weekly newspaper to her mother. "That's the early edition that was supposed to be out on Wednesday, but just came this morning. Interesting, there's a piece there about the thing I want your advice about."

She left Melanie reading the paper and returned from the utility room a few seconds later.

Melanie said, "Let me guess. It's this one about the Calverton Clinic closing."

"Yes, I'd been thinking for a while about needing to find a way to do something worthwhile." She paused. "Not that being here and helping J.D. with the bookkeeping and the breeding records and such aren't worthwhile. And taking care of the kids. I know that's important, but you know how restless I get."

Melanie managed to keep from saying immediately all she thought. Instead, she said, "You're right. What you're doing is important. I'd say it's vital."

Claire shrugged. "I don't know about vital, but having household help a few hours a week like Gran convinced me to, leaves time to think. And what I'd thought was that there are people who need to know how to stay healthy. They need some sort of individual plan of health education with encouragement and continued motivation. There are people with diabetes who know too little to manage their condition. They take pills and that's it."

"Thinking of offering diabetes education?"

"Not only that. It'd have to be a part of some old-fashioned community health nursing. The thing that non-competition agreement I signed keeps me from doing is clinic-based primary care, mainly diagnosing and writing prescriptions. But that was never all I did with the clinics."

She described some of her efforts at health promotion, things that didn't depend on medication and that she usually couldn't charge for because they weren't "medical."

"I believe that's at least as important, sometimes more important, than medication. And if I could do it my way, I'd do it for free. What I don't know is how I'd set up to do it." She'd picked up the newspaper. "They made me sell out and now they've been here less than a year and are closing, leaving people to have to drive more than thirty miles, or farther, just to be seen in a clinic. It just makes me so angry when I think about it." She rolled the paper and swatted it against the table. "I'm not making any sense, I know. Tell me what you think."

Her mother said, "I think you will come to a conclusion when it's time. My only advice would be to remember that you've always moved faster than almost everyone around you. Now that you're a bit older, and a lot wiser, maybe you can try moving at a slower pace when making decisions that affect others."

"I told myself that. But it's hard for me to see unmet needs and not act."

"I'd never tell you not to do what you can to help others, those beyond your family. It's what you do so well." Melanie hoped she hadn't gone too far. But her own experience had taught her that just because she was able to do a thing and to do it well, didn't mean she must always be the one to do it alone. Too often she'd sacrificed family in the process.

Claire said, "It's not even been a year since J.D. nearly died. I have to keep that in mind. His bones have healed. But there may be more healing yet to be done."

Melanie nodded. "I'm not much help, but anytime you want to talk. I'm happy to listen."

Moving from one topic to another quickly, as she often did, Claire said, "You saw that paragraph about the arrest. J.D. thinks that's what may have prompted those signs at the ranch.

The sheriff said the guy's likely to get a jail sentence. Said the others might try to retaliate. I know it's all speculation. But…"

Melanie said, "Oh, wait. I need to tell you. I know you'll keep this confidential, but I think you should know. It could be related." She told about Pastor Goodman's wife's conversation with Justin Reese's wife.

Claire said, "I'll tell J.D., just in case he needs to be convinced to be careful. Chris, too. They'll understand it's not to be mentioned." She sat quietly for a while. "That poor woman."

A few minutes later, as Melanie drove back home, she couldn't help being proud of her daughter, of her kindness and concern for others. That pride was tinged with sadness at the thought that anyone, any woman, and specifically Mrs. Reese, had to live in fear. She repeated Claire's words, "That poor woman."

By the time she parked in her garage, she'd come to a conclusion. She'd find a way to do whatever she could to help Justin Reese's wife.

Floyd County Tribune
Thursday, December 18, 2014

Barker Bull Shooting Trial Begins Today

Jury selection is set to begin Thursday, December 18, at 1 p.m. in County Courtroom 2. A six-person jury will be seated for the trial in the case of the killing of a breeding bull said to be worth at least $4500.00. The defendant, Boyd Barker, was returned to this county after his arrest in Mineola, Texas, last month.

Patient Records Available for Texas Health Solutions Patients

Patients seen at the Jackson's Pond and Calverton clinics operated by Texas Health Solutions are invited to pick up their records as they transfer to other providers. The records are all available at the Calverton location. After December 31, access to the records will be by written request to the corporate office at P.O. Box 2321 Grapeland, TX.

County Junior Livestock Show Entry Forms

Entry forms for the County Junior Livestock Show are available now at the Extension Agent's office in Calverton. Those living out of town can call the office to have forms mailed. The show will be held the third week in January, 2015, at the Calverton Community Center.

Pancho Clos To Visit Jackson's Pond Saturday

Jackson's Pond will welcome Pancho Clos in City Park on Saturday afternoon, December 20 at 2 p.m. Children will have the opportunity to have photos made with the jolly visitor and there will be music and refreshments. All are welcome to attend.

CHAPTER 11

Convictions

Floyd County Courtroom 2 held more people today than J.D. had imagined would care. He'd thought it would be pretty straightforward. The sheriff would testify about the dead bull, the spent shells, the slugs in the bull, and the fingerprints on the gun. It was all fact and plain as day. J. D. had been subpoenaed and so had Chris, but the prosecutor had said they likely wouldn't have to testify.

Yet here he was squeezed in between Marty Broadus's big shoulders and Chris's solid body, with the guy from ATF filling in the last space on the pew. J.D. wondered if they held church in here when court wasn't in session. He and the others were lined up like crows on barbed wire right behind the lawyers and the defendant, Boyd Barker.

J. D. tried to be subtle when he looked around to see where the buzz of conversation was coming from. Turned out about ten guys from around Jackson's Pond and a couple he didn't recognize, probably from Calverton, filled up the back two rows. He wondered if they had nothing better to do on a Friday morning. Sitting off by themselves, separate from the rest, were Justin Reese and a couple of other guys all dressed in camouflage. J. D. knew for a fact that Justin Reese hadn't served in the military. He doubted there was a veteran among them.

Things got underway as soon as they all stood for the judge and she banged her gavel. The six-person jury, four men and two women, had been chosen yesterday. If the prosecutor had his way, Barker would serve a sentence in state jail and pay a fine, one big enough to make him think twice about firing his weapon the next time he came across a breeding bull grazing, not bothering a soul.

Right after opening statements—two different versions of the same day's events, the prosecutor promising to prove that Barker shot the bull, the defense attorney assuring the jurors it was a case of mistaken identity, or if not that, of a lot of circumstantial evidence—the prosecutor called Chris's name. Even though the county's lawyer hadn't thought J.D. or Chris would have to take the stand, he'd walked them through the questions he'd likely ask. "If Barker's lawyer's got any sense at all, he'll get him to plead guilty, even if he has to do it at the last minute."

But when he heard Chris called as a witness, J.D. added "gives false assurance" to the list of reasons he didn't trust attorneys. He knew he'd be called next. As his brother-in-law raised his hand and swore to tell the truth, J.D. felt proud of that man he thought of as his brother. Chris spoke distinctly and slowly and looked directly at the jurors as he responded to the lawyer's request to tell the events of the morning of October 31, 2014. He said, "I was checking fence on our north pasture, the one where we had eight of our registered Angus bulls grazing. They're two- and three-year-olds, growing quickly toward prime breeding age." He paused just then, letting the jury ponder the value of those bulls before he went on.

Then he told about hearing shots earlier and finding spent shells on the Jackson side of the fence. When Chris got to where he'd phoned J. D., the lawyer thanked him and gave the other side a chance, which Barker's lawyer answered with, "No questions, your honor."

After Chris took his time walking back to their pew, J. D. heard his name called. He took a deep breath and reminded himself of how he felt the day they buried that bull. It wasn't as bad as he'd expected, being the target of the jury members' attention. He was pretty sure at least three of the men were hard of hearing, like so many farmers are, so knew their frowns had nothing to do with doubting him, but with straining to hear what he said. The county lawyer led him through arriving at the field, and how he and Chris searched for and found the dead bull. When he got to where he said he called law enforcement, his turn was over. He made a point to stare at Justin Reese and his cronies as he strolled back to his seat. Broadus passed him, ambling up, carrying his Stetson, to swear he'd be truthful. When the bailiff held out the bible, Marty took his time placing his hat, brim up, on the rail around the witness box. Then he placed one hand on the Bible and raised the other and swore to tell the whole truth. The prosecutor waited as the ranger retrieved his hat and sat with it in his lap before running him through his part in the evidence collection.

It went on, with the defense asking no questions of Marty or the sheriff, who was next. The defense attorney sat as quiet as the spectators until the veterinarian came to the stand and testified about the two bullets that killed the bull. The lawyer asked if the vet or anyone he worked with was related to Chris Banks. "Not that I know of," said the doctor.

"Well," said the defense man, "what about your assistant?"

"What about him?"

"Isn't it true that he is the long-time, live-in partner of Chris Jackson?"

"When someone applies for a job with me, I don't ask about their personal lives. I can't answer that."

J.D. was pretty sure the juror sitting closest to the witness heard the animal doctor mutter, "What does that have to do with whether the bullets killed that bull?" If J. D. heard it where he was sitting, he was pretty sure even that deaf man did. The defense lawyer had been facing toward the back of the courtroom, maybe receiving signals from the camo crowd. Too bad, he missed a chance to object.

The prosecutor was paying attention, though, and when the defense said, "No further questions," the county's attorney asked for redirect. Then he asked the veterinarian, "Was anyone else involved in your reaching your decision about the cause of death of that bull?"

"No, I did a post mortem exam right there in the pasture, opened the chest and found one bullet still lodged in the heart muscle and one buried in the muscles behind the right lung. I put them in an evidence bag the ranger handed me. No one else but me."

The doc stepped down off the witness stand at 10:30, and the prosecutor was still on his feet when the judge declared a twenty-minute recess. J.D. thought she must know the tolerance of old farmers for sitting still without dipping snuff or smoking. The bailiff led the jury out. Then everyone else spilled into the hall.

Either some others had arrived or J.D. had miscounted. The camo crowd stood in a cluster near the stairs. He took his time passing by on the way to the restroom, and saw that there were eleven of them now.

He waited until Broadus and Chris caught up with him before they all three entered the restroom. No one followed. He said, "They're coming out of the woodwork."

Chris said, "How do they know Andrew and I are together and where he works?"

After washing his hands for longer than he needed to, Broadus punched the button on the hand dryer which came on with a roar. Then he beckoned them over before he stuck his hands in the hot air to dry. They had to lean in to hear him. He said, "I've got some more on Justin Reese. Things you need to know."

Court reconvened and the two attorneys followed all the steps, presented the forensic evidence, stipulated to the qualifications of the fingerprint expert, so on and so forth, sounding to J.D. like anyone with half sense would declare the guy guilty. And then, the prosecution rested its case.

Loud whispers from the defense table sounded like a swarm of wasps. The lawyer and defendant huddled, facing away from the prosecution and from the judge, too. J.D. strained to hear their words, but could only guess they were arguing about putting Barker on the stand.

The judge banged her gavel. She said, "Is the defense resting, too?"

Barker's lawyer never looked up, just raised a finger. The judge squinted and leaned forward. She said, "For future reference, this court responds only to words, not gestures. Am I clear?"

J.D. had to pretend he was coughing to keep from laughing at the flush that colored the lawyer's face.

The defense attorney said, "No, I mean yes, your honor, I understand. If it please the court, I call Boyd Barker."

The jury returned twenty minutes after they left and handed down a verdict of guilty. J.D., Chris, and Broadus had to work their way through what seemed like all the guys who'd showed up, other than the fake army, just to get out to J.D.'s pickup. With the windows up, they couldn't hear, but they watched as the camo-clad band got in one another's faces.

Chris said, "What would you bet they're trying to decide who gets to beat the shit out of Barker when he gets out of jail."

"I'm pretty sure it's a Klan meeting we're seeing, boys," said Marty Broadus. "Barker getting up there and saying he was framed, and how he never even aimed that gun in the direction of that bull. Which probably wouldn't have upset them much, except he didn't shut up. Going on and saying the reason his fingerprints were on the gun that matched those bullets was because Reese and the other one held him down and made him take hold of it."

J.D. said, "It might be the first time in his life that guy told the truth. Sit tight. I'll drive you over to your pickup, Marty. We've got to get back to the ranch."

As the Special Ranger got into his own vehicle, he said, "I'm going to follow you there so we can talk." He waved at the ATF agent who drove past on his way out of the lot. He turned back and said, "Don't want to discuss this on the phone."

Chris stared out the window, keeping quiet. J.D. thought about asking what he was thinking about, but they'd never done that to one another. When either one of them turned inward, the other one knew to wait. Then when the words might make some sense, the one with a load on his mind would say something like, "Let me say this, then you tell me what sense it makes, or why it doesn't." Since they were kids, that's the way they'd been with each other. They could always count on each other for a dose of hard truth, or if the situation called for it, unyielding backup. Even with Claire and Andrew being as important as they were, he and

Chris had stayed solid with each other for more than twenty-five years. As far as he was concerned, losing Chris would be like losing an arm or a leg. Then he smiled, told himself it wouldn't be a leg, it would be more like losing his liver, real close to vital.

As they passed the pond, Chris said, "I wonder if it'll ever change out here. Over in Taos, even in Austin, being who I am seldom caused a problem. I mean, if I had problems with people, it was because one or both of us was wrong, maybe being an asshole, but I never got the feeling in those places that all my troubles stemmed from being homosexual. Back here, it's as if it's necessary for people to *overlook* my being homosexual before they can even objectively consider what I say or do." He was quiet for a few seconds, then said, "I know. I'm not the only one. And not everyone out here treats me that way. But dammit, that guy implying that Andrew would tamper with evidence. Long-time, live-in partner. And he said it with a sneer."

J.D. said, "How about we turn around right now and go back there and whip that lawyer's ass?" He kept looking straight ahead. "We can take Broadus along for backup."

Chris said, "Hell yeah, why didn't I think of that?"

J.D. slowed down.

Chris said, "Nah, let's go on to the ranch. Marty'd have to take off his hat and wouldn't know what to do with it."

J. D. accelerated again. "If you say so."

"But keep it in mind as a good idea." Chris laughed. Then he said, "Good to know I can always count on you."

As he pulled in at the ranch gate, J.D. said, "Hell yeah. You can always count on me."

They were both laughing as they got out at the ranch office. Broadus parked next to J.D.'s pickup. He said, "What's funny?"

Chris said, "We were talking about you and your hat."

Broadus shook his head. "I get that a lot."

Inside, they listened as the Special Ranger told them about a conversation he'd had with the guy from Alcohol, Tobacco, Firearms, and Explosives. After warning them they had to keep it secret, he recounted how the Fed and his people had been conducting surveillance. He said, "They've even been using a high-altitude drone, occasional flyovers. It has a camera."

J.D. said, "Do they really think they'll catch them in the act of doing some other damage to our place?"

"Not really. They're looking for signs of something else. They think maybe they've seen a beginning."

He explained about what looked from the drone's view like construction, two slab foundations so far, near the bunker. "It's remote from their farmhouse. It looks like they're building a primitive road coming in off the county road on the east side."

J.D. said, "Did I tell you that when Reese asked about buying that north pasture, he said his dad told him that pasture should have belonged to them to begin with. And his dad was PO'd the Jackson ranch ended up with wind turbines and they didn't get any. Of course, I knew the reason for that was he held out for a lease price better than anyone else's and Texas Turbine said, 'No, thanks.' And that's what I told him about selling the north pasture. So, he said if we didn't want to part with that, he'd pay good money for that rough pasture on the east that slopes off the Caprock. It's native grass and some mesquite."

Broadus said, "No, I hadn't heard about that but I'll pass it on." He paused, frowning, then said, "Off on the east, huh?" Another pause. "Let's see. Besides the drone, they've got a couple of people in the county, undercover. I didn't get much on that, but I know one's posing as a seed salesman."

They drank coffee in silence for a while. Then the ranger said, "Oh yeah, and word is that some of their people over in East Texas found out what Reese was doing when he lived over that way. Said a pretty good source had it direct from Reese the reason he moved back out here was because his father's sick, and he's the one to get the ranch when he dies."

J.D. said, "I hadn't heard anything about his dad. Not hanging out at the coffee shop, I miss a lot."

Chris said, "Anything else about him in East Texas?"

Broadus said, "He was number two in an organized Klan over there. Worked at a bank in one of those little towns, a loan officer, if you can believe it. At first glance, he could pass for a solid citizen, if you didn't look past his job. Also has a big interest in hunting, camping, other outdoor activities." He situated his hat and headed toward the door. "Looked to me like his crew was having a dispute in the courthouse parking lot. Trouble in the ranks. It could be a while before they get organized enough to cause you or anyone else more trouble. But if I were you, I'd stay vigilant."

They walked with him to his pickup. As he drove away, J.D. said, "Reckon there's a way to find out the local word on Junior Reese without letting on what Broadus told us?"

"Dad hears lots now that he gets out and about being the mayor. And then there's the Methodist connection. Mom hears plenty before and after choir practice."

J.D. said, "No rush. We'll hear about that sooner or later." He and Chris headed back inside the office. "Doesn't surprise me about that Klan stuff in East Texas, but I can't figure out what kind of construction Justin would be doing on their place."

Chris said, "One thing's for sure. It's harder to hide out here than over there in East Texas with all those trees and year-round greenery. All that moisture leads to rot, but the vegetation can hide a lot."

"That and make a man claustrophobic. I can't see how people live over there. Even Austin's too green for me."

They sat for a while, not saying anything. Then J.D. suggested they'd pretty much done all they could do that day, Chris agreed. J.D. locked up and, after driving Chris back to his place, he headed toward the big house. On the way he let himself focus on ways to keep them all safe. Broadus might be wrong about things staying quiet for a while. Instead of turning in the drive to the house, he took the road up to the north pasture. Since he'd left the other bulls there, they'd checked them at least twice a day. When he got to the north fence line, he reached for his binoculars. East, down the fence line about a quarter of a mile, he saw a sign, posted on the Reese side of the fence, then a second one. Same crude lettering. Same red, white, and black symbol in the corner. One said "No Queers Allowed" and the other spelled "America for Americans ONLY." Those hadn't been there yesterday.

He drove slowly toward the signs and, when he was directly across from them, took a picture with his phone. Then he drove on slowly to the northeast corner and turned south toward the house. About halfway there, his phone rang. Melanie. His mother-in-law seldom called him.

She said, sounding a little breathless, "I thought you should know this, and I'm not sure why, but I just had to call. I heard that Junior Reese is in the hospital in Lubbock in intensive care. The person who told me said Nancy had called her this morning from the hospital. Said they took him in last night and he wasn't expected to live. Massive heart attack. Apparently not his first."

Things might change sooner than expected. "Thanks for letting me know. You were right to call. Let's hope he pulls through. Justin in charge out there could be a bad situation. A worse one."

He didn't offer anything more and she didn't ask. When he hung up, he drove back to the ranch office. It was a good place for him to think, no interruptions.

Floyd County Tribune
Wednesday, December 24, 2014
Early Edition

Preliminary Reports of Jackson's Pond Planning Committees Due January 1, 2015

Mayor Ray Banks of Jackson's Pond announced that preliminary reports of the five planning committees appointed to propose plans for city development will be available for citizen review at City Hall from January 1 through January 15. Input from interested members of the public will be received by the committees at public meetings held two evenings in mid to late January. (Dates will be announced in this paper.)

Following receipt of input the committees will make their reports final and submit them to the City Council no later than February 15.

Speaking of the importance of public input, Mayor Banks said, "Citizen comment has been sought by each committee as they deliberated. This opportunity for input will provide committees with additional public comment before the final reports are proposed to the City Council. We hope that this open process will result in widespread support for the plan that will become Jackson's Pond's roadmap to the future."

CHAPTER 12
New Year's Commitments

Robert and Willa were finishing brunch, working through the Christmas leftovers with a turkey frittata he'd concocted and slices of fruit. The box of oranges and grapefruits sent by a former student of his had prompted him to say, "The man's worried about our getting scurvy out here on the plains. Perhaps he thinks our groceries arrive here by wagon train, and take months."

Earlier he'd made a fire in the fireplace. The scent of slow-burning mesquite laced with chips of piñon made the whole house fragrant. He was stirring the embers to provoke a new flame when the phone rang. As he returned to the kitchen table, he said, "That was Melanie. She asked if I'd come by this afternoon, you, too, if you're available. Her New Year's list includes coming to some conclusions about what, if anything, to do about that poor soul who died here in the last century. Would you like to come?"

"I would," Willa said. She complimented him again on the meal, and began clearing the table. "I never doubted she'd want to pursue the issue. Family reputation means a lot to her. I could tell it disturbed her."

"Even though it's likely no one knows about the episode?"

"She knows. That's enough to propel her."

"Sounds like a lot of us Irish folk. Forgive, likely; forget, doubtful."

She said, "Are you feeding those scraps to the dogs?" At the sound of the word "dogs," the two former inmates of the Lubbock animal shelter rushed from their rugs in front of the fireplace and sat at Willa's feet.

He said, "Maybe just a tiny taste."

She watched the dogs race to where Robert stood at the refrigerator. His training sessions showed. They sat, wagging their tails, but not moving until he gave a hand signal that apparently meant "stand." Each dog was rewarded with a morsel of turkey. Then Robert showed them empty hands and said, "Go." They padded out of the room toward the utility area. The next sound Willa heard was their noisily slurping water.

Seeing Robert working with those dogs and seeing their devotion to him made her remember Frank and his constant companion, Missy, a cowdog. Those two men couldn't have been any less obviously alike, but their care and concern for those dogs told Willa they were alike in important ways. And she knew she had, in her lifetime, chosen to love two good men, one long after the first. Frank had been the one who'd shared his work with her, trusted her, and whose death had left her with grief that only shrank when she immersed herself in her painting and in preserving the ranch. This second one, Robert, was the man willing and able to be with her through the beautiful, bittersweet, hard days of old age.

Robert washed his hands at the kitchen sink. Drying them, he said, "I told her I'd be there at two. Will that work for you?"

"I'll be up from my rest at one-forty and presentable five minutes after, I promise."

Melanie hugged each of them when they arrived. She said, "I'm glad you both came. I didn't know if you might be busy painting, Mother." She led them to the family room. "I've been thinking a lot about whether it's possible to find the grave of Mr. Berryhill. So far, I've come up with nothing. I even wondered about using cadaver sniffing dogs, but it's nearly a hundred years. Even if he'd been buried without a coffin, I doubt there's any scent they could find."

Robert said, "I've done a bit of Internet searching on that subject. A couple of sources specifically mentioned dogs trained to find old remains such as in locating old cemeteries or burial grounds prior to land development. That means it is possible. But my question is, to what end? Suppose we had a dog and found the remains. What then?"

"I asked myself that. The answer is a proper burial and recognition of the wrong that was done."

Willa asked, "Knowing isn't enough?"

"He deserves better. Any human does."

Robert said, "Would a memorial, a marker, serve the purpose if the body isn't to be found?"

Willa watched her daughter stand and pace from the sofa to the dining area and back again. Melanie said, "If it were my family member, I would want to know every effort was made to put the remains to rest properly."

Willa said, "That's your view. Is there a way to find out the Berryhill family's thoughts?" She didn't intend that as a rhetorical question, but neither Melanie nor Robert answered. She said, "For example, if there are living relatives, couldn't we try to contact them? Ask them?"

Melanie sighed. "How would I face them?"

Robert said, "You wouldn't have to. If I can find actual family members, I would be happy to represent you, to see them and ask that question person to person."

Willa started to object. After all, Robert's family didn't do the damage, and it wasn't his people who felt moved to atone. She restrained herself. He offered because it was in his heart. She was convinced, that minute, of what she must tell Melanie, and him, before the day was over.

Melanie sat again, this time next to Robert. She said, "That's so kind of you. Am I cowardly to say I couldn't face them?"

He patted her hand and said, "Cowardly would be attempting to bury the facts of the past. What you are doing is brave and just. I would only be helping with what you feel needs to be done."

Willa noticed her daughter's less-erect-than-usual posture, her gaze focused on her lap, her slow, ragged breathing. Then Melanie raised her head and straightened her spine. "If you can find them, then yes. We should do what they wish."

Robert nodded. "I'll pursue the matter and let you know what I learn. You can count on me."

At that moment, he sounded to Willa less like an Irish art professor and more like a very kind West Texas gentleman. Nothing would suit his romantic soul better than being sent on a knight's mission.

Melanie hugged Robert, then stood again. "I could use some coffee and shortbread cookies. What about you?"

Willa said, "I shouldn't but I will."

Soon the three of them were sitting at the table near the kitchen. Melanie said, "I heard from Claire that J.D. and Chris are installing motion sensitive lights on the houses at the ranch."

Robert said, "That's in addition to the intruder lights already outside the barns, corral, and the garage."

"He thinks the meanness didn't end with the conviction of the bull killer?" Melanie placed her cookie, missing only one bite, on her saucer. "I'd hoped that would send a message."

Willa said, "He found more of those signs up north, on the Reese side of the fence. I agree with him. It's far from over. I'll be more at ease when the workmen finish Chris and Andrew's house. Then there'll be fewer reasons for strangers to be on the place."

Robert said, "That brings up a happy event. The house should be ready for the final walk-through this week."

They worked their way through the plate of cookies and a cup each of coffee. Then they switched to water, as they chatted— gossiped, actually. Melanie passed along the choir-practice mention of Nancy Reese's collapse at the bedside of her husband, Junior. She was only hospitalized overnight. They doubt he'd ever go home. She also mentioned Ray was pushing the sheriff's office for further investigation of the identity of the man who tried to disrupt the Pancho Clos event at the park before Christmas.

She said, "Apparently no one admits knowing him. But everyone seems to remember his shouting, 'Speak English, you stupid spic. This is America.' He yelled several other slurs before some of the parents there threatened him. He left in an old jeep, driving fast, going west out of town. The one deputy who was there had noticed him and thought he was carrying a liquor bottle."

Willa mentioned her search on Amy's behalf for an advanced ballet class. "It will mean she'll have to audition, and if she's accepted, would have to travel there each week, maybe twice weekly for the classes." She said, "It's so sweet. She said she wants to advance but doesn't want to go without Elisa. They're such good friends."

Then Robert tossed in his bit of coffee break information. He'd been contacted by letter from Richard Jesko asking him to consider a consulting engagement to curate a collection of paintings by West Texas artists that would rotate between the corporate office in the Metroplex and the Jackson's Pond facility's offices.

It was nearly three-thirty when he said, "I've enjoyed our visit more than you could know. It reminds me of the way my family would spend time, just talking and being together, when I was young. But now I think we have to go soon. We promised Jay Frank we'd be there when he puts his goats through their paces at four-thirty. He says they're ready for the county show and should get accustomed to an audience. We assured him we'd applaud, whistle, stomp our feet, and make certain they're ready for the big time."

Willa had her coat in her hand, but she stopped and checked her phone for the time. She said, "Wait. Let's sit back down. We have a few minutes. I have something else to say."

Melanie gave her a look she recognized from her daughter's adolescent years, that "What now, Mother?" look that teenagers perfect. Seeing it made her smile. As soon as she smiled, her daughter sat down on the living room sofa. Robert sat next to her and Willa took the chair opposite them. She said, "I doubt you've forgotten the talk we had, the one when I told you that Robert had asked me to marry him."

Melanie nodded. "I haven't forgotten. I've thought a lot about what you said."

"That pleases me. It's been on my mind, as well. Robert's been very patient with my indecision." He leaned forward, but kept quiet. She said, "I've finally reached a conclusion. Having you both in the room at the same time makes this a perfect occasion to tell you. I've decided to accept Robert's proposal."

Willa noticed the faintest frown on her daughter's face, but it quickly disappeared. Robert sat back, smiling, and shaking his head. He said, "This is truly a surprise. And a welcome one. Willa, my dear, you've made me a very happy man."

She winked at him. "You can't back out now that there's a witness."

Melanie said, "Robert, I'm as surprised as you. I have to ask, what made you decide to tell us together, and why today?"

"The decisions about marrying, about telling you both, and telling you today came to me as we sat here talking. I can only say it came directly from my heart."

"That's good enough for me, my dear." Robert pulled out a handkerchief and wiped at his eyes. He offered it to Melanie.

She shook her head. "I'm happy for you both. Please forget any previous objections I made and replace them with my congratulations and best wishes."

Willa said, "There's one other thing. We should begin planning now. I think Valentine's Day would be right. What do you think?"

She knew it would be a rush, and expected Melanie to object, but she and Robert both agreed with the date. Melanie asked where, and the three of them discussed the merits of a ceremony at the Methodist Church, which Willa vetoed; a civil ceremony in a Justice of the Peace office, which Melanie rejected; and the big house at the ranch, which sounded like a good idea to Melanie and Robert.

Willa said, "Yes, that's a possibility, if Claire and J.D. are willing. But before we go further with that, with a traditional ceremony, there's one thing."

The other two both said, "What?" simultaneously.

"I would want you to give me away, Melanie. Will you do that?"

The expression that registered on her daughter's face struck Willa as reflecting something true. But she couldn't tell if it was distress or simply surprise. She waited to hear the words that went with it.

The answer came slowly. But neither she nor Robert broke the silence.

Melanie finally said, "I hardly know what to say."

Willa said, "'Yes,' would be the best."

Melanie gazed at her a long time. Although she could usually predict Melanie's mood and anticipate her words, this time Willa truly had no idea what to expect.

"Yes. I am honored and humbled that you would ask me."

Willa crossed the room faster than she imagined she could, and pulled her daughter to her chest in a hug. She said, "Thank you. That makes me happier than you can know."

Robert said, "I'm sorry to say we are going to have to leave. We made a commitment to a young man I would not wish to disappoint."

Willa said, "Certainly not." As they neared the front door, she turned to Melanie and said, "Thank you again."

As they walked toward Robert's pickup, her phone rang. She stopped to answer it. Then she said, "We're on our way home from Melanie's. We'll be right there."

She said to Robert and Melanie, "You'll want to come with us, Melanie. That was Claire. Jay Frank's goats are missing, and he's off somewhere trying to find them. She's frantic because she doesn't know where he is. Apparently, after he called her and took off, he either turned off his phone, or lost it."

Robert sped faster than the limit all the way. Willa didn't speak her thought, her fear that her great-grandson might have been kidnapped. The only words spoken were Melanie's. She said, "Please, God, don't let anything happen to him."

Less than fifteen minutes later, they pulled into the drive at the big house. Claire stood on the porch, her phone to her ear. Amy, wearing her tights and leotard, her face blanched, eyes full of fear, stood close to her mother. Melanie rushed ahead to Claire and Amy.

Claire said, "That was Chris. He said the fence on the goat pen was down and looked like it had been cut." She heaved a deep breath. "After Jay Frank went to exercise them, a little later he called and said the goats were out, pen broken, and he thought he'd find them grazing close by. He said he'd call again if he didn't find them soon. 'Don't worry,' he said.' When he didn't call, Chris and J.D. took separate pickups, going opposite directions from the pen, honking and shouting. I stayed here in case he came back while they were out."

Willa said, "Robert and I can help search." She hesitated, then said, "If we don't find him in the next thirty minutes, you should call J.D. and tell him to call the sheriff. It'll be dark before long."

Claire agreed. Willa told Robert she knew the place best; she'd drive. She heard Claire crying and turned to see Amy with her arms around her mother, Melanie standing nearby with her eyes closed. Willa knew she was praying.

Willa took the road that passed the pond, planning to turn east from there, along the track inside the ranch's outer fence, then if they saw no sign of Jay Frank or the goats, to turn back north along the eastern outer boundary fence. She said to Robert, "Call Claire and ask what Jay Frank's wearing."

The pasture on the ranch's east side had never been cultivated. The soil was rocky and thin. Plowing would leave it open to wind erosion. Native grass grew abundantly during periods of adequate moisture, as long as the mesquite was kept under control. Most people had given up on ever eradicating the invasive tree, and knew that control meant cutting or spraying mesquite at regular intervals. The result was a pasture good for the slow grazing of mother cows and their small calves. J.D. had bisected the pasture with a gated fence, and moved the cattle from side to side to give the grass time to recover between grazings.

When she was a child, her father had let her roam that pasture, even though at the time it wasn't part of the Jackson ranch. She'd spent hours pretending she was on the frontier, discovering arrowheads, and imagining she was in charge of leading her family west. It had been that lonely young motherless child's playground. She never felt fear there, but now, with night approaching, danger seemed to lurk among the scrubby trees.

As the road steadily declined toward the east, following the natural change in elevation between the Caprock and the rolling plains below, Robert's phone signaled a text. He said, "Melanie. The boy's wearing a tan coat, red knit hat, Wranglers. No word from J.D. or Chris."

At the eastern boundary fence, the road leveled out. Willa turned north, then stopped the pickup. She honked the horn, short bursts of three, repeated several times. Then she sounded a sustained tone, flashing the lights from dim to bright. Robert rolled down his window, shouted Jay Frank's name again and again. As the sun dropped lower, the temperature had changed quickly from around forty-five to near freezing, according to the truck's thermometer. Then they waited a couple of minutes in silence. Finally, Willa said, "I hope that coat he's wearing is warm."

She drove north at a crawl, with her window rolled halfway down, hoping she'd hear Jay Frank or his goats. The only sounds she heard were the steady breeze, blowing from the north, and occasional coyote calls, sounding like mothers calling their pups, their higher-pitched yips answering. Stopping again, going through the same routine—honking, lights, shouting, waiting— then Willa saw a flash of white, moving behind a stand of mesquite, then another. She said, "Look there, the goats." Seconds later she and Robert were both out of the pickup, calling, "Jay Frank, we're here."

A hoarse voice answered, "I found them. Don't move. I'm herding them your way."

Robert said, "I'll call." Then seconds later, she heard him say, "J.D., Robert here. We found him and the goats. Here's Willa. She'll tell you where we are."

Willa took the phone and told J.D. where to find them and to bring a stock trailer. Jay Frank and the goats made it to them seconds later. His face was tear-stained and he shivered when he stopped still. As they wrapped him between them, Willa said, "Are you all right? Were you afraid?"

His voice near a whisper, Jay Frank said, "I yelled and yelled while I followed their tracks. My voice wore out. I was so mad, I couldn't help crying. Someone cut their fence. I never leave it unlocked. And the goats never tear it up."

Jay Frank refused to warm up in the truck while they waited for his dad. So they stayed with him and his goats. Once he was warm, he said, "Thank you for finding me, Gran. Thank you, Robert."

She couldn't help her tears' falling then at how that sweet brave boy always remembered his manners. Crying, she couldn't speak. Robert said, as if talking to a grown man, "You'd have made it back on your own. But I'm glad we saved you the walk. I wonder if you'd do me a great favor."

Jay Frank said, "If I can."

Robert said, "Please don't call me Mr. Stanley or Robert. From now on, please call me *móraí.*" The word sounded like MO-ree.

"Sir?"

"That's an Irish word for Grandpa."

Jay Frank leaned against him and repeated the word.

They heard the pickup and stock trailer clattering over the seldom-used rocky road, then saw its lights. Jay Frank talked to his goats, telling them to stay put. They huddled, milling around as a tight group. Willa noticed there were only three.

When J.D. stopped the truck, and he and Chris bailed out, Jay Frank ran to him. He said, "Dad, I tracked them all the way. I tried to call, but my phone wouldn't get a signal. I tried a lot of times. They'd been out a long time because they were a long way down here before I found them."

"It's okay. You did a good job. Let's get them loaded and get back to the house."

"We can't leave till I find Rivera. He wasn't with the others. I haven't seen him at all. I can't leave him. He's my third best goat."

They loaded the three, and J.D., Jay Frank, and Chris searched the area for a while. As they walked back, Willa, sitting in Robert's pickup, heard Chris say, "Goats tend to stay together. I don't think he was ever with them."

J.D. said, "You're right." Then he said to Jay Frank, "Son, I think we'll go on to the house. If he doesn't come back on his own tonight, we'll come look in the morning."

Willa felt weariness press on her. She asked Robert to drive. "I need a bit of rest," she said. "Lots of excitement today."

Back near the house, everyone met at the goat pen. The sheriff's deputy had arrived. Tag had turned up and stood waiting with a fence-mending tool in one hand and fence wire he'd cut into two-foot lengths in the other. Willa heard him say to J.D., "If I was a bettin' man I'd a bet there was cabrito cooking up at that place north of us." Then he raised his voice and said to Jay Frank, "I come to help you splice that fence. That fancy wire's not as easy to work with as good old two-strand hot wire electric fence."

She knew he was right about that. The four-foot-tall goat fence had twelve strands, each four inches apart both height and width. A goat's head seldom got stuck in those squares and unless someone made the mistake of putting a structure nearby they could climb on, they almost never went over the top.

After the deputy took some pictures of the fence and nearby ground, the men helped Jay Frank fashion splices to hold it together. When they finished, J.D. headed out of the pen behind the deputy. Tag followed them, and stopped to shut the gate. As he passed Willa, Tag lifted his hat and said, "Good to see you, ma'am." As he walked on, she heard him mutter, "No, sir, nobody can tell me them goats got out on their own. It took wire cutters."

Jay Frank wouldn't leave until he'd fed and watered his goats, so everyone, including the deputy, milled around until the livestock was taken care of.

When they returned to the big house, Claire and Amy hovered around the boy as long as he'd tolerate it, which wasn't long. Then Claire herded everyone inside. She and Amy had made sandwiches as soon as they heard Jay Frank had been found.

Willa and Robert stayed until the deputy left. Then the two of them moved toward the door. Jay Frank followed them and said, "Thanks again for finding me. You were right, Gran. I was a little afraid." Then he turned to Robert and said, "Tell me that

Irish word for Grandpa again. I want to say it right."

They practiced together a couple of times and he whispered something to Robert. Then the boy said, "Hey, everybody, I have a MOree now and so does Amy—that's an Irish Grandpa."

Willa took Robert by the arm, turned him toward the door and pushed him forward. She turned to the others and said, "Grandpa and I are going now."

In the pickup, while he fiddled with the ignition key, she leaned over and kissed his cheek.

The next morning, she was up earlier than usual. Nautical twilight had not yet created shadows, but as she stood at the kitchen sink, the newly installed motion-sensitive light activated. Seeing nothing from her window in the light's glow, she moved to the door, opened it a crack, and still saw nothing. Then the light on Chris and Andrew's house cast another glow across the back of their house, and she saw Andrew walking her way, wearing jeans and a short-sleeved t-shirt, apparently coming from the east, out of the mesquite pasture.

She stepped outside. Speaking in a whisper, she said, "Did you hear something?"

He shook his head. "Aren't you cold?"

"Probably no more than you."

"I came back for gloves. I woke up thinking about Rivera, about where he would have gone. Only thing that made sense was that someone took him. Otherwise, we would have found him with the rest of them. So, I hiked toward the county road on the east."

"What did you find?"

"Tire tracks, the goat's halter." He hesitated, then said, "And a lot of blood and some hair." He shook his head. "I didn't want to disturb any evidence, and I forgot my phone. So, I came back to let J.D. know."

She handed him her phone from the pocket of her sweater. He nodded, punched in some numbers, and then pointed toward his and Chris's place. He said, "Back in a minute."

She heard him speak into the phone as he walked away. Finding Robert making coffee when she returned to the kitchen surprised her. She'd avoided waking the dogs, but apparently not him.

When she reported Andrew's discovery, Robert said, "Poor Jay Frank." He left the room saying, "I'll get dressed. They may need help."

He'd left without putting water in the coffee maker. Thinking how he'd taken on the family's problems as his own, she smiled as she finished what he'd begun.

Andrew and Chris met her and Robert on the front porch. Just then, J.D. drove up with Jay Frank, who jumped out almost before the pickup stopped.

"Dad said you found Rivera's halter. Where? Let's go find him."

J.D. put a hand on his son's shoulder. "Hold up a minute, son." He gave a slight shake of his head that told Willa he hadn't had the heart to tell the boy any more. He said, "Broadus and that deputy who was here last night are coming out. I told them where. We can meet them there.

She and Robert followed in her pickup behind the four in J.D.'s, riding the few miles to the spot near the county road on the east boundary of their property. Again, when J.D. stopped, Jay Frank was the first one out. But he stopped short, not moving past the front of the vehicle, and stood shaking his head. He said, "He's dead. That much blood, and see over there, they dragged him away."

No one disagreed. In fact, no one said a word. Not even when Jay Frank slammed his right palm against the pickup fender and said, "Dammit, Dad."

J.D. put a hand on his son's shoulder, and the boy leaned against him, his head down, breathing hard. Although she wanted to comfort Jay Frank, Willa held back. He was learning a lesson about being a man, that it's complicated and sometimes unjust and painful. She shouldn't interfere even though she did hate for him to learn those lessons so young.

Broadus pulled up and the deputy drove in behind him seconds later. While they conferred with J.D and Andrew, Jay Frank came and stood between her and Robert, watching. She leaned down and kissed the top of his head. He said, "Thanks, Gran, MOree. Don't worry about me. I'm just very angry right now."

They continued watching while Broadus took over collecting evidence—the halter, samples of blood and hair, photos of tire tracks from what appeared to be two separate vehicles, and a single boot print clearly apparent in the blood-tinged dirt.

The ranger stood and packed all his gear and evidence bags into his pickup, then turned and said, "This is one more thing to add to the other counts we'll eventually be able to get that bunch for." He and the deputy conferred for a second, then Broadus said, "Right off we can see that some of these tire tracks match ones that were up by the goat pens."

Then he came and stood in front of Jay Frank and said, "I promise we'll find out who did this. I'm sure sorry about your goat."

Jay Frank raised his head and held out his hand to shake the ranger's. "Thank you, sir."

As Robert drove back to their house, he said, "That boy is going to make a fine man one day. I was proud of him just now."

A few minutes later, as they had breakfast at home, Willa said, "It appears that marrying me, you're about to join up with a family in trouble."

Robert said, "Life is full of trouble. The difference is that when it arrives, a good family turns toward one another to help instead of turning away. I've joined a good family."

She nodded. "We do help one another, now more than ever before. But I think I might have been hasty in choosing a date for our wedding."

He put his head in his hands, slumped his shoulders. "Is this your way of letting me down gently? What next? Will you start with, 'It's me, not you?' and finish with 'and here's the ring back?'"

He leaned back, and she saw the twinkle in his eye, and

realized she'd have to listen to more before he was through. She couldn't help smiling.

He said, "Oh, that's it! There's no ring. Would you believe me if I told you it's at the jewelers? I designed it especially for you. No, wait, it's an antique, and it's in the vault at the bank." The dogs ran into the room, alerted by the sound of his voice, she supposed.

She said, "You're upsetting the children."

"Please, darlin', tell me there's not another man."

"If you ever quit talking, I'll tell you. It's not you, it's the date."

"I'm so relieved to hear that." The dogs sat watching them. Robert cut his eyes toward the dogs. "They were as worried as I was."

She said, "Are you finished?"

"Yes, my dear, I am."

She handed him a slice of apple. "Prove it."

He stuck the whole slice in his mouth.

"As I was saying, I think Valentine's Day is too soon, given all that's going on. There's the stock show, Melanie and Claire and I have to make plans for the house since the wedding is to be there, and most of all, this meanness going on needs to be settled."

He nodded as she ticked off the reasons to delay. "I agree. But only if we choose another date now."

"What about May first? That's a Friday. We could have it in the evening."

"Fine with me." He stopped and handed each dog an apple slice, which they promptly carried away to their beds. "To tell you the truth, working on my search for relatives of Mr. Berryhill, I've wished for more time. If we wait until May, perhaps by then I can have accomplished what I promised Melanie. We could honeymoon with our calendars clear of obligations."

"Who said anything about a honeymoon?"

"I just did."

"Well, we'll talk about that later."

Floyd County Tribune

Thursday, January 15, 2015

Junior Livestock Show Results

The 71st annual county junior livestock show, held Tuesday, January 13, 2015, was a success, according to Show Superintendent Ricky Adams. "We had more entries than ever before, even though there were none in the steers division. The swine, lambs, and goats more than made up the difference," Adams said. "Raising and showing livestock is a great way to interest young people in careers in agriculture."

Winners include the following:

SWINE—Grand Champion-Billy Cox
Reserve Champion-Karen Bullard
Showmanship-Carlos Gutierrez
LAMBS—Grand Champion-Monique Avila
Reserve Champion-Bobby Scott
Showmanship-John Parker, Jr.
GOATS—Grand Champion-Jay Frank Havlicek
Reserve Champion-Rhett Compton
Showmanship-Jay Frank Havlicek

Management Personnel at RBJ on Board

A press release from RBJ this week announced the names of the first five employees hired for mid-management positions for the company's new facility in Jackson's Pond. They are: Chief of Security-David Montoya; Shipping Manager-Quentin Washington; Production Manager-Callie Burson; Quality Control Manager-Samir Krishnamurthy; Data Center Manager-Carson Brubaker.

Local HR office personnel said that three of the five are relocating to the Jackson's Pond area, one each from Dallas, Lubbock, and Midland. Montoya and Washington currently live in the area. All five begin their new positions on site next week.

CHAPTER 13

Property Matters

When Melanie got home from the preschool, a red Jeep Cherokee sat parked in front of her house. By the look of its big tires and mud flaps, the vehicle could deal with any terrain including muddy mountain roads. Surely that wasn't Nancy's. By the time Melanie parked in her garage and opened her front door, her mother had pulled into the driveway and Nancy stood waiting outside the door. Melanie waved to her mother and Claire to come in and said, "I'm sorry if I'm late, Nancy. Have you waited long?"

"You're not late. I'm early."

Willa and Claire greeted Nancy and followed her inside. As Nancy shed her coat, Melanie got a good look at the woman who'd been her high school friend. The last time she'd seen her, Nancy must have weighed well over 200 pounds, far too much for her frame. That had been a year or more, and then she'd only glimpsed Nancy leaving Claire's clinic, walking as if every step required effort. Today, she appeared almost gaunt. Loose skin drooped below her chin, her slacks could have fit a woman fifty pounds heavier, and the most striking difference was her hair. The high school redhead had kept that color all these years, the few times Melanie had seen her at a distance, and she'd always worn up-to-date hairstyles. No one saw her in public without perfect makeup. Even as she'd gained weight over the years, she'd tended to her appearance. But today her faded red hair showed about three inches of gray roots and was pulled back with a tie at the nape of her neck. She wore no lipstick.

Hoping her own face didn't betray her, Melanie led the other three into the family room. She said to Nancy, "I was surprised to hear from you."

Nancy said, "I didn't know who to turn to, just you three. Mrs. Jackson, you were always so kind. And Claire, I know I can trust you. I don't have any other friends. Not anyone I can trust."

"I usually snack when I come in from school," Melanie

said. "Would you like some fruit and cheese, or something to drink? Hot chocolate sounds good to me."

"That would be nice. I don't remember eating today."

In the kitchen, as she stirred the milk and added chocolate, Melanie tried to recall the last time she and Nancy had been together, had done something friends might do. Nothing at all came to mind past high school graduation. Then, as she took four cups from the cabinet and placed them on a tray, one that her mother had decorated with a watercolor scene as a graduation gift, a specific occasion flashed in her memory. Nancy had spent the night with her, as girlfriends often did. Melanie recalled prattling on about going to Tech, pledging a sorority, getting away from home. Nancy had listened, but not had much to say. When Melanie finally took a breath, Nancy paced around the bedroom, frowning, and then finally asked Melanie if she could keep a really important secret.

Melanie stirred the hot chocolate, sneaking a glance at Nancy. She hadn't moved from the dining room table where she sat, leaning forward, elbows on the table. Melanie kept stirring, remembering what happened that night more than forty years ago.

That was when Nancy told her she was going to marry Junior Reese and asked Melanie to be her maid of honor, her only witness. Junior would bring his own, some other man. "We don't want a church wedding. It will be in a Justice of the Peace office in Lubbock. He knows someone there."

Melanie had been so stunned she didn't answer. Nancy said, "Well, will you do it?"

"I can't believe you're saying this. Junior Reese is old. Why would you marry him?"

Nancy looked away, then said, "I can't stand living at home another minute. My parents can't pay for college, and besides, Junior says we'd make a good couple."

"I mean it. He's at least ten years older than you are."

"I'll have my own house, and I can do what I want, when I want."

"Tell me the truth. Do you love him? Do you actually even

know anything about him?"

Nancy had turned and looked at herself in the mirror over the dresser. She said, "Junior says I'm beautiful." She'd patted her teased hair and turned and showed Melanie a beauty queen smile. "I'll be so sad if you won't be my maid of honor. Please say yes."

As Melanie poured cocoa into two of the four cups she'd set out, she remembered telling her, "I can't do it without telling my parents. They don't like for me to leave town unless they know where I'm going."

From the look on Nancy's face, she knew she'd chosen the right excuse. Later, after graduation, an announcement that Nancy and Junior had married appeared in the paper.

Melanie added a plate of cheese and apple slices to the tray and carried it to the table.

When the four of them were all seated, Willa, then Claire, raised an eyebrow at Melanie. Nancy focused on her hot chocolate, staring, not drinking.

Finally, she said, "I feel like such a fool, having to ask for help, but the truth is, I just don't know what to do."

More silence followed. Then Willa said, "Nancy, it's been a very long time since I've seen you. Tell us what's troubling you and how we can help."

Her mother's tone carried a note of comfort that Melanie hoped would help Nancy. So far, it seemed to Melanie that her old friend began slipping away the minute she'd stepped in the door.

Nancy said, "I may as well just say it—Junior and I separated last year. I've been living most of the time at our house in Red River. I couldn't stand it another day. Living with him, his constant criticism, and all his demands were killing me. He'd gotten worse than ever since Justin moved back out here. So, one day I packed up and left while they were gone off to East Texas to get some of Justin's equipment. I've expected every day that one or the other of them would come and evict me. The house isn't mine. Everything we have is in his name. Always has been."

She stopped and ate an apple slice and a piece of cheese.

Since she'd begun telling her story, a bit of color had come into her cheeks.

Willa asked, "Have you been living alone over there?"

Nancy nodded. "I was afraid at first, but relieved not to have Junior at me all the time. And the mountains in New Mexico are beautiful. I know a few people there. Well, I have acquaintances. None of them really know me. They think I'm a widow." A trace of a smile passed across her lips. "I encouraged that. And after I got past being afraid, then I was just sad. Nobody, not Junior, not Justin or his wife, not even my daughter, the missionary, called or wrote. No one cared that I'd left."

Claire asked, "Have you felt better since you've been away?"

"You recall when I came in to see you at the clinic last year and told you I'd been in Red River all summer. By then I didn't feel better, I felt worse. But I was too stubborn to take your advice. I left your clinic and got the clothes I'd come back for, and drove on back to New Mexico. I probably would have just stayed up there until I died."

Nancy picked at the peel on an apple slice, leaving little bits on the plate. She said, "Then when they put Junior in the hospital, Justin called. It surprised me. Since he was a teenager, he and I haven't gotten along. I came back just in case Junior dies. There would be arrangements to make."

Melanie said, "Appearances to keep up?"

She saw a spark of the young Nancy, the redhead who only had to roll her eyes to communicate as eloquently as pages of prose. This time it was a nod and those eyes that said, "You still know me, Melanie."

"I was going to stay at the house, out at the ranch, but the first night I was there, I got scared. The next day I moved to town to the little house my parents left to me. I didn't care if it did smell like dust and mildew. It was better than being out there."

She pushed her cup away and leaned back. "Here's what frightened me, the reason I called. Justin has several men out there. He calls them friends. I call them thugs. They come and go at all hours and they all carry weapons around. They're building something out beyond Justin's house. I asked his wife what they're doing and who they are. She just shrugged and mumbled something like, 'The less I know the better.' Then she scurried away."

Melanie said, "I can see why you'd be frightened."

Nancy went right on. She knew about the bull killing and the trial from the newspaper. "It's the only news I get from over here, so I subscribe," she said. "When I read that, I couldn't figure out what possessed them to kill that bull. Then I remembered Junior wanted that pasture of yours, always did. Said his Daddy told him they ought to have control over that patch of land, said if he'd taken a mind to a long time ago, he could have made C.C. Jackson sell it to him for a dollar. So maybe Justin wants to get you to sell for his own reasons. I wouldn't put anything past that boy. Well, he's a man now, and he's just like Junior. Bigoted, self-important, and downright mean. I pity his wife. If she wanted to leave, I'd find a way to help her. She should get those kids away from him before they learn to be just like he is."

She stopped talking because she'd started crying. "It's my fault. I should never have married Junior Reese in the first place." She looked at Melanie. "I wouldn't blame you if you said, 'I told you so' and sent me away."

More tears followed. Melanie brought a box of tissues and set it beside Nancy. She looked at her mother and Claire, gave a tiny shrug.

When Nancy collected herself, she took a deep breath and drank some of her no longer hot chocolate. She said, "Junior's going to die. The doctor told me it's just a matter of time before a decision has to be made about life support. He breathes on his own now, but his lungs are going bad. You'll think I'm as awful as he is, but I'm worried Justin may have gotten him to change his will so I don't have power of attorney. If he changed it, he could have cut me out completely. I won't have anything. I wouldn't be able to stop whatever he's doing out there—that building, bringing all those thugs."

She started crying again, sniffled loudly. Claire said, "How can we help?"

"You already have. I needed to tell someone." Nancy's gaze flitted around the room. "I don't think I've ever been here before. This is a nice house."

Melanie saw Willa look at her watch.

Her mother said, "It seems to me that you need a good attorney to give you advice. Do you have one?"

Nancy shook her head. "No, Junior took care of anything legal. I hate to admit it, but for years I didn't even have a checkbook." She closed her eyes and leaned back against the chair. "You have no idea how crafty I got finding ways to save little bits for myself out of the house and food money Junior gave me." She sat up straight again. "You're right, Mrs. Jackson. I need to quit thinking about the past and get focused on what to do now."

Melanie said, "If you've been crafty before, you can do it now." She patted Nancy's hand. It belonged to an old woman.

Nancy left about thirty minutes later. By then, Willa had contacted Kay Henry, her attorney in Lubbock, and gotten Nancy an appointment for the next morning. Melanie had called the sheriff's office in Calverton for an appointment for Nancy the next afternoon. Melanie agreed to ride there with her. As she opened the door to leave, Nancy said, "Thank you. It means so much to me that you haven't abandoned me. And, Claire, I'll see that doctor you suggested. But as soon as you can, I want you to take care of me. I'll be a better patient than I was before."

"We'll help you get through this," Melanie said.

After Nancy drove away, Claire said, "We promised her we'd keep this among ourselves. If anyone asks, what are we going to say about why Nancy wanted to see us? I told J.D. where I was going when I left."

Melanie said, "I'd thought about that, too. It wouldn't be wrong to say that she's upset and wanted to talk to people she feels are friends. Needed to have someone listen."

Willa said, "That's good. It's true, so far as it goes."

Claire said, "I hope she has time to get the legal situation clear before Junior dies. If not, she may need a lot more help than we were able to give today."

The next morning, Melanie was on the road to Lubbock, even though she'd intended to meet Nancy in Calverton later in the afternoon. Things had changed. Last night, she'd told Ray the edited version of Nancy's visit, and mentioned she was to meet her in Calverton this afternoon. Those words were just out of her mouth when Nancy called from the hospital. Justin had come to Junior's room, along with a man Nancy didn't know.

She'd said, "He had on camouflage pants and a black shirt and black leather jacket. His head was shaved, and tattoos covered most of his neck. There was a scar on his face, on the left side from his ear to his mouth. Everything about him looked evil. I might as well have not been there for all the attention they paid to me. Justin glared at me and asked when the doctor expected Junior to regain consciousness. I tried to explain that he might or might not.

The other one left the room and for a little bit, Justin sat by Junior's bed. I stood in the doorway because I didn't know what else to do. He looked like he might break down, the way he would when he was a little boy, when Junior would yell at him. I remembered then how often he'd come to me for comfort after Junior did that." Nancy's voice dropped to a near whisper. "I couldn't help it. Right then I wanted to hold him, rub his back the way I had then, to settle him down and . . . if I'd been a better mother." After a ragged breath, she went on. "Justin hasn't always been the way he is now, not until he got to be a teenager. After he had his growth spurt, Junior got interested in him, taking him places, teaching him how to shoot a rifle. He called it training him to be a man, like his daddy had taught him, quoted the old man saying, 'One day they'll need us again. Every one of us needs to be ready.'"

Nancy went quiet for several seconds. Melanie wondered if she'd lost the connection, or if Nancy had hung up. Then she said, "Justin was talking to Junior. I couldn't hear what he was saying, but I could see he did start crying. I knew then he was afraid of that other one, the one with the scar. About that time that thug stomped back in. He started talking in a loud whisper, like he was giving orders. I got so nervous I left the room. When I came back they were gone. I'm going to sleep here at the hospital in Junior's room. I'm afraid to go out to the parking lot alone."

Eventually, she came to her point—asking if there was any way Melanie could be there when she met with the lawyer instead of waiting to go with her to Calverton in the afternoon. She'd sounded timid and frantic. Melanie agreed and arranged for Claire to go to the preschool today and help Dolores. Claire had understood without an explanation. Dolores agreed without asking any questions.

Melanie parked in the lot at Kay Henry's office. No sign of Nancy's big Jeep, so she spent the time thinking about Nancy as she had been in high school. The one word that came immediately to mind was spunky. She'd been a better-than-average student, lively, always smiling. And she'd been a beauty. The only thing she hadn't been a part of was athletics. Instead, she'd been a twirler in the band. Then after she married, it was as if she'd disappeared instead of moving fourteen miles out to the Reese ranch. But Melanie admitted to herself now she'd been so wrapped up in her own activities at Tech, she'd never tried to stay in touch.

When Nancy got out of her Jeep, Melanie saw she was wearing the same clothes she'd had on yesterday afternoon. If she'd slept any in that hospital room last night, it didn't show on her face or in her posture. She looked like a tired, old woman.

Kay Henry got right to business as soon as they were seated in her office. After confirming that Nancy wished Melanie to be present for their discussion, she asked Nancy a series of questions about her problem. Nancy had apparently gathered some gumption overnight, even if she did look beyond worn. Her clear, factual answers impressed Melanie. If she was as anxious as she'd said, she was doing a good job of covering it.

Nancy explained that with her husband in critical condition, she was concerned about knowing the position she was in legally, given that he was unconscious and might not recover. She handed an envelope to the attorney and said, "This is the copy of the will that was in his desk drawer at home. I see that it was made in 2004, but it was never discussed with me. That's not a surprise, as he never discussed business with me."

The attorney scanned the pages. When she looked up, she said, "On first reading I can answer some of your questions. According to this will, you have health care power of attorney, so you can receive information about his condition and make decisions as needed in conjunction with his doctors. No one else is mentioned in regard to that responsibility. Second, there is an end of life decisions paragraph that indicates your husband does not want heroic measures employed. If he is deemed by physicians to be in a terminal condition, he does not want resuscitation. I assume those are the immediate concerns."

Nancy nodded, then said, "I'm sure the doctors will want to see that or something to know that I'm the one responsible."

The attorney called an assistant to make two copies of the relevant sections. Nancy was to keep one and the other was to be given to the hospital for their records. "If there are questions, have them contact me. I indicate on this attached sheet that I am your attorney and that this will in its entirety was filed and recorded with the County Clerk, and, as far as we know, is the only will. Agreed?"

Nancy nodded again.

Ms. Henry waited before moving on. "Do I understand that you are concerned about the possibility that some other will may have been filed?"

A series of answers and questions between the two of them made it clear that Nancy had no way of knowing what had gone on in the past several months. Melanie noticed she never said they'd been living apart. But she did mention that their son had moved back to the family ranch in the past eighteen months. Their daughter, a missionary and wife of a missionary, was living in Africa and had been for the past six years. Nancy's words were, "We seldom hear from her. It's not surprising to me. She and her father never got along."

The attorney said, "The next step is to search the Floyd County records to see if a more recent will has been filed. I will . . ." She stopped when Nancy's phone rang.

Nancy apologized and answered. She hung up soon after. "I'm sorry. That was the hospital. The doctor says my husband's condition is worse and decisions need to be made. I have to go."

Melanie hurried to the Medical Intensive Care Unit as soon as she reached the hospital. She saw Nancy speaking to a female physician, standing outside the doorway to one of the patient rooms—Junior's she guessed. Nancy saw her and waved her over. "I left in such a hurry, I didn't get those documents. Could you . . ."

Melanie handed her the folder she'd brought. If she ever needed a lawyer, Ms. Henry would be her choice. She'd been a bit concerned, remembering her encounter with her years ago, when she and her mother had been at odds. Now she appreciated the fact that Kay Henry had stood fast as her mother's advocate then. Today confirmed she always put her clients' interests first. After handing Nancy the folder, Melanie moved away. She'd want privacy if she were in Nancy's situation.

She watched as Nancy followed the doctor into Junior's room. Soon the doctor left and Nancy stayed behind. Through the doorway, Melanie could see her sitting at the bedside, watching the inert figure in the bed. Her face composed, hands in her lap, she'd obviously assigned herself to watch through his final moments, no matter how long it took.

Melanie stepped to the door and beckoned. "Do you want me to call anyone, or stay here so you can get a shower and change, maybe eat something?"

Nancy said, "I called and booked a room at a hotel three blocks from here. I'll check in, clean up, and come right back. Thirty or forty minutes. If Justin hasn't called by then, I'll call him from here later. My daughter can't come, but I'll let her know, if I can reach her." She took a long breath. "You probably shouldn't stay. It's okay to leave him alone. The doctor said it's likely to be gradual, over a day or two." She fished in her pants pocket, pulled out a piece of paper and read from it. "Renal failure, the kidneys are shutting down. Heart failure after the myocardial infarction, obvious long-standing hypertension, cerebrovascular accident, a stroke." She wadded the paper and stuck it back in her pocket. "I should feel sorry for Junior. A decent person would."

Melanie knew Nancy was right in suggesting she should leave. There was no sense adding fuel to Justin's volatile temper. She said, "I'll stop by the sheriff's office on the way home and let him know you'll come another time." She hugged Nancy and said, "Call me if you need anything. Or if you need to talk."

Nancy said, "Thank you for everything. You're a good friend."

Driving home, Melanie thought about the strength that Nancy was summoning from somewhere inside. Knowing it was likely that Justin would do all he could to seize control of the Reese ranch, she'd proceeded to take a first step to protect herself and possibly to prevent her son from managing to complete whatever plans he had underway. Plans that surely included creating misery for others. All those years of being Junior Reese's wife, a different person than the one she'd been when they were girls, hadn't fully erased Nancy's strength. Part of that spunky girl had shown up today. Before she arrived home, Melanie had resolved to help Nancy find the rest of herself.

Floyd County Tribune

Thursday, February 12, 2015

Obituary—Silas Reese, Jr.

Silas Reese, Jr., of the Reese Ranch near Jackson's Pond, died January 30, 2015. Reese was the son of Silas and Oveta Reese. He was born January 30, 1939.

Mr. Reese was well known in the county as a rancher and principal in other agriculture-related enterprises. He had served on the Board of the Jackson's Pond Elevator (now closed) and the Board of the Floyd County Coop Gin (also now closed).

The deceased is survived by his wife Nancy, a son Justin of Floyd County, and a daughter Charity, of Kenya, Africa, where she serves with her husband as a missionary. A private family graveside service was held February 8, 2015. The family suggests that memorials can be sent to the Jackson's Pond Baptist Church Mission Fund.

Vandalism Mars County Businesses

County sheriff's deputies and Calverton City Police have no identified suspects in several reported cases of vandalism in Jackson's Pond and Calverton in the past week. Since the Tribune's last edition four businesses, two schools, and a private residence were struck by paint-wielding vandals. The cases all had in common the use of a circular red symbol typical of Ku Klux Klan materials and messages consistent with white supremacist and other hate groups.

A sheriff's department spokesperson said, "Both the Calverton City Police and the Floyd County Sheriff's Department have stepped up surveillance and police presence during night and weekend hours and are actively investigating the incidents. Evidence, including fingerprints, provided several clues that will aid in finding and apprehending those responsible. We encourage anyone with information about the incidents to contact law enforcement."

CHAPTER 14
Discoveries

In her studio, a cup of coffee within reach, Willa sat near her easel. Something about the painting she'd begun two days earlier, different from her usual work, had sent her to her armchair to ask herself that question an artist hopes to answer— what does this want to be? Lurking just beyond that question was its companion—where has this come from?

Moving away from her paintings to view them as she worked her way through their development was a habit she'd cultivated. The perspective created by a slight distance helped her know where to work next, what to add. It also gave other less specific, yet entirely substantial, guidance about the process of creating her art. Never one to glorify her way of working as something mystical or unique, she still found it hard to explain where her choices came from. She wouldn't utter the word inspiration—that was for artists seeking to attach importance to themselves rather than the work. Instead she studied what she saw in silence.

The quiet didn't last long. She recognized Chris's voice, then Andrew's, and the barking of both the dogs that told her she wasn't the only one up and underway this chilly morning. Then Robert's command hushed the dogs, but not their two neighbors. She didn't move from her chair. There was work here that called her to stay.

After a few minutes of silence, she heard Chris's pickup start and Robert saying, "Load up." The three of them, plus the dogs, were surely off on an adventure. Her grandson, Chris, had spent many of his childhood hours roaming the ranch. And he'd often spent time on the acres to the east that J.D. had years later bought to add to the Jackson Ranch holdings. Although that was a rough pasture, never plowed, and dotted by cedar and mesquite, the native grass served well now for grazing pregnant cows and their unweaned calves. Even though back then it wasn't their property, young Chris had been given access by their neighbor.

Weary from his travels, he'd sit with her, telling of his day in that pasture tracking bobcats and coyotes, of following the trails of outlaws, and other tales that only the imagination of a child can picture so vividly. It was no wonder because, unlike the plowed acres or the grass pastures, that land held rough breaks and gullies and squat trees good for hiding out.

She closed her eyes, recalling how, almost every weekend from the time he was about six, before he'd been old enough to do heavy work, Chris would arm himself with his BB gun, a sandwich, and a canteen of water and spend his days exploring. Later, from the time he was eleven, he'd followed his Granddad Frank, learning the skills a rancher and farmer used to tend the livestock and the land. But he never neglected his Gran, often seeking her help as he occupied his evenings with creating drawings of scenes from his day. She'd known then he had an artist's vision.

Eyes open now, she studied the painting she'd begun. As always, she'd started with the background, spreading a wash over the entire piece. Never routine, her choice of tint always felt as if it emerged from somewhere other than her mind. In this case, the result was a pinkish hue. She stood and returned to her easel. People belonged in there, and the beginning of a building. Her brush moved almost automatically to hint at the scene. A small child, female, appeared along with two adults, a man and a woman. She worked quickly, then stepped back. This was the point at which she often felt compelled to rush ahead, painting quickly to capture what she could only describe if she painted it first. But experience had taught her moving slowly produced the best result.

A fresh cup of coffee in hand, she returned from the kitchen to her chair. Focused on that beginning scene, she saw herself as a child, "helping" as her mother and father added a room to the small house that had, over many years, become the place she now called home. She couldn't have been more than three then. Her mother had stitched her a child-sized carpenter's apron to hold nails. Her job had been to place any fallen or bent nails in one pocket of that apron. In the other, where she carried a flat yellow pencil identical to the one her father used to mark lumber for cuts, were new nails. Those she handed to her parents as they worked together erecting the frame for the new room. Her room.

Not aware of when she crossed the line from memory, she moved into nostalgia, a shift she felt when the scene of the past presented itself against a background glowing warmly in the pink of a full dawn. The long rays of an early sun lit everything, with none of the harsh contrasts of reality, none of the distinctions between aspiration and accomplishment to mar the scene's serenity. She drifted, but only for seconds. With a quick intake of breath, she pulled her thoughts to the present.

She knew that in nostalgia, all is perfect and much is untrue. That didn't mean that her painting a nostalgic scene was wrong, but only that she mustn't stay there too long, hiding from the present. Her childhood had not been perfect, but there had been perfect moments. Returning to the easel, she returned to her memory, smiling as the scene emerged in the painting. This scene was one of those moments. After several minutes, she left the studio, satisfied she'd made a good beginning. The sound of a pickup's motor, then a dog's bark, told her the men had returned.

First Laddie, then Peggy burst into the kitchen, slowed, and stood, bright eyes searching Willa's face until she told them to sit. Tiny dog biscuits, one per dog, that she produced from her smock's pocket, settled them to rest at her feet, tails wagging. The three men followed. Robert said, "I guess they told you we were back."

"And where did your travels take you this morning? Was breakfast served there?" she asked.

Both dogs hauled themselves up and trotted to where Andrew sat at the dining table. He petted a dog with each hand and talked to them in a soft voice. Willa couldn't hear, but whatever he said apparently told them they were the best dogs ever. For him, they would try to be lap dogs. Chris had told her the vet said Andrew had a magic touch with animals. "Instant calm," he'd said.

Willa lifted a coffee mug and said, "Anyone?"

All three nodded. She poured the coffee, and they came to the bar where she had filled a plate with banana muffins.

Chris said, "The dogs and Robert took us on a field trip. They may have found something important."

"What?" She tensed, thinking it could be another dead animal. One breeding bull and a show goat slaughtered were enough.

Robert said, "We won't know until we do some excavating. Although the muffins and coffee are important, and much appreciated, we actually came back for supplies and tools— water, two shovels, a pickaxe, my gloves, the dogs' longer leashes."

"Where?"

"Come along and we'll show you," Chris said. "It's just this side of the east fence line on the original ranch property.

"I'll get my boots on while you three finish."

She came back wearing boots and Levi's, two thermal shirts, layered, and a barn coat. She picked up her walking stick and beckoned the dogs to her. "Let's take my pickup, too, so we won't be crowded."

Robert drove her and the dogs, following Chris and Andrew. They took the ranch's road south to the county road, then turned east and soon after stopped at a gate about a hundred yards from the southeast corner of the old boundary fence. Inside the gate, Andrew waved Robert on through and closed the gate behind them. They continued following Chris north along the pasture road that stopped at a stock tank. From there, he proceeded north along a path worn by cattle coming to water, then angled slightly east and drove to a spot about sixty feet from the east fence line.

Willa said, "Did the dogs lead you up here?"

Robert pointed toward the west. He said, "See the top of the house. It's about a half mile, but seems farther because of the little elevation, and then the slope off between that rise and here.

When we go walking, I let them off the leash when we leave the house, and follow behind. If they go out of sight for too long, I whistle. Today they didn't return, so I went looking. They both were scratching at the ground. I thought they might have found a dead rabbit. But when they saw me, it was as if they wanted to show me something. They ran back and forth between me and the spot they'd been digging, yipping as if they were excited and trying to talk."

"Don't keep me in suspense. What did they find?"

"Could be nothing. But the dirt they scratched up was pretty soft. I got down close and looked to see what might be in the small piles they'd made." He drove with his left hand, reached in his jacket pocket with the other. "Here's what I found."

He showed her a piece of what appeared to be a six or seven-inch length of old, dry tape of some sort—black on one side; dirt brown, dry, and cracking on the other. She said, "That looks like what we used to wrap bicycle handlebars with, years ago."

Robert said, "Friction tape. Yes, that's exactly what I thought. The dogs dug it up from several inches down. If I hadn't held them, they'd be digging still. They must have smelled something."

Laddie barked from the back seat of the pickup. Then Peggy joined him, and the two of them continued, taking turns. Robert said, "When we stop, I'll put them on their leashes. Maybe they'll settle down out here with us."

Chris and Andrew stopped, and Robert parked behind them. He led the way to the place they'd dug, Chris and Andrew brought the shovels, and Willa followed with the dogs on their leashes. Robert said, "Maybe if you enlarge from both sides of where they unearthed this tape, we'll see if there's anything else to be found."

Andrew said, "I went on an archeology dig one summer down in the Big Bend. They had us dig down only three or four inches at a time in grid patterns. If we make a square, say three feet with the dogs' marks at the center, then we can stop and take out the dirt, sift through it, then do the same each time we go deeper."

Robert nodded and signaled the dogs to sit and stay. Willa said, "I'll supervise."

She watched as Chris and Andrew dug, shovel by shovel, then she heard a clink. They both stopped and squatted, began sifting the turned dirt, lifting it out and placing it to the sides. Andrew held up something in his hand. He said, "A perfectly preserved arrowhead."

Willa said, "When I was a child, I found many of those in the pasture east of here."

They resumed sifting, finding nothing more. Then they dug another several shovels full and stopped again. Chris lifted another piece of the brownish tape. They proceeded that way until the hole was about eighteen inches deep—finding occasional bits of the tape, nothing else. Then one of them hit something that made a different sound, dull and hollow. Sifting through the dirt, they turned handful after handful that yielded nothing. As she watched, however, something dark brown and almost round fell with the dirt Andrew dropped. She said, "Is that a button?"

Chris held it up. "Yes, about three-quarters of an inch in diameter, four holes. It's old, looks like horn."

They pulled more dirt from the hole, now close to two feet deep. Andrew, on his knees beside the hole, said, "There's something larger, looks like wood, still down here." He straightened up, reached into his jeans pocket, pulled out a pocket knife. "I'll see if I can work it out intact."

Chris stepped away from the hole. "Maybe we should enlarge the perimeter." He used his shovel tip to draw a larger outline around the current site, resulting in a five-foot square with the hole Andrew was digging in at its center. "I'll start out here on the edge and work in."

Andrew, his arm in the hole, said, "I think this is a baseball bat. A handle, which looks like it has some of that tape on it. The barrel is splintered and decayed. I'm trying to get it to come out all in one piece."

Robert whispered to her, "Shall we call Melanie?"

Willa said, "She'll want to know." If even one bone turned up, it would be right to call the sheriff first. "Let's wait a bit, see if there's anything else."

Shoveling dirt to the edge outside the new border, Chris said, "I'm fading. I should have eaten more before we left."

Andrew said, "Let me get this out, then we can go eat. This isn't going anywhere." He kept his head down, working in the hole. About a minute later he raised up, holding the prize he'd freed in his gloved hands. Apparently, the friction tape had protected the handle, which was mostly intact. The lower part of the belly of the bat was splintered and riddled with holes. "The rest of it fell to pieces, but it looks like enough to be the rest of the whole bat." He placed the handle in the large plastic zip-top bag that held the button they'd unearthed. Then he stood and stretched. "That was more work than it looked like."

Chris said, "What do you think, Gran?"

"I think your mother will want to see this and see the hole where it was found."

Chris went to his pickup, came back carrying his camera. "I'll document this with photos. Give me a few minutes. Using gloves and bagging those pieces may make DNA analysis possible—maybe."

Shortly after noon, the four of them took Melanie to see the place where the button and the bat had been unearthed. As they stood together near the overturned earth, none of them spoke. Then Willa said, "Do you have any thoughts about what to do next?"

Melanie said, "Based on Grandmother's diary and those clippings, I doubt that the body was buried here. I think the bat was buried at the time of the murder. The body was supposedly buried later, undisclosed location, that clipping said. I have no doubt that guilt made Great-Grandfather donate a place somewhere on this ranch."

Robert said, "That makes sense, given the documents you've found."

"Chris and Andrew, if you'll dig deeper and as wide as the space Chris outlined, we'll have an idea if there's anything more," Melanie said. "If there's not—well, either way, then we'll have to decide what to do next."

Chris said, "One possibility is to do nothing. Think about it, Mom. All this vandalism, the threats. Why stir things up worse than they are right now?"

Willa watched Melanie's jaw tighten, and waited, wondering what she'd say next. Chris could be correct—stirring things up might have disastrous results.

Melanie raised her head, and seemed to study her son's face. She said, "Would it stop you? I doubt it."

"But you're not me. You're . . ."

"I'm what? Weak?"

"I was going to say vulnerable." Chris shook his head.

"You know, probably better than anyone, I've fought on the wrong side of some things before. But this is right. We all are vulnerable. But I won't let these current thugs and bullies keep me from trying to right this wrong. We'll decide together, after you finish digging, what to do next. But we will do something, not nothing."

Willa had seen the two of them argue before, seen Chris storm away, slamming doors, cursing. Had seen Melanie's back stiffen and her heart harden. But now they were both different. She hoped the past wouldn't overshadow that for either of them.

Chris seemed to be focusing on the contents of the plastic bag. Then he looked up, and smiled faintly in Melanie's direction. He nodded and said, "Okay, I'm with you."

Robert said, "Meanwhile, I will continue searching for family of Mr. Berryhill. Census records and the Internet grave finding site gave me a clue to the existence of one living family member. I left a message on the phone at the only number listed to a Berryhill in Bosley, Oklahoma, asking for a return call. If I don't hear back, I'll call again this afternoon."

Melanie nodded. Willa recognized her expression.

Persistence, it said.

Back at the house, Melanie and Willa studied the baseball bat remnants closely. Willa said, "I'll put it here, up on this shelf, so the dogs won't bother it. It will be here when you decide what to do next."

Melanie sat in a chair facing Willa's easel. She studied the tinted canvas and the beginning sketch. "Were you painting today?"

"I've begun a new one. But I don't know yet what it will be"

Melanie said, "I envy your ability to move forward without a clear path. This whole business about the murder frustrates me because I can't see a direct way to do what's right."

"Just trust the fact that in your heart and mind, doing the right thing is foremost. It will come to you."

For a few minutes, the two of them sat quietly, each with her own thoughts. When Chris and Andrew drove up next door at their house, Melanie said her goodbyes and went over to their house. Not long after, Willa saw her drive away.

That afternoon, soon after she got up from her midday rest, Willa heard Robert's phone ring. Soon after, she was at the kitchen counter making a pot of tea when he called her name. Before she could answer, he came and sat at the kitchen table. "I just talked with a relative of Mr. Berryhill. From the sound of her voice, she's an elderly one. She's willing to have me visit and promised to show me family keepsakes and clippings. However, she's not certain there's anything there about Lincoln Berryhill other than his name in the family Bible. She said there was a lot of material that she'd never looked at, just put in a cedar chest when her grandmother passed."

"When will you go?" Willa poured tea for both of them and slid a plate holding three shortbreads toward Robert.

He took one and sipped his tea. "Thank you, my dear. Monday, unless you need me here." He bit the cookie and chewed slowly.

"I'll soon need a new wardrobe if I don't change my eating habits."

She said, "Some gain weight when they're depressed, others when they're happy."

"Then I could be absolutely rotund before the year is out. I'm definitely not depressed." He pushed the plate toward Willa. "I'll stop with one."

That evening they got out the atlas and a Texas roadmap. Neither of them trusted the GPS in Robert's Land Rover since the day it steered them forty miles out of the way on a scenic drive to Palo Duro Canyon. That was the last time Robert insisted his new vehicle knew the way to everywhere. Willa had kept quiet the whole time, never even allowing so much as a smirk to let on that she could have driven the route blindfolded.

Bosley, they had learned from an Internet search, was one of several historically African American towns in Oklahoma. Although it was smaller than at its peak, the last census listed the population as 545. Willa watched as Robert highlighted his route on the map. Not looking up, he said, "I know you're watching. You're invited if you'd care to go along."

"No, this is your mission. The dogs and I will tend to things here."

Monday morning, she handed him a six-can cooler after he loaded his briefcase and overnight bag in his vehicle. She'd packed a turkey sandwich, an apple, cheese, two bottles of water, and three shortbread cookies. "Road food," she said.

He handed her a sheet of notepaper on which he'd written the name of the person he was to see and her telephone number in Bosley. He said, "Vital information."

After he was in the driver's seat, belted in, she leaned in the window and kissed him. "Drive carefully. We'll be right here when you get back."

He started the engine and rolled up his window. She stepped away and raised her hand to wave. He rolled the window down again and beckoned to her. When she was close, she asked, "Did you forget something?"

"No," he said, "just something I needed to tell you. I love you, Willa."

Then he rolled the window up again and headed toward the county road.

Floyd County Tribune
Thursday, February 12, 2015
Committees Report to Jackson's Pond City Council

The five special committees charged with making recommendations to the Jackson's Pond City Council on city development presented their reports at the February 11, 2015, meeting of the Council.

Key recommendations from the committees include the following:

Education and child care—Gain agreement from Floyd County Independent School District to reopen Jackson's Pond Middle School. Develop a city-sponsored after-school arts program for school-age children.

Housing—Seek developers to create at least twenty-five new family housing units within the next year. Provide incentives in the form of cost shares to local property owners to rehabilitate vacant properties as rental units. Short term (within 90 days), seek vendors to provide temporary housing units for at least thirty new residents.

Business development—Form an advisory and support committee to assist the City Manager in efforts to entice new business to the city. Support efforts to revive the efforts to entice new business to the city. Support efforts to revive the Jackson's Pond Chamber of Commerce. Within the next twenty-four months, add at least one each of the following types of businesses: full-service grocery, general merchandise and sundries, auto repair, laundry and dry-cleaning, pharmacy, and restaurant. Explore need for and interest in reopening the local grain elevator and local cotton gin.

Public health and safety—Find a provider to reopen the local health clinic. Develop a local, assisted-living facility. Form a city police department to provide 24-hour local law enforcement. Explore establishing a local Emergency Medical Service station in conjunction with the Calverton EMS/911 district.

City infrastructure—Charge the consulting engineer with performing an assessment of city water capacity, sanitation services, and street improvement needs in light of projected population growth. Partner with RBJ Data Solutions to identify necessary upgrades to broadband access to meet city and school needs in conjunction with future business requirements. Analyze additional personnel and equipment requirements consistent with identified needs. Consider a bond election to support necessary upgrades to areas as identified by the assessments. Provide full-time library service for the city.

The council accepted the reports and promised action to begin implementing the recommendations as soon as the next council meeting.

Mayor Banks thanked the committees for their work and encouraged interested citizens to review the full reports, available in the City Manager's office.

CHAPTER 15
Gang of Four or More

Finally, by noon, Melanie had managed to calm herself after the morning's rocky start at Banks Preschool. As if the earlier encounter with Justin Reese hadn't been enough, another couple arrived demanding a refund. Although her pulse rate eventually returned to normal after the episode, she still hadn't been able to erase the image of the mean-faced son of another long-time Jackson's Pond family standing in her office and announcing, "I won't have my boy mixing with mongrel races."

Then he demanded a refund for the remaining two weeks' tuition his wife had paid. His choosing to stop his child's attending pained Melanie. Each morning the child arrived solemn and watchful, but daily she'd seen him begin showing signs of playfulness with other children and of joy in learning. She knew her sorrow about that child's situation would abate. But his father's words pierced her to her core.

Stabbing pain had shot through her stomach as she mustered control. He said, "It's people like you that have to learn this is our country, white American country. These Spics and all the other mongrels trying to take over, intermarrying. We will drive them out and all you communists that preach brotherhood and one world along with them. One way or another, you and them, you'll all be punished. My wife and her mother put my boy here without me approving. She's learned her lesson. Now give me my money, you ignorant old bitch. I hated you and your queer son all my life. You'll not poison my boy's mind."

She said, as if she'd rehearsed it, "I will not tolerate that kind of talk here. This is a private establishment. You have no rights inside these walls. I will write your refund check and you will wait silently until I finish. If not, I will call the sheriff. Not another word. Your choice."

After she handed him the check, he stomped out. She followed him and locked the door. At least the mother and the child hadn't been there to hear his rant.

Then as he left, she'd had to answer the question Dolores asked. "It's me, isn't it?"

Melanie said, "No. This has nothing to do with your being African American and married to a Hispanic man. It's definitely not you. It's him. I'm embarrassed to say I knew him when I was school counselor at the junior high here. He's always been the type to follow, was never independent. He's probably joined Justin Reese and that bunch responsible for all the vandalism here and in Calverton."

Dolores said, "This can't go on. I'll resign. That'll solve the problem."

"That would only tell them they won. Please don't even think of resigning."

Dejection showed in Dolores's slumped shoulders, the sadness in her face. "I should be teaching my own children at home. I worry they aren't safe in the school at Calverton. If I resign, it will solve two problems."

The preschool day was beginning, so Dolores and Melanie agreed they'd talk more after school before making any changes. Until a few minutes ago, they'd both been occupied filling their young pupils' day with fun and educational play. Now, they sat together in the break room with the lunches they'd brought from home. The bright curtains and the cheerful yellow paint on the walls were meant to make the room cozy. Today they were no help. Gloom hovered over them both.

Melanie said, "Is it possible we could have your children here for their homeschooling?"

"When I teach them, I focus entirely on their learning. I couldn't do that and do justice to our young pupils at the same time."

"What about the afternoons? With only clean up and preparing for the next day each afternoon, you could concentrate on yours, and I could do the rest."

Dolores shrugged. "It might work. I give them assignments to complete on their own. They could do those in the mornings. But that means more work for you. When would you do the record-keeping and all the rest?"

"I haven't thought about it. But I will. If you'll talk with your family, then we can discuss this again next week." She ate some of the salad she'd brought for lunch, pushing aside lettuce that looked as wilted as her spirits. Then she said, "Is it only your boys you're concerned about, or Elisa, too?"

"Mostly the boys. The older one said last week some boys from his class tried to start a fight on the playground and Jay Frank and some other boys—I think they are African American—stood up for him. I don't want them to have to go through that." She wadded the sandwich she'd been nibbling and its waxed paper wrapper into a ball. As she took it to the trash can, she said, "Elisa may have just not told me. She loves being with Amy, riding the bus, being in the same classes. I'd hate for her to have to give that up."

"Mother and Claire are stopping by around two. Maybe Amy's told Claire something. Hard to say with teenagers. The main thing I know is that backing down only encourages bullies."

Dolores nodded. "I know. But I have to protect my children."

Melanie remembered the times Chris had fought and how J.D. had helped protect him until her son grew large enough and able to defend himself, for being himself. She also remembered that she'd blamed him, not the bullies. Try as she might, forgiving the person she'd been back then continued to challenge her. She'd told herself starting the preschool, demonstrating positive values, was one small way she could erase the blame she carried for her own earlier lack of understanding and tolerance. She said to Dolores, "You're a good parent."

She and Dolores had just finished clearing away their lunch remnants when Claire and Willa knocked at the school's front door. On the way back to the break room, Claire said, "I have news! You're going to be so surprised."

Melanie overcame an urge to turn to look at her daughter, to see if her face showed the same excitement she heard in her voice. Claire could encourage almost anyone into believing the best was on its way. That ability was an asset with her patients. But sometimes she put a positive spin on a situation just to manage to get through it. Claire had even fooled her during the time the clinic had been threatened with a hostile buyout and again when there'd been trouble between her and J.D. Melanie had promised herself then that she'd pay closer attention.

When the four of them were situated at the table, Claire bounced up from her chair and said, "Pretend you hear a drum roll." Then she spread her arms wide and said, "Announcing! Gran and I have a plan."

Before either she or Dolores could speak or encourage Claire to spill her news, her daughter sat back down. She said, "I'm so rude. Sorry. I didn't even say hello or ask how your day has been. Please forgive my lack of manners."

Dolores said, "You're excited. Tell us."

"It's really Gran's idea. Then it got bigger when we heard the city planning committee reports. Gran, you tell it. I'm too excited to make sense."

Willa wore the same smile that Claire always brought to her face, a mixture of joy and indulgence. Melanie knew that Amy and Jay Frank saw the same from her. It was a grandmother's smile, one that says, "You are perfect in every way."

"I've never told this before, but it won't hurt, as long as I leave out a name. You probably recall when June's Apparel closed down. June was in a bind. She needed to sell in a hurry. Her elderly parents needed her near them in Central Texas, but she still owed some on the building and all the inventory. I happened to know she and a man here in town, a married man, had been seeing each other now and then for years. I think I might have been the only one she ever told.

"I meddled. I told him the situation, because I knew she wouldn't. June clung to her pride, no matter what. Shortly after that, she told me she'd managed to find a buyer, inventory and all.

Off she went. Every time I've passed by, all these years, I've felt bad for that poor mannequin she left behind in the window."

Melanie said, "He bought it?"

Willa nodded. "I'm pretty certain. And I think someone might be able to convince him to donate that building, now that his wife's long dead."

Melanie shook her head. "I had no idea."

"There was never any reason to tell."

Claire leaned forward. If excitement made some people glow, it made Claire almost sparkle. "Gran figured out how the building can be remodeled to hold a small gallery and the rest can be the home of an after-school arts program." She paused for a breath and then said, "I know, it's going to take a lot of planning. So, if we start the process right away. Well, what do you two think?"

Melanie imagined the mountain of planning that would have to go into getting a program of that sort started. But if it were sponsored by the city, not the school system, it would be far simpler. She said, "Who would convince this mystery man? Who'd operate it?"

Willa said, "Those are details we need to deal with right away. That's why we're here—to get the broad strokes down on paper so we can more easily deal with the details. Do you have time to start?"

That was all it took. An hour and a half later, they had identified a list of areas to be developed further, including organizational structure—non-profit; personnel required—many volunteers and a paid director; how to acquire the building at little or no cost; programs that would be included at first—dance, drawing and painting, children's theater; and names of people to involve early. The topic of funding slowed the flow of ideas until Willa said, "To be practical, to assure the program would continue, there has to be a source of money."

That stopped the conversation. The four sat looking at one another; it seemed to Melanie like several minutes passed before anyone said another word. Finally, her mother spoke. "Assuming we get the building, if we begin with finding interested people to serve on a board, then they can help identify possible sources of funds. Meanwhile, I believe I may know some people in arts who'd be willing to provide a one-year seed grant. That would give us time to work out the details of more permanent funding."

Melanie didn't give any hint that she knew her mother could fund the program herself if she chose to. It would be better overall to have more than one "angel." She said, "I think we should go ahead with planning and know that funding can be worked out somehow."

Claire, who'd been making notes as they chose assignments, said, "I'm the only one without an assignment. If it's okay with everyone, I'll talk to the building owner."

Willa said, "You're probably the perfect person for that job. He's always had a soft spot for a pretty face."

Claire said, "I can check the property records and find the owner's name. That way you aren't involved, and if he asks, it'll be the truth when I tell how I got his name. Is that okay with everyone?"

Melanie said, "Have at it, and good luck."

She saw the smile Willa tried to hide with a fake cough.

Before long, they agreed they'd made a good beginning and planned to meet again in a week. As she and Dolores walked toward the front with Claire and Willa, Melanie said, "Now we've enlarged our gang to four. There's no stopping us." Her phone rang. She said, "Wait a second. Let me get this."

She answered and heard Nancy Reese's voice, sounding frantic. Melanie said, "Yes, Nancy, come right over. We're all here."

Melanie waited at the door while the other three returned to the break room. She'd explained to the others that Nancy needed help, right away. She heard Willa, in the other room, giving Dolores background information about their past association with Nancy, her husband's recent death, and her difficulties with Justin, with whom Dolores was all too familiar.

Coming from her vehicle toward the school, Nancy gave the impression of a woman whose load had been lightened. Unlike the last time Melanie had seen her, Nancy stood erect and walked steadily. Her hair had been cut in a short, curly style and she wore lipstick. She even smiled as she approached. When she reached Melanie, Nancy greeted her with a hug, the way old friends do.

As they walked through the classrooms toward the break area, Melanie told her about the other three waiting. She said, "You said there's a problem. But you look good. Really good."

"Until this afternoon, I felt good. Better than I have in years."

After introducing Nancy to Dolores, Melanie said, "Tell us the problem and how we can help. We're thinking of going into the helping business, so you can be our first case."

They sat around the dinette table in the kitchen-like room while Nancy told of a telephone call she received from Pastor Goodman's wife, Sue Jane. "She had called Holly, Justin's wife. She said she was concerned because since Holly's earlier call she'd not heard back from her. So, Mrs. Goodman called, and Justin answered, told her his wife was busy, and not to be calling there. Then later that same day, yesterday, Sue Jane answered a call, and it was Holly.

"She told the pastor's wife she was afraid of Justin and wanted to run away. But she had no way to get herself and the children out. Sue Jane said Holly's exact words were, 'He never hit me until the last three weeks. But now it's every day. I'm afraid for the kids.' She asked Holly if she was injured and Holly said, 'Only bruises. He mainly hits me to keep me from talking.' Here's the worst part—Sue Jane said that in the middle of a sentence, the connection broke and the phone's been busy since then anytime she tried to call."

After she spilled out that story, Nancy sat back, both hands clenched on the table. "I know it's my family's problem. But I don't know how to solve it alone. Holly chose to marry Justin. But those children had no choice."

After those words, she began crying, but quickly checked herself. She searched the faces of the other four women. "How do I begin? What could the sheriff do, if Holly's never made a complaint? Where could she go that Justin wouldn't come after her?"

Dolores spoke first. "In the Air Force, when there were cases of domestic violence, we women found it was more effective to get the wife and children out first and then call the police. Legally, there are rules for when law enforcement can intervene."

Claire said, "Do you mean the women banded together and took the wife and children to safety? That's brave."

"At our last base, there were about twenty of us who worked together. We protected one another. We let the police know just before we intervened. It takes planning—knowing where the women's shelter is, how to get someone in there, having an attorney ready if needed. The most difficult part was always getting the woman to agree to leave. They were all afraid."

"There's a women's shelter in Lubbock," Melanie said. "I recall a staff member from the school district in Calverton who left her job abruptly. We learned afterward she'd gone there and later had moved to another city after getting a divorce."

Willa said, "I don't know if the five of us could get her away from that house, if he didn't want her to leave. Do you have any idea about their routines, when she might be able to get out to the gate so we could get her away?"

Nancy shook her head and said, "He's never even let her drive, not even get a license. She'd have to walk at least a quarter mile. And those kids."

Willa said, "We need a Jehovah's Witness."

The others all looked her way. Melanie said, "What?"

Claire said, "I don't think religion will help right now."

"Wait," Dolores said, "I get it. Someone to take her a message, a way to let her know she's not alone. Who goes door-to-door these days? Doesn't have to be a real Witness, just someone to slip her instructions."

Nancy perked up. "It's been so long since I felt like I could accomplish anything. You give me hope."

Melanie said, "I'm thinking of others who'd help us. I know Laverne would."

"Mamie would go along for support," Willa said.

Claire, always one to think through steps needed for any plan, said, "We need to work as two teams. Three of us collect the local information we need—Dolores should lead that."

Dolores agreed with a nod. Nancy said, "I'll work with her."

Melanie said, "I'll make three. We can work here tomorrow afternoon."

Claire said, "Gran and I will recruit at least four other people who agree, without knowing who or what, to help rescue a woman and her children who are in danger. Then we get together, the five of us plus the ones who agree to help, and work out the final plan. In the meantime no names are mentioned, no one contacted who'd have to tell her husband before she could help."

The four of them walked with Nancy to the front door. She repeated her earlier thanks, then said, "In all this excitement, I forgot to tell you that it's nearly certain Justin's contest of Junior's will is going to fail."

Melanie said, "Has he threatened you, Nancy?"

"He's said a lot of hateful things, but no outright threats. I don't answer anymore if he calls. The lawyer told me to avoid contact until this is settled. She called him volatile. She didn't need to tell me—I lived with him from the day he was born. I watched him turn into the image of his father, from the time he was a teenager until he left home at twenty. He was lost to me." She stopped walking, and looked at each of the others, one at a time. "That's not true. No, the truth is I gave him away by being weak and stupid."

Melanie put a hand on Nancy's back. "You aren't weak or stupid now. So, stay focused. Do you feel safe living at your parents' house—deadbolt locks, window locks, security lights?"

"Yes, except I don't have the lights, yet. And my cell phone and the landline both have 911 on speed dial. I'll tell you one thing, when this will business is over with, I'm going to Africa. My daughter invited me. I might just be a missionary for the rest of my life."

Melanie watched as Nancy went to her Jeep. Willa and Claire left soon after. Melanie and Dolores cleared away cookie crumbs and coffee cups. When they finished, Melanie went to her desk and pretended to organize the papers strewn there. In fact, it was her thoughts she wanted to organize. There'd been so much that day.

Dolores, on her way out, carrying the Mickey Mouse lunchbox her youngest boy had outgrown—she and Melanie had laughed about mothers hating to toss out their children's once-beloved items—stopped at the desk. She said, "Before we go, I wanted to tell you, I've decided I'll wait about homeschooling for now. I was being selfish. Spring Break is soon and shortly after that, school's out. Things could change for the better before the next school year begins."

Melanie said, "Let's hope. Just know that we can work it out if you decide to do it. And, Dolores, thank you. In case you don't know it, you're vital to me and to this school."

Driving home, even with all the problems of the day, Melanie found herself smiling. She imagined their gang of three expanding, turning into a force for good in Floyd County— bringing arts education to Jackson's Pond, rescuing women from danger. She entertained herself with thoughts of costumes to fit that image. Then as she pulled in the drive at home, she laughed as she pictured her mother masquerading as a door-to-door evangelist.

Floyd County Tribune
Thursday, February 19, 2015
Jackson's Pond City Council Endorses Reports

At its February18, 2015 meeting, the Jackson's Pond City Council formally endorsed the recommendations of the five committees charged with proposing goals for city development. Mayor Ray Banks spoke on behalf of the council in thanking the committees for their hard work. "Without the dedication and effort of citizens such as those on these committees, Jackson's Pond could not thrive as a city. With their effort, this group has provided the council with clear direction about the wishes and the dreams of local citizens. I know the City Council and City Manager will do all in their power to see that these goals are met."

Chamber of Commerce Reformation Effort in Jackson's Pond

Mr. V.I. Patel, owner of Jackson's Pond Motel, announced a meeting to be held Tuesday, February 24, 2015 at 7 p.m. at the City Offices. The purpose of the meeting is for any and all interested parties to discuss reviving the Jackson's Pond Chamber of Commerce.

Patel said, "I urge all current business owners and any who are considering developing businesses to attend this meeting."

Cross Burning at Cowboy Church

Pastor Heath Goodman of the Cowboy Congregation, which meets in Floyd County midway between Calverton and Jackson's Pond, reported vandalism at the church building sometime after their Wednesday night service February 18. Evidence collected included photographs of a partially burned cross in front of the church. Also retrieved was a sign saying "We're watching you. Repent Now or Suffer."

CHAPTER 16
Winter Storm

Robert had only been gone two days, but as soon as he opened the front door, both dogs greeted him as if he'd been gone two years. The usually calm adult dogs behaved like puppies—leaping, barking, and bumping against Robert and one another. Willa's indulgent smile did nothing to slow their celebration. If she were their age, she might leap, too. She'd also missed him as if his absence had been far longer. The routines that marked their days together held little interest to her when he was gone. Who wants to sit and drink coffee and eat shortbread alone? And apparently, the dogs felt their world had tipped also. Both of them had paced the house, looking in each room. When she let them out to run, they returned soon, not waiting to be called. They left their bowls half-full of food.

"Ah, I see its first things first." Robert spoke directly to the dogs. They promptly sat still at his feet. From his jacket pocket, the man who held all their attention produced two large dog biscuits. They settled, wagging tails and making crunching sounds as they ate.

Robert wrapped Willa in a hug. He whispered, "I missed you."

She said, "I admit it; I missed you, too. I'm glad you're back safely." Telling him how she'd lain awake both nights, wishing she could hear the sound of his breathing, or admitting that she'd eaten supper standing at the kitchen sink—cheese, apple, and crackers the first night and a peanut butter sandwich with milk and corn chips the second—wouldn't do. So, she hugged him tightly a second time. Living alone for years, she'd enjoyed the solitude, but now, after months of Robert's constant companionship, she'd behaved like someone new at being on her own.

She followed him to their bedroom. As he unpacked the few things he'd taken along, he said, "What went on while I was gone?"

"A lot. Too much to tell until you've had time to relax. Plus, I guess you noticed the clouds. A winter storm's on the way. We need to make ready."

"What does that involve? This will be my first winter storm in this part of Texas."

"These days, not much, other than seeing that the water doesn't freeze and that there's wood for the fireplace and candles in case the electricity goes out. We have food to last at least a week, so that's taken care of." She watched him stow the clothes he'd worn in the hamper in the closet. When he finished, he sat beside her on the bed. She said, "If the weather service is correct, the front should arrive later this afternoon, and if there's snow or ice, it will be heaviest late tonight and early tomorrow. Of course, there will be wind, piercing bone-chilling wind. It'll make you wonder why you ever left Austin. I had other plans, but weather trumps almost everything, so instead, I'll make a giant pot of chili and another of beans. We can feed the entire family, have a storm party."

"That's one of the many things I admire about you. Some women, strike that—some people—would fear a storm, and fret about the preparations. But for you it's a diversion, and in this case an excuse for a party."

"It's been a long time since I've feared a storm." Someday she might tell him about the tornado the day baby George died. Standing on the porch of this very house, watching the tornado come directly at her and Frank and their dying baby, thinking it would be the end of them all, and then seeing the storm abruptly change its path had altered her forever. Not only because it coincided with her baby's death, but also because it was a moment in which she had fully surrendered, accepted that Baby George would never recover and that she and Frank were likely to be killed there, standing together with their tiny son in her arms in the face of an elemental force. She marked that as the day on which she understood that no human was fully in charge of his or her own life's course. Someday she might tell Robert that story.

During the months of the depression she endured following that day, she acquired a sense that one must learn to welcome the inevitable. She learned that one only influences how and whether she examines her motives, chooses the best possible decisions, and acts responsibly. After that, she must be at peace and accept what comes. In the case of this coming storm, she chose to make chili and let Robert, Chris, and Andrew take care of the rest.

She felt Robert watching. He'd finished unpacking and held out his hand. "Let's check the wood supply and count the candles. Then I'll tell you about my trip and listen to your tales." They walked together to the family room. From behind her, she heard him say, "By the way, did I mention that I missed you?"

They checked the wood and found that Chris and Andrew, being good next-door neighbors, had laid in enough at both houses to last far longer than the storm was likely to. And there were candles and holders sufficient for a long dark spell, as well. Satisfied they were in good shape, they returned to the kitchen. Willa chopped onions while Robert made coffee. As they worked, he began the story of his trip with a preface. He said, "I believe Melanie will be pleased with the result of my little sojourn."

"She'll be coming out just after noon. Do you want to save the details until then, tell it only once? Now that I know you were successful, I can wait."

"Good idea. But I will tell you about my travel to and from. I learned much from that, none of which has to do with the man whose remains rest here somewhere." He searched two cabinets, then the pantry and finally found a tin of shortbread cookies. He said, "I can see I need to bake soon."

"A leprechaun was here looking for those. I hid them there to throw him off."

He counted aloud from one to five. "He found them. There were eight in here when I left."

"I might have eaten one or two."

"My countrymen, the leprechauns, often get a bad rap." He sat at the table, nibbling a cookie and sipping coffee. As soon as she finished chopping, and had the onions and beef sautéing, she joined him.

He said, "Taking the route we mapped out, I stopped in several small towns in the Texas Panhandle and in Oklahoma, all the way to Bosley and back, giving myself two days. My plan was to make the trip serve two purposes. Of course, the more important was to gather information about the deceased who was deprived of his life here on this land. But almost as important to me was to soak up the culture of these rural areas and the people who live here.

She could tell he was warming to his topic. He leaned forward, both hands surrounding his coffee cup. He said, "It's too simple to uncritically accept the idea that people in rural areas are dull-witted and backward, bigoted and uninformed, the view that some in metropolitan areas hold about rural folk. To me, that's just as biased as is a racial prejudice. Not all rural people are alike, I am certain. No more than are all members of any racial or ethnic group alike."

"And now, Professor, have you sufficient information to reach any conclusions?"

"I do go on, don't I? Please give a signal, such as holding your hands over your ears or fleeing the room, anytime I edge toward pontificating."

"I love your way of looking at life, and I enjoy hearing you tell about it. You know I'm joking. Please, go on." She pointed to the cast iron Dutch oven sitting on the stovetop. When she lifted the lid, both dogs arrived, noses held high, then seated themselves near the stove. As he continued, she shook chili powder, comino, and dried cilantro into the mixture, then added a small can of tomato sauce. The dogs were right; it smelled good already.

Robert said, "Certainly I must collect further examples before reaching any firm conclusions. But my preliminary reactions are these: waves, smiles, handshakes, and pleasant utterances are common, with no apparent purpose other than friendliness, an interest in others. People notice one another and also any stranger in their midst far more than in more densely populated places; speech and action move at a leisurely pace, generally; verbal interchanges often have as their only purpose a shared experience—no exchanges of goods or any vital information are needed for "visiting" to occur; considerable time is often invested in trivial conversation, less on issue-driven topics.

"People I encountered greeted me as if I were a welcome guest. They offered hospitality, much like I recall from home as a child. When I arrived in New York so many years ago, it was as if all the ease and comfort disappeared from my life. Now I've found it again.

"I am open to revising these findings as I collect more data. In summary, reaching well-founded conclusions will probably require most of the rest of my life. And as this location is perfect as a base for my research, I fear you are stuck with me."

Willa had returned to the table by then, followed by the dogs. "That's exactly what I thought when you asked me to marry you—I'll be stuck with him."

He put on a mock-sad face. It lasted only a few seconds. He said, "And speaking of marrying. We should decide on a place to honeymoon. How's New York?"

"My preference is no honeymoon. Let's travel when we have the urge, not because the ceremony was performed." She took a cookie from the tin, dunked it in her coffee. Frank had taken her on the only honeymoon she ever wanted back when they were young and each experience was memorable, if for no other reason than it was new.

It wasn't that Robert appeared relieved, but she didn't detect any sadness. He said, "As you wish, my dear. Staying home suits me fine. All the people I love are here."

At the word "people," both dogs stood as if they'd been called. Then Willa heard a knock at the door. "Excellent guard dogs need treats."

When she returned to the kitchen, Melanie followed.

After Willa added more ingredients and covered the pot of chili to simmer, she joined Melanie and Robert at the table. They had already begun talking. She heard Robert say, "I believe you will be pleased."

"If you made contact, I'm pleased already."

Robert told her in detail about the woman he talked with in Bosley, Oklahoma. Miss Martha Jane Berryhill was Lincoln Berryhill's grand-niece, the granddaughter of his younger brother. She had shown Robert the family Bible which included names of the family members beginning with her great-grandfather up to the current time. According to that record, she was Lincoln's only living relative. He had no children and because he'd had only two siblings, the one brother—Miss Martha Jane's grandfather—and one sister, who died young and childless, only Miss Martha Jane's family line had carried on the Berryhill name. Robert said she'd commented, "Our family tended to die young, it seems, except for me. I consider myself lucky to have made it to seventy-one."

She also showed him a clipping from the Bosley newspaper in 1921 mentioning that the family was searching for the missing Lincoln Berryhill who had been working his way down to Fort Stockton, Texas, and had not communicated for more than a month. "She allowed me to make a copy of that clipping."

She explained why her family had settled in Bosley. It was one of several of those towns in Oklahoma populated by people who were freed slaves, many having been owned by some of the Native American tribes that lived in the territory. "The area was home to our ancestors when they were freed, and so our family has stayed ever since."

Robert said, "Hoping not to upset her, I had only told her that we believed we had information confirming that Mr. Berryhill had died here in Floyd County. Before I even began to tell her a little about the circumstances, she said that the family had given him up as dead. She said, 'You have no idea how bad things used to be for us. White people killed us for any reason, or no reason.' Then I told her we believed, based on family records and newspaper clippings, that her family's fears were accurate, that Klan members had killed him."

As Melanie and Willa listened, he told of Miss Berryhill's asking if anyone was punished for the murder, and how she shook her head when he told her those arrested had been acquitted. Finally, he ended by saying she'd been brought to tears by Melanie's wish to have a memorial service for Lincoln Berryhill, as a way of atoning, even though no remains had ever been found.

"After she collected herself, she told me she appreciated that and would be happy to attend a service whenever it might be held." After a long pause, he said, "Then she did the most amazing thing. She invited me to stay and have lunch, just the two of us. She served an excellent meal and was a gracious hostess."

He left the room and returned with a folder he handed to Melanie. "Her contact information and the clipping she gave me are in there."

Melanie grasped his hand. "You can't know how much it means to me that you did this. Will you help me later with planning the memorial? Sometime in May would be good. There's too much happening now. Maybe by then, things will be calmer."

Willa said, "What about our plan to get together today, get the rescue organized?" Robert's reaction—widened eyes and alert posture—didn't surprise her. She gave him credit for his silence. "The temperature's already fallen about twenty degrees. I could tell when you came in the front door. And if it snows as predicted, it could be as unsafe to try to help Holly leave as to make it a day or two later."

Melanie said, "That's part of why I came out—to tell you Nancy came by just after the school day was over. She doesn't want to put anyone else at risk trying to get a message to Holly. She's going out to the ranch on the pretense of collecting some things she plans to take back to Red River. If Justin's there, that's what she'll tell him. One way or the other she plans to tell Holly to meet us at their mailbox at two-thirty tomorrow."

"It's risky rushing into this, especially with the weather threatening. Did you try to talk her out of doing it this way?"

"I tried. She's intent. She said, 'It's at least partly my fault that Justin's the way he is. I never had the courage to stand up to Junior. But those are my only grandchildren. They need to have a chance to turn out to be decent humans. We have to get them away.' Nothing I said would convince her to wait."

"Do the others know?"

Melanie had told Dolores before they left school. She'd talked to Claire before she came out, and Claire was going to be in touch with Sue Jane Goodman. "Nancy's probably already out at the ranch. She'll call when she gets back. If she succeeds in getting Holly to agree to walk away tomorrow, we have no choice but to be there to take her to the women's shelter in Lubbock, snowstorm or not."

The sound of Willa's pushing back her chair brought the dogs to their feet. She said, "I'm going to call Nancy this minute. I hope she hasn't left. Maybe I can convince her to wait." She left the room. Less than a minute later, she was back, shaking her head. "No answer. I left a message to please call one of us as soon as possible." She put her phone on the table. "If she's hell bent on doing this today, then we have to be ready to help. Do you agree?"

Melanie said, "Yes. As soon as we hear from her, we should get our plan in order." She turned to Robert and said, "I don't mean to be impolite, speaking as if you're not here. Mother, I think we should tell him."

Willa had intended to all along. She said to Melanie, "If you think so, certainly, tell him. Meanwhile, I'll start the beans." As she set the beans to soak, and cut two slices of bacon into small pieces, she listened to Melanie's summary of the situation. Robert listened without asking questions.

After slicing half an onion and removing the seeds from three jalapenos, Willa filled a large soup pot half full of water, and returned to her chair at the table. "While you two were talking, I was thinking. Earlier we'd intended to involve some other women. Now that Nancy's moved ahead, I believe we'd be better served to limit the group to no more than seven, the six who already have committed to help and, if we need, one more. Then, as soon as Nancy's back, we'll get organized without having to explain again to anyone else. We know the six of us are committed."

Melanie frowned a bit, then said, "That makes sense. I'll call Claire and then the others. Meet here?"

Robert spoke up. "I'll be happy to stay out of sight if you want to meet here. And I'm more than willing to help if you need me to."

Willa went to tend the chili and Melanie made a phone call. When she finished, she said, "Claire agrees. She'll have the others here as soon as we hear from Nancy."

Robert said, "I'm going to check the fuel levels in both our vehicles, just in case."

It was close to three when Nancy called. From Melanie's side of the conversation, Willa guessed Nancy had had a change of heart. When she ended the call, Melanie said, "Nancy sounded completely unhinged, talking so fast her words ran together. She was about to leave when snow began falling and she realized we were right. We need good weather and a solid plan. I'm going to get her and bring her back here."

Willa said, "I'll let Claire know to delay the others by thirty or forty minutes."

After Melanie left, Robert bundled himself in a heavy coat, hat, and muffler, and took the dogs out for a walk. The beans and chili simmered, wafting the aroma of chiles and onions to mingle with the scent of mesquite and piñon from the fireplace. Willa caught herself smiling as she added yet another fragrance to the atmosphere by starting a fresh pot of coffee. The place smelled like home.

Soon after the pot signaled the coffee was ready, Willa felt a rush of chilly air followed by Claire's voice. "I'm coming in."

Then she hurried into the kitchen, pulling off her heavy coat and scarf as she entered. "I wanted to tell you before the others are here." She sat and nodded yes when Willa raised the coffee pot. "J.D. told me this morning that his friend, the Cattle Association Ranger, had called and told him he'd heard from his friend in the ATF. The task force that's been investigating Justin Reese and his cronies are close to the point of being able to make arrests. He didn't have details, but said they felt sure they'd be able to make a case this time."

Willa said, "Did they have something to do with the vandalism at the Cowboy Church?"

Claire shrugged. "I don't know. That's all J.D. knew, but he did say he thought it was about time. Since the goat was stolen, he and Chris have seen people coming and going on that back road Justin built onto the ranch. They were concerned there might be more people out there than before. J.D. said he'd been having a hard time keeping himself from driving up there to investigate. The only thing that held him back was knowing about the task force."

A knock sounded at the front door, just as Robert and the dogs came in the back. He shushed the dogs and called them to follow him to his study. Claire said, "Don't mention what I told you to the others. J.D. doesn't want to get Marty Broadus in trouble."

Willa let Dolores and Sue Jane in, telling them to join Claire in the kitchen. "I'll be there in a second. I see Melanie and Nancy coming up the road."

Even though she doubted their plan would be flawless, being a part of this group of women working to help someone who needed a new start gave her a warm feeling and a surge of energy. Watching as the other two came up the walk, she noticed occasional snowflakes blowing in the gusts of frigid wind.

Floyd County Tribune
Thursday, February 19, 2015
Editorial
Silence Is Consent
by B.R. Connally, Editor

Recent incidents of vandalism in our county, both in Calverton and Jackson's Pond might have been overlooked by many. If you noticed, you might have said to a friend, "Kids. Someone needs to get them under control." After that first one, at a ranch outside Jackson's Pond, several businesses in Jackson's Pond, and more recently in Calverton, have been struck with paint smears on windows, broken glass, and various slogans, many of them threatening, painted on property or on signs posted on private property.

Most recently, a place of worship in our county has been the target of these misdeeds. The Sheriff has stepped up patrols in business areas and increased police presence during hours of darkness, when these crimes (call them what they are) have been perpetrated. And still, no suspects have been identified.

This newspaper's archives include reports from 1920 and 1921 telling of the killing of a man whose only crime was having been African-American. Although his death was ruled murder, and the reports of the trial found in county records indicate that three masked men were implicated by a fourth who found the body on his property, no one was found guilty.

We would like to think that sort of thing cannot happen in the 21st century. Unfortunately, that is not the case. The Southern Poverty Law Center, based in Alabama, now tracks the emergence of hate groups.

Their records for 2014 show one such group active in Amarillo and several as near as the Fort Worth area and other parts of the state. Are these crimes in our county the work of some group, calling itself Klan or some other name, hiding behind masks, and striking in darkness?

Such actions have no place in a civilized society, where diversity of race, ethnicity, religion, and sexual orientation are fact. There is no place for hate and intolerance directed toward individuals and groups based on their being other than the majority. Differences in personal opinion and preference are welcome in an open society; violence and intimidation based on those opinions are not.

It is incumbent on all of us to speak up, to voice our respect for the rights of all and to report intimidation and violence as well as what at first might seem simple vandalism. Silence can imply consent.

If one has remained silent due to intimidation, it's all the more reason to report the threats to law enforcement. Each of us must also report any attempts to recruit people to join groups spreading hate and violence.

We may not individually be able to keep all the church bombings, hate killings, and other acts of violence from happening throughout our country. But as citizens of Floyd County, we can surely join together to work with law enforcement to assure that they do not happen here. So far, all that's occurred has been property damage and intimidation. Let us each be aware and speak up to prevent its escalating into major violence.

CHAPTER 17
Shelter

After leaving her mother's, headed home, Melanie had just passed the ranch gate when she stopped and called Nancy. When she answered, Melanie said, "I'm on my way. Until I get there, you need to relax. You did the right thing. Are you at your parents' house?"

"Yes. Should I be somewhere else?"

"Stay there. I'm on the way."

"Maybe we . . ."

"Just relax. Sit down, take deep breaths. I just left Mother's. I'll be there in fifteen minutes. Sit still until I get there."

Melanie had visions of Nancy working herself into a high blood pressure crisis, having a stroke, or something worse. She pulled back onto the road and sped toward town. On the way in, she thought through the steps needed to complete a plan—drivers and vehicles, with full gas tanks; how to notify Holly; contact the women's shelter; contact Kay Henry to be available; safety for Nancy afterward; Sheriff notified after the rescue. Had she forgotten something? Someone had to be organized. She might as well be the one.

As she neared town, the snow flurries stopped and the sun made a brief appearance before the sky turned completely gray. The wind picked up, blowing the few collected snowflakes in swirls across the pavement. She turned in at the house where Nancy had grown up. Before Melanie could get her door open, Nancy hurried down the walk from the front door. Her lips were moving, but Melanie couldn't hear for the wind.

As Nancy opened the passenger door, a rush of cold air told Melanie that this storm's clouds might drop ice pellets instead of snow. One more reason Nancy's change of heart had been a stroke of good luck. Melanie said, "Do you have your purse and house key?"

Nancy nodded. She said, "If you think I need a keeper, you're probably right. I couldn't sleep last night, thinking about Holly and those children. I hope she'll file for divorce. I'm going to let her know she'll not have to worry about money to live on. The more I thought about going out there alone, and the weather, all that, well I just couldn't make myself start the car. I was sitting there, crying, saying to myself all the things Junior used to say about how useless I am."

Melanie reached across and squeezed her friend's hand. "That's something you'll have to work on, forgetting all those negative messages. You've been through a lot, and you still have much to do. We'll help."

"I know, but . . . you don't know how it is after trying to keep up appearances all those years. It's hard to change overnight."

"Living the truth won't be hard compared to that."

"I hope you're right." She took a deep breath. "What will the others think? Me changing my mind, all that?"

"They'll probably think the same thing I do—that you made a good decision to wait."

She parked behind the navy blue Suburban situated behind Claire's black one in Willa's drive. Anyone driving by might think there was a club meeting going on. But this house, three miles from the big ranch house, suited their purpose best— making plans without giving explanations—because it sat on a separate side road that ended a couple of miles north, just past the ranch office. No one drove by here on the way to somewhere else. She'd tell Ray after they'd accomplished the rescue. Her guess was the others would also wait until afterward to let their husbands know.

As they entered the family room where Claire, Dolores, Sue Jane, and Willa sat, Melanie noticed that Robert and the dogs were out of sight. Likely they'd gone next door to Chris and Andrew's. Claire barely gave them time to get their coats off before she began. "I hope it's okay with everyone if I'm a little pushy. We all have lots to do, so I made a list of the things we need to decide in order to have a final plan. Plus, we don't have time to waste if this snowstorm actually arrives." She handed a single sheet of paper to each of them. Melanie smiled when she saw that Claire's list was the same as hers, plus a couple of items she'd not thought of.

Dolores said, "Deciding on the date for the actual removal from the home is first on your list. But before that, I need to hear from Mrs. Reese about whether she believes this is still a good idea."

"Call me Nancy, everyone. The short answer is yes, I'm more convinced than ever. I know, without any evidence, that Justin and that gang are behind the cross burning at your church." She'd been looking at Mrs. Goodman as she spoke. "His wife wants to leave and we need to help her. Otherwise those children don't have a chance."

"I'm Sue Jane, Nancy. I want to help because I know Holly wants out."

After a couple of minutes of discussion, they agreed that Monday would be the day for their rescue. According to the weather service, snowfall would be primarily tonight and tomorrow. That would leave Saturday and Sunday to get word to Holly. Any residual snow should be either melted or plowed by Monday afternoon. That meant the pick up of Holly and the children would be at two-thirty p.m. Monday at the Reese Ranch mailbox, on the county road a quarter mile from the ranch house.

Nancy nodded and said, "No trespassing on the ranch. That's one less possible complaint. And that's safer for the people picking them up."

Claire moved the discussion to who would get word to Holly and how. Nancy said she wanted to go to the house, using gifts to the two children and packing up the last of her clothes as her excuse. She said, "If Justin's there, I'll make an excuse to get Holly outside, and help me load things."

Willa said, "Has he confronted you directly about the will? Even if he doesn't suspect there's anything else up, he's likely to use your being there as an excuse to try to intimidate you. We know he's physically attacked Holly. What's to prevent him from doing the same to you?"

"He never has before."

Melanie waited while the others kept silent. She felt her mother watching her. Sue Jane Goodman clasped her hands as if in prayer. Dolores studied the paper Claire had handed out. Finally, Melanie said, "The most important thing is getting Holly and the children out and to the shelter in Lubbock safely. I believe we should find another way to get that information to Holly. Does anyone else agree?"

As if they'd been holding their breath, Claire, Dolores, and Sue Jane all spoke at once, echoing, "Yes, we'll find another way."

Nancy slumped where she sat. Shaking her head, she said, "He's my son, my fault. I should be the one."

Willa said, "That's exactly why you shouldn't. And, Nancy, he's no one's fault. Blame has no place in this. We have a job to do."

After that, Claire said, "If everyone will bear with me, I think we should move on to the details of the actual rescue, then come back to how we'll notify Holly." Then hardly hesitating, she plunged in, getting everyone to discuss each small step in the process. They were listed on the sheet she'd handed out.

Pride in her daughter's ability wedged itself near the front of Melanie's thoughts. For once, she didn't find herself thinking she could do better than the person leading the group.

They worked steadily until they'd decided who would ride in what vehicle, the positions of the cars, what to do if there was any pursuit. They each had assignments and phone numbers and addresses for attorney Kay Henry and the shelter—each to be notified ahead of time. When there was a pause, Willa said, "Anyone need the restroom?"

Claire nodded. They all stood as if choreographed. All except Nancy. She sat still, smiling a sad smile. She said to Melanie, "No matter what happens, I am so thankful that you're still my friend."

Soon they had filed back into the room and set to work again. Only one more item had to be decided. Before Claire said a word, Sue Jane said, "I want to take the message to Holly. She reached out to me first. She trusts me. Justin's never met me, and I have no doubt he's behind the cross-burning at our church. Plus, I have four-wheel drive and snow tires."

"What excuse will you use to get inside?" Dolores asked. She'd been taking notes as each decision was made. "In my past experiences, notifying the abused person was always our most difficult job. We learned that having at least *two* plans—to get the same message delivered twice—was the best way. So even if Sue Jane gets a message to her, we also need to try to get a repeat to her."

Sue Jane said, "Nancy, you said you thought he was likely to be gone from the house after breakfast. I'll go at nine on Saturday morning. If Holly answers the door, I'll say she and the children are to meet us at the mailbox at two-thirty on Monday, that we'll take her to safety. I'll tell her if he asks who was there, she should say it was me delivering a message from our congregation inviting the family to church."

Nancy spoke up. "What if he's there, and he opens the door?"

"I'll invite him to church and deal with whatever hateful things he says by offering to pick up the children for Sunday school, and repeating that I came in peace."

Melanie said, "Are you prepared in case he becomes violent?"

"I've prayed about this ever since Holly called me. I'm confident it's the right thing to do. That makes me brave."

Willa said, "Brave is good. Just in case, some pepper spray in your purse would be a wise addition."

Sue Jane rolled her eyes and said, "I carry that with me everywhere I go. I grew up in Houston."

After more discussion, Claire, Dolores, and Melanie each were assigned to phone Holly on Saturday afternoon with the same message. Their final task, at Dolores's suggestion, was drawing a telephone circle. Each of them was assigned one person to report to, who would then report to her assigned person, and so on until the final person called the one who initiated the report. The circle closed with that last call.

After each one entered the name and number of her assigned call partner in her phone, Claire said, "Before we stop, before the snow starts falling, let's summarize by going over each item on the list."

Minutes later, as they gathered their coats, Melanie saw excitement in her daughter's eyes. Willa stood, relying on her walking stick, and wished them each a good evening as they returned to their cars. Leaving last, Melanie waited, listening while Nancy said to Willa, "I can't thank you enough. But I will try to find a way."

That night, and all day the next day, snow fell in lazy, intermittent showers. It was the light, dry sort of snow that blows with every gust and leaves little moisture behind. The temperature rose to forty around noon on Friday and the snow turned to misty rain; then as the temperature fell, snow began again. Saturday morning, a light frozen crust atop approximately four inches of snow covered the sidewalk in front of Melanie's house. Hardly the blizzard the television weatherman had speculated might arrive.

After stepping out into brilliant early morning sun on Saturday morning, Melanie felt one worry lessen. The weather seemed to be in their favor—the temperature already rising toward the upper twenties. By afternoon, the powder-dry snow should pose little problem for driving on Monday. After a breakfast of a boiled egg and dry toast, waiting to hear if Sue Jane had succeeded in delivering the message and made it home safely, she occupied herself by exercising on her elliptical trainer. She worked hard for thirty minutes, until ten o'clock, then took her phone with her when she went to shower. Ray was catching up on some work at the city office, and for once, she was glad. No need to explain what was occupying her mind. She wondered if he could smell worry. Somehow, he always knew.

Her hair dripping, she stepped from the shower to answer her phone. Caller I D showed Willa, Melanie's "notifier" in their phone circle. Her mother said, "I don't know how she accomplished it, but Sue Jane succeeded in talking to Holly on the front porch. According to Claire, Sue Jane said Holly had a bruise on the side of her face and that the little boy held onto her skirt the whole time they were talking. Holly understood we'll be there on Monday at two-thirty and that she's to bring nothing but her purse and the children."

"Amazing. Justin must have been gone from the house. So far, so good. I'll call Nancy now to tell her, and remind her to call Sue Jane to close the circle."

Near four o'clock, as planned, Melanie called Holly's number. After ten unanswered rings, she hung up. She immediately called Claire and was relieved to hear that Claire had spoken to her, briefly, and repeated the instructions and that Holly had said, "You must have the wrong number. There's no one here by that name. No, I understand all that, but no one named Mendoza lives here." A child had been crying in the background.

That night, Melanie dreamed all the steps in their plan. She woke twice, frustrated each time by the ending, which was fuzzy and out of focus, not as clear and sharp as the parts where a woman and two small children, one carrying a backpack, hurried up the road toward a waiting Suburban.

Sunday, because she was tempted to pace, she arranged her clothes for school on Monday morning and loaded her briefcase with a new lesson plan for that day, plus two cans of soup and a package of saltine crackers for the break room pantry. Then, to keep from wearing a track in the carpet or spilling out the plans to Ray, she took a nap. Two hours later, she woke, calm for the first time in three days. She invented a headache as an excuse to go to bed early. A twinge of guilt about hiding her activities from Ray assaulted her. She promised herself she'd tell the whole tale tomorrow evening, without fail. He'd forgive her.

School on Monday went smoothly from their morning opening to waving goodbye to the last child leaving at noon. She and Dolores ate the lunches they'd brought and focused on school, talking about the children's progress in reading readiness. Then, clearing their dishes, they reviewed their plan. At Willa's suggestion, the group had included having Robert wait in Willa's pickup near the county road as lookout, prepared to call the sheriff's office in case anyone followed them. He'd be an extra measure of safety. And they'd agreed that an all-female presence at the actual rescue could likely reduce any sense of threat if any of the men at Reese Ranch happened to see them. Without saying it, Melanie thought it insured Willa would have Robert to drive on the way home. She'd noticed Willa's slowed gait and reliance on her walking stick on Thursday afternoon.

Dolores and Melanie, in Melanie's car, picked up Nancy and drove to the pond to meet the others. Seconds later, Sue Jane arrived, followed by Claire, driving Robert's Range Rover. Robert and Willa arrived last, in her pickup. The time, according to Melanie's phone, was one-twelve, right on schedule. Sue Jane made a weak effort at a smile. Claire, ever the one to encourage others, made the rounds, patting each person on the back and whispering, "We're doing a good thing. We'll be fine."

They took their assigned positions in the vehicles. Sue Jane would drive her Suburban, accompanied by Nancy, who could help comfort her grandchildren, and Dolores, a veteran at rescuing abused women. Holly and the children would ride with them. Claire, driving Robert's vehicle, which was unlikely to be familiar to Justin, should he see it, would precede Sue Jane. Claire was to drive past the Reese Ranch and, after one mile, make a U-turn and park, idling. Willa and Melanie rode with Claire. They would notify Dolores by phone whether there was any sign of Justin or others near the house or mailbox. If not, Sue Jane would drive past it a half mile, then turn and go back rapidly to the mailbox.

Just as Claire started the Range Rover, J. D. parked his pickup at the end of the dirt road to the pond. He and Tag got out, then both ambled toward the group assembled for the rescue effort. Melanie heard him say, "Somebody call a meeting out here?"

Claire waved him to the driver's side. She opened the window but didn't turn off the engine. She said, "I'll explain when we get back. It'll be near dark." As Claire and J.D. continued talking, softly, Melanie saw Tag checking out the occupants of the other two vehicles. He nodded to her when he caught her eye. J.D., speaking loudly enough that Melanie heard, said, "You have no idea what you could be getting into. None of you do. I'm telling you, leave this to the law. And turn. . ."

Claire interrupted. In a clear, strong voice, she said, "I don't have time to argue. I'm going. We're all going. Now."

Claire's window rolled up. Melanie didn't say a word and neither did Willa.

J.D. rapped his knuckles on the window, and Claire rolled it down halfway. He said, "Okay, but . . . please call me from Calverton. I need to know you're safe. Don't forget." Then he leaned in the window and kissed Claire. He said, "Stay safe."

He and Tag moved faster getting back to their pickup. As soon as they left, Claire drove from the pond to the county road, then turned right, away from their ranch. The others would follow at five-minute intervals. The slushy condition of the county roads would make it slow going. Claire said, "Mother, please call Dolores and tell her I'm going to drive thirty-five on the county roads and fifty on the highway. Sue Jane should do the same. Okay, buckle up. Here we go."

To calm herself after making the call, Melanie calculated the time it would take to position Sue Jane at the Reese gate. The bulk of the Reese ranch lay north of theirs, but since no county road passed directly through either property, their route was first south two miles on County Road 12 to State Highway 53. Then west for two miles, then north on County Road 13 four miles, then east two miles to the mailbox at the driveway to the Reese ranch house, a quarter mile away. She estimated seventeen minutes according to Claire's plan. Then she repeated the calculation. They were leaving too early. It was only one forty-five now.

She said, "We're ahead of schedule."

Claire said, "I'm leaving some slack. It'll be okay."

Willa nodded. Melanie took a deep breath and watched her daughter's profile. Nothing hinted she was anything but perfectly calm.

When they turned off the state highway onto CR 13, Claire said, "We're going to need that slack." The gravel road,

usually a tight two-lane, had been cleared in the center, only
the width of one vehicle. Low drifts humped along the sides,
and spots in the deep ditches beyond held foot-high clumps
in some places. "It must have snowed more through here."

It was two-twenty when they passed the Reese's
mailbox. The last two miles hadn't been plowed at all and now
it was thick, muddy slush. Melanie gritted her teeth to keep
from speaking as Claire proceeded ahead, according to plan.
Willa, equipped with binoculars, pronounced the coast clear.
No Justin in sight. Melanie's chest tightened as she called
Dolores with that message.

The Range Rover held tight to the road and didn't slide
an inch as Claire made the turn back toward the rescue site.
Sitting, waiting to hear that Sue Jane and the others had Holly
and the children on board, seemed eternal. Then Melanie's
phone rang. Dolores said, "Mother and children on board.
Took a bit getting situated. See you in Calverton."

They waited another five minutes and then retraced
their earlier route, easier this time since they'd made tracks.
But they were tracks that Justin could follow if he chose to.
At the point where the road turned south heading to the state
highway, they passed Robert, who waved and joined the
parade following behind. Willa said, "Claire, you are an
excellent driver."

In the rearview mirror, Melanie saw Claire's smile as
she said, "Gran, I've never forgotten the lessons you gave me
on how to drive in rain and snow."

For a second, Melanie wished she'd been the person
Claire would have trusted to teach her when she was fifteen.

They passed the time silently the rest of the way to
Calverton. Melanie relaxed slightly when they pulled into the
school parking lot and saw Sue Jane's vehicle. They would
trade vehicles there. She, Claire, and Nancy would go to
Lubbock with Holly and the children, in the Range Rover,
with Claire driving. Sue Jane and Dolores would return to
Jackson's Pond. Willa and Robert would go back to the ranch
and wait for word that the rescue was completed.

When Nancy, Holly and the children got in, Melanie could see that something was wrong. Claire said, "Does he often wheeze like that?" She pointed to the older of the two children, the little boy who'd briefly attended Banks Preschool.

Holly said, "He wouldn't leave the kitten behind. The wheezing started when he began crying. I just gave up and let him bring it."

As if on cue, a weak meow came from the backpack on the wheezing child's lap. Melanie said, "Troy, can I see your kitten? I like cats a lot."

He smiled through the tears that had made dirty streaks down his face. She wondered why Holly hadn't dressed him more warmly. And his little sister, who looked to be between two and three, wore only a pair of overalls and a sweatshirt, no coat, hat, or gloves. Looking at Holly, she realized she could barely care for herself, given the black eye and bruises that showed on her face. No wonder the children were in this condition.

Troy said, "He's my friend."

"I'd like to see him. He sounds sad." He lifted the flap on his backpack and a tiny black and white kitten poked his head out. The little boy gently patted him. "His name is Spike."

"Sounds strong. I'll bet you're strong, too."

The youngster focused on petting the kitten.

Holly said, "I know we shouldn't have brought him, but I didn't know what to do."

Claire asked if Troy took medicine for his wheezing. Holly shook her head. "He never did wheeze until last year, when we moved out here. Justin said he just did it to get attention and he'd outgrow it or wish he had."

Melanie could tell Claire wanted to ask more, but didn't. She watched as Claire sent a text message, likely to J.D., and then started the motor. The road to Lubbock was nearly free of moisture. They made the thirty miles in close to thirty minutes. As they entered the Lubbock city limits, Melanie called Kay Henry and the shelter. Both had expected her call. The lawyer would meet them at the shelter.

When they arrived at the site, which was located in an area that combined small businesses with rental houses and apartments, a woman stood inside the locked gate. Melanie got out, identified herself to the shelter director, and asked what the next steps were.

The woman led the six of them inside to an office on the first floor of what had once been an apartment complex, decent, but definitely not fancy. The director asked if they'd been followed and if the husband knew where his wife and children were. When Holly didn't answer, Nancy said, "Holly, she needs to know, so she can help."

Holly faced the woman and said, "I left a note saying I was going back to my parents' house in Mineola and not to try to get me to come back. I thought that might throw him off my trail."

"It could help," the director said, "but there are other measures we can take to see that you aren't abused again." She then said that Holly should give her the cell phone to disable. "It's possible to trace a person's location from the phone, so we'll give you a different one. You can keep it until you relocate. Then return it to us."

Holly, who must have been accustomed to following directions, handed her phone over without a question. Before saying any more, the director opened the phone and lifted out the battery, then released a fingernail-sized card from a slot inside.

After handing Holly a different, older-model phone and a list of the rules for the shelter, she said, "Please read through those and keep them to refer to."

Troy, his backpack over one shoulder, stood close to his mother, holding onto her arm. The little girl sat on her lap. Looking at the sad little group made Melanie thankful for her own grandchildren. She looked at Nancy, who somehow appeared composed. Nancy had been the one who decided she would stay in Lubbock to be near the children and Holly until they got settled. And she'd also thought of leaving her Jeep in Jackson's Pond. If Justin attempted to find her, he'd think she was still in town. After all these years, resourcefulness and courage seemed to be blossoming in her friend. She watched as Nancy took her cell phone from her purse and turned it off. She whispered to Melanie, "Just for safety's sake. Tomorrow I'll get a new one and let you know the number."

Claire, who'd stayed outside to wait for Kay Henry, came in just as the director started discussing the house rules, which she emphasized were for safety for everyone living there. Claire leaned down between Melanie and Nancy and spoke in a soft voice. "Ms. Henry's outside. I told her about the black eye and bruises. She said she'll take Holly to file a complaint. They'll photograph the injuries."

As the director finished going over the rules, Troy let go of his mother's arm. Since they'd been inside the shelter office, his wheezing had stopped. He said to the director, "Please, Miss, can my kitty stay with us? He's my friend."

Before the woman could answer, Nancy surprised Melanie again. She said, "I'm going to be staying here in town for a while. If it's possible for the kitten to stay with him tonight, then Troy and I can decide if he and the kitten want to come and stay with me for a little vacation. Or maybe he'll just send the kitten to stay with me." The child had listened intently. Nancy said, "Would that be all right with everyone?"

The kitten meowed; Troy frowned. "I guess. But my mommy needs me."

The director said, "Just for tonight. Only." She reached behind her into a toy box and retrieved two large stuffed toys, a rabbit and a lion. "Because you're our new guests, I have something for you and your sister. It's easier to sleep if you have a friend. And you can talk to them." She held the toys near the children. She said, "Troy, you can choose first, since you're the oldest."

He chose the lion. His sister latched onto the rabbit, clutching it like a life preserver, one of its fluffy ears under each of her arms.

Claire beckoned the attorney inside. Holly agreed to file a complaint and request a restraining order against Justin. She said, "When I get a job and some money, I want to file for divorce."

Nancy said, "Don't worry about the money. You and the children will be taken care of."

The director suggested they get settled in their rooms while Ms. Henry contacted the police. Nancy said that if Claire and Melanie would take her to the airport to get the rental car she'd reserved, then they could get home by dark. "I have a room reserved for a week at a hotel near here. Don't laugh, but it's in my maiden name, and I'm paying cash so I'll be harder to find. Tomorrow I'll go shopping and get them some clothes."

On the way home, Melanie remembered that no one had called the sheriff to tell him, in case Justin should report his wife missing. The response she got when she called surprised her. The call was transferred directly to the sheriff. He said they'd done a good thing and that since Holly was filing an abuse complaint in Lubbock, he'd be able to fend off any pressure from Justin to have the County Sheriff's Department help him find his wife.

By six-thirty, Melanie was home explaining to Ray where she'd been and why she hadn't told him. He said, "I doubt this will be the end of it. But I'm glad that that woman and those children are out of there." He patted the seat next to him on the sofa and she sat close to him, leaning against his chest. He said, "I would have worried about you if I'd known, even though I trust your judgment. It's usually better than mine."

As they were getting ready for bed, Claire called. She said, "I'm glad we did that today. I know Nancy is convinced now that she has friends she can rely on. I called to let you know that J.D. heard today from Marty Broadus some things that may explain why Holly was able to get away. He didn't have details, but said to keep an eye out because Justin and his crew are likely to be desperate before long. The federal officers are building their case and beginning to close in on them. You should keep the doors at school locked and your car in the garage. Have Dad drive you to work. We're taking extra precautions out here, too."

When Melanie told Ray, he said, "It can't be too soon to suit me. We have too much good to accomplish here in town to have the kind of trouble he stirs up." He put his shirt back on. "I'm going to go check all the outside lights and locks."

She rested well that night, her only dream one that included a frail-looking four-year-old petting a black and white kitten named Spike.

Floyd County Tribune
Thursday, March 19, 2015

RBJ Data Solutions Workforce Increase

According to a press release from company headquarters, the Jackson's Pond site of RBJ Data Solutions workforce will increase by fifty employees on April 1, bringing the total to eighty. Although eighteen of the new employees already live in the area, the rest are moving from locations as far as India and as near as Austin and Dallas. Company officials estimate there is an immediate need for permanent housing for thirty families.

RBJ has arranged for temporary dwellings, mobile homes, to be set up on company property near the worksite and will leave those in place for an undetermined number of months.

The release states, "Clearly, the most desirable solution would be for existing and new housing to be made ready as quickly as possible so that those new to the area would be able to choose whether to rent or buy, and where they wish to locate. But until other housing is ready, RBJ will provide reduced cost access to company owned housing."

Vandalism Reports in the Area

Local law enforcement officers were busy this past weekend with reports of vandalism. There were two reports in Jackson's Pond of broken windows, one at Banks Preschool and another at the RBJ Data Solutions offices' Welcome Center and Employment Office. In both of those cases, bricks had been thrown through windows. County Sheriff's deputies are analyzing the fingerprints data and other evidence recovered.

In and near Calverton, two churches reported their outdoor signs had been defaced and then chopped down. The Cowboy Congregation, site of a cross burning recently, made one of those reports. The other was from the pastor of the Bethel Temple, a predominantly African American congregation in Calverton. Calverton city police and county sheriff's officers responded to the Sunday morning reports and concluded that the property damage had occurred in the early morning hours.

Motley County sheriff's personnel reported similar damage to three businesses in Matador, and one church, a Spanish-speaking Baptist congregation. A spokesperson for the sheriff's office stated, "We've been cooperating with nearby officers in other jurisdictions and conclude that these attacks on property likely all took place simultaneously late Saturday night and early Sunday morning."

When asked if the incidents were being viewed as racially motivated, the spokesperson said, "Based on the things that were painted on the churches, that's our conclusion. We're pursuing all leads. This hurts everyone."

After-School Arts Program a Possibility

Several Jackson's Pond citizens are assessing interest in and need for an after-school arts program. A meeting will be held March 25 at 7 p.m. at the Jackson's Pond Saint Anne's Catholic Church fellowship hall. All interested persons are invited.

For further information prior to the meeting, contact Marisol Quintero or Claire Havlicek. Leave a message at the Jackson's Pond city office with your contact information and one of them will call you.

CHAPTER 18
Spring Break

Claire's excuse for the party was the fact that Spring Break for the schools would begin with dismissal at the end of school that day. Everyone she invited would surely enjoy an opportunity for some fun. The past few months had been full of unusual activity, some positive, some threatening. Good food and pleasant company could be just what they all needed. At least that was the explanation she'd given J.D. when she'd told him. He'd agreed.

So here she was at two-thirty with all the food preparation completed, waiting for the other women in what she'd come to think of as "our gang" to arrive. Sue Jane Goodman had been there since just after noon when she finished her day's volunteer job at the city office. Together they'd assembled all the food and set up tables in the upstairs room that years ago had been the scene of Claire's great-grandmother Jackson's fancy parties. Although the room now served as a dance studio for Amy and Elisa, all it took to turn it festive was some crepe paper streamers and a banner saying "Spring Break!!" They had set up three long tables and chairs, enough to accommodate the twenty or so that had been invited. Seven of that number were children who'd likely not care to sit with the grownups, so one table had a RESERVED, NO ADULTS ALLOWED sign decorating its center, balloons and streamers taped to each table corner.

Sue Jane straightened the checkered gingham table cloth on a fourth table they'd set up near the door from the stairs. It would serve as the buffet table. She said, "I hope the weather holds. It's been so nice the past three days. My boys want to see Jay Frank's goat pens."

"With luck, it'll stay warm enough for them to play outside for an hour at least after they get here from school," Claire said. She stood against the mirrored wall, arm resting on the barre she'd used when Gran had taught her basic ballet. Now that she didn't have the clinic demanding her attention every day, she often spent a morning hour here working through the same exercises that Willa had Amy and Elisa perform as the first part of their twice-weekly lessons. At first, her hours in the ballroom alone had been something to replace the excitement of her days in clinic. Now they'd become an important part of allowing herself to become more than who she'd been.

She said, "I hope everyone enjoys themselves this evening." Even if her wish came true, she knew that the past few months' tensions weren't likely to disappear because of one party, especially since the additional vandalism this past weekend.

Sue Jane said, "I know Heath and I will. It's the first time in months we've been to anything not church related. He'll appreciate the chance to relax without having to be in charge."

Claire waited, thinking her friend might need to talk more about the attack on their congregation's church and sign. But Claire saw her studying the paned-glass doors opening from the side rooms to the ballroom. Sue Jane said, "This must have been a grand place."

Claire told her about the dumbwaiter that had been closed off and recounted the story Gran had told about the first party held in the ballroom, back when she was a girl. "Granddad Frank's high school graduation party apparently made quite the big splash. Gran had worked that evening as part of the serving help. She said she'd wanted so badly to be able to dance with him that night, but that his mother, my great-grandmother, would have never allowed it."

Sue Jane looked at her phone. "What time do you expect your mother and Dolores? It was so nice of them to volunteer to bring my boys from the elementary. Saves me a trip."

Claire said, "About three-fifteen. The other kids will all be on the bus from Calverton. The Montoyas usually pick up their children at the bus stop in Jackson's Pond, but today they'll all get off here. Since we're at the end of the route, it will be close to four. Your boys will get first chance at testing the cookies and fruit we set up to keep children from starving." She cocked her head toward the stairs. "I'm ready to sit for a little while. I think everything's ready."

A few minutes later, the downstairs living room held five women, and at least three separate conversations competed for attention. The Goodman boys had been perfectly mannered six- and eight-year-olds, working their way through the snacks, then clearing their plates and thanking Claire. But as soon as their mother told them they could go play on the porch until the others arrived, they raced out the door and began a game of "catch me if you can" that extended far from the porch into the front yard.

When Claire returned from the kitchen, where she'd set out snacks for the next wave of sure to be hungry youngsters, she sat in the chair next to her grandmother. Willa said, "We need to get together soon and make plans for the wedding. Your mother, too."

Just then, Melanie stood. For seconds, the conversations halted in mid-air. She said, "I don't want to stop the fun, but there's something important everyone needs to hear at once."

Claire whispered to Gran, "Just tell me when you're ready to meet." Then she turned her full attention to her mother, who now sat again, in the center of the sofa, Dolores on one side and Sue Jane on the other.

Melanie said, "Nancy called just before we came out. She's sorry she won't be here today. But she did tell me that Holly has filed for divorce. She's leaving Lubbock tomorrow to move to Brady. She has a cousin there with a husband and two children. Justin hasn't ever met them, so she believes he won't find her three hundred miles from here. Nancy asked that I check on her house and vehicle to see they haven't been tampered with."

Willa asked, "How did she sound?"

"Still strong. Wanted me to thank everyone again. And she said she's going with Holly and the kids. She bought a used car for Holly, and said she'll let us know to pick her up at the airport when she's ready to come back. It will be a couple of weeks, at least. She plans to take us all to dinner. Her words were, "It's the least I can do.""

Sue Jane said, "I hope the children recover from all this without any major scars. Living in domestic violence had to be hard for them, even if they weren't ever physically harmed."

They all went silent for a moment. Then Claire said, "J.D. was proud of us for helping her. I think he actually was glad I hadn't told him ahead of time, though. By the time he knew, it was too late to stop."

"David got very quiet when I told him. Then he said, 'I'd hoped you could leave that behind when we left the military.'" Dolores shook her head before she spoke again. "He remembers the sad stories of those women that I'd told him." After a pause, she said, "I told him I would never stop as long there are children at risk or women who need the help."

Claire said, "If no one minds, I have something on a different subject… and it's good news. You probably saw the notice in the paper yesterday about seeking interest in the after-school program. I already have had conversations with two parents who are coming to the meeting. They seemed very eager."

That started a more detailed discussion about the status of information on building renovation, Marisol's agreeing to head the initial phases of the program, Claire's mention that Marisol would join them for supper later, and Gran reporting on Amy and Elisa's audition with the ballet teacher in Lubbock. "She told them they were far past the entry level for the corps de ballet, and that they would fit in the advanced class. I have to admit I felt a bit of pride in that."

They all stopped talking when J.D. came through the front door. He said, "I didn't mean to stop the conversation, but my wife told me I had to clean up before the party." He started down the hall toward the bedrooms, then returned. "One more thing. My friend the ranger called just a few minutes ago. His information, and this is all off the record, is that there's been a lot of additional activity up on the northeast part of the Reese place. The law enforcement people who're watching say there are at least ten vehicles there most of the time, coming and going on that road they built in from the east. They believe they're planning something. I'm telling you so you can let your families know to be alert."

Sue Jane asked, "Did he know anything about the attacks on churches?"

J.D. said, "That's all he said. He always reminds me he's not officially a part of the investigations, and that he'd stop getting any information if the feds find out that he's telling people." Then he shrugged and headed toward the bedrooms. About two steps farther, he turned again and beckoned Claire. When she got close, he said, "I'll pick up the kids from the bus at the gate, so you don't have to leave." She nodded. He said, "This time I mean it. I really am going to shower." And he disappeared into their bedroom.

When she returned to the living room, the others were talking about the latest attack on the Cowboy Congregation's meeting place. She heard Dolores ask if there were people of color in the congregation, or if something in their doctrine might be the target. "For example, do you welcome gay and lesbian churchgoers?"

Sue Jane said, "We've talked as a group, all of us who attend there, about why our church has been targeted. It's easy to see the predominantly African American church in Calverton as being a typical target. Our church is diverse. Everyone is welcome, cowboy or not. That could be the reason we've been targeted. We're not affiliated with any specific denomination. We only expect that those who attend want to learn about the life of Jesus and what it can teach us for living in today's world."

Listening to Sue Jane, watching her intense, yet calm, eyes, the way she exuded kindness, Claire concluded her new friend had chosen the perfect role in life. She fit the part of pastor's wife to a tee.

Sue Jane said, "I could see how someone in a white supremacy group would see our diversity as a threat. For example, some of the people who recently began attending came from a similar congregation in the Dallas area, people who work at RBJ. I don't know what ethnicity or nationality they are, but I would say they are people of color. And two same-sex couples attend. They come out from Plainview, and have since we began." She shrugged. "Heath's working on a lesson for next Sunday, looking for ways that the Lord's example might help us as a congregation deal with the threat."

Willa said, "Have the attacks affected attendance?"

"Actually, it's increased. Ordinarily between thirty and forty attend, not always the same people. We meet regularly only once a week, a morning-long meeting, singing, Bible reading, and a lesson brought by Heath, followed by lunch and fellowship. Now and then there's a Wednesday night song service. Last Sunday there were fifty-two, and after lunch, everyone stayed to work on repairing the damage to our building and the sign. Afterward, we all held hands and promised to be strong and to care for one another."

Claire didn't say anything, but she decided right then that it might be time for her family to attend church, and that the Cowboy Congregation might be the one for them.

J.D. walked through the living room on the way out the front door. He stopped and said, "I'm going to pick up the kids. Is there anything we need to do while we're out?"

Claire followed him to the porch and kissed him goodbye. "Everything's ready. See you soon."

The rest would arrive around six-thirty. Marisol; Tag Burley, his wife and two nearly grown, large-appetite sons; David Montoya; Robert; Chris; Andrew; and the vet Andrew worked for, along with his wife. It would be a full house. Until moments ago, Claire had been relaxed and happy. Now, as J. D.'s pickup went out of sight, the fine hairs on her arms rose and she shivered. Maybe another cool front was on the way.

In the living room, talk and smiles among her friends and family there told her everything was fine. She passed behind the sofa and walked toward her bedroom. Gran called after her. "Claire, are you okay?"

"Just chilled. I'm getting a sweater." She moved slowly, letting her family and friends enjoy their visiting as she searched for her yellow sweater. Then, as she entered the living room, her phone rang.

J.D.'s voice sounded strangled and far away. Claire heard the words he said but held the phone away from her ear, staring at the screen. "They've taken our kids!"

Why would he say that, sound that way?

Her mother, standing next to her, said, "Claire, answer him! I heard what he said."

Claire couldn't breathe or speak. Melanie grabbed the phone. She said, "J.D., what happened, where are you?"

Claire pulled the phone from her mother's hand. She said, "Tell me."

"The sheriff's on the way," J.D. said. "I'm at the bus. The driver's hysterical, said she got here early. Three men boarded the bus and put a hood over her head, tied her up, and took the kids. I'm going after them."

As soon as his voice disappeared, she said, "Someone's taken our children." It was her strong, nurse-in-an-emergency voice that spoke. Determined not to cry, she said to the people with her, "Deputies are on the way. J.D.'s searching. We need to stay here and be calm. Dolores, call David. He'll know what to do. Tell him the bus is at our gate."

Everyone in the room seemed to speak at the same time. She couldn't understand a word as she stared at the mute phone in her hand. She watched her mother open her purse, lift her phone, put it to her ear. Claire saw her speak, her face stiffened into a frowning, fearful mask. Gran came toward her, hands out, reaching to hold her. It happened like a slow-motion sequence in a movie she'd never choose to watch.

Chris and Tag and one of his boys came in the front door, spoke to her mother, then left, engine sounds promising they'd gone to help. But Claire could only observe from a distance as the other women in her living room moved toward the front door, as if that could draw the children back. She heard them all talking.

Not a word made sense. She stood useless, huddled in her grandmother's arms.

How much time passed, she couldn't say. Maybe it was minutes. No, it had to be hours because sometime, Gran still holding her, they sat near the front windows, watching the sky change as the sun arced neared the horizon.

Then people poured in the front door. J.D. walked toward her and when he held her, he whispered, "We have the boys. They're safe."

Then she gathered her strength and they joined the others. Jay Frank and the two Montoya brothers followed J.D. in. They, and all the waiting women, men in uniform, other men wearing dark windbreakers with alphabets of acronyms in bright yellow across their backs, and a woman, the bus driver Jay Frank called Miss No Horseplay, moved in a mass toward the center of the living room.

For no reason she understood, she counted—the three boys, a woman, four men. She heard herself saying, "Please, bring eight more chairs from the dining room. Everyone sit down."

People moved, still in slow-motion, following her instructions. All but one sat; a man wearing a Homeland Security windbreaker remained standing. He said, "County deputies and a state trooper did an excellent job of finding these children and the driver. We've agreed on which of us will collect physical evidence and how we'll share the reports of the agencies involved. Mr. Havlicek offered your place for us to debrief the witnesses, which we have to do one by one. It'll take a while. Others who aren't involved directly can leave if you want."

No one moved.

Dolores said, "Our girls. Where are Elisa and Amy?" Before an answer came, she wailed and began sobbing. "Where is David?"

J.D. said "He and other state troopers are searching."

Jay Frank, who'd been silent since coming in the door, said, "Those men threw us out and left with Amy and Elisa. We tried to stop them. But . . ."

J.D., standing next to Claire, said, "I'll have to give a statement. Tell everyone I'll come upstairs and tell what happened as soon as I'm finished."

Claire stood near Dolores, her arm around her. She wanted to offer her hope, but no words came. As they huddled together, the three boys gathered near, Claire heard Sue Jane say to Melanie, "Heath will be here soon. I hope they'll let him in."

As if they'd agreed to, she, Dolores and the boys followed Sue Jane and Melanie to the kitchen. The clock there showed six twenty-five. Claire paced as she watched her mother and Sue Jane place sandwiches on trays.

Wondering why they would try to rescue this day and turn it into a party, Claire realized that others had been invited, and it was too late to call them off. As Sue Jane started toward the staircase, Claire went to the kitchen door and beckoned a deputy who seemed to be in charge of standing near the front door. She told him the names of the others who were expected. He shrugged and said, "I'll send them upstairs. Everyone in town's going to know before morning anyway."

To keep from wandering or breaking into tears, she went up to the ballroom with everyone else. The three extra law enforcement people stood together near the top of the stairs. Her mother, Gran, Sue Jane and her two boys, and Dolores had pulled chairs into a tight circle near one of the tables, which stood full of food and ignored. Claire skirted the edges of the room, a sleepwalker searching for a way out of a dream. Finally, she sat in a chair near one of the balcony windows.

The three boys' statements were taken first, then the bus driver. When they came upstairs one at a time, silence greeted each of them, then when they were all there, a chorus of, "We were so worried—You must have been frightened—So brave," gave way to their telling what happened.

It unfolded in bits. Or that's the way Claire heard it, alternately listening and not believing. Thinking she should do something more for Jay Frank, who sat huddled in a chair next to her. Telling herself she should be a better hostess. Knowing she should be a better wife and mother.

She heard snatches of the stories, as if she'd gone deaf in first one ear, then the other. Someone said a panel van—old, dull green, with Chevrolet on the front, two doors on back, and no windows, followed the bus all the way from the county road. Jay Frank noticed and took pictures of it with his phone. "When those men in masks got on the bus, I hid my phone in my backpack, and left it on the back seat. Mom, will the sheriff give me my phone back? He said it was evidence."

She didn't have an answer. All she could do was wrap her arms around him and hold him close.

The driver had stopped at their gate. Thinking ahead to what she'd cook for supper, she hadn't noticed the men get out of the van. Three of them banged on the door. They aimed guns at her and yelled to open the door. When she did, two jumped in, wearing white hoods with eyeholes. They threw a burlap bag over her head. She said, "I thought I'd smother. They cuffed my hands with plastic ties. Couldn't breathe." She looked toward Claire and Dolores. "Please believe me. There was nothing I could do."

One of the Montoya boys spoke for the first time since coming upstairs. He said, "They pushed us all in the back, and we fell on top of each other. All three had on dirty lace-up boots and green jackets, like the army."

Jay Frank said, "That's right. They drove off, but pretty soon, they stopped and pushed us out again. We didn't know where we were. With those hoods and our hands tied, we couldn't do anything but stay there and yell. And then they drove off fast with Amy and Elisa still in the back."

Jay Frank edged up next to her again. He said, "Mom, how did the trooper find us so soon?"

She didn't have any answer for him. She wondered too, how the trooper knew so quickly. When J.D. finished his statement and came upstairs, she had her answer. As soon as the men got on the bus, Amy had dialed the sheriff's office, her emergency contact number. Then she'd called J.D. He got there first. "I got the hood and wrist ties off the bus driver, then drove on hoping to catch the van. The trooper heard the message on the sheriff's frequency. He was just outside of town on the county road. So, he came immediately."

None of it made sense to Claire. But she didn't have the will to ask questions. It took all her strength to hold onto Jay Frank and J.D. And to hold fast to hope that Amy and Elisa would be found safe, soon.

The ballroom filled up as the others arrived at what they'd expected to be a party. People retold the story, and she watched and listened as if from a great distance. Jay Frank and J.D. stayed near her. One of the windbreaker-wearing lawmen, Homeland Security, eased over to them. He said to J.D., "There's likely to be more. This was intended as a distraction. Our other people see something going on, lots of movement near the bunker. FBI and state troopers are following up with the hunt for the van and the two girls. We've issued an Amber Alert. They'll get word to you as soon as there's anything to report. We're leaving, except for the sheriff's people. Keep your eyes open."

J.D. nodded and cut a glance toward her. He said to the lawman, "Should we send everyone home?"

"No rush. The deputies'll stay till people leave. They'll follow them out, staying behind them to the edge of town."

The Goodmans were the first to leave. Their young boys had both stretched out on jackets in the side room, worn out from their game of tag and all the other excitement. Their goodbyes signaled the others to do the same. Dolores and David Montoya left last, each holding onto one of their boys. David promised to call if he received any word from his law enforcement friends. Dolores said, "I will be awake, praying, until they are home."

Claire nodded, but could only cling to her friend as they hugged goodbye, wishing words could bring their daughters back, wondering if there was some right thing to say.

Shortly after, Melanie and Ray; Willa and Robert; Chris and Andrew; Tag Burley, whose wife and boys had gone home;

and the three Havliceks sat together in the living room. J. D. repeated the message from the Homeland Security man. "I'm going to call my friend who knows one of the Federal guys. We need to stay together tonight if that bunch up at Reese's had something to do with grabbing the kids."

J. D. went toward the kitchen to make his call. Willa said, "Robert and I have the dogs to tend to. We'll get them and come back."

Ray said, "If we're needed here on the ranch, we can stay."

J. D. came back holding a six-pack of beer, handed it around. He, Chris, Andrew, and Tag ended up with one each. J.D. said, "I talked to Broadus. He thinks it would be a good idea to move our cattle off the north pasture and the east, if we can do that right away. Just in case. He said there was some speculation, no firm evidence, that crew might be planning something to do with the wind turbines on our place."

Chris said, "Let's get on with it."

Claire stood at the front door watching as they drove away.

Soon Robert and Willa left, and then returned with the dogs. Gran kissed Jay Frank and said goodnight and went to the guest bedroom. Robert followed, but only after hugging his new great-grandson and telling him how brave he was.

Melanie and Ray volunteered to sleep on the couch in the family room, but Claire told them to take Jay Frank's room. Jay Frank would sleep with her and J.D.

Jay Frank said, "Yeah, and the dogs, too. Mom, I can't go to sleep yet."

Claire found she could speak again. Her son needed her to. She said, "You can help your grandmother and me clear away upstairs."

Upstairs, Jay Frank tracked her step for step as they disposed of food scraps and crepe paper.

Melanie said, "I wish I didn't know they were going out there to move the cattle in the dark."

"It's not the dark I worry about. The cattle will go where they push them without much trouble. They'll probably put out some hay where they want them to go. I just hate not knowing who grabbed the kids and why, and whether they're part of that Klan group, or whatever they call themselves. Most of all I hate that Amy and Elisa are out there."

Jay Frank said, "They'll find them, Mom. Amy's brave. I'll bet she gets away."

She knew crying wouldn't help her or help find the girls, so she kept busy until the ballroom was straightened up. Back downstairs, the living room was empty. Jay Frank asked if she'd go with him to bed. She lay beside him, and in only a few minutes he was asleep. Both dogs had situated themselves next to the bed.

She checked on the others—her mother and dad were in Jay Frank's room, probably pretending to sleep; Gran and Robert's door was closed; and J.D. and the others hadn't come back yet.

Claire went back up to the ballroom. She opened a pair of the French doors on one of the balconies and stepped outside, hugging a throw from a family room chair around her to ward off the late March chill. Looking north, she watched the steady pulse of the wind turbines' red lights reflecting against the slowly rotating blades. She sat, leaning against the balcony rail, watching, listening, then hearing faintly the occasional whistle—high-pitched, two-note warbles—punctuated by leather slapping on leather. J.D. and Chris both learned that from Granddad Frank, their way of urging the cattle along—whistle, then softly clap their gloved hands together. Now and then, someone added, "Yah, yah, yah, move on." She wished she'd ridden with them. Pegasus enjoyed working, and she loved riding at night. And she needed to be doing something, anything that would help. But her family needed her here more than there.

That thought sent her downstairs to check on Jay Frank again. He was asleep, dogs snoring, now both in the bed with him. She didn't mind that she and J.D. would be crowded when they were all in that bed together. She wished it would be four—that Amy would be returned by magic. But she knew better.

She trudged upstairs again, and sat on the same balcony. The distant, faint hum of the wind turbines continued. The cattle and horse sounds had stopped. She wouldn't sleep until J.D. was safely back. But she would close her eyes, take the same advice she'd given her dad—relax, focus on breathing.

In the space between full, acute awareness and sleep, the wish to find a way to feel whole again visited her. In fits and starts, in between other activities in the past months, she'd sketched a plan for a part-time community health service. There would be no medical practice, no insurance companies restricting access, no threat of takeover by people who saw healthcare as a commodity not a service. Pure nursing was what she wanted to do. She would be in control.

Her breathing accelerated and her eyes opened. The words "in control" mocked her. As if her family would never present a need only she could meet, as if the only external threats were insurance companies. Now was all she had and control was a myth.

She closed her eyes again, focused on her breathing. For now, being whole for her would mean meeting challenges as they arose. If they got through this, if Amy was found safe, she'd never, promise to God, she'd never be so selfish again.

Later, J.D. woke her. She'd nodded off there on the balcony. He told her the cattle hadn't minded moving. He and the others were going to stay up a while downstairs. Just in case, he said. Broadus had told him there was a lead on the van. Someone reported one like it seen out near Sundown, headed west. She wanted to ask a thousand questions and knew he wouldn't have any more answers. He helped her to her feet, then held her to his chest. She couldn't help it. She held onto him tightly and let herself cry. He said, "Don't worry. They'll catch them and the girls will be fine. Everything else is going to get sorted out."

"How can you be certain?"

She heard the fear he was covering up as he answered, his voice husky. "I'm not certain. But right now, hoping and believing is what we can do."

He kissed her forehead and squeezed her even closer. He said, "Come downstairs. I need you beside me."

Lubbock Journal
Online Edition
March 19, 2017
Posted at 8:15 p.m.

Amber Alert Issued

Two fifteen-year-old females were abducted in Floyd County. They were last seen being driven away from a roadside near the Jackson Ranch near Jackson's Pond at approximately 3:15 p.m.

Suspects are three white males, in their thirties to forties. The vehicle is an old model, dull green panel van with upright back doors and no back windows.

If you see a vehicle matching this description, contact local law enforcement immediately. Do not attempt to detain the suspects, as they are armed.

CHAPTER 19

Kidnapped

Amy whispered to Elisa, "Stop crying. It won't help."
Her friend sniffled, like a baby's snotty effort to stop
tears after a tantrum. "I can't. I don't want to die."

"We're not going to die. We just have to stay alive until
we're rescued."

"It's been a long time."

One of the men in the front of the van said, "You two
shut up, or I'll shut you up permanently."

Amy said, "My hands are getting numb. Would you
loosen these ties? Please." She made her voice small and pitiful.

Elisa squirmed and said, "I need to use the bathroom."

She probably wasn't lying, Amy thought.

A different man said, "If I have to stop, you'll both be
sorry. Now shut up."

She whispered again to Elisa. "If you need to, just go
ahead and pee. It won't make any difference. Try to keep quiet."

The phone she'd hidden in her bra poked at her chest.
Her hands really were getting numb. When the men grabbed
them off the bus, they put bags over their heads and pulled their
hands behind their backs and put plastic ties on like handcuffs.
Then, when they dumped out Jay Frank and Elisa's brothers and
the bus driver, one of them got in the back and tied their ankles
with ropes, too. But those were pretty loose; if she tried, she
could probably slip out, but . . . She moved a little to get off her
stomach and onto her right side.

Someone turned the radio on. An announcer said, "This
is KWJX in Roswell, New Mexico. The time is seven twenty-one
p.m. Now here's an oldie by George Strait."

The radio went silent and one of the men said, "Nothing
but country music. Leave it off."

So, they'd been in the back of this stinking van, smelling
grease and gunpowder and something else, maybe beer, for four
hours. No, five—that was Mountain Time. They must have gone

two hundred miles or more. She and Elisa would have to testify when these men were caught. She had to remember everything she heard them say and everything that happened. They picked the wrong girl to kidnap. With her testimony, she would personally see they got major prison sentences. Life probably.

The only sounds she heard for a long time after that were the tires humming against the road. At first, they had made a lot of turns, like they were just driving around close to home, but in the last who-knows-how-long, it had mostly been straight roads.

Only once or twice did she hear a car passing, and another time it sounded like a truck had passed them. Like a country road, hardly any traffic. If she kidnapped someone, she'd stay on country roads. She closed her eyes beneath the bag, not willing to sleep, but working to memorize all the sounds she heard.

As the silence stretched on, she pictured her family, all of them together, waiting for her to come home. There was such a thing as telepathy; she'd read about it, and knew that messages could be transmitted mind to mind. It was something else she could do right now, so she would do it as hard as she could. She moved away the picture and imagined the words, FIND US.

"I've got to piss. And we're nearly out of gas." That must be the one driving.

Another one said, "Stop in Tatum. We'll get gas. I'll call my contact and get directions to the meet point."

A third voice, the whiny-sounding one, said, "I'm tellin' you, this is a bad idea. Not part of the plan. We were in charge of distractions. We should already be back at headquarters."

"Messing with locals may be your idea of the big time. Not mine. Those two in the back will bring good money in Mexico."

The whiny one said, "You heard what Horst said. Our money comes soon as the shipments get to the camp. When we're established as the West Texas center of operations for the Klan."

"Horst, my ass! I've known him since he was Dwight Taylor in Tomball, Texas. I'm getting mine and living on a beach in Mexico. You don't like it, I'll leave you in Tatum."

"I don't like New Mexico, and I sure can't live in Mexico. I hate spics."

Elisa made another sniffling sound. Amy whispered, "Pray. Pray as hard as you can."

All Amy could see through the bag covering her head was light or dark, and until just now, it had been dark for a long time. She felt the van slowing. This must be Tatum. She moved closer to Elisa and felt something wet on her leg. She whispered, "They'll stop soon. We're coming to a town. If we get a chance, any chance at all, we have to scream."

Elisa moved a tiny bit, so Amy knew she'd heard. Slowing, the van turned to the right, and then stopped. The man who sounded like a boss said, "I'll pump."

Whiny said, "Leave me here. I'll get back on my own. Horst's gonna make me his lieutenant. There's work to do, cleansing West Texas, making it great again for the white race."

The boss said, "Okay, Jerry, sure. Before you go, do one more thing to help out. Get back there and retie their hands in front of them. Damaged goods don't sell."

Amy heard the door near her feet open. Someone pulled on her arm and flipped her from her side to face-down again, then loosened her hands. Next, he jerked her onto her back and pulled her hands in front of her and snapped plastic ties on again. "Don't make a sound," the whiner said.

She felt him move a little and heard Elisa groan as he rolled her over.

He said, "Damn, this dark one pissed on herself."

The sound of the gas pump stopped. The boss had finished filling the tank. She had to do something now. She pulled her knees toward her chest and kicked hard toward the whiner.

"You little bitch!" He hit her head, but it only stung her face. For a second, she was glad for the hood.

She screamed, "Help! We're being kidnapped!"

Elisa wailed, "Help us, please."

A hand grabbed her, pushing the hood into her mouth. She couldn't get a breath. Then she heard something solid hit something else not quite as solid, and the man holding her down fell onto her legs, limp and heavy as a sack of feed.

The boss, now in the back with them gave an order to the one up front. "Drive out, take your time, don't attract attention. If that woman minding the counter looks up, wave and smile."

The driver said, "I still need to piss."

"Go about two miles toward Roswell, and then turn south on 206, the road to Lovington. Then go about four more miles and pull off the road. Somewhere dark. You can take care of your weak bladder, and I'll drive from there. Jerry'll be staying here in New Mexico."

Then she heard another thud and something crunching, bone maybe. The boss said, "He's not going to mind a bit."

The weight on her legs lifted, and she felt Jerry's body crowd between her and the side of the van. The boss, somewhere near her feet, between her and Elisa, said, "You're a feisty one, aren't you? That's good. You're going to need it when we get to Mexico. Now, make another sound and I'm covering your mouths with duct tape. Both of you."

Amy worked on visualizing flashing lights and sirens, but the dark covered her again and the tears running down her face made imagining impossible.

The van came to a halt again, and the man in the back got out. Then the driver got out and said, "Be right back."

Wind drifted in the open back doors. It dried the tears on her face, even with the hood in place. A coyote howled and pups yipped in answer. The body beside her, alive—she knew because she felt him breathing—moved, sliding toward the van's back doors. He made no sound. Grunts from the boss told her he was dragging Jerry out of the van. She didn't let herself think what might happen next. She'd seen guns when they boarded the school bus, which seemed like days ago.

She froze when a single gunshot sounded, and she heard heavy footsteps approaching. Seconds later from the open doors at their feet, the boss said, "Either of you two give me any trouble and you'll end up like him." The back doors slammed, gravel crunched, and a front door opened, then slammed closed. The engine started, gravel spewed against the fenders, and the van sped away. She whispered, "Don't worry, Elisa. Now there's only two of them. Work on getting your feet loose. We may get a chance to run."

A phone ringtone sounded. Amy startled, hers was on vibrate, she was sure of it. The boss said, "Yeah, all fine. By ten your time, no problem. The goods I offered are on board. Cash on delivery was the deal, right? Good." He went quiet, then in a minute, he started humming.

She wanted to choke him.

If she could look at her phone, she could see how much time passed. Maybe thirty minutes. Every minute put them closer to whomever he talked to on the phone. She wouldn't let herself think about what would happen then.

A siren! Flashing lights! She sat up, knowing she shouldn't, and even though she couldn't see anything except dim light. Then she crouched back down. The van stopped. The lights behind flashed, red, blue, faint.

"Sir, I've stopped you this evening because you have a taillight out. Are you aware that's a violation?"

"Sorry, officer, I didn't know."

"Get out of the vehicle, please, and I'll show you. And I need to see your license and registration."

Another car engine roared, then stopped. More lights flashed. Heavy footsteps crunched on gravel, coming near. More voices raised. One said, "Both of you get out of the vehicle. Show us your hands above your head."

Without being told to, Elisa began screaming—not words, but the sounds of fear; not the whimpering, sniffling sounds of a baby, but of a grown woman screaming for her life.

Amy's screams echoed hers and carried pleading, warning words. "Help, we're kidnapped! Guns! They have guns! Save us!"

They both screamed; it felt like forever that they screamed.

Lubbock Journal

Friday, March 20, 2015

Hate Crime Arrest at Gun Show

In joint action with FBI agents, Lubbock police officers arrested Dylan Burrows, of Amarillo, at the Gun and Knife Expo at the Civic Center Thursday night.

According to witnesses, exhibitors were just completing set up when Burrows approached one of the exhibitors, an African American man from Oklahoma City whose booth offered handmade knives and beaded leather items. Burrows, carrying a heavy-duty stapler, had placed posters on several areas throughout the exhibit hall.

The witnesses reported that the African American man left his booth and stood in front of the nearest poster, which he then ripped down. Following that, he tore down several more of the posters in the hall.

Burrows approached him, shouting racial slurs, and hit the exhibitor on his left shoulder with the stapler. A fist fight that followed was broken up by private security officers, who notified the Lubbock Police Department.

Officers arrested Burrows and confiscated the posters as evidence. Because of the content of the posters, which included such phrases as "Keep America White," "whites arise," "prepare now, arm and train," and an address for a website designed for recruiting members, FBI agents subsequently collected witness statements. Burrows was charged with assault and Federal offenses listed as hate crimes.

The exhibitor was transported by ambulance to Lubbock County Hospital for treatment of injuries and was subsequently released.

CHAPTER 20
Dark Night

J.D.'s phone vibrated. He jumped and the rattlesnake in his dream disappeared. He rolled to his side and put his feet on the floor, hoping to make sense when he answered. The phone showed eleven-fifteen. A voice said, "Mr. Havlicek? This is FBI Special Agent Hulen calling from Lovington, New Mexico. We have your daughter. She's safe."

Before he could answer, Claire grabbed the phone, and turned on the speaker. "This is Amy's mother. Let me speak to her."

After a brief silence, Amy said, "Mom, I'm okay. They caught them. Please let me give a statement . . ."

Claire said, "Did they hurt you? Is Elisa okay?"

"We're both fine. My hands are still shaking. Before, I was shaking all over, I was so scared."

Hulen came back on the line. He said, "If you'll give us permission to take Amy's statement, with a female officer present, we can bring Amy home, and have her there in approximately four to five hours."

Claire handed the phone to J.D., and said, "I think we should let them get the statement. She needs to come home right away."

J.D. said, "If Amy agrees, we agree. What about Elisa?"

"Another agent's on the phone with the Montoyas as we speak, asking for their permission. Hold on." In a few seconds, he said, "They agreed. We'll get them both home as quickly as we finish here. The three men were all apprehended. One's here in custody, another's being brought here from near Tatum, and the third is on the way to a critical care unit in Lubbock, under guard. A woman at a convenience store in Tatum saw the Amber Alert and phoned police."

"Can you tell us any more? Why they did it? Where were they taking the girls?"

Hulen said, "Preliminary questioning has given us little. The two who are able to talk refuse to implicate anyone else but do admit to taking the children and the bus driver, and leaving with the girls. We hope Amy and Elisa heard something that can help explain the motive."

J.D. waited, hoping the agent would say more, but he said nothing. J. D. thanked him for the rescue and for the call, and hung up. He hugged Claire and in a lowered voice said, "They're safe. We can relax a little bit. But I have to leave again. Marty said we needed to keep a watch starting around midnight. Chris, Andrew, Tag, and I'll be at headquarters. They're pretty sure something else, something big's going down tonight."

As he talked, he pulled on his Wranglers and the shirt he'd left on the floor. Jay Frank stirred, then settled. Claire grabbed her clothes off the chair nearby. In a whisper, she said, "I'll tell the others. I doubt if anyone's actually sleeping, except maybe Jay Frank and the dogs."

She stepped into the bathroom where she splashed water on her face. "Did Marty say what they expect to happen?"

"Best he can tell, the undercover guy gave the Feds information that the white supremacy stuff is only part of their purpose. The rest is all business—guns and drugs. Apparently, the grunts who do the work aren't clued in on everything. They think it's all about setting up a training camp to get people ready for the race war that's coming." He shook his head. "It's all hard for me to imagine, but we're living right here next door to it." He started out of the room and said, "When you give the others the good news, tell Ray and Robert if they hear anything near the house, to call the sheriff."

She kissed him and said, "Be careful."

Soon after, J.D. stood on the porch of the ranch headquarters, the house that had been his childhood home. Growing up here he'd thought his dad's job, farming for the Jacksons, couldn't be beat. As a kid he'd never dreamed of being a partner in this ranch and part of the Jackson family. Never thought of it until Claire grew up, and then marrying her was all he thought about. Now he was responsible for this place and the family he loved. He intended to make it all safe again, if it was the last thing he did.

The sound of a pickup on the road, but no visible headlights, told him one of the others was on his way. A person driving this far on this road only had one possible destination. The road dead-ended a ways past the headquarters, at the gate to the north pasture.

At midnight, as they'd agreed, Andrew drove up and parked in front. Chris made it to the porch in three long strides. Andrew, carrying the saddle gun, followed.

Andrew said, "I haven't driven lights off, on a country road, in the middle of the night, since I was a teenager. I used to be better at it."

Chris said, "You got us here without hitting a jackrabbit or running into a cow. That's good enough." Chris turned west in the direction of the big house four miles away, which showed only the bluish glow of the outdoor intruder lights. "The ranch house with the burglar lights was my beacon when I was a kid. The way I could always tell where I was. I used to love roaming around the ranch in the middle of the night. Lots of wildlife activity."

J. D. said, "As I recall it, you were the wildlife. Drinking and smoking weed out in the country occupied a fair number of your young weekends." He gave a backward nod toward the headquarters' front door. "Just so you know, the FBI called right before I left the house. The girls are safe. I'll tell you all I know, as soon as this, whatever it turns out to be, is over. Let's wait for Tag and Marty inside."

J.D. had made coffee and cleaned his twenty-two while he waited for them. Chris, pouring himself a cup, said, "I see you had the same thought I did. Guns. Between the two of us, Andrew and I only have the saddle gun and this." He produced a snub-nosed .38 revolver from his pocket. "Reckon we actually need any firepower, with the Feds and their arsenal?"

"I doubt it, but it can't hurt to have them just in case." J. D. had a notion Marty might quash the idea of their carrying, but planning ahead never hurt. He saw Tag pull up, and just behind him, Marty came to a halt out front.

.

As soon as he walked in, Tag said, "I had a hell of time gettin' away from the house. My wife didn't want me to leave, and both the boys wanted to come with me."

Marty shook hands all around, the way they'd all learned as kids—didn't matter what the occasion, unless they're close kin, men shook hands. He said, "First, I have to say I was glad to hear just a minute ago on the band the Feds use, about the girls being safe."

J.D. nodded. He said, "Tag, I'll tell you and these other two all I know when this business here's over."

Tag, silent for once, nodded. Broadus said, "I guess y'all have questions. I couldn't afford to tell J. D. much of anything on the phone, since my buddy in Homeland Security wasn't supposed to be feeding me information the way he did. Then, since they use local law enforcement for backup, he got me a ticket to the show, so to speak. I thought quick and came up with a reason why I needed to come and tell y'all.

"Officially, you're keeping an eye on your property to prevent the possibility of fire. The Feds agreed since they want to concentrate the men they have on the road on the east, the bunker, and the turbine towers on that north pasture. You'll stay over beyond the gate on your east pasture. If anyone comes that way, you'll be there to slow 'em down."

Tag said, "You're looking stouter than usual. You wearing body armor, Broadus?"

Marty pulled aside the Homeland Security windbreaker he was wearing, thumped the vest covering his chest. "Feds didn't issue it to me. When I started carrying a gun, working for the Cattle Association, I thought I probably ought to have protection from other guys carrying guns."

Tag said, "Well, I feel lots better knowing you can stop a bullet, even if I can't."

Andrew said, "Any idea how they know the plan that bunch has? J.D. said something about blowing up those two wind towers in the north pasture."

"I didn't know this for sure until today. FBI's had a guy undercover in there. Bad guys've been recruiting. At least three from Calverton are in. The undercover fellow joined up a few weeks back. They welcomed him like a brother when he talked about stuff he'd been in on down near Houston—intimidation, particularly some Vietnamese people; church fire; cross burning."

"Well hell, what do they have against those towers?" Tag shook his head. "I thought the Klan was just out to get anyone who's not a *white* American."

Broadus said, "I hear it's either because there's a lot of foreign money behind those towers—Swedish, I think—or maybe they're still pissed at J. D. over that thing with the bull."

Chris had been in the bathroom when Marty came in. J.D. hadn't noticed until he heard flushing and then Chris reappeared, that he had a camera mostly hidden in his pocketed vest. If you didn't know what you were looking for, you'd miss it, in that pocket in the back. Chris said, "One o'clock's when things start, right?"

"Around then. That's the intel the feds have. You guys are going with me. We'll meet the others down where that east pasture drops off into the breaks, and stay out of sight till they say go. Then the bunch I'm with will intercept anyone who turns up at the turbine. The others are ready, up on the Reese ranch's north side, to raid the bunker. I expect this time they'll find more there than the last time."

Chris said, "So we stay back at the east gate when you go in?"

Broadus nodded. "That's the plan. And try not to catch any bullets."

They went in on foot, tracking east from headquarters and over the fence into the pasture, then after about a quarter mile, turning back north, then west again to approach the gate. Even though the thorny trees weren't yet leafed out, the mesquites' spiky branches formed barriers in the spaces where they'd taken hold. Between the mesquite patches, emerging spring grass suggested the cattle down here would eat well.

A lone coyote howled, farther east from the sound of it. Their trek was slow going. Walking over uneven ground in the dark, J.D. and the others stayed close behind Broadus, who wore night-vision goggles. About twenty minutes after they left the headquarters, they approached a group of—best J. D. could tell in the dark—eight men in dark windbreakers.

"Phones mute or off," one of the Federal guys said. Since dark fell, around eight, the wind had blown intermittently. Now, not a breeze stirred and every sound seemed magnified. Someone sneezed and whispered, "Damn." The voice made J. D. think of his dad, and how he'd wipe his nose with a blue and white bandanna a lot every spring. It's been a long time since he'd thought about him.

Marty told them to stay put. He joined the other law enforcement types clustered near the gate, all wearing black, faces smeared with black grease paint. Tag raised a finger, then disappeared behind a clump of mesquite. About a minute later, he returned and said, in what passed for a whisper from him, "Sorry, boys, I had to pee. You'll understand when you get older." He came back and stood close to J.D. "I still don't get what they've got against the turbines." He shook his head. "About now I'm wishin' I'd brought a gun. Sons a bitches that dumb might decide to shoot a conscientious objector like me, just for standing close to you."

He turned silent when one of the Feds raised a hand and said in a whisper, "Something's going down near the RBJ plant. Fire department and sheriff's been called out." He covered his right ear with his hand. J.D. supposed he had an earpiece communication device of some sort. Then the man said, "We're to stay here, go on with the mission."

Just as he said that, another one of the lawmen, wearing night goggles, said, "Check it. Three men coming over the north fence, two with assault rifles, one wearing a backpack. Get ready."

Marty turned around the ball cap he was wearing, raised his rifle, and peered through the scope. He said, "I see 'em. You guys stay back here. Don't let anyone get out. It's show time."

J.D. and the other three watched as the dark-clad group spread out just inside the gate and began inching forward toward the tower about 400 yards away. As they closed the distance, the leader dropped down and began crawling commando style. The others followed suit.

Chris edged forward. He had his camera out, large lens attached. He said, "Don't worry. I'm not taking pictures. We don't want a flash. The lens lets me get a close view." He handed the camera to J.D. "Take a look. They're getting near that first tower out where the concrete pad starts."

Figures his naked eyes only saw as dots of movement, the lens brought near enough that he flinched. He said, "I think that guy with the backpack must be carrying explosives."

For once, Tag had nothing to say.

J.D. reached for his phone to check the time, then realized it was turned off. He said, "This is like watching a bad movie, or a dream where you're stuck in a long tunnel and can't get out. Seems to go on forever. Right?" He didn't expect a response. He was talking to himself in a whisper.

A west wind would have carried sounds from the tower their way, but as it was, the only sounds were the four of them shifting from foot to foot. Then J.D. heard three shots, in a burst.

As if they'd been cued, all four of them squatted down. They were near the gate, on land as flat and bare of trees as the pasture. Anyone with night vision could see them. J.D. said, "Our job's to keep anyone trying to leave this way from getting out. Let's back down that slope a little bit. No sense getting shot waiting for someone making a getaway."

The sound of two more bursts of gunfire pierced the still air. Chris said, "I heard someone yell, 'Federal Officers, stop where you are,' just now. Did you hear it?"

J.D. admitted he hadn't—too many hours driving noisy tractors. Andrew was the only one who agreed he'd heard. Tag said, "Huh?"

Chris stood and moved nearer the gate, searching through his lens. "There, I see them. One's in an FBI jacket. I think they've got all three of the thugs on the ground. Two for sure. No, only one, the guy with the backpack. He . . ." The sound of a shot interrupted him. They all crept forward, then squatted down again.

J.D. saw movement near the turbine. Chris belly-crawled forward, then stood in a crouch, peering through his camera again. He said, "That sounded like a handgun. Now the other two are up. One still has a gun."

J. D. said, "Chris, get down, move back." He saw figures moving their direction. Three shots sounded, in quick succession, followed by a burst of automatic weapon fire.

Chris, now down with them, said, "Damn. Mesquite thorns got me on the neck." He rubbed the back of his neck, looked at his hand.

Voices in the distance said things J.D. couldn't understand. Andrew said, "Looks like they've got them now. They're marching all three of them south, toward the road in front of headquarters."

J.D. got close to Chris. "Turn around. I'm not so sure that was mesquite thorns. Andrew, take a look."

Andrew pressed two fingers around the wound on Chris' neck. "Painful?"

Chris shook his head.

Blood on his hand, Andrew said, "It's too dark to get a good look. But I think we have a casualty here."

Chris said, "It's nothing. A scrape. Let's get another look now."

J.D. remembered all the fights Chris had gotten into as a teenager. His friend had never admitted to pain, not once. J.D. doubted he was a reliable witness now.

Tag, talking faster than usual, said, "Damn, boys, that was excitin'. What are we supposed to do? Go back to where we come from or wait here? I want to see their faces. Wonder if they was wearing hoods."

They stood together inside the gate, watching the prisoners stumble along in front of the group of lawmen in the distance. Then, a loud explosion shook the air, and they all turned toward the sound. The marching group stopped. A fireball, orange followed by black smoke, rose from the Reese land, in the direction of Justin's bunker.

J.D. and the other civilians all began walking back the way they'd come, toward headquarters. None of the four of them said a word. J. D. turned on his phone.

When they made it back, four black SUVs filled the rest of the space in front of headquarters. The Feds and Marty stood in a cluster in front of one vehicle, where a man sat in the second seat, separated from the front by heavy wire screen. One of the Homeland guys nodded toward the prisoner and said, "That's the only casualty. Just needed first aid. We put a pressure bandage on a through-and-through wound on his leg."

The other two prisoners occupied two other vehicles. Best J. D. could tell, they were both in their late twenties or early thirties. Neither one was Justin Reese.

J.D. checked his phone and saw a text message from Claire, sent minutes ago at two fifty-eight a.m. He called her. After he'd assured her he was fine, there was no damage on the property, and the thugs were all in custody, she told him Ray had been called to town when the fire department was called. She said, "He hasn't called or come back. Mother's trying to look calm and not doing a very good job. Jay Frank and the dogs are still asleep. Robert checked all the doors and windows again. Gran's up now and we're having coffee."

He promised he'd be there as soon as he could. He said, "This day has been about fifty hours long already."

The Fed standing next to Marty said, "Word is, that explosion didn't take out the bunker. Blew up a vehicle one of them was trying to escape in. I suppose he was their explosives expert." He smirked as he said that. "And get this. Word is they've impounded two cattle trucks, a few heifers and three old cows, and a lot of marijuana packed in a compartment in the truck." He shook his head. "But here's the best part. Some genius hid a bunch of bags of cocaine inside those old cows, if you get what I mean."

Tag said, "I've heard stranger things, but not in a while. Damn!"

Andrew took Chris inside and they both returned in a couple of minutes, with Andrew holding a wad of paper towels against the back of Chris's neck. Andrew said, "This isn't a puncture from a thorn. Based on the width and depth, I think a bullet grazed him. I have dressing supplies at the house. He'll live until we get there." One of the lawmen took a look. He agreed and said he'd need a statement.

Another of the Federal officers said, "I just heard a report about the fire in town. One suspect in custody. A house on the RBJ property, one of the temporaries, burned to the ground. Unoccupied. The volunteer fire department kept it from spreading to the others. Montoya and his security men had been patrolling the property twice as often as usual. They detained the guy, who'd apparently stayed to watch the fire, until the sheriff's men got there."

J.D. stood off to one side, apart from the gaggle of Kevlar-wearing men in black sharing bits of conversation and speculation. He was ready to get home. Others must have felt the same, because the officer in charge said to him, "Thank you for your help; your property is safe. Members of our task force have taken the rest of those apprehended at the bunker to Calverton to sort out the charges. Our undercover man said, and it was confirmed by video from the drone, that all who were out there are now in custody—somewhere near thirty. We have more work ahead of us tonight, so we're leaving."

He and the other federal lawmen began sorting themselves into the four SUVs. Then he returned to where J. D. stood and said, "One more thing. This isn't official until the sheriff's department finishes their work. But our undercover man confirmed those three that abducted your kids are part of the group we busted up tonight. Rest assured every possible charge will be brought against each one. We have lots of evidence."

After they drove away, Marty following behind in his big diesel pickup, Tag said, "Guess I'll call it a day. Mind if I come to work late tomorrow?"

J. D. said, "Take the whole day off. I plan to."

At home, Claire met him at the door with a cup of coffee. The aroma gave him hope he'd make it inside before falling asleep. She gave him that nurse's once-over he recognized. Then she poured her brother and Andrew coffee. Everyone except Jay Frank and the dogs waited in the kitchen. Claire said, "The explosion woke us up. Then Daddy got the call to come to town because there was a fire at RBJ. We've done a good job of telling each other you were all fine."

She sat next to him as he repeated an abbreviated version of the evening and ended the tale with the Homeland Security man's assurance that the men who had taken their children off the school bus were part of the same gang of thugs, a diversion for the raid on the tower and the RBJ facility.

J.D. had just finished his recitation when Ray returned and told all he knew about the fire. One house was destroyed. The arsonist had posted a sign far enough from the house not to burn that said, America for Americans.

Claire whispered to J.D., "Don't you need to get some sleep?" He admitted he did. They left the others recounting their several views of the day's events, and walked to their bedroom. Jay Frank and the dogs occupied most of the space on the mattress.

J.D. said, "Let's don't wake them. I can fit in there on the edge, or the floor would be fine. I can rest till Amy gets home."

He had gotten his boots off and stood unbuttoning his shirt when the doorbell rang. Sockfooted, rebuttoning, he hurried behind Claire toward the front door.

Dolores and David Montoya began apologizing almost as soon as the door was open. Their sons, wearing pajamas, stood behind their father. David said, "Elisa and Amy wanted to ride home from New Mexico together. We couldn't say no."

Dolores said, "We told the FBI man we would meet them here. I hope that was all right. We wanted to be here."

J.D. pushed open the screen and said, "Of course, come in."

Claire and Dolores hugged, and he heard them murmuring about whether the children should all see a counselor. He ushered David and the boys into the living room. Jay Frank, rubbing his eyes, stood in the doorway, with the dogs by his side. Soon everyone was seated, boys on selected laps, and dogs near Robert and Willa, Melanie and Ray on chairs nearby. It appeared that everyone was talked out, and now they were just waiting for the two girls to complete the families.

No sooner had J.D. thought that, than the doorbell rang again. The boys beat everyone else to the door. Jay Frank flung it open and Elisa and Amy were met with a jumble of words and hugs and tears. FBI Special Agent Hulen introduced himself. He said, "You should be proud of these two girls. They remembered everything. Their statements filled in all the details we couldn't."

Amy and Elisa were surrounded in the living room by family. The agent stood with Claire and J. D. watching the reunion.

He said, "Amy showed great presence of mind, even though she must have been terribly frightened. She'd hidden her cell phone in her bra as soon as the men boarded the bus. When we started our search, using GPS, we located a weak signal from her phone. But then it disappeared. The problem was the battery had died. We gave her the phone back. Probably needs a new battery.

"I know all of you are worn out. The girls have eaten and they slept a little on the way back, but they deserve a long rest. So, I'll leave them in your care."

He handed cards to the Montoyas and J.D. and said, "You can reach me at this number if you have any questions or concerns. We'll be in touch."

He shook hands all around and nodded as the families thanked him. Glancing again at Amy and Elisa in the living room, he lowered his voice and said, "I'm sure you know this has been terrifying and stressful for them both. You might consider getting them some counseling."

Claire said, "You must be a parent yourself."

He nodded. "Yes, ma'am, three girls, now in their twenties. Their mother's the expert on raising girls, but I know being a teenage girl's not easy, even under the best circumstances."

When the agent left and they'd all returned to the living room, the women took over. Dolores said, "I give thanks to God that this long day and night are over and everyone is now safe and back home."

Melanie said, "Amen to that."

Willa said, "Most of all, we're thankful to have all the children safe. Now, everyone needs rest after this long day and night."

Claire said, "I agree with all of that. But before we all get back to our own beds, please come into the kitchen. We should go to sleep on full stomachs. I'm a nurse. I know these things."

Everyone followed her. J. D. stood by, his arms around their two children, as Claire and the other women set out cereal, milk, and juice, and toasted a full loaf of bread.

The group made short work of the food. The children tolerated hugs from all the adults. Amy and Elisa clung to each other, whispering their goodbyes. And then the house emptied out, almost as if nothing had happened.

In the now quiet kitchen, Amy said, "I'm really tired. I've talked all I can." Sounding calm and mature past her age, she said, "But you need to know I'm okay. I was never really hurt, just afraid of what might happen later." She started to leave the kitchen then turned back. "I'm going to bed now... but first, there's one thing I need to tell you. I don't think I can go back to school next week. Please don't make me."

J.D. nodded. Claire said, "We understand. Go on to bed. We'll help you figure out how to put this all in the past. There are lots of possibilities. Homeschooling is one."

Jay Frank said to Amy, "When bad things happen, it takes a long time to stop being afraid. Remember when you saved me from the snakebite? You helped me after that. I'll help you now."

J.D. turned his head. They didn't need to see him crying. But watching those two growing up right there in front of him, he couldn't help it.

The kids went to their rooms, and he didn't move from his chair at the kitchen table while Claire cleared away the dishes. He said, "I'd help, but I'd drop something and break it. I haven't been this tired in a long time."

Claire put the final plate in the dishwasher. Then she pulled him up from the chair and pushed him toward the bedroom. She said, "Go. Get undressed and in bed. I'll be right there before you know it."

When she slid in beside him, she said, "I am so glad you're my husband, and that you're safe, and the kids are safe. Now sleep as long as you can."

He wrapped his arms around her. The last thing he remembered was saying to her, "When I wake up, I hope everything's back to normal and none of this was real."

Floyd County Tribune
Thursday, April 2, 2015
Hate Group Arrests

Thirty-one men apprehended by a task force that included officers from several Federal law enforcement branches and local authorities were arrested on March 20 and 21 at locations in and near Jackson's Pond and Lovington, NM.

Each of those arrested has been charged in relation to at least one of three separate incidents. Those were the attempted destruction of a wind turbine outside Jackson's Pond, kidnapping of five children and one bus driver from a Calverton ISD bus, and arson of a residence in Jackson's Pond.

In addition to charges related directly to each of those incidents, thirteen of those arrested have been charged with various Federal hate crimes and all thirty-one with conspiring to commit acts of domestic terrorism.

Further, one of those apprehended in New Mexico has been charged with murder in the death of one of the three charged with kidnapping. Indictments were issued on all those charged.

Authorities report a large amount of evidence was seized from a remote site outside Jackson's Pond, including unregistered assault weapons, computer equipment, ingredients for making explosives, printed material recruiting members for the group, plus computer evidence of plans for a training camp to teach "survival and triumph of the pure white race in the USA." That material mentioned weapons training would be offered at the camp. An opening date in August, 2015, was prominent in the materials.

Additional items confiscated in the raid were a large cache of firearms, several head of cattle, and an undisclosed amount of marijuana, cocaine, and heroin, all related to smuggling and other related charges which are pending. The site of the raid, the Reese Ranch, has been sealed as a crime scene until full investigation is completed.

All those indicted were denied bail on the basis of the severity of the alleged crimes and the likelihood of their being flight risks.

Of the thirty-one in custody, ten are Floyd county residents. They are: Justin Reese, Robert Lee Thomas, Terry Parson, Barney Hughes, Don Roy Walker, Robert Nelson, Brad Thornton, Marshall Thornton, Perry Wheelis, and Larry Mack Wheelis. The others gave addresses at other locations in Texas and adjoining states. (See Crime Report, page 3, for additional information on charges filed.)

Guest Editorial

Editor's note: *This arrived as a letter to the editor. However, its message defines the issues and points to the hopes we hold for our communities so well we choose to offer it as also representing the opinion of this newspaper's editor.*

With the approach of the Easter season, I find it important to pause and reflect on the many changes and problems that have occurred in our area in the past few months. I share these reflections in hope that others will consider the importance of a renewed spirit of community and a rebirth of the hope that was the spark on which these communities were founded.

First, those who came here early, in the late 1800s and the beginning of the twentieth century, were a diverse group. Early settlers came from many areas, not only from other parts of Texas but also from other states. Among those many, if not most, were only one generation from immigrants who came to this country seeking a better life. We only need search our own family trees to find the name of the first arrival in the United States.

Second, those early settlers brought varying religions and ethnic backgrounds, but they all had in common a desire to work the land or to support the work of those who did. Land for agriculture was the primary attractor and in those days that work required much manual labor to achieve a living. Now much of that work is mechanized, yet we cling to a sense that agriculture is who we are and what this area can produce.

Third, we are in different times now. Other work and other workers with different skills can help keep alive the communities that agriculture developed. People of other backgrounds, with different religions and other ethnicities are some of those who can become part of our communities and help them thrive.

Fourth, and finally, the changes necessary for our small communities to remain vital are not so different from the changes those first settlers had to endure. They had to make new friends, accept different viewpoints, and trust others whom they did not know.

I hope for all of us, that this season can be a time of reflection and dedication, of being a part of the necessary rebirth of a sense of commitment to our communities and their survival.

May God bless us all.

Pastor Heath Goodman

CHAPTER 21
Renewal

Melanie had managed to push aside all the things that had happened in March. By daily acts of sheer will, she focused on events on the horizon, the future, not the past. Today she and Dolores had permitted themselves a few minutes of reporting to one another bits of details of their families' lives. A therapist would probably call their recitation of such common things as appetites returning to hearty, sleep patterns uninterrupted, and smiles and laughter in their homes a form of mutual reassurance. Probably best of all was their relief that the children, all five who'd been kidnapped, had all returned to school after Spring Break. Each of them had seen a counselor. The man who worked with the boys had felt four visits were sufficient. The girls' counselor recommended eight, and their final sessions were scheduled for this week. Melanie let herself believe that the lives of her family and friends were edging back toward normal.

She and Dolores weren't the only ones eager to return to calm days and restful evenings. The people around them all showed a special eagerness for the coming month of May. Parents of their students mentioned vacation plans; Melanie's fellow choir members threw themselves into polishing their renditions of hymns of peace and joy; and Claire and her grandmother immersed themselves in planning Willa and Robert's wedding.

Even though she'd hoped to be a part of those preparations, Melanie had agreed that her plate was full. This coming weekend, on Saturday night, May 9, the ranch house would be the site of the wedding, an event she'd long since accepted as a positive next step for the whole family.

Today, she and Dolores planned to put the final touches on the end-of-school program for their eighteen preschoolers and their parents. In less than three weeks, eight of them would graduate, each receiving a diploma sized to fit small hands, wearing caps and gowns rented for the occasion. A photographer would offer group and individual photos for an affordable price. As soon as the children arrived this morning, they would rehearse their program.

So far, they'd never actually been able to get to the end of the songs the three-and four-year-olds would sing, much less having the four-year-old graduates march forward one at a time for diplomas. Some of the threes had broken out in tears when they were left empty-handed last week at their first rehearsal. Plus, standing in straight lines for fifteen minutes taxed the children's concentration. This morning, Melanie had devised a new plan she hoped would keep the children attentive and satisfied until the brief ceremony ended and refreshments were served. She'd often thought how nice it would be if punch and cookies solved adult problems as easily as those of small children.

She said to Dolores, "I think I've come up with a way to make the program work."

Dolores rolled her eyes. "After Friday's attempt, I'm ready to try anything."

Melanie handed her the revised program. "If we break the activities into even shorter segments—pledge of allegiance, song seated, song with gestures and dance steps, then marching with rhythm instruments, then receiving diplomas and certificates—I think they'll be able to stay on task. And if they don't, we smile a lot and I'll say something about their being eager for summer vacation. Then we'll have each child show their parents their art and demonstrate what they do in the learning centers, then pass out the diplomas and, so everyone will have something in hand, we'll award certificates to the three-year-olds."

"If you say so." Dolores shook her head. "It amazes me how any one of them can stay occupied in any learning center for fifteen minutes or longer, easily. But put them all together, they want to scatter like chickens." She smiled again. "I guess that's emerging leadership behavior."

"Great line. I'll remember to use that. What parent could be disturbed by hearing they have a four-year-old leader in the family?'

Dolores went to unlock the front door. When she returned to the larger classroom where Melanie was working on a certificate to award the three-year-olds, she rearranged the pictures of colored shapes along with their English and Spanish shape and color names, moving them to a space near the activity center that held a child-sized replica of a kitchen. As she worked, she said, "Do you really think the trouble's over?"

Melanie straightened from leaning over her desk, rolling sheets of paper into "certificates of completion" for the three-year-olds. She said, "I think we'll never have people spreading hate and fear here again. That's hope speaking."

Dolores said nothing more as she continued posting azul—blue, red—rojo on the wall near the stove and sink built for tiny hands.

Seconds later the first child arrived. Others soon followed. She and Dolores greeted each child and parent with smiles. By the time they began the day's activities, Melanie had convinced herself that these children were the best reason for hope.

The day of the wedding arrived with a sunrise promising a beautiful day. The grass pastures at the ranch wore a shade of deep green, echoed by the ready-to-mature wheat growing nearby, a complement to the bride's chosen color, emerald. Last week's thunderstorms had brought only showers, without hail or threat of tornados. Melanie and Ray both fell silent while driving past the fields on the way to the big house. Not the silence of dread, but the all's-right-with-the-world-and-I'm-lucky-to-be-alive-to-share-this-with-the-ones-I-love calm that she'd cultivated over the past few weeks.

They would dress for the wedding at the house and be ready for guests' arrival at six. With three hours to spare, they joined J.D. and Jay Frank on the front porch at the big house. Their grandson ran to hug them both. The child who'd worn worry like a too-heavy backpack following the abduction had been replaced by this young man, smiling and eager to perform his duty as Best Man at the wedding. He said, "Guess what! Hopper, my favorite doe, is having twins. Maybe today. Andrew's checking her every two hours. When they're born, that's the last ones in my first herd."

Ray said, "You'll be busy keeping up with... what will it be now, seven goats?"

Jay Frank nodded. "And guess what else! I get to help with wheat harvest this year."

J. D. said, "Yep, no sense paying strangers to do the hard work when we can pay a relative."

"Tell them how much I'll earn. Listen, Grandmother. This is good."

"I told him it'll be like in a John Wayne movie—a dollar a day and found. And if he turns out to make a hand, then he'll get two bits more. His job title is swamper."

Jay Frank jiggled from one foot to another. "Granddad, were you ever a swamper? I'll get to learn to drive the pickup. Not on the roads at first. Just in the pasture. But still! Amy didn't learn until last year. Girls . . ."

Melanie said, "Uncle Chris learned when he was your age." She stopped short of telling that the second day Chris drove, he took out a gate and dented the right front fender on his Granddad's farm pickup. She said, "We need to take our clothes in and see if there's anything we can do to help before the guests arrive."

Jay Frank followed them in. He said, "You know I get to wear a tuxedo. Rented it in Lubbock." He struck a pose he must have seen in an advertisement for formal wear. "The Best Man gets to carry the ring. It's an important job."

She said, "You'll make a handsome Best Man. Uncle Chris will take your picture."

When she turned back from hanging her dress in the guest room closet, Jay Frank had disappeared and Amy stood in his place. "Grandmother, tell the truth. Does this make me look fat?"

Melanie said, "Step back, then turn around, slowly." She waited until Amy had made a full turn. "The dress fits perfectly. No puckers, no pudgy rolls above the waist. The shade of green highlights your eyes, and I see you've added a light touch of eye shadow. Some overdo when they begin using cosmetics. But yours is just right. No, the dress doesn't make you look fat. What it does is show that you are becoming a beautiful young woman."

Amy hugged her, then sat on the bed, careful not to crush the tulle of the ballerina-styled dress. Melanie sat beside her. "Anything else on your mind?" Amy shook her head no. Melanie said, "Sure?"

Amy said, "I'm happy for Gran and Moree. Are you?"

Melanie took her time responding. She tried always to tell children the truth, and to tell it in ways appropriate to their age. But Claire at fifteen and Amy at fifteen were two very different girls. Things in her granddaughter's world posed issues her mother had never known at the same age, dangers Melanie never had to warn her own daughter about. For instance, the threat of kidnapping was never something she had to discuss with Claire. But these children were resilient. Here was Amy, concerned about her dress, just like any other teenager. Melanie said, "To tell you the truth, at first I didn't know how to feel. But now I'm very happy."

Amy smiled and said, "Me, too. I'm going to go wait for Elisa now."

Melanie found Claire at the kitchen table, checking over a list. Beyond the countertop kitchen bar, a woman and two young girls spoke to one another in whispers as they arranged canapés on trays. When Melanie asked if Claire needed help, the answer was, "I don't think so. But go through this list with me one final time." She nodded to the woman making hors d'oeuvres and said, "Mother, meet Margretta, our lifesaver from Calverton. She and her daughters have the catering all taken care of. No worries there." Melanie and the caterer, obviously busy, nodded a brief greeting to one another. Claire lifted the paper she'd been poring over. She said, "I'll read the list and you ask questions and tell me what I've forgotten."

She ticked off the items: catering, including the wedding cake, all in hand; music, string quartet from Lubbock to arrive at five; flowers from the florist in Matador in place—absolutely beautiful; Jay Frank instructed on when to bathe and dress, to report for inspection at five-fifteen; Amy probably already dressed, Elisa to arrive, dressed to match at five-fifteen. Melanie said, "No need to worry about Amy, she's dressed and wearing a tiny bit of makeup."

Claire continued the list: minister to arrive at five, has called to confirm; two guests from Austin, arrived yesterday evening, stayed with Chris and Andrew, thrilled to be here; Pat Carmichael arrived this morning from Taos, will also stay with Chris and Andrew; recorded music for the reception and dance, previewed, cued up, amplifier in place, power connected."

Melanie saw Claire's shoulders sag as she continued toward the end of her list. She asked her daughter, "Have you eaten today?"

Claire's head came up and she said, "That's what I forgot! I haven't fed myself or the family since early this morning and then it was only toast and cheese."

Melanie said, "If you'll eat, I'll go check to see if the others need something."

A couple of minutes later, she returned and found Claire leaning back in her chair, apple in one hand, a hunk of cheddar in the other. Melanie said, "J.D. sneaked a sandwich while you were upstairs, as did the kids. They're fine."

Claire checked her watch. She said, "The only thing lacking is arrival of the wedding couple. Chris will bring Gran here to dress at five. Then at five-thirty, he'll drive Robert over in his Range Rover. They'll be able to use that to leave after the reception on their three-mile honeymoon journey. They both said that's what they wanted."

Melanie said, "I'll keep an eye on things if you want to shower and take a short rest before the festivities. You've done an amazing job. Give yourself a treat."

Claire surprised her by agreeing. Soon Melanie sat alone in the living room, alert for any small disasters, but none emerged. Willa arrived, looking rested, her gait steady even without her walking stick. She went directly to Amy's room to dress.

Melanie and Ray dressed and stood ready to greet any early arrivals by five-thirty. Even though the invitations showed the ceremony beginning at six-fifteen, in West Texas, guests often arrived early.

Then the next minutes passed in a blur. She'd have been hard pressed to say who did what, when, or where. She would recall that the quartet from Lubbock played continuously as people entered the ballroom and took seats. Then at precisely six-fifteen, all those present stood as the opening chords of the wedding march sounded.

As Melanie accompanied her mother, Willa Lofland Jackson, from the ballroom doorway down the aisle between seats arrayed on either side, she heard murmurs, "beautiful, so youthful," from those assembled, words she'd heard spoken about her mother all her life. As they continued down the aisle, she also heard her mother whisper, "Thank you for this, Melanie. It means so much to me."

She heard Heath Goodman ask, as part of the traditional wedding ceremony, "Who gives this woman in marriage?"

Her own voice surprised her. She responded, "I do."

The next surprise came when she heard the entire family say in unison, "We do."

After she moved aside and the bride and groom joined hands, she took the opportunity to fix the scene in her mind. Chris would have photos, but she wanted her own images, colored by all her emotions. Jay Frank in his tuxedo, standing next to his new great-grandfather; Claire, so much the image of her grandmother, as her matron of honor; the bridesmaids, Amy and Elisa, both wearing light green dresses with skirts like long ballerina tutus. Four matching arrangements of mixed flowers in shades of purple, each with one perfect bird-of-paradise as the focal point, flanked the sides of the small riser that held the minister's podium.

The centerpiece of the memories she'd store was the wedding couple. Robert stood tall, as erect as a sentry, white-haired and handsome in his tuxedo, with an emerald green bowtie. Willa's dressmaker in Lubbock had created a simple, long-sleeved, shirtwaist style dress with a portrait collar, made elegant by the fabric, emerald green silk shantung. Its waltz-length hemline made it perfect for dancing. She wore with it a simple strand of pearls and pearl earrings. Her bouquet echoed the arrangements in the room—one bird-of-paradise with mixed flowers in shades of purple. They each spoke the traditional vows in voices strong and unwavering, gazing directly into one another's eyes.

Watching her mother take another in a long line of steps into something new, continuing a way of being that in the past Melanie often had misunderstood, seeing her starting anew, again, Melanie felt more love for and understanding of her mother than ever before.

Symbolism Attributed to the Bird of Paradise Flower

Flower lore attributes much symbolism and many positive attributes to the striking blossoms of the bird-of-paradise. The plant, native to South Africa, has been chosen by florists as the traditional flower for the ninth wedding anniversary because legend conveys that it represents faithfulness. In addition to its anniversary designation, the gift of birds-of-paradise from a woman to a man are said to convey her faithfulness in their romantic relationship.

The appearance of the bloom, with its striking combination of purple, yellow, and orange petals and its striking erect plume suggestive of the birds from which its name was taken, also imply royalty through their regal appearance. The fact that the flower resembles a bird in flight suggests freedom and the ability to travel. Less directly tied with appearance, other symbolism attached to this exotic bloom are joy through both challenges and successes, and optimism about the future.

Based on the symbolism attached to bird-of-paradise flowers, they are suitable for a variety of occasions as part of display arrangements, as bouquets, or individually, as personal gifts.

Retrieved from an Internet search accessed April 13, 2015

CHAPTER 22
A View to the Future

As she and Robert passed down the aisle toward the ballroom door to the sounds of applause from those assembled for their wedding, Willa realized she'd been holding her breath. She exhaled slowly, in time with the music, and felt her shoulders relax. Now that the ceremony was over, the party would begin.

Following their exit, they paused on the stair landing, just as Claire had instructed. Willa heard the sounds of chairs being moved. The caterers, along with guests, were striking the lovely set that Claire had created for the ceremony, making ready for the next scene. Now that the ceremony was over, the party would begin. She smiled, thinking of the party scene in "The Nutcracker," in which she had danced many times years ago.

When Claire opened the door, they returned and took their places as guests of honor at a long table situated near the French doors to the balconies. Ray offered a wedding toast, saying that it was from Ireland by way of the Internet. He said, "May joy and peace surround you, contentment latch your door, and happiness be with you now, and bless you forevermore."

Jay Frank had performed admirably handling the ring as Best Man. He did equally well with his other Best Man function, offering a toast. A *Star Trek* fan to his core, he prompted the crowd to laughter by solemnly giving the Vulcan salute and saying, "Live long and prosper."

Then he disappeared into one of the side rooms, and the background music changed. Classical gave way to the song that she and Robert first danced to. The first notes of their song, "I Could Have Danced All Night," brought Robert to his feet. With a courtly bow he led her to the center of the ballroom. He led her in a waltz every bit as polished and as thrilling as the first time they danced that night on the cruise ship. She felt all eyes on them and hoped everyone could see Robert was as perfect a man for her at this time in her life as he was a dance partner.

They returned to the table and when the next song began, another waltz, she saw Ray take Melanie's hand. Ray, the steady, faithful man who'd weathered the storm that had been Melanie years ago. He'd let her find her own answers and become the person Willa admired more with each passing year.

As Melanie and Ray danced, Claire and J.D. joined them. She saw Chris lean close and whisper to Andrew, who hugged him briefly and nodded. Then Chris began moving around the room, taking photographs from every angle. Jay Frank, Amy, Elisa, and her two brothers danced holding hands, a moving circle in the center of the floor. Willa whispered to Robert, "Our family is happy for us, and happy with one another. Thank you for making this happen."

He said, "It's entirely my pleasure. You've given me everything I ever wanted." He lifted his champagne glass and said, "To my partner."

She lifted hers and said, "And to mine."

"Would you care to dance again, or to watch?"

She said, "I want to watch, so I can remember every moment."

Briefly, she smiled, wondering if Delia Jackson's spirit might be hovering, shaking her head. She knew Frank's was, and that he was happy for her and for their family.

The wedding guests, somewhere near fifty in all, took turns stopping by the head table to congratulate the newlyweds. The music switched from waltzes to western swing, and people continued dancing, odd pairs of different ages, genders, races, and dancing abilities told her times had changed and perhaps people had, as well.

She whispered again to Robert, "Look at Melanie and Claire. Working the room together. Making everyone welcome and the evening memorable."

Robert said, "It's no surprise to me. You, my dear, have set the best example they could have ever learned from."

She focused on J.D. standing with Andrew and Pat

Carmichael. If Frank had lived, he'd have chosen him, as she had, to be the person to keep the ranch a thriving enterprise. As if he'd heard her thinking his name, J.D. crossed the room to where she and Robert sat. He said, "I hope you know that all the Jacksons, including those of us with different last names, are happy for you two, and proud to be your family."

It must have been obvious that she couldn't answer, not without crying. Robert leaned forward, his hand on her back, and said, "Thank you, J.D., from both of us."

A few seconds after J.D. left the table, she said, "Okay, I have my voice back now. It'll soon be time to cut the cake. And I'm warning you, Muldoon, none of that cake-in-the-face business."

"Duly noted. I shall be a model of deportment."

After the cake was cut and everyone served, she and Robert waited a decent interval and then stood to leave. Once again, applause and good wishes filled the air as they made their way to his Range Rover.

On the drive home, he said, "Tell me what you're thinking, Willa darlin'."

She said, "I'm glad you asked. I'm thinking how fortunate I am. We have one another. And I know now that whenever the time comes, after we're gone, this family will continue to be in good hands."

LUBBOCK JOURNAL
Online Edition
May 11, 2015
Posted at 6:00 a.m.

Severe Weather Watch

The National Weather Service in Lubbock, Texas, has issued a severe weather watch in effect from ten a.m. May 11, until seven p.m. May 11.

A severe weather watch indicates that conditions will be favorable for the development of heavy rains, damaging winds, and hail. If threatening storms develop, a Severe Weather Warning will be issued.

A low pressure system moving in from the west will create conditions for severe weather events in an area that spans southern Kansas, the western part of Oklahoma, and the Texas Panhandle and some parts of the South Plains.

This watch includes the following South Plains counties: Lubbock, Crosby, Lynn, Dickens, Garza, Floyd, Motley, and Cottle.

Residents of these areas should access National Weather Service radio, local broadcast outlets, or Internet weather sites for current conditions as the day progresses.

CHAPTER 23

Storm Watch

Yesterday, the day after her mother and Robert's wedding, Melanie had slept late, at least late for her, which was 7:45. She and Ray had taken home a bottle of champagne—no sense letting it go to waste, she and Claire had agreed, so they each took one. Ray and she had treated themselves to most of the bottle when they got home. He'd said they deserved to have their own party, and she'd agreed. In fact, Melanie had felt agreeable all of yesterday and again this morning when she woke up.

Then she opened the online site of the Lubbock newspaper and saw the weather alert. Traveling in stormy weather set her on edge. But Miss Berryhill expected her today, so she would go. Last week, Melanie's mother had asked if the plans for the memorial service were all in place, and if there was anything she could do to help. When Melanie showed her the short agenda she'd developed, her mother had asked if Miss Berryhill had approved the plan.

Melanie had not even talked to Miss Berryhill since Robert had secured her agreement to be there. What a terrible oversight. She'd thanked her mother for asking and immediately had called Miss Berryhill. After apologizing for not contacting her sooner, Melanie had asked if she could visit this afternoon. Face to face would be the only way to let her know her wishes would be honored.

She'd packed an overnight bag, but hoped she could make the trip and accomplish her purpose all in one day. Bosley, Oklahoma was 271 miles from Jackson's Pond. Leaving at nine, she should be there by two and be able to be home again by eight or nine.

As she got in the car to leave, Ray said, "Please keep an eye on the weather. If it looks stormy, stay overnight somewhere." She nodded. He kissed her and said, "Keep in touch. I'll worry until you get back."

The morning was bright and the sky cloudless. Maybe the

National Weather Service had it wrong. It had happened before. By eleven, she had crossed into Oklahoma, and at 1:30, directed by her GPS, she reached the address Miss Berryhill had given her. Two cars sat in the driveway and two more were parked out front. She pulled in behind the pale green minivan.

Miss Berryhill opened the door as soon as Melanie rang the bell. Welcomed inside, Melanie saw that she and Miss Berryhill would not be alone. Four other women were seated on the floral sofa and two leather armchairs. Her hostess invited Melanie to sit in one of the two other armchairs situated near a small glass-topped table, and she took the other. Miss Berryhill introduced the others, each of whom she addressed as Sister. She said, "We're members of the same congregation, and the choir at the church. They are my best friends."

Small talk, focused on her appreciation for Miss Berryhill's willingness to help, on the other women's long friendship with her, their shared interest in the church choir, and the weather. One of the women, Sister Etta Jane, left the group and came back with a tray of cookies, a pitcher of iced tea, and glasses.

After a bit more conversation and attention to the refreshments, Melanie said, "I am so pleased that you've agreed to be part of the memorial service. It's important to me that what is planned meets with your approval."

Two of the church sisters nodded. Miss Berryhill smiled and said nothing. Melanie felt her hands shake as she opened the folder which held the agenda. "I'm sorry I only have these two copies. I'd have made others, but . . ."

Sister Eleanor said, "That's fine. We can share."

Melanie handed her one of the copies and gave the other to Miss Berryhill, who said, "You and I can share, too."

Since she'd walked into the room, Melanie had felt one of the sisters' scrutiny more than the others. Sister Collette had watched her continuously and hadn't spoken. After Melanie read through the few items on the list—opening prayer, songs from the choir, placing of flowers on the memorial marker, remarks from her, remarks from Miss Berryhill, and closing prayer—Sister

Collette finally uttered her first words.

She said, "Why are you doing this? And why should Sister Martha Jane help you by being part of it?"

Melanie took a deep breath. Before she could answer, Sister Collette continued, "No one can help Lincoln Berryhill now. Not you, not anyone. He was murdered, and no one was punished. That's the way it was then, and that's the way it still is lots of places. You just want to make yourself feel better."

Melanie said, "I don't disagree with anything you've said. But . . .."

Sister Etta Jane said, "Let her speak, Sister Collette. She's come all this way."

Thunder, sounding nearby, rolled for what seemed like a full minute. No one spoke until it stopped.

Melanie said, "You're correct. One reason I want to have this memorial *is* to make myself feel better. I feel guilt for what my great-grandfather and those other men did."

Sister Collette smirked and said, "Like I thought."

"But, Sister, that's not the only reason. I hope it will also demonstrate to others in our community that our past is stained, not just with Lincoln Berryhill's blood, with injustices done to many others down through the years. And I want them to see that if we are ever to atone for those wrongs, we must first be aware and must admit to them." She paused and took a drink of her tea, glancing at the faces of the others. She said, "Do any of the rest of you feel as Sister Collette? That nothing we do will help?"

Another who'd been silent much of the time said, "Yes, in a way I do. We live here in our own town. None of us need any people in your town trying to take care of our hurt, our bad feelings. They're ours and they've been passed down to us and relived by us all our lives in one way or other."

Miss Berryhill cleared her throat. She must be the choir director; the others gave her their attention immediately. She said, "I don't feel the same. Although, I understand your reasons. I've prayed over this since that nice man visited some time ago to tell me this story. I hope you all will do the same. I plan to attend and

I hope you will go with me."

Melanie kept her eyes on the agenda she and her hostess shared. After a three-breath silence, she said, "Miss Berryhill, what would you like to add to the agenda or how might you want it changed?"

Lightning flashed against the dark clouds she could see through the window. Thunder followed, an orchestra composed entirely of tympani. She waited through another silence. Miss Berryhill said, "I don't feel called to speak at the service, but if my sisters agree, I would like us to offer some songs, perhaps near the end, after the flowers are placed."

Melanie saw Sister Josephine nod. Then two others nodded. Sister Collette held out, her stern expression not changed. Miss Berryhill said, "You can count on us, Mrs. Banks."

Her throat parched by now, Melanie took a long drink of her iced tea. She said, "Then let me summarize what we've agreed to."

She added the songs to the agenda as she read from the sheet. "I am concerned that you might get caught in a storm on your way home, so I won't take any more of your time. But please know how much I appreciate this visit and how I look forward to seeing you at the end of the month."

Although Melanie felt she'd said those words as if reading from a script, the sisters stood and each offered her hand, including Sister Collette. As she left the front porch, Miss Berryhill held her hand and said, "I can't thank you enough for coming."

Melanie called Ray as she left Bosley, heading south. He told her the storms had passed to the north and that she should have clear roads after she crossed the border. She told him she'd be home just after dark. She drove on, heading toward a bank of dark clouds, and soon had to turn on her windshield wipers. Finally, after reaching Childress, she met sunshine again.

Today, with just over a week left until the memorial ceremony for Mr. Berryhill, Melanie immersed herself in efforts to make that day perfect. The promise of a quiet, lazy seven days in Red River the first week in June glittered like a prize she'd receive for May's full month of important and tiring activity.

When Nancy Reese had called and offered Melanie and Ray the use of her house there for the week, she'd said yes without stopping to call Ray. Later, he'd said he was more than ready. Nancy had made the same offer for other weeks in the summer to all the other women who had helped rescue Holly and the children.

Now that Nancy was back, living in her parents' house in town, she'd stopped by several times to visit briefly. Each time, Melanie saw more of the liveliness that had made Nancy notable in high school. More than once, she'd mentioned her sadness about Justin's conviction and assignment to the Federal prison in Colorado. But more often than that, she said she felt free and hopeful for the first time in years.

The last time she'd stopped in, they'd sat and chatted over coffee. As Melanie suspected, Nancy had something to tell her. Before many minutes passed, Nancy said, "I've made some decisions, and I want you to know. First, I don't intend to stay in Africa like I said earlier. This is home and I'm coming back to the ranch. Right now, I'm getting one of the Burley boys to be a caretaker until I get back and get permanent help to run the place."

Melanie said, "I'm glad to hear you're coming back." Then she waited. Nancy had that expression she'd worn so often as a teenager, the "here's a great idea" look that made her a good cheerleader.

Sure enough, as soon as she finished her coffee, Nancy said, "Here's the other thing. I was going to offer your mother the use of the Red River house, like I did you and the others. But I changed my mind. Tell me what you think about this."

Melanie leaned forward, but didn't interrupt.

"I'm going to tell her that if she wants that half-section of land that joins the Jackson Ranch, the one where Justin and his people shot across the fence and killed that bull, I will give it to her free and clear. If even a part of what I've heard about the things Junior and his father and now Justin did to your family over the years, it's only right."

Melanie knew her mother wouldn't ever accept such a large gift. A half-section of that land could be worth close to three hundred thousand dollars. She said, "That's very generous. But I doubt Mother would accept."

"The will's not settled entirely anyway. Nothing can be changed, probably not before mid-July. I wouldn't mind if you mention it to your mother, just to see what her reaction is."

The old Nancy was back, the girl she'd known in high school—full of ideas and determined to make things happen. Melanie said, "How about offering to lease it to the Jackson Ranch for one dollar per year for a multi-year lease?"

Nancy clapped her hands and said, "Yes! That's great. Thank you for that! If she agrees, I can get the paperwork taken care of before I leave for Kenya the end of August."

A few days later she'd called to let Melanie know that Willa and J.D. had agreed to the arrangement and the papers would be signed as soon as the will was settled. Melanie was happy for Nancy to have some things go her way, after so many years of misery. She suspected there would be days to come when Nancy would need her support again, and she intended to be there whenever that was.

Melanie made herself focus on the memorial ceremony to be held on May 30. Memorial Day travel would be over; no other town events were scheduled on that day. After the service, she and the rest of the family would gather at the ranch house for lunch with Miss Berryhill and the three women traveling from Oklahoma with her.

Claire and Willa had shushed Melanie when she asked if they'd mind helping with lunch. Her mother had said, "Lunch is under control. It will be time for you to relax and enjoy your visitors. Claire and I, with Amy and Elisa's help, will take care of it all."

This morning, she'd driven out to the ranch, to the pond pasture. J.D. had fenced a twelve-foot by twelve-foot area under a mesquite that had been allowed to grow there. Over the past ten or so years, with frequent trimming, it had gained enough height to cast some shade. Though the tree was not in the marshy area that had once been the pond, it was perfect as the background for the plot that, with the rustic fence he'd installed, now appeared much like an old family cemetery. The granite marker had arrived and been set in place yesterday. The four bulls that usually lounged in that pasture had been moved.

As she drove back toward town, she continued thinking about the comments she would make. Pastor Goodman would offer opening remarks and a prayer. Hers would be the only other remarks. Having settled the arrangements, she realized the burden that rested on her to say just the right things. She wanted above all to convey her family's sorrow for the injustice her great-grandfather had been part of. And beyond that, she hoped to speak to the others who would come, to say the words that . . . Well, she wasn't sure now what she hoped to accomplish, exactly.

When she reached home, she went directly to the bedroom, lay on the bed, and told herself that taking a nap could help her find the words. She might dream what to say.

Thursday morning, she still had only notes, no coherent organization. She was staring at the pages when her phone rang. It was Willa. She said, "Is there anything I can do to help?"

"Write my remarks?"

"You'll know what to say. Just speak from your heart."

Robert had volunteered to go to Bosley and drive Miss Berryhill and her friends to Jackson's Pond. But one of them was younger and was comfortable driving, so they would arrive late Friday morning. They'd accepted Melanie's invitation to stay with her and Ray.

Dinner Friday evening was pot roast and vegetables with rolls, salad, and cherry pie. Melanie relaxed when their guests complimented her cooking, said it reminded them of home. The younger one asked for her pie recipe. After dinner, as they sat in the living room, Melanie told them all the plans for the program were set as they'd discussed and described the memorial marker.

Later, when their four visitors were readying for bed, Melanie heard four beautiful voices, a perfect quartet, humming, harmonizing without words. Miss Berryhill had been correct. Their songs would complete the ceremony in the best possible way.

Saturday morning, when they arrived at the pond pasture, Melanie counted the cars parked along the road. Eighteen! Chairs. She'd forgotten to supply chairs. But by some miracle, someone had remembered. She said to Ray, "The chairs?"

He said, "I thought we might need some. I borrowed from the school."

She wanted to kiss him right there, but settled for squeezing his hand and repeating her thank you.

She'd invited the members of the church in Calverton that had been defaced and had announced the ceremony to her Sunday School class two weeks ago. Ten members of her church choir were present, wearing their robes. She'd left the selection of hymns to them. She ushered their Oklahoma visitors to chairs in the first row. As they were seated, Miss Berryhill whispered a compliment to Melanie about the hat she was wearing. All four of the sisters wore hats, as well. Miss Berryhill said, "I believe you would fit right in at our church."

By the time the service was to begin, all forty of the chairs were occupied. The Patel family was there. Richard Jesko and his wife sat in the second row. All five members of the City Council sat in a row together. The Goodman family and several members of the Cowboy Congregation occupied two more rows. The Jackson family sat with the Montoyas and Nancy Reese. Marty Broadus, Tag Burley and his family, and several others stood.

At ten-thirty, Melanie stepped before the group and welcomed all, noting the presence of neighbors from Jackson's Pond and from Calverton, and recognizing by name the four women from Bosley, Oklahoma.

She introduced Pastor Goodman who then stepped forward and said, "Today we will honor the life and memory of a man none of us knew personally, Mr. Lincoln Berryhill, who died in Floyd County in 1920. As we begin this memorial, let us bow our heads in prayer."

His prayer was simple and direct, asking blessing on the departed and on those assembled.

At Melanie's nod, the Methodist Church choir sang the brief hymn, "Goodness Is Stronger Than Evil," then followed with "He Leadeth Me," and ended with "I'll Fly Away."

A light breeze blew steadily from the southwest as Melanie spoke again. Fixing her gaze on each of the members of her family, one at a time, Melanie found strength that made her voice rise above the wind. She said, "Family documents, long forgotten, which were found in the past few months, plus a search of official records convince me that a terrible injustice occurred here, somewhere on the land that is our family's ranch, many years ago. Some might think it better to let the past stay forgotten. But I could not. I enlisted others in the search for more information. This is the story I believe to be true, and it is the reason all of you were asked to join us here today."

Having given up on writing a coherent speech, she followed her mother's advice, telling from her heart not only the events of 1920 that she knew but also the documents that verified them. She said, "This man, Lincoln Berryhill, seeking work and a place to call home, passed this way. At the time, the Ku Klux Klan had begun activity in this county, as in other parts of Texas. They cloaked themselves in secrecy and preached separation of the races. They intimidated through violence any who were other than white, and many of other ethnic and religious groups. African Americans were their primary target, but their hate spewed onto others as well.

"Although my great-grandfather was not a mask-and-robe-wearing part of the group, apparently he participated, along with four others, in killing Mr. Berryhill. By their lights, he didn't belong here. They killed him and no one was ever punished for the crime. No justice was ever provided nor was a decent burial conducted.

"Recent events in our area have convinced us that such things continue today. So, it's important not only to provide some atonement for the wrongs of the past, as we do here today, but also to commit to working together—here and now—to eliminate the seeds of prejudice and violence that remain.

"Today we dedicate this memorial marker, which is our promise to never forget. It bears Lincoln Berryhill's name and dates of birth and death and the words 'Justice too long delayed, no longer denied.'"

As she rejoined Ray standing near the fence around the plot, the children—Jay Frank and Amy, and Elisa and her two brothers—laid five small bouquets of mixed spring flowers at the marker. Together they formed a single arrangement.

Miss Berryhill and her church sisters rose and faced the group. She raised her hands and hummed a tone. Then she and the others performed a flawless gospel version of "Swing Low, Sweet Chariot." Hearing the phrase "… coming for to carry me home," started Melanie's tears falling. After the final chord, Miss Berryhill said, "We thank you for this memorial and for the fellowship here today. We'll end on one final song. Please join in."

The song they'd chosen was "We Shall Overcome."

Close to noon, the final visitors drove away from the pond pasture. Miss Berryhill and her friends, along with the family and the Montoyas rode the short distance to the ranch house, where a lunch of fried chicken, potato salad, coleslaw, and other picnic food waited. Around two, the women from Bosley waved goodbye after a session of final photo-taking by Chris. With a long lens, he'd captured images of the service and all who attended. Now that he had the close-ups of the four church sisters, he promised to send each of them a set.

Melanie felt she had no words left, that she'd spent so much care and concern and energy the past month, all she wanted was a glass of wine followed by about eighteen hours of sleep. Relief and satisfaction mingled with fatigue as Ray drove them home. May had been a month worth doing, and now it was over.

Tomorrow morning, they would officially begin their vacation. They'd planned to sleep late and drive at a leisurely pace through the pleasantly vacant spaces of West Texas and New Mexico to the mountain town of Red River. As she lay drifting toward sleep, her last thought was of the diverse group of people assembled that morning and the enormous sense of community and goodwill that had lifted her spirits after several difficult months.

She woke the next morning at seven-thirty, a full hour and a half later than usual. Intending not to disturb Ray, she turned on coffee to brew, then opened the front door. She would bring the hanging basket of fuchsia-colored petunias inside to leave in a shady spot while they vacationed.

She glanced at their car, sitting where they'd left it in the driveway last night. A chill passed through her as if she'd seen and heard a rattlesnake. On the side of their car, the words THIS ISN'T OVER in white paint and that hateful red and black symbol taunted her. She stepped out onto the porch and looked both ways up and down the street. No one in sight.

Her hands shook as she opened the screen and rushed back into the house. She got as far as the bedroom, about to wake Ray. Then she stopped, and retraced her steps to the front door.

Running away, fleeing in fear, a primitive instinct, could save a person from some types of danger. True. But not all fear was based on the sort of danger one should run from. This was not a rattlesnake. This vandalism was the work of one, or a few, whose main triumph was in creating fear, spreading hate. In her, today, they'd accomplished prompting anger, briefly. The thing they hadn't intended, she was sure, was strengthening her resolve.

These past months had shown her strength she hadn't known she could muster. Not only had she faced fear, she'd taken action to rectify wrong. The greatest surprise during those months was learning how many people shared her hope, how many truly cared for others and valued the importance of living together as civilized humans.

That was paint on the car. It could be cleaned away. Ridding their community of that poison would take unity and the strength of many. She would persist, and now she knew that others would also.

Appendix

CONNECT WITH THE AUTHOR

For more information about the author or to contact her about presentations and book signing events, please visit www.tjoneswrites.net, and https://www.facebook.com/Jacksons-Pond-Texas-the-Series-632471517373701.

Made in the USA
Monee, IL
15 October 2021

123c40f7-5fd0-44df-92fa-7f9549234241R01